BONNIE K. WINN
A Family All Her Own

&

Child of Mine

Love Inspired

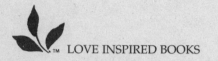 LOVE INSPIRED BOOKS

ISBN-13: 978-0-373-65148-1

A FAMILY ALL HER OWN AND CHILD OF MINE

A FAMILY ALL HER OWN
Copyright © 2001 by Bonnie K. Winn

CHILD OF MINE
Copyright © 2006 by Bonnie K. Winn

www.LoveInspiredBooks.com

Printed in U.S.A.

CONTENTS

Books by Bonnie K. Winn

Love Inspired

A Family All Her Own
Family Ties
Promise of Grace
*Protected Hearts
*Child of Mine
*To Love Again
*Lone Star Blessings
*Return to Rosewood
*Jingle Bell Blessings
*Family by Design

*Rosewood, Texas

BONNIE K. WINN

is a hopeless romantic who has written incessantly since the third grade. So it seems only natural that she turned to romance writing. A seasoned author of historical and contemporary romance, Bonnie has won numerous awards for her bestselling books. *Affaire de Coeur* chose her as one of the Top Ten Romance Writers in America.

Bonnie loves writing contemporary romance because she can set her stories in the modern cities close to her heart and explore the endlessly fascinating strengths of today's women.

Living in the foothills of the Rockies gives her plenty of inspiration and a touch of whimsy, as well. She shares her life with her husband, son and a spunky Norwich terrier who lends his characteristics to many pets in her stories. Bonnie's keeping mum about anyone else's characteristics she may have borrowed.

A FAMILY ALL HER OWN

Hope deferred makes the heart sick,
but desire fulfilled is a tree of life.
—*Proverbs* 13:12

Dedicated to my mother, Tex Yedlovsky, who taught me the value of faith, and who showed me every day in every way a lifetime of her belief.

ACKNOWLEDGMENTS

To Ann Leslie Tuttle and Tracy Farrell for sharing that faith. And to Karen Winkel, pastor of the Bountiful Community Church, for sharing the truth about being a woman in the ministry. Any flights of fiction are strictly my own.

Prologue

"So. What do you do for a living?"

Although the conversation had been going well up until that moment, Katherine Blake glanced at the attractive man with the inviting grin and felt her hopes evaporate. She had visited Nichols Grocery many times, but this was the first time she'd met such a good-looking, apparently eligible man at the store.

Unfortunately she had heard this particular question before. And it was always a killer.

Guessing how he would react, still Katherine smiled. "Actually I'm the minister of Rosewood Community Church."

The man's face shifted from confusion to incredulity to discomfort in under fifteen seconds. It was a new record. At the same time, he stepped backward at her off-putting admission.

"Right. Maybe I'll see you there sometime."

"I look forward to it," she replied, knowing the

flirtatious encounter had skidded to a halt and it was time to change hats. "All are welcome."

Nodding, the man edged away. Clearly he wanted to escape. Katherine's lips curled in an ironic smile. Apparently the man thought she might come after him. *Not to worry,* Katherine wanted to tell him. She recognized that uncomfortable look, one often tinged with pity. The men she had met over the years couldn't understand why a woman without a hump or a third eye would choose to become a minister. As a result they treated her much like a nun out of her habit—sort of a non-woman, one they couldn't get away from fast enough.

Katherine couldn't squash a familiar feeling of hurt. She was accustomed to the reaction, but she also longed for that one special man who would respond differently, who would embrace the choice she had made. One who wouldn't be too intimidated to embrace her, as well.

It wouldn't be this man, though. Mr. Good-looking and Eligible was wheeling his cart away as though piloting a race car in the Indy 500.

Unfortunately, he wasn't that good a driver.

In his haste to escape, the man crashed into the week's special: canned tomatoes. Cans toppled and slid down with a force only towering stacks of tin could achieve.

Unable to stop the avalanche, Katherine gasped as the momentum continued, dismantling the top half of the display. Dozens of cans crashed into her cart while others rolled haphazardly down the aisle.

Then, as she watched in stunned disbelief, the man sped away from the scene of his crime.

Tempted to throw a can after the retreating coward, instead Katherine swallowed an equally unflattering thought and bent to pick up the mess.

Suddenly, someone knelt down beside her. For a moment she thought her coward had repented. But glancing up, she met a far more handsome face, concern written in his deep blue eyes.

"Are you all right?" he asked.

At the same time, three small children surrounded them, gaping at her in wide-eyed astonishment.

The lone boy was the only one to speak as he stared at the mess. "Wow!"

"Are you okay?" the man repeated.

Dragging her gaze from the children, Katherine met the man's eyes. "Yes, I'm fine. The cart got the worst of it."

"This is really cool," the boy told her in admiration. Then, before either his father or Katherine could anticipate his next move, he pushed the man's cart forward, toppling the remainder of the display, most of which fell into Katherine's cart.

Her lips twitched when the child crowed with glee at the mini-disaster. It was a remarkable sight—especially to the young driver.

"David!" his father admonished.

The boy shrugged and said with childlike reasoning, "The thing was already coming down, Daddy."

It looked as though the man were silently counting to ten. "And now you've doubled the damage. Tell the lady you're sorry."

"Sorry," the youngster told her, not looking particularly repentant. Instead, he looked even more impressed by the massive spillage.

Katherine clamped down on her bottom lip and tried to look appropriately serious. "No damage done. I got into my share of accidents when I had my beginner's permit, too."

"He's not old enough to drive," one of the girls told her in a conspiratorial tone.

"And David knows better," the father added, his glance rebuking the boy.

Katherine met the man's eyes, again noticing their deep blue color. "As I said, no harm, no foul." She turned her attention back to the cans. "If we all pitch in, it won't take long to put this back together."

A harried stock boy approached. "It's okay, lady. I can do that."

"We insist on helping," the man replied. Then he directed his compelling gaze to Katherine, again impressing her with both his looks and his consideration.

Now, why couldn't he be single? Katherine lamented. Instead of the ill-mannered boor who had left her with the disaster. But that was her luck, always had been. The good ones were either taken or uninterested. Like this one. He had a small flock of children, and a discreet glance at his left hand showed a simple gold band. *Lucky woman,* Katherine thought with a silent sigh of longing.

Soon, with all the large and small hands helping, the cans were restacked. And the stock boy insisted on completing the display.

Grateful, Katherine smiled at them all. Then, impulsively, she held out her hand to young David. "I'm Katherine Blake. It was nice to run into you."

The boy grinned at her choice of words. "I'm David Carlson." He shook her hand, obviously pleased to be treated like a grown-up.

His father hesitated a moment, then offered his hand, too. "Michael Carlson."

Katherine accepted his handshake, startled by an unexpected shiver of awareness at the contact. Trying not to be obvious, she pulled back, alarmed at her reaction to a married man. She was accustomed to shaking many hands each week. It went with the professional territory. Why had this one seemed so different?

One of the little girls tugged on her father's sleeve.

"This is Annie." The man shifted his hands, placing one on the other girl's shoulder. "And Tessa."

The girls squirmed, grinned, and then dug the toes of matching purple tennis shoes against the grocery cart.

"You two look like you're the same age," Katherine replied, thinking one of the girls looked familiar, but she couldn't place where she'd seen Tessa before. "Fraternal twins?"

The girls giggled in obvious delight.

"Actually they're friends, not sisters," the man explained. "But they might as well be twins. They're always together."

Katherine winked at the girls in understanding. "It's a girl thing, isn't it."

They nodded, grinned again, and then bounced up and down.

Seeing that they were still blocking the aisle and that the stock boy was looking even more harried, Katherine pulled her cart backward out of the melee. "Well, it was great meeting all of you."

The man nodded, but the children waved enthusiastically as she headed the opposite way down the aisle. Now, those were the kinds of conquest she could handle, Katherine decided wryly—the under ten-year-old variety. Kids and safe, married men.

Chapter One

The smallish town of Rosewood blossomed in the summer. Located outside Houston, the village-turned-town was situated on the gradually sloping lands that marked the approach of the Texas hill country. Children, playing with abandon, filled the streets and parks, euphoric with the months of freedom stretching out before them.

Katherine Blake felt equally enthusiastic about summer. Especially since it meant vacation Bible School this first week of June. It was one of her favorite activities at the church. There was much to love about being minister of the warm, caring congregation, but there was something so very special about anything involving the children.

And she really loved it when she got to sub in one of their classes. She rarely had the opportunity to step out of her administrative role. However, because they were short of volunteers, everyone had been reined in to help on this first day. And Katherine had drawn the class of five-year-olds.

Surely it was one of the Lord's many wonders—the amount of energy a room full of five-year-olds could generate. With no children of her own, Katherine appreciated every moment of her time with the many who belonged to the church. And she tried not to think about how much she longed for children of her own.

"Katherine, can you round up the paints and brushes for the art project? Oh, and the clay, too. I want to get started and take attendance."

"I'll get right on it, Donna." Katherine didn't mind the grunt work. She admired Donna Hobbs, the teacher of the class. Twenty-seven years old, bubbly, a pretty blonde, she was one of the best Sunday School teachers in the church.

As Katherine collected art supplies, she checked out the children still entering the classroom. As they continued parading inside, she suddenly recognized two of the miniature faces. Tessa and Annie from the grocery store collision!

It dawned on Katherine why Tessa had looked so familiar. She was new to the church—her family had just joined recently. The Spencers had changed churches because they wanted a stronger youth program for their family, which included a teenager and two younger children. Tessa had been visiting her grandparents when the family joined Rosewood. Katherine had only glimpsed the youngest child last

Sunday, when her parents had retrieved her from the children's church service.

Pleased to see her new friends, Katherine approached them. "Tessa, Annie. Great to see you."

"Hi!" they greeted her in unison, still somewhat shy. But their grins were welcoming.

"Are you the teacher?" Tessa asked, her face puckered in anticipation.

"Actually, I'm the helper."

"Daddy says I'm his best helper," Annie confided, losing a touch of her shyness.

Katherine smiled as she met Annie's large blue eyes, which were filled with bashful pride. The child was a charmer. "I'm sure you are the very best helper," Katherine agreed.

"I help, too!" Tessa added, not wanting to be outdone by her friend.

"Oh, I'm sure you do," Katherine replied seriously, although her eyes danced with amusement. What a pair!

Since Donna was trying to quiet the class, Katherine left them with a wink. But throughout the morning, she found her gaze wandering toward the winsome duo.

The time spent with the five-year-olds was as much fun as Katherine had anticipated. When Donna called for the closing prayer, Katherine was nearly as disappointed as the children to see the class end.

A few parents were lined up in the hall, chatting among themselves as the session ended. Donna had asked Katherine to man the classroom door while she escorted some of the children out to waiting cars at the front drive.

Glancing down the hallway, Katherine recognized Annie's father striding down the hallway. His purposeful gait didn't match his surroundings. Michael Carlson looked like he belonged atop a steed or perhaps the modern-day version—a massive Harley. She shook her head at the notion.

"Mr. Carlson—" she began with a smile.

But he cut her off. "I'm here to pick up Annie and Tessa."

Although his words were controlled, she could see that he was angry. She wondered why.

"Of course. They're right here. We certainly enjoyed having them today."

"This one time had better last Annie."

Confused, she watched as he began to shepherd the girls out of the room. She snagged his sleeve. "Mr. Carlson? I don't understand. Is something wrong?"

"Annie was here without permission. Tessa's mother didn't mean anything by it, but Annie won't be back."

"But why not? She seemed to enjoy it so much and—"

"We don't go to church. Ever."

Katherine felt his distress in her own soul. "Oh, surely you can't mean that!"

"I said it and I meant it."

"Perhaps if you and your wife discussed it—"

"My wife's dead."

Stunned, Katherine was silenced for a moment, even though her eyes flicked to the ring he still wore. "I'm sorry. I didn't mean to be insensitive. But I do hope you'll reconsider about Annie." She paused, sensing his loss, knowing words couldn't dilute it. "I'll be praying for you and your family."

His blue eyes met hers, the darkness in them hiding what she guessed was a wealth of pain. "Don't bother."

The children in tow, Michael strode through the hallways, slowing down only long enough to accommodate Annie's and Tessa's shorter legs.

He kept up the pace as they left the church and drove rapidly toward home.

But he couldn't stop thinking about Katherine Blake. He had been aware of her in the grocery store when they met. In fact, she'd lingered in his mind. And again today when he spotted her, he'd felt an unwelcome jab of attraction. It wasn't something he was ready for.

Michael could still see the compassion in Katherine's eyes. But he had seen similar expressions all too often after Ruth had died. He didn't need the pity of do-gooders, certainly not from lady Sunday School teachers.

He and Ruth had just moved to Rosewood and only attended the local Methodist Church a few times when she became ill. Staying home to care for her and the kids, Michael hadn't realized then it would be one of the last times he'd enter a church.

No, he and his kids didn't need anything from anyone…not anymore. There had been a time when he had begged, pleaded. But that time was gone, never to be recovered.

Once at home, Michael took over for the baby-sitter, Mrs. Goode, who was happy for the rare opportunity to leave early. Tessa and Annie retreated to the world of Barbie dolls and make-believe. His son, however, was more practical.

"Dad, I'm hungry," David announced, shifting from one leg to the other in an impatient dance.

"I know. You'll have to wait until it's cooked."

David tried to finagle. "We could order pizza."

"By the time the pizza could get here, I'll have dinner cooked."

"But if we order pizza, you wouldn't *have* to cook. You could read the newspaper or watch TV."

"Nice try, David. But you need your vegetables."

David sighed, a heartfelt groan of disappointment. "Then, can I eat at Billy's?"

Michael stared suspiciously at his son. "Any special reason?"

"Well…" David hedged.

"Why?" Michael insisted.

"His mom's a *really* good cook," David finally admitted.

And it went without saying that Michael wasn't. So much about their lives had changed since Ruth's death. So many things he felt his children had been cheated out of—things he couldn't compensate for or replace. But he had to try.

"It's important that we eat together as a family. Why don't you see if Billy wants to come over, instead?"

"Uh, if he does, could we have something *good?* Like pizza?"

"We already covered that, David. No pizza. So, you going to call Billy?"

"Nah." With seven-year-old resilience, David scampered away.

Dinner was a quiet affair. The children picked at the overdone pork chops and soggy cabbage. Clearly David could picture the pizza he'd been denied. And Michael dreaded the difficult task ahead of him.

Once the dishes were stacked in the dishwasher, Michael approached Annie, who was in her room enthralled with her new toy stove. "Hey, princess, you have a minute?"

She looked up, her sweet smile melting his heart. "Sure, Daddy. You want to play?"

Obligingly, Michael sat down next to his daughter, trying to fit his long legs into the cramped floor space between the stove and all its accessories: miniature bowls, pans, silverware and mixer. "What are we playing?"

"Dessert. I'm baking a *huge* cake."

Feeling his love for his precious daughter swelling, Michael smiled. "What kind of cake?"

"Chocolate!" she chirped, opening the door to the

play oven, her imagination filling in where reality stopped.

"Good. My favorite."

Again she looked up at him. "I know. That's why it's chocolate."

His heart completely undone, Michael accepted the small plastic plate filled with part of an Oreo cookie. He took a bite, then waited a moment. "This is delicious, Annie."

Obviously pleased, she broke into a grin. "Thanks, Daddy."

For a few moments he enjoyed the bites of cookie, accompanied by water served in tiny teacups. But he knew he had to tell Annie, to get this over, even though he dreaded doing so. "Princess, I need to talk to you."

"About what, Daddy?"

He paused. "Honey, you can't go with Tessa to vacation Bible School tomorrow."

At first Annie's small face reflected only confusion. "But why not, Daddy?"

"We don't go to church," he replied, not wanting to meet the questions in her eyes.

Then her lips quivered as her face crumpled. "Why can't I, Daddy? Tessa gets to go. And she's my very best friend in the whole world!"

"I know. But Tessa's family belongs to the church. We don't."

"Tessa's mom said that's okay. That Jesus wants everyone to come to His house."

Michael's throat worked, remembering a time he,

too, had believed that to be true. "Annie, it's different for us. So, I'm sorry, but you can't go."

Tears rolled down Annie's cheeks. "But I want to go, Daddy!"

Again Michael fought a wave of emotion, swamped by the bitter irony of his words. "Honey, we don't always get what we want in this life."

But Annie was beyond logic. Crying loudly now, her eyes and words accused him. "But you could let me go if you wanted to!"

Feeling helpless, Michael hated to hurt his child, but he could not budge on this point. When it had mattered most, God had let him down, let them all down. And Michael couldn't ever forget it.

The following morning Katherine watched the children pouring through the hallways, searching for little Annie Carlson. She had prayed for the troubled family, hoping the Lord would soften Michael's heart.

Brightening, she spotted Tessa Spencer. Still searching, she didn't see her other young friend. But maybe they hadn't come together.

When Tessa was close enough, Katherine knelt down beside her. "Morning, Tessa. How are you?"

"Okay," Tessa replied without her usual exuberance.

"Where's Annie today?"

"She couldn't come. Her daddy wouldn't let her."

Katherine suspected her own disappointment equaled Tessa's. "Maybe he'll change his mind before vacation Bible School ends. We have almost two weeks left."

Tessa didn't look convinced. "Her daddy said she couldn't come back, ever."

Katherine winced. The man was a tough case. Then, seeing how forlorn little Tessa was without her friend, Katherine reached for her hand, linking it with her own. "How about if you're my special helper today?"

"But I thought *you* were the helper. What would I do?"

"Help me pass out the art supplies, get the juice and cookies ready."

Looking somewhat comforted, Tessa nodded. "Okay." Yet she kept her hand within the safe confines of Katherine's.

Michael Carlson's stubbornness was hurting two little girls very much. Katherine could only imagine how much he was hurting himself.

It had been a long day, one which Michael had spent thinking mostly of his daughter and how he'd denied her request. He couldn't erase the image of her tears. But he also knew his children were adaptable.

Regrettably, it was late. Michael had hoped to be home earlier, but the workday hadn't cooperated. He hated that his contracting business often meant working long hours. It was a double-edged sword. As a single parent he had sole financial and emotional responsibility for his children. Yet it seemed he was always sacrificing one for the other.

And Mrs. Goode, the baby-sitter, was getting tired of working overtime. She had warned him again this evening when he'd come home that if it continued, he'd be looking for another caregiver.

The house was far too quiet. He expected it from Annie—he knew she was still upset. Mrs. Goode had confirmed that. But David could be counted on for his share of noise no matter what else was going on in the house.

The sitter had reported that the kids were in their rooms. Michael hoped David wasn't brewing up another excruciating scheme. His son was long on imagination and fearlessness, but short on caution.

Michael poked his head into David's room. His son was organizing rows of toy soldiers. "Formulating a battle plan?"

David shrugged.

Concerned, Michael stepped inside, then crouched down beside David. "Is something wrong, son?"

David continued to line up the green plastic warriors. "Annie's still crying."

"Still?"

"Yeah. She's been crying a lot."

Michael frowned. "Mrs. Goode said she'd been quiet today."

"Yeah, well she didn't want Mrs. Goode to see her cry."

Placing an arm around David's shoulders, Michael hugged him. "Thanks for telling me. Caring about your family is a true sign of responsibility."

David shrugged. "I don't like seeing Annie cry."

"Me, either. A man never wants to see a girl in tears." *Or to be the cause of them,* Michael reminded himself.

"I wish things were like they used to be," David mumbled. "When Mommy was here."

When he was certain David was all right, Michael hurried down the hall. Pausing at the doorway of Annie's room, he was sickened by the sound of her quiet sobs. In a few quick strides he was inside, scooping his daughter off the bed and into his arms.

She resisted for a moment, and then her baby-soft arms wound around his neck. "Oh, Daddy!"

Her words and agony crept into his heart. "Shush, Annie, it'll be okay."

He cradled her until the sobs lessened into a few hiccups. "Annie, you mustn't go on like this."

"But Daddy, I want to be with Tessa and Katherine. I want to visit Jesus's house."

The pain ripped through him at her innocent words.

"Oh, Annie…"

"I don't want to be left out again!"

"Left out?"

"I don't have a mommy to help in kindergarten or Sunshine Girls. And I'm the only one. I don't want to always be the only one!"

Heart fracturing, Michael held her close. He knew Annie and David desperately missed their mother, but it hadn't occurred to him that the lack of one would make the children feel singled out. And now, denying his daughter vacation Bible School was making her feel even more an outsider.

Though he was a strong man of principle, Michael didn't want those principles to inflict further pain on his children. And Annie had cried for nearly twenty-four hours. She wasn't simply throwing a tantrum— she was deeply hurt.

He pulled a handkerchief from his pocket and tenderly wiped the tears from Annie's face. "I think I could use some hot cocoa. How about you?"

She nodded, her lips still wobbling. "What about Bible School?"

He lifted Annie into his arms and carried her from the room. "I guess we'd better talk about that some more." He smoothed back the hair from her flushed face. "Maybe we can work out something."

After all, vacation Bible School only lasted two weeks. If it meant that much to Annie, he could bear it for a short time. It wasn't as though he planned on signing up hook, line and sinker. In two weeks they would walk away from the church, just as the Lord had walked away from them.

The next morning Katherine reprised her role as teacher's helper for the five-year-old class. Even though Donna had enlisted another volunteer, Katherine managed to head the other woman in the direction of a different class. She simply had to learn what was going to happen with Tessa and Annie.

Praying about it the previous evening, Katherine had asked for guidance. Was it time for her to pay Michael Carlson a visit in her official capacity? Or should she wait and see if he relented on his own?

Anxiously studying the doorway of the classroom, Katherine spotted Tessa. A happy-looking Tessa. Not a foot behind her, Annie appeared. Her shy, sweet expression was in place, along with a blossoming smile.

Sweeping forward, Katherine enveloped both girls in her own smile. "So. The twins are back in action!"

Matching grins replied.

"That's right. You're not *really* twins," Katherine continued.

The girls giggled.

"We're not really even sisters," Tessa reminded her in a loud whisper.

"Sometimes friends are like sisters, though, aren't they? Almost better, because we get to choose them."

Annie's sweet smile grew. "I would always pick Tessa."

"And I would pick Annie," Tessa added loyally, not to be outdone.

"Then, I'd say you're both very lucky. Come on in. I think we're about ready to get started."

The girls blended in, and the lively session went well. The time flew quickly, and soon it was time for the parents to pick up the children.

Katherine watched for Michael Carlson with a

mix of anticipation and dread. She wondered how he would act today. She hoped he realized that he was serving Annie's best interests in allowing her to attend vacation Bible School.

Since Katherine had lived in Rosewood less than a year, she hadn't met everyone in town. And she was certain she would have remembered him. It was easy to spot him in the crowd. His tall, well-muscled build set him apart. He was a handsome, distinctive-looking man in every sense. Thick, dark hair at odds with his blue, blue eyes…and features that were arresting, strong, memorable. No wonder she had been so aware of him at their first meeting.

It took a giant dose of conscience to remember that his need was spiritual, not romantic. Not that she had forgotten. But she couldn't shake that initial spark of attraction.

Compromising, she simply smiled. "It's good to see you, Mr. Carlson. We were very happy to have Annie with us today."

Obviously ill at ease, he avoided her gaze. "I haven't changed how I feel, but she had her heart set on coming here."

"I think you'll both be glad she did."

He didn't reply, but Katherine suspected what he wanted to say—that her attendance was against his better judgment.

Instead he absently ran his fingers over the old-fashioned light switch just inside the door.

"I guess they haven't made that kind of switch in

years," she commented rather lamely, wishing she could find just the right words to reach this man.

"You're right." His fingers paused over a ragged patch in the wire that ran up the wall. "Is this the original system?"

She shrugged, her knowledge of building structure nonexistent. "Probably."

"You should get someone to check it out." Again his fingers lingered over a frayed wire. "It might not be safe."

"I'll mention it to the Deacons' committee."

"Good."

At that moment, Annie and Tessa rushed up to the doorway, all smiles.

Katherine told them to fetch their backpacks, then caught Michael's gaze again. "Whatever your reasons, you made them both very happy." She swallowed. "Actually, all three of us. And for that, I thank you."

Meeting his gaze, she saw something unexpected there—a light she couldn't quite define, but something that seemed to reach out between the two of them.

The girls returned, bouncing and bubbling with energy. Knowing it was uncertain ground, Katherine didn't press about seeing Annie again the following day. She had glimpsed the love Michael held for his daughter. Katherine doubted he could deny permission for her to return.

Somewhere in the exchange, she had glimpsed something of Michael Carlson, as well.

Just then he paused, turning back. "It's you I should thank."

Before she could reply, one of the other parents reached the classroom. "Afternoon, Pastor."

Acknowledging the greeting, Katherine glimpsed the shock in Michael's expression and could imagine the mental wheels whirling.

Katherine wanted to reach out and detain him, to prevent him from walking away. Impulsively, she blurted out the first thing she could think of. "There's a picnic!"

Michael's eyes widened but he didn't speak.

"On Sunday afternoon," Katherine continued. "It's open to everyone."

Michael's lips tightened.

Still Katherine rushed on. "It's not a service, just lunch on the lawn. The kids really enjoy it, and even the adults—"

"Thank you for the invitation, Pastor," Michael replied frostily.

It didn't take a mind reader to see he was angered by the invitation, especially since it had been delivered in front of his daughter. Katherine mentally pedaled faster, trying to think of a way to smooth over the words. "Actually, we're having a picnic here in vacation Bible School tomorrow, in case you can't make the one on Sunday."

Annie and Tessa both looked excited at the prospect.

"If you'll have the girls each pack a sack lunch,

we'll provide drinks and dessert," Katherine continued. "There's a note with Annie's Bible story."

Tessa bounced a bit on her brightly colored tennis shoes. "Wow. Two picnics!"

Meeting Michael's stern expression, Katherine felt her diplomacy falter. And guessed she'd just hit rock bottom on his list.

Chapter Two

What was it about that church woman that got under his skin? Michael wondered when he got home. It wasn't just that she had a colossal talent for saying absolutely the worst thing.

He'd noticed, again, that she wore no rings on her left hand. That wasn't all he'd noticed. Her intelligent brown eyes had softened, seeming to see beyond the surface. It was disturbing, yet at the same time intriguing.

Michael wondered what her story was. How in the world had such an attractive woman come to be a minister? He ignored a niggling voice that said he once would have admired her choice, the strength of character it required.

But he didn't linger over that last thought. Grudgingly he admitted that she radiated energy. He just wished she wouldn't direct it all at trying to get his family to attend vacation Bible School and church picnics.

"Daddy!" David charged into the kitchen at full steam.

Pleased, Michael stooped down to pick up his son.

After a quick hug, David wriggled to get back down. He was growing so fast, Michael realized. Not too many hugging years left.

"Daddy," David repeated. "I want to go tomorrow, too!"

"Too?" Michael asked, his mind on what to prepare for dinner. Maybe he would relent and order pizza this once.

"With Annie!"

Michael stopped thinking about pepperoni versus combo, and concentrated on what his son was saying. With Annie? To vacation Bible School? At the *church?*

Feeling sucker-punched, Michael took a fortifying breath. "What do you mean, David?"

"Annie just told me about her day. It sounds fun, Daddy!"

"What kind of reason is that?" Realizing how idiotic he'd just sounded, Michael placed one hand on David's shoulder. "You don't want to horn in on your little sister and her friend."

Puzzled, David stared at him. "Huh?"

Michael's eyes flickered shut for a moment. What was he doing? He'd always encouraged his children to interact together. In fact, he'd taught David to include his younger sister whenever possible.

So he took another tack. "This isn't for you, David."

"Then, why can Annie go?"

Why, indeed? Because his daughter's tears had gotten to him. Because he hadn't believed things would get so out of control. Because he thought he could stop his children's curiosity and order their thoughts.

"David." He tried again. "I don't think this vacation Bible School thing is for you."

"But why not?" David screwed his face into a heartfelt grimace.

Because I don't want you to be hurt when everything you learn to count on betrays you.

"Daddy?" David implored.

"Why don't we think about it some more?" Michael suggested, knowing it was a losing proposition, knowing he could do little to change that.

"But I wanna go tomorrow!" David protested.

Michael knew he couldn't rationalize, even to himself, that he would allow his daughter to attend but not his son. It wouldn't be fair, and David knew it as well as Michael did.

Defeat was tromping over him with relentless abandon.

"Please, Daddy? Please?"

"I was thinking about ordering pizza," Michael said weakly.

But David wouldn't be distracted. "I had some at Billy's. Can I go tomorrow?"

Michael had lost and he knew it. "Why don't we see how you feel tomorrow?"

"I'll still wanna go," David insisted.

And Michael didn't doubt for a moment that his son would. Again he thought of Katherine Blake. It seemed since he'd met her, she'd started an impossible landslide. And now he had to figure out how to halt it.

The following afternoon Katherine could see the trepidation in Michael's face. Not only had his daughter attended vacation Bible School, but so had his impish son. And clearly, David had enjoyed the session.

Just as clearly, both of his children were loving the Thursday afternoon picnic. Unfortunately, the same couldn't be said of their father. Michael looked like a man caught in the crosshairs of his own making.

While other parents either relaxed at the tables or lounged on the grass with their offspring, Michael sat with rigid precision, as though expecting disaster. For a fleeting moment Katherine wished she hadn't issued the invitation. But she knew she had had to take this step.

She also had to take another.

"Mr. Carlson?"

He met her eyes and she admired that it was an unflinching gaze.

"Yes?"

"It's just a picnic." She gestured toward the swing set and slide where some of the children, including Annie and David, were playing. "And it's good for them to have other kids to play with."

When he didn't reply, she pushed a bit more. "Don't you think so?"

"Pastor, I'm sure you mean well—"

"Katherine," she interrupted gently. All her parishioners were on a first-name basis with her. "Call me Katherine."

For a moment that nameless, undefined tension hung in the silence.

Then he spoke, but for Katherine the timbre of his voice only increased the tension. "Katherine."

Why did he have to say it that way, with an inflection that seemed to ring in the quiet?

Swallowing, she managed to secure the smile that had faded from her lips. "That's better."

"Not necessarily." His tone wasn't antagonistic, but the resignation tinged with bitterness seemed even worse. "I don't want to get to know you, *Katherine,* to get on a first-name basis. It's not personal. It's necessary."

Even though he maintained it wasn't personal, inwardly Katherine flinched. Why did she always champion the impossible causes? And why was she attracted to the impossible men? Ones who could never be part of her future.

Katherine glanced again toward the playground area. "You're doing a remarkable job with your children."

His expression grew wry. "You think so?"

Concerned, she drew her gaze from the children and back to Michael. "You don't?"

"They're missing a lot. Things I can't do and can't make up for. Things only their mother can provide."

"But you're providing love. That's what they need the most."

"I'll be sure to tell Annie that when she's in tears because she's the only one in Sunshine Girls without a mother for mother-daughter day."

Katherine swallowed her immediate response. It would be too pat, a cop-out she wasn't willing to take. Instead she glanced again at his children. "They're so beautiful, and seem so perfect. But it's what you don't see that hurts."

Michael looked at her in surprise. "No platitudes?"

"Would you want one?"

For a moment his mouth edged upward a fraction. "I've had more than my share."

"I imagine you have." She drew an unsmiling face in the droplets of condensation that clung to her paper cup. "I'm sorry about the picnic. My intentions were good, but I didn't mean to put you on the spot."

"I've been on the spot since their mother died."

Katherine added eyebrows to the face on the cup. "Has that been very long ago?"

"A year-and-a-half," he admitted bitterly.

It was as though his voicing the fact made it that much more painful.

"You miss her very much," Katherine said gently.

He acknowledged this silently.

"How did you meet her?" Katherine asked.

He looked surprised at the question. "At a church mixer, actually. We lived in the same small town, but her family had just moved there."

"You were young then?"

"In retrospect, very. At the time I didn't think so. I was all of twenty-one. But I knew the first time I met Ruth, she was the one for me." His eyes took on a faraway expression. "She was so sweet, never had an unkind thought for anyone. And it was genuine, nothing she put on to impress people." He laughed briefly, a little caustic sound. "When she got sick, she didn't complain. Her concern was for us, especially David and Annie. She was worried about how *we* would cope."

"Are the children adjusting?"

"I'm not sure that ever happens."

Katherine guessed it would, but it wasn't her place to say so. Since Michael was pushing the church away, she knew that any pushing of her own would only make him that much more resistant. "Annie's a sweet child."

"She's a lot like her mother," Michael acknowledged. "Ruth was all about giving and caring."

"That's a special legacy."

"Pity that's all Annie has. A legacy, instead of a flesh-and-blood mother."

Katherine winced before she could stop herself.

"Too graphic an image for you?"

Katherine considered her next words, then plunged on nevertheless. "No. But I was wondering if it's an image you portray for David and Annie at home."

"This a typical preacher's question?"

"No," she replied truthfully. "Not in any sense."

"Since you're being candid, I will be, too. No, I don't insist on daily morbid reminders for my kids. They remember their mother, they know what they've lost. I want to help them, to make it easier, not more painful."

"Which is what you've done by bringing them here," Katherine said.

"You're very certain of yourself, aren't you?"

She nodded. "It's a curse, I'm afraid. Most mothers in my neighborhood encouraged their daughters to be meek, gentle and unassuming. My mother taught me to be courageous, outspoken and very much myself." She shrugged with a touch of undisguised irony. "I didn't break a mold. My mother refused to allow me to even glimpse the mold. In fact, she was convinced it had been broken and discarded years before."

"So your mother was very influential?"

Katherine smiled, keeping the rueful, not as optimistic, thoughts to herself. "She certainly was."

"Then, tell me, Katherine. How is it you think my children should be able to grow up without a mother of their own?"

Katherine pondered Michael's words long after the picnic ended, long after she'd bid his family a good-night. Even now, Katherine wondered if she should have told him the complete truth about her mother and the uneven upbringing she'd had.

As a pioneering female minister, Victoria Blake had possessed definite opinions and convictions about many things. One of those had been to teach Katherine the value of giving to others, the importance of generosity and service.

But there had been a downside, one Katherine didn't like to dwell on. Her mother's strong personality and equally dominant occupation had been difficult to balance with marriage. Everything in the family had paled in comparison to her duties and obligations. Family vacations were postponed, often never taken. Time alone with either Katherine or her father, Edward, was nonexistent.

Edward's career was always downplayed, given second consideration after Victoria's. And after a time it was apparent that Victoria's only true concern was her ministry.

Katherine's father tried for as long as he could, but after a time he could not continue to take a backseat to his wife's ministry. Their marriage didn't so much break up as break *down* from lack of care, communication, and time spent with each other.

While Katherine despaired over the loss of family, her mother was philosophical. Victoria wasn't bitter toward Edward, instead believing that her sacrifice was worth the rewards of her career. In Victoria's opinion, the help and guidance she gave her congregation ranked higher in importance than her marriage. It never occurred to her that the Lord would have expected her to value her own family, as well.

Despite her mother's flaws, Katherine had never doubted Victoria's dedication to the Lord. Nor had those flaws affected Katherine's faith. Both of her parents had given her a long-lasting legacy of deep-rooted belief that even their individual mistakes couldn't weaken.

Yet she had often wondered what would have happened if her mother had simply given in a little bit, allowed her husband a place in her life. But that hadn't happened. It wasn't in Victoria Blake to give in, to consider that she might be wrong.

Consequently, Katherine wondered at her own ability to have a successful relationship. She had seen firsthand what happened to a marriage when one of the partners was a headstrong female minister.

Just like she was.

And now she was trying to counsel a man whose children no longer had a mother. How could she possibly give him unbiased advice? How could she explain that not every maternal legacy was a good one?

But then, she didn't think Michael Carlson wanted to hear anything from her. Which was going to make it that much more difficult to tell him that the following evening was a special gathering for all the parents and children to recap the first week of vacation Bible School. It was something they had discussed during class, something that all the children were excited about. Something she didn't want Annie and David to miss out on.

Grappling with the dilemma, Katherine could think of only one possible course of action.

However, even after she got into her car and pointed it in the direction of the Carlson home, Katherine wondered if she was doing the right thing. And as she turned into the driveway, the doubts were barreling through her mind.

And when she reached for the doorbell, an entire colony of butterflies chose to migrate to her stomach.

That wasn't in her nature. She'd never been a timid soul. If anything, she was too assertive. Besides, this was a pastoral call, one to benefit the children.

Then Michael pulled open the door and all her thoughts turned to mush.

"Hello," he greeted her, the solitary word as much a question as a statement.

Luckily, a fraction of her composure returned. "Good evening. I hope I'm not interrupting your dinner."

He hesitated, then opened the door a bit wider. "No. Actually, we just finished, and I was doing the dishes."

"Let me help!" she offered hastily, latching on to that excuse.

"Pardon me?"

She smiled through her nerves. "Really, let me help. Since I live alone I don't have much KP duty."

"So you're going door-to-door to find some?"

"You must admit, I could corner the market. Not too much competition," Katherine countered, knowing she must sound every bit as foolish as she felt.

He angled his head, studying her. "Church work doesn't keep you busy enough?"

"I'm guessing you must be tired of doing solo dish duty. You going to turn me down?"

"You guess right." He pointed past the casual dining room to a swinging door. "Kitchen's this way."

Once inside, Katherine began rinsing the dishes he carried from the table. It was a cozy kitchen, warmed by lots of distressed pine and welcoming framed homilies. The wallpaper was a diminutive plaid, the colors mild and unobtrusive. Obviously decorated by a caring woman who had seen this charming room as the heart of her house, it was a kitchen that cried out for a happy family.

Michael began stacking the rinsed plates in the dishwasher. She reached for a sponge, but his hand closed over hers. The butterflies in her stomach morphed into hummingbirds. Yet all she could do was stare, absently noting how much larger and more tanned his hand was than hers. At five foot ten inches tall, it wasn't often she felt petite. But Michael's six-foot-four-inch frame towered above her.

And now his hand lingered on hers.

She tried to clear her suddenly clogged throat and realized she'd made a sound that resembled a bashful bullfrog.

"You don't have to do that," he was saying.

Trying again, she managed to clear her throat, yet her voice still sounded husky. "Do what?"

"Wipe down the kitchen. Despite your offer, I doubt you came here to clean house."

Katherine collected her rattled thoughts and managed an almost convincing chuckle. "I really don't mind."

He lifted his hand from hers. "But I want to know why you're here."

Show time.

Katherine smiled, then called on the Lord to guide her through this conversation. "Actually, it has to do with your kids."

He waited.

"Well…and Bible School."

His eyebrows raised in question but he didn't speak.

Still gripped by nerves, she rattled uncharacteristically. "I was going to talk with you today when you picked up the girls, but we got sidetracked, so that's why I thought I'd better come by tonight."

When she finally paused, he spoke, his tone droll. "Lots of detail, but I still don't know why you're here."

Katherine stared at him, wondering if a pair of incredible blue eyes was making her lose all sense of reason. So she took a deep breath. "You see, we have a special evening on Friday night for the vacation Bible School kids and their parents. It's pretty informal, but the kids always love it."

"I think I've made it clear how I feel about my children attending church events. I'm allowing them to come to vacation Bible School against my better judgment. However, that's it. Nothing else."

"But this *is* part of vacation Bible School," she explained. "Everyone participates in the program, and the kids will be terribly disappointed if they can't be there."

His expression was skeptical. "Are you sure the kids know about it?"

She nodded. "It's on the church calendar, so all the members have known the schedule for some time. And we sent home a note today. It's probably with the kids' Bible stories or artwork. But we've been talking about it all week…practicing songs and skits. Annie and David definitely know. And they'll feel left out if they can't attend."

He winced, and Katherine realized she'd hit a tender spot.

"All right—"

However, it wasn't resignation she heard in his voice, but determination.

"But this has to end. I agreed to let them go to vacation Bible School, not every event the church holds."

Although she wanted to argue, Katherine knew she would have to take this battle step by step. This small victory was enough. For now.

Chapter Three

Since Rosewood Community Church had a two-week vacation Bible School program, they treated each week as a separate unit and had a celebratory conclusion to each week so no one would feel left out.

It wasn't an elaborate ceremony. One of the members of the congregation owned a pizza business, and he donated scores of pizza for both Friday night get-togethers. Another member brought a snow cone machine. And another a cotton-candy maker. Mothers brought cakes, cookies and every imaginable dessert. The atmosphere was festive, much like when the church held its autumn carnival.

And the kids loved every moment.

Including the Carlson kids. David took one look at the endless tables of pizza and went into pepperoni frenzy. The more delicate Annie was intrigued by the intricate webs of cotton candy.

Michael watched them both, feeling them being

sucked deeper into the church. As he did, he experienced a familiar pang, one he'd never completely left behind. A pang that reminded him that he had once had a church home, as well. One he valued. One he missed.

But he couldn't just forget what had happened. And he certainly couldn't forgive.

Katherine was making her way across the room, stopping to speak to nearly everyone—but then, as minister, she knew all the members. In fact, it was her job to round up those who had strayed from the flock.

But he was no lost lamb.

Michael approached his son. "Why don't we get a table?"

David studied his overloaded plate. "Think I have enough to start with?"

"And finish," Michael agreed.

"We have to get some lemonade, too," David insisted. "And cotton candy, and—"

"Let's start with the pizza, okay, bud? I'll grab the drinks, if you'll find your sister and pick out a table. She'll probably want to sit with Tessa."

"Okay. But Tessa's gonna sit with her family," David told him, before heading toward the sea of tables.

Michael joined the growing line of people waiting for punch and lemonade. It took some time to collect the drinks. When he looked for David and Annie, he didn't see them at first.

Then he spotted his daughter's luminescent

face—as she gazed in admiration at Katherine. Katherine, too, was animated, laughing with the children.

Why was it that every time he turned around, she seemed to be there—and looking so remarkably attractive? She stood out among the other women like a brightly colored robin surrounded by wrens. Perhaps it wasn't a fair comparison, but just her energy alone radiated an appealing aura. Pity she was a linchpin in the church—

The thought brought him to a sudden and complete stop. He hadn't believed he was ready to feel any serious attraction to another woman.

Michael forced himself to move forward, to regain his steadiness. As he reached the table, another wave of laughter erupted. His children seemed equally charmed by Katherine. He had to admit he couldn't remember ever seeing them laugh so much.

Annie spotted him first. "Daddy!"

David was only a beat behind. "Over here, Daddy!"

Since the children sat on each side of Katherine, that left the spot directly across from her at the four-person table.

Katherine reached over, helping him unload the drinks from his tray. The automatic gesture surprised him. He had become accustomed to doing things on his own with his children.

He was even more surprised when David pushed over a plate filled with Michael's favorite—combo pizza.

"You're lucky, Mr. Carlson, the combo goes pretty fast because we have mostly cheese and pepperoni for the kids," Katherine said with a smile.

"It's 'Michael,'" he told her, remembering her insistence that he call her Katherine.

Her eyes warmed in a way that made his insides do somersaults. "Michael."

It seemed ridiculous that in the noisy, crowded room he suddenly had the sense that there were only the two of them, sharing an unnamed tension, an unfathomable connection.

"Aren't you going to eat your pizza?" David asked.

Pulling his gaze from Katherine, he turned to his son. "I sure am. Thanks for getting mine." He was touched that his son had been so thoughtful.

"It was Katherine's idea," David told him without hesitation, digging back into his own pizza.

Michael met her eyes.

She shrugged. "No point in your fetching the drinks, then having to fend for yourself in the pizza line."

Still it was a thoughtful gesture, Michael acknowledged to himself. So, she was beautiful *and* thoughtful.

Katherine stood to hug one of the elderly members of the congregation, making the woman beam with pleasure. Michael couldn't deny that her behavior was a good example for the kids. They both looked so relaxed, so happy. Katherine was right. This had been a good experience for them.

And that thought ran riot.

Michael slammed on his mental brakes. He couldn't allow himself to believe she was right. Then, he might be duped into permitting his children to make the same mistake he had, to trust as he had—to be betrayed, as well.

Just then, Katherine met his gaze, her own urging him to join in the fun his children were having.

It was difficult, considering the proximity, for Michael to avoid her gaze. It was equally difficult to remain stern, when Katherine kept his children in stitches.

She was explaining anchovies to David, and the expressions on both their faces had even Michael fighting a chuckle.

"Tell you what, David," Katherine said with a laugh. "We'll have pizza again, my treat, and I'll find the squishiest, saltiest little fishes in town."

"Ick," Annie added with a shudder.

"No one *has* to eat them," Katherine told her with a smile. "But David *wants* to taste anchovies."

David grinned. "Neat!"

Michael rolled his eyes. This was his child? The one who wouldn't try most foods unless coerced? And, he realized, Katherine had just managed to insert another invitation into the conversation.

Then her laughing eyes met his. "So, are you an anchovies man?"

Michael realized he hadn't tasted anchovies in years because Ruth hadn't liked them. "Actually," he admitted, "I love them."

"You eat squishy fishes, Daddy?" Annie asked with a mixture of horror and admiration.

"Yeah, I'm pretty tough, sweetheart."

Katherine's laugh bounced around him. "A real macho man."

Her spirit, at once compassionate and uplifting, touched him. And he found himself reluctantly grinning.

Katherine's and Michael's gazes met, their laughter erupting simultaneously.

Unperturbed, David shook his head and attacked another piece of pizza. Annie chose the same moment to try her cotton candy. Clearly they were unimpressed.

This time, amusement and instant understanding bloomed in the glance between Katherine and Michael. It was a family sort of moment—the kind parents often shared with their children.

And that didn't seem right, Michael realized, not with a preacher.

Katherine was urging Annie to tell him about her participation in the art project.

Delighted with the attention, Annie told him about being Katherine's helper and how the teacher had praised her work. The mood lightened with her recitation.

After polishing off their pizza, Katherine gestured toward the game setup that lined two of the long walls in the church hall. "We consider this sort of a carnival preview, for the one we hold in the fall.

There's a ring toss and apple bob, that sort of thing. They're simple but fun games."

"Can we do that one?" Annie pointed to a group that was holding balloons beneath their chins. The object was to pass the balloon on to the next person without using any hands. The entire group was laughing loudly at the antics the game demanded.

Michael wanted to refuse, to wind up the evening. But Annie was jumping from foot to foot, tugging on his hand. It simply wasn't possible to crush her excitement. As least, it wasn't in Michael to do so.

So he and Katherine walked with the children over to the balloon relay. The players greeted Katherine warmly, obviously fond of their minister.

The relay was popular, eliciting bursts of unrestrained laughter and much good-natured teasing. The balloons slipped as they were passed, some squeaking, some drifting to the floor.

Annie and David giggled with delight as they managed to successfully relay their balloon. Michael cheered their accomplishment, then started to turn away.

"No Daddy! You have to play, too!" Annie exclaimed.

"Yeah, Daddy!" David chimed in.

"I'm too tall," Michael protested, giving Annie a hug.

"You can play with Katherine. She's tall enough," David told him.

"Yes, Katherine!" Annie cried.

Michael shook his head, but to his surprise, Katherine was smiling gamely.

"I'm willing if you are," she said. "And I think I'm tall enough."

She was, Michael realized. His wife Ruth had been a petite woman. Katherine was very different, tall and willowy.

Dismissing that thought, he wanted to dismiss the game as well, but his children were begging him to participate.

"Then our team will have enough points to get a prize!" David told him.

Michael glanced at Katherine in question.

"The prizes are small—puzzles, comic books, bubbles—that sort of thing," she explained. Then she ruffled David's hair. "But I was hoping to get enough points for bubbles. I blow killer bubbles."

"Then, you hafta play, Daddy!" Annie responded.

Realizing he was outnumbered, Michael decided it was time to give in gracefully. "It probably won't kill me."

"Now, that's the kind of enthusiasm that lights up the night," Katherine responded wryly.

Again her humor was infectious, and Michael took his place in the relay line. In moments he held a neon-orange balloon beneath his chin, wondering if he had completely lost his mind. But with his children jumping up and down in excitement, he turned to Katherine, to pass the balloon. To end the game, the silliness.

Then she was beside him, her face lifted up

toward his to allow the balloon to slide beneath her jaw. She *was* tall, Michael acknowledged. It was as though her entire body was a tall challenge, one now only inches from his own.

Trying to ignore that fact, he scrunched the balloon more firmly and angled his head to pass it to Katherine. Obligingly, she tipped her head to one side to facilitate the relay. But it wasn't as easy as it looked.

Not without touching each other.

And Michael was determined to prevent that at all costs. Katherine was doing her part to remain at a discreet distance, as well. Consequently the balloon wasn't going anywhere.

Feeling like a fool, Michael moved a bit closer, tipping his head the other way. Rolling the balloon closer to her, he had just about completed the relay when their cheeks grazed.

For a moment they both froze.

Michael's gaze flew to meet hers. And he read the matching awareness in her expression.

"Don't drop the balloon, Daddy!" David yelled.

"Move closer!" Annie shouted.

Michael couldn't have moved closer if jet-propelled. But his children's voices brought him out of the frozen tableau. Carefully, he moved back, allowing Katherine to capture the balloon.

She held up the balloon in victory as she turned away from Michael.

For an instant he was disappointed, wondering

what he might have seen in her expression. Just as suddenly, he realized he didn't dare find out.

Michael soon learned that he didn't have time to worry or wonder. His children surrounded Katherine, dragging her to the next game.

In a short time they splashed through the apple bob, laughed through the ring toss, and quickstepped past the games of twister.

Then Annie begged for face painting, and Michael tried not to look pained. His youngest could play at that for hours.

To his surprise, Katherine's expression softened. "Why don't we give the boys a break? They probably have some he-man stuff to do. I'll take you to the face painting."

Annie clapped her hands. "Are you going to get your face painted, too?"

Michael grinned at the prospect, but Katherine surprised him again. "I'll give it a shot. I've always thought a butterfly resting on my cheek might be nice."

It probably would be, Michael realized. The instant he had that thought he remembered the feel of her cheek against his. Then she was walking away, Annie's small hand in hers.

David tugged at his jacket. "Can I have some more pizza?"

"Aren't you about to blow up?"

David shook his head. "Uh-uh. I love pizza. 'Sides, you didn't eat very much."

No, because he'd been too aware of Katherine.

"You're right, David, let's see if we can rustle up a few more pieces."

"Maybe they even have some with green stuff on it."

Michael laughed at his son's description of combo pizza. "Now, that sounds appetizing. Tell you what, I'll even eat plain."

"Not me," David announced, never one to vacillate. "I want pepperoni."

"A man who knows his own mind," Michael murmured, leading his son back to the pizza tables. *Just like his father.*

Annie's expressive eyes grew even larger as she watched the woman create a butterfly on Katherine's cheek.

"Ooh, purple!" Annie murmured, totally intrigued by an adult willing to have her face painted.

"And pink, too, I hope," Katherine replied, winking at Annie.

"Absolutely," the face painter told her, and then grinned mischievously. "I could paint a hummingbird on the other cheek."

Katherine kept her own grin in check. "I think I'll go with just the butterfly for now."

"It looks pretty," Annie told her softly. "Like magic."

At her words, Katherine imagined silvery unicorns and soft swirls of girlish pink. And she could picture Annie deep in their midst. "I bet you have a pink room."

"Yes. My mommy fixed it for me. She was always making stuff for me."

Katherine sensed the depth of this child's loss. "I'm sure it's real pretty, sweetie."

"It is. Can you come see it and play with me?"

Incredibly touched, Katherine felt herself melt. What a precious child Annie was. "We'll have to see, okay?"

"Okay. Do we match now?"

The face painter handed them each a small mirror. "See for yourselves."

Katherine and Annie studied their reflections, then turned to each other with a grin. "Matched," they said in unison, looking at the identical butterflies on their cheeks.

Annie had requested matching designs, and Katherine had seen no reason to disagree. Briefly she wondered if this was how most mothers felt with their daughters—sharing little things, taking joy in something as simple as face painting. Then Annie reached up to hug her, and Katherine knew it must be true.

As they left the face-painting area, Annie spotted her father and brother.

Michael had noticed Katherine and Annie, as well, walking hand in hand, sharing smiles and secrets. When they neared, he studied them in surprise. He hadn't really expected Katherine to allow her face to be painted. But she was nonchalant about the butterfly. Annie, however, was excited, her blue eyes shining. And he could see that his daughter was equally captivated by Katherine herself.

Taken aback, Michael wondered how this had happened so quickly. Only days ago they hadn't even met Katherine. Now both his children were involved with church activities, something he had sworn wouldn't happen. And he was having thoughts he hadn't experienced since Ruth died. Thoughts about a minister. Thoughts that had to end now.

Chapter Four

Despite the warmth of early summer, the grasses and foliage surrounding Rosewood remained vibrantly green. Not the blue-green of drier western climates, but a lush, fertile green. Sturdy native flowers that had survived beyond spring added luscious color.

Katherine took in the surroundings she enjoyed so much, gently tugging at her dog's leash to guide him away from some thorny-looking weeds. "Snowy, those weeds are taller than you are."

Leaning over, Katherine petted him affectionately. He was her family, and her most consistent companion. There hadn't been a steady man in her life since shortly after college. Oh, men admired the dedication of her calling and what they guessed was her purity of heart.

But they didn't want to date her.

At least, not in what she considered the normal fashion. True, she had the occasional date. But most men made it clear she was a woman they respected, not one with whom they wanted to become involved. Katherine had grown to recognize the look, one that said, *admire but don't touch.*

She was accustomed to how men reacted to her profession, but she still longed for that one special, different man. Her past should have told her a relationship wasn't possible, that no man could take the pressure of a wife who was also a minister. But one persistent niggle of hope continued to hang on, like a weed in an immaculate rose garden refusing to die no matter how often she tried to yank it out, stomp on it, even bury it.

Katherine tried not to think of herself as lonely. She had plenty of friends and the fellowship of her congregation, and they were extremely important to her. But when there was no one special in her life, no one who shared her dreams, no one with whom she expected to share her future, it was hard to dispel the loneliness. And it was equally difficult to still the longing.

Glancing down the road that seemed to stretch forever in the flat plain, Katherine spotted a bright red convertible Mustang approaching. And she felt a smile erupting.

The car skidded to a halt, and the driver tooted out a friendly greeting on the horn. "What are you doing out here in the middle of nowhere?" Cindy Thompson asked, tossing back her flame-colored hair. "Hop in and I'll buy you a soda, maybe even a root beer float."

"I've got Snowy," Katherine replied, not certain she was ready to give up her solitary walk.

"We'll get him a milk bone," Cindy replied without concern for the immaculate car interior. "Besides, I met a man."

Katherine's grin grew, suffusing her face. "You say that like it's new."

Cindy didn't take offense. "So, don't you want to hear about him?"

Katherine picked up her dog, deposited him in the backseat, and then hopped inside. "I'm all ears."

As they drove down the road, Cindy described her new and, as always, temporary Mr. Right.

Katherine listened patiently, and Cindy finally paused. "So what do you think?"

"I think I don't know much about him other than his looks."

"Katherine, I barely met him. I don't know his life history yet!"

Katherine smiled gently at her best friend, one of the few people in the small town who viewed her strictly as a friend, rather than a minister. But they went back a long way to the time when they'd both lived in Houston. In fact, when Cindy had needed to escape her big city life, she'd chosen to relocate in Rosewood because of their friendship. Cindy had never stood on ceremony with her, and Katherine appreciated every irreverent bone in her body. Also, she was aware of her friend's painful past, one she disguised with humor and outlandish behavior.

Years before, Cindy had fallen hopelessly in love

with Flynn Mallory. But he had chosen Cindy's sister over her. Cindy had hoped her feelings for Flynn would fade. When they hadn't, she'd fled Houston, moving to Rosewood where she could be near her best friend. But neither time nor distance could obliterate that love. And since her parents had died, she had no other family with which to fill her life. "I didn't mean to criticize."

Cindy sighed. "I know my track record isn't good, but I also know my prince is out there. I just have to keep looking. Maybe from here to Kalamazoo, but I'm going to find him."

"Tenacity is a good quality."

Cindy threw back her head, a gust of laughter combining with the wind that skimmed over the open top of the car. "That's subtle!"

Sheepishly, Katherine grinned. "I didn't mean it quite that way."

"Pshaw," Cindy retorted. "At least I'm still looking. I haven't seen you dating anyone lately."

Katherine couldn't contain a grimace. Cindy was right on target.

"You'll meet someone."

Katherine didn't reply.

Cindy jerked her attention from the road, staring at her friend. "You *have* met someone! Who? Details! I want details!"

But Katherine hesitated. "It's not what you think. He's the father of one of the children in vacation Bible School."

Exasperated, Cindy glanced back at her. "And that makes him unacceptable, why?"

"It's more complicated than that." Briefly Katherine outlined their meeting and her subsequent discovery of Michael's feelings.

Cindy gave a low whistle. "Whew. That's tough. You can see why he's all closed off. Losing his wife and having two little kids to raise on his own."

"Of course. But he's turned his back on the Lord."

"And who better to set him in the right direction, Katherine?"

"I know it's my job—"

"It's not just your job, Katherine. It's who you are. Wouldn't you want to help him even if you weren't attracted to him?"

"Of course!"

"Then, what's the problem?"

Katherine stared straight ahead, but her composure slipped a bit. "The first time I saw him I was immediately attracted to him, which appalled me since he had three children with him and I guessed he was married. And now that I know how he feels about his faith, I'm even more disturbed to find that I'm still thinking about him in more than a spiritual way. Perhaps I should be listening to my initial feeling of alarm. Maybe it's the Lord's way of telling me that Michael is not someone I should be attracted to."

"And maybe He's telling you that this is a very special man, who needs you in more ways than you've considered."

Reluctantly Katherine turned and met her friend's

gaze. Despite Cindy's frivolous appearance, her roots were grounded. "You really think so?"

"Katherine, let yourself be both a minister and a woman. You'll know which direction the Lord wants you to take. Don't just assume it's either-or. Perhaps this is a dual role."

It wasn't something Katherine had considered. For such a long time now she had stood on the outside of the relationship circle. Could it be that that was changing?

The following morning Katherine stood inside the sanctuary, glancing around at the church she loved. It was something she did early on Sunday mornings. It was a way to seek the quiet, reestablish her connection to the congregation. And today she felt a special need for that.

As was her custom, immediately before services began she slipped away to pray. And the Carlsons entered into her prayer.

When she looked up again, she was surprised to see Pastor James McPherson, the wise and Godly man with whom she had interned after seminary. As her mentor, he had guided her throughout her ministerial career.

"James! What a wonderful surprise! Is Jean with you?"

"She stopped at the nursery. You know how my wife is about babies."

That she did. James's kind and gentle wife would have a dozen babies if she could. So far they'd been blessed with only two boys. "I know they'll welcome an extra pair of arms. You should have told me you were coming to Rosewood."

"It was just an impulse. Classes are out this week at the seminary. Jean and I decided to take advantage of the break, and the boys were thrilled about a trip. Besides, it's been too long since we've seen you."

Touched by his words, her smile wobbled a bit. "It's so good to see you."

James angled his head, studying her. "Is anything wrong?"

"Not wrong, just a little heavier burden than usual."

"You know we're only two hours away, Katherine. And you can call on us anytime for help. That's what friends are for."

He and Jean were that and more. His mentoring had grounded her ministerial career, given her the direction she'd needed. "I know. But this is one problem I'm afraid I'll have to deal with on my own."

Again he searched her expression. "You know best. But don't forget we're always available."

"I'm counting on it," she replied.

He glanced at the people who had begun filing inside. "We'll talk more after the service. I'd better find a seat."

Katherine nodded, taking her place on the dais.

The pews filled rapidly even though it was early summer, a time when attendance typically dipped. Katherine found herself watching for the Carlsons, wondering if Michael Carlson could possibly have begun to relent. Even though she guessed it was far too soon for that to happen, she was disappointed that he and his family were absent.

Silly, she knew. Michael Carlson had been adamantly clear about his feelings. Still, she had hoped. She knew the Lord was working on him. But He possessed far more patience than she did.

Even though her sermon went well and almost everyone gathered on the lawns afterward for their Sunday picnic, Katherine couldn't lose her nagging feeling about the Carlsons. She wondered if Annie and David had asked to attend the picnic, if they were disappointed at not being allowed to come.

Despite her concern, she was able to interact with James, Jean and the church members, to join in the children's laughter as they romped with one another, and to be charmed by the babies.

It was one of those picture-perfect days. But Katherine couldn't fully appreciate its beauty. Tomorrow was the beginning of the second and last week of vacation Bible School. If she didn't convince Michael to allow his children to attend church beyond the week, she might never see them—or him—again.

On Monday afternoon, Michael approached the room where Annie's vacation Bible School class was held. But his feet dragged a bit as he approached. Glancing at the ceiling of the educational building, he frowned. The water stains that bled through the paint were a sign of trouble. Coupled with the antiquated wiring system, a leaky roof could cause serious trouble. And from what he'd seen of the electrical system, it could well be already compromised. Which meant the building's structural integrity might also be compromised.

Then he shook his head at the train of thought—dodging reality for his own comfort zone of contracting problems. What did they matter?

What bothered him was Katherine. He was pretty sure she would be at the door of the classroom, as she had been every day. On the previous occasions, however, he hadn't just spent two days thinking about her.

But since Friday night, she had crept relentlessly into his thoughts. It was hard to shake the image of her making his kids laugh and forget the gloom they'd been living with. It was equally easy to remember Katherine hugging Annie, then turning around to present their matching butterflies. It was an unexpected moment of whimsy, a breath of something so fresh he hadn't known what to say.

And he still didn't.

But when he arrived at the classroom, Katherine wore her usual smile. So perhaps she hadn't attached any special significance to the evening.

Not certain whether to be relieved or disappointed, he collected backpacks and children. Ready to leave, he saw David flying down the hall toward him.

"Aren't you supposed to wait until I get to your

room?" Michael asked him, corralling the youthful bundle of energy.

"Teacher said it was okay when I saw you right here," David explained.

Coming up behind him with Annie in hand, Katherine smiled. "His class and ours played outside together today. His teacher knows that Annie's his sister."

With all the frightening things happening to children in the news, Michael didn't approve of the practice. "Next time wait, young man."

Recognizing the serious tone in his father's voice, David sobered a bit. "Okay, Daddy."

Michael draped one hand over his son's shoulder. "We'd better get going."

"Are we still having a barbecue?" David asked anxiously. "You don't have to work late again, do you?"

"Nope. We're having my world-famous hamburgers."

"It's the only thing he really knows how to cook," David told Katherine candidly.

"I'm sure that's not true," Katherine replied.

"Afraid he's right," Michael conceded ruefully.

But Katherine didn't respond in the sympathetic tones he had expected.

Instead, she burst into laughter. "Sorry," she finally managed to say. "Most men aren't usually so honest."

"My daddy's always honest," Annie told her, forever the loyal child.

"Oh, I'm sure he is," Katherine responded. "And I bet he's a champion hamburger cooker."

"He is," Annie agreed. Then her small face lit up. "Why don't you come taste?" She turned to her father. "Katherine can come eat hamburgers with us, can't she, Daddy?"

And how was he supposed to say no?

Especially when David chimed in. "Yeah, Daddy. She could see you're the best!"

Katherine looked a bit embarrassed, but she smiled at the children. "I don't want to intrude."

"She wouldn't be 'truding, would she, Daddy?" Annie questioned.

Michael stared helplessly at his daughter, who was positioned between them, looking from one uncomfortable adult to the other.

"Of c-course not," Michael stammered.

"If you're sure," Katherine murmured.

"We're sure," David answered for him. "Can you bring dessert?"

Michael rolled his eyes in embarrassment, but Katherine was laughing again. "Two honest men in the Carlson family! I'd be happy to, David."

"It's just that Daddy's not so good on dessert," Annie whispered to her.

Katherine hugged her lightly. "It'll give me something to do. Dessert's my thing."

"We like lots," David told her.

Michael glanced down at his son, hoping the boy could read the admonishment in his expression. "Let's remember our manners, David."

"But I thought she'd wanna know," David protested.

Tactfully, Katherine bit her lip and refrained from either laughter or a defense for his forthright child.

"We'll eat around seven," Michael told her. "I think you know the address."

A bit of color crept into her cheeks. It surprised him. He didn't think a direct, candid woman like Katherine would blush.

She cleared her throat. "Right, I do. I'll be there with bells on."

"And dessert," David reminded her.

Unable to resist the laughter lurking in Katherine's eyes, Michael repeated David's words. "Lots."

Her laughter spilled out. David, Annie and Tessa joined her.

Funny. He'd just been hog-tied into inviting the woman to dinner, and yet it was difficult to remain provoked. Belatedly Michael remembered that Katherine was the reason he now stood in the church hall. And he told himself it would be easy to regain his annoyance. Then his glance strayed back to Katherine and somehow he doubted his own resolve.

The summer days were long, spilling sunshine past the huge trees in Michael's yard. Spreading branches provided canopies of shade while bougainvillea crept across the fence and trailed over an ancient arbor.

The yard was old and somewhat softened, like the

house, a weathered Cape Cod that boasted a wide porch running around the entire perimeter.

Katherine thought the home was filled with charm and character. She believed that houses, like people, were more interesting with a bit of age. Personality didn't develop overnight, and this one had mellowed delightfully over the years.

Michael had greeted her with reserve, and Katherine keenly felt her occupation standing between them. It was a barrier neither could ignore. But for the children's sake, Katherine was determined to be upbeat. She sensed they needed more laughter. And that was something she could provide, regardless of Michael's resolve.

Katherine wrapped the last ear of corn in aluminum foil and added it to the platter. "This should be yummy."

"I like stuff cooked outside," Annie agreed.

"Me, too." As she took a deep breath of the fragrant air, the smell of mesquite chips lured her to the grill.

With Annie at her side, together they handed the corn to Michael. While he hadn't requested that she bring a vegetable, Katherine had thought the kids might enjoy it.

Michael eyed the corn on the cob dubiously. "You and I will probably be the only ones to eat it, but we can toss it on the grill."

"I'll eat some, Daddy," Annie insisted.

Katherine shared a smile with her, realizing that

the child had a special gift for always wanting others to feel happy. It was remarkable for one so young.

"Should we set the table?" Katherine asked David and Annie.

"Sure," they replied in unison.

Michael's eyebrows rose. "That's a first."

"Usually we take turns," David explained.

"And they don't volunteer," Michael added.

Hearing this, Katherine decided to make a game of the chore. "How about a contest? Let's divide the table in half." With her hand she drew an imaginary line down the middle of the tablecloth. "You each have half a table to decorate."

"Decorate?" Annie asked. "You mean like Christmas?"

"Not exactly, sweetie, but something like that. I'll leave it to your imaginations. You have plates, napkins, glasses and silverware to work with."

"Is that all?" David asked.

She thought for a moment. "I guess not. You can use other things, too, but nothing too big or too messy."

Together the three of them carried the dinnerware from the kitchen. A second and then third trip yielded all the condiments and hamburger buns. Another trip brought lemonade and chips. Katherine noticed that Michael remained at the grill, as though using it to keep the distance between them.

Then the children scattered to collect what they were using for the table-decorating contest.

"Don't look!" David and Annie cried as they brought their loot back to the table.

Obligingly, Katherine sat in one of the overstuffed lawn chairs away from the table. And she couldn't help noticing that Michael didn't move from his spot at the grill. Katherine wondered if he intended to spend the evening there, perhaps munching on his burger from a safe distance.

As she watched him, he lifted his gaze, almost as though he sensed her eyes on him. Again that nameless tension hung in the air. Wildly attracted to him, she wondered if the feeling was one-sided. But if so, why did the pressure seem to radiate between them?

Katherine smiled a trifle tenuously, wishing she could ban her uncharacteristic uncertainty. But his gaze remained thoughtful, neither antagonistic nor welcoming.

She was a threat, Katherine realized, and one he wasn't certain how to banish. When he looked at her, she guessed, he must be constantly reminded of the church, and the loss that drove him from it. In a purely feminine fashion, she wondered if he saw more…wanted more.

The minutes passed and the hamburgers cooked, their smell a tantalizing aroma that brought all of Katherine's hunger buds to life, despite her nerves.

"Burgers are done," Michael announced finally and the children ran toward him. "Hope you guys remembered the mustard."

"And pickles," Annie replied happily. "And cheese, too!"

He smiled fondly at his youngest. "Good." Then he glanced at Katherine. "Why don't you two escort our guest to the table."

"Okay, Daddy," Annie replied.

"Then you guys have to judge the table," David insisted. "Before we eat."

Michael raised his brows at Katherine. "Another first."

But he walked over to the table with his children. Initially, surprise held him in silence. He had seen the children playing by the table, but he hadn't guessed they would glean so much from Katherine's suggestion.

"Whose side do you like?" David demanded.

"Oh, my," Katherine murmured.

Michael stepped closer to the table that now resembled a fantasyland that could only have been dreamed up by children.

David's side looked as though it had been plucked from a miniature army bivouac. Tiny soldiers guarded each plate, reinforced by a row of tanks. A helicopter had landed amidst the napkins, while silverware resembled a bridge, crossed by foot soldiers.

And Annie's side was as whimsical as David's was realistic. Barbie, Ken and their friends sat by each plate. Barbie's swimming pool and slide looked poised for a party. On each plate either a tiny hat or equally minuscule pair of shoes decorated the center. Annie had draped her toy pink feather boa atop her makeshift centerpiece, a final piece of whimsy.

How had so much creativity flowed from his children?

As he continued to stand mute, Katherine draped her hands over their shoulders. "This is wonderful!" She gazed at the table again, then emitted a low whistle. "Just wonderful. Both sides. I knew you'd both do a fabulous job, but this is even better than I expected. It's Barbie World And G.I. Joe Land!"

David and Annie both grinned at the praise, then turned to their father.

"What do you think, Daddy?"

Jerked from his startled silence, Michael crouched down between his children. "It *is* wonderful—just like you guys."

Annie looped her arms around his neck. "Thanks, Daddy."

"But who won?" David asked.

"Both of you," he replied. "You made something fabulous and you worked together to do it. And now we have a beautiful table to sit down to. We're all winners."

"But you weren't in the contest," David pointed out practically.

"Of course he was," Katherine inserted gently. "As your father, he's always with you in everything you do, cheering you on, feeling what you feel. And he's always on both your sides."

"I like it that we both win," Annie replied generously.

"Yeah, it's okay," David agreed.

Michael watched Katherine's interaction with his

children and again he wondered, How was it she managed to say just the right thing? As remarkable was his children's reaction. Perhaps they were simply craving a woman's attention. But if he were honest, he had to admit Mrs. Goode hadn't elicited the same response.

"Then, if your dad's ready, maybe he'll let us dig into those burgers," Katherine suggested, lightening the mood.

"Yeah, burgers!" David replied. "My daddy makes the best."

"It's one of those macho guy things," Katherine confided to him.

"But girls eat 'em, too, don't they, Katherine?" Annie asked seriously, her hand poised above the buns, hesitating.

"We *devour* them," Katherine replied, pretending to reach out and tickle her.

Annie giggled.

The more practical David trotted back to the grill, retrieving the plate that held the burgers.

"They smell heavenly," Katherine declared.

Michael searched for a hidden meaning to that particular description, but she was helping the kids put the plate on the table, not waiting for a reply from him.

When Michael took his seat, he saw Katherine glance at him in question. No doubt she wondered if he planned to say a blessing over the food. Deliberately he set his mouth in a thin line. Not anymore.

Instead, he reached for the hamburger platter. To

his surprise, Katherine assisted him, even though her eyes told him she thought the food should be blessed first.

He offered the first burger to her, and soon every gooey condiment was opened and being poured. Katherine capitulated easily when Annie suggested they build identical burgers. She only flinched mildly when Annie heavily covered both buns with sliced sour pickles, and gamely followed suit.

Michael found himself enjoying the sight.

"I almost forgot the corn!" Katherine exclaimed, popping up from the table. Pulling on his chef mitts, she retrieved the corn from the grill. "Any takers?" she asked, returning to the table.

"Me!" David shouted.

"Me!" Annie chimed in.

Michael guessed they would agree to anything she suggested. But he still didn't think his son would actually eat the corn.

Katherine peeled away the aluminum foil, then buttered each ear. "It's best when it's almost dripping butter," she told them seriously.

"Sold me," Michael said, not wanting her to feel too rebuffed when the kids didn't dive in.

She smiled. "I love fresh corn. When I was growing up, we often got donations of corn that had just been picked."

"Donations?" Michael asked.

For a moment she looked uncomfortable. Then she reached for the saltshaker. "My mother was involved in a lot of charitable projects, and people often gave us the overage from their gardens. And they always brought some for my family, too."

"Do you have a big family?" Annie asked.

Katherine shook her head. "Just my mom and dad."

"No brothers?" Annie asked with great concern, as though this were a terrible and unjust misfortune.

"Afraid not," Katherine replied. "You're lucky to have each other."

An only child, Michael thought. Yet she seemed overly generous, not at all like the stereotypical only child.

But his attention was pulled away from her when he saw his son take a bite of corn. Then another. And another.

Katherine didn't look triumphant, only pleased. "A friend gave me the corn. And it was just picked today."

Michael took a bite, too. Sweet and moist, it was the best corn he'd tasted in longer than he could remember. "Can't beat fresh. Thanks for bringing it. I can't believe David's not only eating a vegetable— he volunteered."

"It's just something different," she dismissed with good grace.

They all polished off the delicious ears of sweet corn, chins dribbling with butter and rivulets of corn juice.

Michael reached over to wipe David's chin. "And I *really* can't believe you're on your second ear."

"This doesn't *taste* like vegetables," David explained. "It tastes *good*."

Katherine laughed. "That's how I feel about grilled squash."

"Ick," David replied without hesitation. "Nothing you can do to squash would make it taste good."

"I thought so, too," she agreed. "Then I had some on a grilled shish kebab."

"What's a shishbob?" Annie asked.

"Lots of yummy stuff on a stick."

"Will you make it for us sometime?"

Michael cleared his throat. "Annie, you don't invite other people to cook for you."

Katherine smiled diplomatically. "My fault again, I'm afraid. Tell you what, if you decide you'd like 'shishbobs' for dinner one night, I'll be happy to cook."

Michael studied her face, wondering at hidden motives. They were either nonexistent or he was too out of practice to tell. That or she was so consumed with bringing his family back to church that she hid her true motive well. And it was that final thought that bothered him.

But before he could think of a way out of this newest invitation, David spoke. "Can we have dessert now? What'd you bring?"

"Actually, I brought two things. I wasn't sure what you'd like so there's a choice."

"You shouldn't have gone to so much trouble," Michael protested, knowing this treatment might spoil his children, actually get them used to edible food.

"It wasn't any trouble," Katherine replied. "Although I don't do a lot of cooking, I enjoy it. But I'm always putting a twist on standard recipes. When I was a kid I tried everything. For a while I went through a stage where I tinted everything I cooked with food color. My father was a very patient soul, but even he had a hard time going through the blue food stage."

"Blue?" the kids asked together, fascinated.

Katherine met Michael's eyes, sharing his amusement. "And I wouldn't recommend it—nothing looks like it would taste too good in blue. Trust me."

"What else did you make?" David asked.

"Well…I think I tried every single flavor of jelly mixed with every imaginable thing I could find in the fridge."

"Your mom didn't mind?" Annie questioned.

For a moment a strange, almost unhappy look passed over Katherine's face. Michael wondered why.

"My mom wasn't into cooking much, so she didn't mind my experiments."

"My mommy was a good cook," Annie told her.

"I'm sure she was, sweetie. I bet she was the best."

After she spoke, Katherine met Michael's eyes, and he saw the compassion there. Michael again felt the sense of loss his family continued to endure. Yet, somehow, with Katherine seated across from him, it didn't seem so bad.

"Why don't we get the dessert?" Katherine suggested. "I could use two helpers."

Annie and David immediately rose, scampering beside her as they headed back into the kitchen.

Michael couldn't still his sense of amazement at how completely his children seemed to accept Katherine. She wasn't anything like their mother, yet they seemed drawn to her shelter much like baby birds to their nest.

Soon the trio returned from the house, each carrying something.

"We're doing s'mores, Daddy!" Annie announced, putting the marshmallows and chocolate bars on the table.

David plunked down the box of graham crackers and, surprisingly, a jar of chunky peanut butter.

"My little twist," Katherine explained, catching his glance resting on the peanut butter. "I love chocolate-peanut butter cups, so I thought, why not?" As she spoke, she put an elaborate glazed, fresh fruit tart in the center of the table. "And I've always loved these."

He glanced appreciatively at the exquisitely prepared dessert. "It looks delicious."

She bent a bit closer, lowering her voice. "I brought the s'mores in case the kids don't like it."

"I think they'd like anything you do," he told her truthfully.

Again, surprising him, she colored a bit, her

hands suddenly nervous, fussing with the dessert plates. "I'll help the kids with the s'mores."

As she headed toward the grill, Michael found himself following. *To supervise the kids,* he rationalized.

He noticed that she had brought long metal hot dog holders with safe wooden handles. She'd thought of everything. And that bothered him. He didn't want to like her as a person. She represented the church that his children were already enjoying too much.

"Mine are almost done," Annie was saying.

"Those aren't cooked enough," David dismissed.

"You want yours charred," Katherine commented. "I like them well done, too, but they're great on the s'mores when they're just gooey like Annie's."

"So they'll work both ways," Michael told them.

"I could cook mine a little more," Annie said, not quite ready to give up her place at the grill.

"Whatever you think, princess," he told her.

"Aren't you going to cook one, Daddy?" Annie asked.

"Oh, sure. I love a good s'more." He picked up one of the roasting sticks, pushed a few marshmallows on the end and joined their circle around the grill.

When they had assembled the graham crackers, chocolate and marshmallow, Katherine gave them the option of peanut butter, as well.

Michael watched as Annie readily agreed. David was another matter. He was a member of probably one of the most minuscule groups in the world—children who don't like peanut butter.

But Katherine took it in stride. "I like s'mores both ways, regular and peanut butter. It's the differences in this world that make things interesting. Just like people."

"People?" David questioned, still not certain he wasn't being teased about his peanut butter aversion.

"Don't you know some people who aren't a lot like you?" Katherine asked.

David thought a moment. "The kids that live by the place Daddy's working on. We go there sometimes when Mrs. Goode can't watch us."

"Did you see them do anything fun while you were there?" Katherine asked, wiping marshmallow goo from her fingers.

David brightened immediately. "They hit a paper donkey that was hanging from a tree."

Katherine met Michael's gaze, and they both smiled.

"A piñata," Michael told him, remembering how all the workmen had paused to watch and grin as the children attacked the piñata, joining their laughter. He hadn't realized David would remember the moment so vividly.

"And that's different," Katherine added. "In a good way, don't you think?"

David nodded. "It looked like lots of fun."

"Maybe sometime your dad would let you and Annie have a piñata. One of the best things about the traditions of other cultures is that we can borrow some of them and make our own lives more interesting."

Michael enjoyed her analogy nearly as much as her positive outlook.

"I think my s'more needs another marshmallow," Annie announced.

Katherine reached for a roasting stick. "Let me make a few more. I like to eat the extras."

"I don't know," Michael observed. "I could skip the graham crackers and marshmallows and go straight for the chocolate."

"But then they're not s'mores, Daddy," Annie protested.

"So they're not, princess. Tell you what. I'll help Katherine make a few more marshmallows, and then you and David can both have another s'more."

"Yea!" David cheered.

He noticed that Katherine's glance slid toward him as they stood beside the grill. A breeze drifted through the trees teasing tendrils of smoke between them. Even though the children were only across the yard, it seemed oddly as though they were alone in the approaching twilight.

Even Katherine's voice was quieter, softer. "Thank you."

"For what?"

"This evening—allowing me to enjoy your children."

He shrugged. "Just a barbecue."

"Maybe so. But I've really had a good time."

Michael wasn't ready to agree with her, to admit that it had been a pleasant evening.

In the silence Katherine fussed with the roasting stick. Suddenly she jerked one hand away. "Ouch!"

"What did you do?" he asked, setting his own roasting stick on the cart beside the grill.

"Oh it's nothing," she replied, still holding the tender spot.

Michael reached for her hand.

"It's so silly," she protested. "I shouldn't have touched the metal."

But he was already turning over her hand. "It's blistering."

To his surprise he felt a trace of trembling in the hand he held.

"I'm such a klutz," she apologized, an odd note in her voice.

He traced the outline of the burn. It wasn't serious, just a reddening of her pale skin. Her very pale skin.

Glancing up, he met her eyes, fielding the questions there, staggered by the ones forming in his own thoughts. Her lips parted in a little *O,* and he sensed trouble. Trouble in the form of a minister. An intriguing, beautiful minister. One whose hand he still held. Worse, one whose hand he wanted to continue holding.

Chapter Five

Three days later Katherine was unusually quiet. As she had been all morning and the preceding two days and nights. She couldn't stop thinking about the Carlson family. More specifically, Michael.

She thought it was telling that he hadn't picked up the children from vacation Bible School either day. But surely it was too much to imagine that he was equally uncomfortable. She doubted that he had read more into the simple touch of their hands than was warranted.

But she couldn't forget the look that passed between them.

And that had all her alarm bells clanging. Despite her longing to have a special man in her life, she knew it wasn't to be, and it certainly couldn't be Michael.

He was a father, a family man. And she knew what happened to men like that when paired with women like her. She could easily remember her own father's pain, the bewildering realization that he counted so little in his wife's estimation. It had been devastating to him. And in Katherine's opinion, he had never truly recovered.

Equally important, she couldn't ever forget Michael's spiritual needs. Needs he continued to deny. Needs that as a minister she should be concentrating on.

Instead, she was agonizing over her personal failures, her own needs. Immersed in her thoughts, she barely heard the knock on her office door.

Cindy entered, her voice equally jarring and cheering. "Well, you look like yesterday's leftovers."

"Thanks."

Cindy stepped closer. "Any special reason for the gloom and doom?"

"Just thinking."

"Morbidly, from the look of you."

Katherine grimaced. "That bad?"

"Yep." Cindy dropped into one of the chairs across from Katherine's desk. "This have anything to do with the seriously good-looking man you think you shouldn't be interested in?"

Katherine was startled into a smile. "What makes you think he's *seriously* good-looking?"

"Because I, my friend, am an optimist."

"Do you suppose that's why we're hopeless romantics?"

"No doubt," Cindy replied with an unflappable calm. "But what would you rather do? Buy a rocker, support hose and a cat in preparation for your future?"

Katherine glanced out the window that offered a wide sweeping view of the church grounds. "Snowy might not take to a cat."

"Then, what are you going to do about this man?"

"Do?" Katherine fiddled with the word in her mind as she had all morning. "He's wounded, Cindy. In so many ways."

"Then, he's lucky to have met you."

Katherine searched for any teasing in her friend's face. But she didn't see any. "I'm not so sure." Quickly she recounted the evening at Michael's house, the barbecue, her own awareness of him.

Cindy's voice was gentle. "It sounds like a really nice time."

Katherine lowered her head. "I thought so, too. But he's avoided picking up his children from vacation Bible School for two days now."

"Maybe he's just been busy, had work conflicts."

"Could be."

"But you don't think so."

"Not really. But perhaps I'm making more of it than I should. Maybe he hasn't given the evening... or me a second thought."

"Then, why is he avoiding you?"

"I keep coming round to the same point, Cindy. First I tell myself it's my imagination. Then I'm convinced that I'm failing him as a minister."

"Maybe he'll be at the picnic this afternoon."

Katherine stared again out the window. "I hope you're right. I really need some answers."

But Katherine didn't get her answers that afternoon. Or the next. Michael appeared determined to stay away. Even though she knew it wasn't sensible, she felt a familiar prick of hurt.

Yet Katherine couldn't help hoping he would accompany his children tonight to the Friday night wrap ceremony. The church had already filled with volunteers who were bringing food and supplies, setting up games and tables. Although she was surrounded by people, Katherine felt a shaft of loneliness so deep the ache resonated through her senses.

It seemed everyone was paired off or grouped into family units. However, she was expected to be a strong leader, the person with all the answers. And so she smiled, greeting people, asking all the right questions, listening as best she could.

Her gaze skipped across the crowd, though, searching. Yet she didn't see the Carlsons…no Michael. Determinedly she kept to the task at hand, making certain everything flowed smoothly.

The minutes passed, and it was nearly time for the program to begin. Children had filled the first few rows of folding chairs, waiting for their opportunity to be front and center. Tessa, was seated on the first row, precocious as always.

Someone caught Katherine's attention, and she turned away for a few moments. When she looked back, to her delighted surprise, both Annie and

David were sitting with Tessa. David was speaking to another boy, but Annie waved immediately, seeking her attention.

Unable to repress her own answering grin, Katherine waved in return. Her stomach flip-flopped as she searched nonchalantly for Michael amidst the surrounding adults. At first she didn't see him, then a pair of broad shoulders and a casual pose caught her eye.

The rush of blood that warmed her face was anything but nonchalant.

But he wasn't meeting her gaze. Feeling incredibly foolish at the snub, Katherine turned away, heading across the room to take her seat.

Within a few minutes, the program began. The children sang several songs, their enthusiasm camouflaging any forgotten words or missed notes.

Then the children chosen to recite Bible verses lined the front of the room. To Katherine's surprise, David was among the children. Immediately concerned, her eyes sought out Michael once again. What would he think of this? Would he believe she had engineered his son's inclusion in the recital?

She couldn't tell. Michael's gaze was focused on his son.

David recited a verse, his voice steady and confident. Katherine found herself smiling fondly—more so than her usual reaction to the children in the congregation.

Then she glanced again at Michael. His face was tight, his expression closed. Immediately she wondered at the pain he held deep inside, the pain that motivated each action, each decision.

The program continued, ending with a charming tune sung by all the children. Then they walked from the front of the room, dispersing to claim parents and friends.

Annie skipped toward Katherine, her eyes shining. "Hi!"

"That was wonderful!"

"Could you hear me sing?" Annie asked earnestly.

"Of course. How could I miss such a sweet voice?"

Annie beamed. "Come with me to see Daddy, okay?"

Katherine tried to think of a kind way to refuse the request, but she couldn't crush the expectation gleaming in the child's eyes. Instead, she called on the strength of her faith, knowing it was time to step into her dual role.

David had reached Michael first, clearly seeking his father's approval. Katherine met Michael's gaze, her own beseeching him to not crush David's enthusiasm.

Michael dropped his hand on David's shoulder, a wordless gesture of approval.

And Katherine released a breath she hadn't realized she had been holding.

"Daddy, can we go to our classrooms so we can see what we made?" Annie asked, bouncing in her excitement.

"Don't you know?" he teased her gently, tapping her head.

She giggled. "Uh-huh, but you don't!"

"Good point," he conceded.

"It's just a casual walk-through," Katherine explained. "Much like open house at school. And the children can take home their art projects tonight."

Annie clapped her hands.

Michael finally met Katherine's eyes, but he disguised his thoughts well. "Then, I guess we'd better see them."

Together they headed down the hallway, Annie clutching her father's hand, urging him to walk faster. Once inside, she became a mini tour guide, making them all smile.

But it was when she reached her art project that her enthusiasm peaked. Carefully Annie picked up a small clay picture frame and handed it to her father. "It's for you, Daddy."

Taking the frame from her outstretched hands, Michael then knelt beside her. "For me, princess?"

"Yes, Daddy, to show you how much I love you. Like Jesus loves us."

Michael's throat worked, then he hugged his daughter tightly. "Thank you, baby." His voice was husky; he sounded nearly undone.

Knowing how the effort must be costing him, Katherine felt her own chest clog with emotion.

"You can put a picture in it, Daddy."

"And I think I know just whose picture," he told her, hugging her again.

"Do you really like it?"

"It's the best present I could get."

She beamed. "Then, does this mean I can come to Sunday School?"

His head jerked up, meeting Katherine's startled gaze, his own accusing. And she couldn't think of one word of explanation.

The late evening seemed empty of its earlier promise. Everything appeared dimmer, even the coffee shop in which Katherine and Michael now sat.

She was prepared to offer conciliatory words, but the waitress appeared quickly, taking their order, chatting amiably.

The coffee arrived with equal speed. Each delay dried Katherine's throat that much more. Fiddling with the cup, she added cream even though she usually drank her coffee black.

"You asked for this meeting," Michael began, his voice void of inflection.

But sensing his underlying anger, she reached inwardly for strength. "I know you were upset earlier this evening." Glancing up, she saw the quiet irony reflected in his eyes. She rushed to fill the tense silence. "More than upset. But I want you to know that I had no idea Annie would ask to attend Sunday School."

"Not even a stray suggestion?"

She couldn't miss the sarcasm in his voice, but she also couldn't rise to the challenge. Instead, she remembered the pain he harbored, the pain that had taken over his life. "No, but it must be equally clear to you that Annie loves going to church. Most children do. We teach love and kindness. Things Annie's obviously already been taught, so it feels natural, welcoming."

"A difficult point to argue, but you knew that. Now, what am I going to say to Annie? How am I going to tell her no?"

Katherine leaned forward, pushing aside the coffee cup. "Does it have to be no?"

"I think I've made it clear how I feel."

"You've told me how difficult things have been since your wife's death. Perhaps having more people to interact with can help Annie through this time."

"Not those particular people."

"Like me?" she asked, unable to completely repress her hurt.

Exasperation flickered in his eyes. "That's not what I meant. I've been honest about my feelings. Yet my children have been sucked further and further into the church."

"Only because they want to be," she reminded him gently. "I know how difficult your loss has been, but please don't punish the children because they're drawn to a healing place."

"If God had answered our prayers, they wouldn't need healing."

Compassion filled her heart, misting her eyes. "There are many answers. Even more than all the questions we have. Please remember that, Michael.

And don't make the solution more difficult than the problem."

Michael met her gaze without speaking. And Katherine knew he was battling both past and present. She could only pray that the Lord would show him the path.

An hour later, Michael kept his tread light as he walked down the dimly lit hallway. Mrs. Goode had put the kids to bed, and he didn't want to waken them. The baby-sitter had warned him again that if his hours didn't improve, she would quit. It was yet another problem to tackle, one for which he had no answer.

Luckily, Tessa's mother was still willing to pick up the kids from any activities. But he hated to depend on others. Often, he'd had to take David and Annie with him on the job when Mrs. Goode wasn't available. But it wasn't a good situation for any of them.

Entering David's room, he smiled at his young soldier. Apparently David had been playing with his army toys until the moment he'd fallen asleep. He was surrounded by miniature tanks, jeeps and infantrymen.

"So the battle wore you out," Michael whispered, smoothing the hair back from David's forehead. Then he lifted the toys from the bed, soundlessly replacing them in plastic crates. Turning back to the bed he pulled the blanket up, smoothing it over bare arms.

It was remarkable how vulnerable a child looked when sleeping. Inside him arose a fierce need to protect and love. It seemed the world was full of more pitfalls and challenges each day. How was he to shield his children from them all? Especially now that he didn't have God to count on anymore.

"Dream of better tomorrows, son," Michael whispered before retreating quietly.

Annie's room was as girlish as David's was all boy. Michael crossed the pale pink carpet to the white canopied bed, which was awash in ruffles.

He was bending to check on Annie, when her voice startled him.

"Is that you, Daddy?"

"Yes, princess. What are you doing awake?"

"I was hoping you'd come tuck me in."

He sat on the side of her bed. "You were?"

"Uh-huh. Daddy, did you really like your present?"

He flinched, grateful for the darkness that camouflaged the motion. "Yes, sweetheart, I loved it."

"Katherine said you would!"

Michael paused. "She did?"

"Uh-huh. She's so nice, Daddy. She makes me feel special."

"Special?"

"Like Mommy did."

Michael's heart stung, knowing how much his daughter needed a woman's attention, also knowing how much they both missed Ruth. Why, though, had Annie glommed on to Katherine? It frightened him to think that breaking this attachment might hurt Annie even more. "But she's not like mommy, sweetheart."

"But she makes me feel good inside, like Mommy did."

Michael sighed. "I'm glad you enjoyed your time with her."

"I'll see her some more, Daddy, when we go to Sunday School."

"Annie, I'm not sure about Sunday School."

"Then, when will I see Katherine?"

"Sweetheart, I'm not sure she has time—"

"Katherine said she'd always have time for me!" Annie wailed.

Michael strove for patience, for a way to make his daughter understand. "Grown-ups often say things like that, but—"

"She meant it, Daddy! She wouldn't lie in Jesus's house!"

Michael blinked. Of course he and Ruth had taught their children the commandments. He just hadn't expected Annie to use one in Katherine's defense. "I didn't say she lied."

"Then, you know she'll see me when we go to Sunday School."

"Annie, families go together to church."

"David wants to go, too. He really likes Katherine. He says she's funny. She made you laugh, too, Daddy."

Yes, she had. But he hadn't expected that to be

another nail in his coffin. Michael made one last attempt. "What if she doesn't have time on Sunday?"

"She will," Annie replied confidently.

Michael didn't know what to tell Annie. Perhaps Katherine wouldn't have the time she'd promised. After all, a minister had obligations. And if Katherine let the relationship wither, rather than him having to force the point, maybe his daughter wouldn't be as crushed.

However, that meant allowing Annie and David to attend Sunday School. And that was only a day away. A day until he gambled with his children's lives.

Chapter Six

Harmeniah Goode was much like her name—a good woman who was a bit of a contradiction. She enjoyed her job caring for the Carlson children, but she also had responsibilities of her own, which included an ailing sister. Harmeniah was getting on in years, and the long hours were taxing.

Yet she was torn because she was genuinely fond of young David and Annie. Harmeniah had been pleased when Michael had allowed his children to attend vacation Bible School. And she'd been downright stunned when he had agreed to let them go to Sunday School. They had attended twice now. Heartened, she'd thought it was a sign that he would be spending more time with his children. But he was still working long hours. Hours Harmeniah no longer had to sacrifice.

Which was why she had called Katherine Blake. Both children had spoken of the minister continually. But that wasn't surprising to Harmeniah since she knew Pastor Blake to be a warm and personable woman.

The doorbell rang, and Harmeniah wiped her hands on her apron, rushing to open the door. "Thank you for coming."

"Certainly, Harmeniah. It sounded urgent."

"It's my sister, Evelyn. She needs to go into the hospital, Pastor."

Katherine didn't bother asking the woman to call her by her first name. She'd tried before to no avail. Harmeniah had said she was too old to change her ways. Instead, Katherine laid a comforting hand on the older woman's arm. "And you need prayer?"

"Actually I need to leave, and there's no one to watch the kids. Since I know you and the Carlson children know you, I thought maybe you could stay with them until Mr. Carlson comes home from work."

"Certainly—if you're sure it will be all right with him."

"It'll have to be," Harmeniah replied frankly. "I've warned him again and again that I can't work these long hours. And I told him about Evelyn's appointment with the specialist today. But his mind's never quite there, if you know what I mean."

Katherine drew her brows together. "Not exactly."

"His mind's always on either work or how to keep his family together."

"I'm sure it's been difficult since he lost his wife," Katherine murmured.

"But it's time he moved on," Harmeniah announced.

"Excuse me?"

"He's too young to stay married to a memory. And his kids need a mother—someone like you, Pastor."

Katherine swallowed, coughed, then swallowed again. "Excuse me?" she repeated.

"Never did understand why you aren't married, Pastor. Need to put the both of you in a bag and shake you up, see what falls out."

"That's a whimsical thought, Harmeniah, but not very practical. Besides, how do you know Mr. Carlson isn't happy as he is?"

"Does he look happy to you?" Harmeniah asked bluntly.

Katherine hesitated. He looked anything but happy. "Still…"

"You take my advice, Pastor. And don't wait until it's too late, if you know what I mean." She raised her graying eyebrows to emphasize her point. "But for right now, can you watch the kids?"

"Certainly, Harmeniah. My schedule is free tonight. Should I try to contact Michael?"

"Don't think it'll do you any good. I've been trying his mobile phone for two hours. I get a message saying it's out of area. I have to be honest with you, Pastor. Sometimes he's a lot later than he expects to be."

"Where are the children?"

"Out back. I didn't want to tell them about you

until I was sure you could stay. No point in getting their hopes up in case you had other plans."

Katherine felt an unexpected flicker of something she couldn't quite define—a combination of disbelief and surprising joy. "You really think they would have been disappointed?"

Harmeniah waved one hand in dismissal. "This family needs you, Pastor, all of them."

Katherine lifted her eyes, meeting the older woman's knowing gaze.

Harmeniah untied the strings of her apron, then pulled it off. "I was just planning to get dinner started."

"I don't mind cooking."

"It's up to you, but I don't want to cause you extra work. Fact is, I never had to ask anyone for help before to do my job."

It occurred to Katherine that the woman was feeling both guilty and a bit incompetent. She shouldn't be, but there it was.

"Harmeniah, you're not asking for help in doing *your* job, you're asking help for Michael in doing *his.*"

To Katherine's surprise and apparently Harmeniah's mortification, tears appeared in the older woman's eyes. "You do have a way with you, Pastor." Then, embarrassed, Harmeniah fled to the next room.

Katherine waited until she heard the other woman collect her things before entering the kitchen. "Harmeniah, perhaps you should come with me to tell the children why I'm here."

Now composed, Harmeniah nodded. "Good idea, Pastor." Not wasting another moment, she marched into the backyard. Katherine trailed behind.

"David! Annie!" the older woman called. "Come here!"

The kids ran toward them from the far end of the deep yard. When they spotted Katherine, they grinned, running even faster.

"Katherine!" they both shouted.

"Hi, guys!" Katherine greeted them.

"What're you doing here?" David asked. "Did you bring dessert?"

Katherine hooted, but Harmeniah plopped disapproving hands on both hips. "Where are your manners, young man? She's not here to bring you dessert. She's here to watch you till your dad gets home."

"Really?" Annie breathed, her face shining in excitement.

"Yes," Katherine replied, inexplicably thrilled by the children's acceptance.

"Wow!" David echoed. "Can you have dinner with us?"

"I think I'll be cooking dinner," Katherine replied.

"Up to you," Harmeniah commented, crimping the handles of her purse together and tugging at her cotton sweater. "Fine, then."

Once the baby-sitter was on her way, Katherine returned to the kitchen, flanked by her willing helpers. Soon she had a stir fry of chicken and vegetables started.

She glanced over at the table. "Great job. I like the pink napkins with the yellow plates."

"I picked those," Annie confided.

"I guessed you had," Katherine replied. In a moment of instant understanding, they both giggled. In typical male fashion, David rolled his eyes, but a grin lurked on his face, as well.

At that moment, Michael walked in, his gaze darting from his smiling children to a flushed Katherine. And the kitchen smelled like heaven. Certainly not like Mrs. Goode's boiled dinners. And certainly not like his own burned attempts.

But what was Katherine doing here?

She spotted him, and her face registered a variety of expressions before settling into a calm smile. "Hello, Michael."

"Katherine." He didn't keep the question from his tone.

"Harmeniah called me."

"Mrs. Goode?" He didn't know anyone had the nerve to call the woman by her first name.

Katherine smiled. "Yes. She had a personal emergency and asked if I could watch the children until you arrived home. She left you a detailed note on the hall table. It's about her sister."

"Oh." Deflated and more than a little confused, Michael nodded. Then he remembered Mrs. Goode telling him about a special doctor's appointment for her sister. Was that today?

Annie and David flung themselves at him, and he knelt down, hugging them both.

Katherine washed her hands, then turned back to him. "Well, I guess I'll be on my way."

"No!" both children protested.

"It looks like you've cooked dinner," Michael responded, still thrown by how natural she looked in his kitchen. How bewitching her flushed face appeared.

"Well, yes, but—"

"Then, won't you eat with us? Whatever it is, it smells wonderful."

She smiled again. "I think it's a little different from what the kids are used to. I hope it's okay."

"Katherine said I could eat just the chicken and rice if I don't like the vegetables," David told him.

She half shrugged an apology, but Michael couldn't find it in himself to complain. Not when she'd rescued him from possibly losing his babysitter.

To his further surprise, when they began eating, David did try the vegetables. Remarkably he seemed to like them. But they were crisp, fresh and tasty. What was not to enjoy?

"This is like eating in a restaurant," Annie remarked.

Katherine smiled. "Not quite, but thanks, sweetie."

Michael bristled for a moment at the familiarity. But Annie's smile was a rainbow. One he couldn't banish with words or a look.

"That was delicious," he told Katherine honestly,

as they finished. "I can't remember when I've had anything so good."

"I'm glad you enjoyed it." Katherine fiddled with the spoon in the rice bowl. "I'm sorry I didn't think about dessert."

"We could go get ice-cream cones!" David suggested gleefully.

"I want vanilla," Annie joined in. "With sprinkles."

Katherine looked at Michael helplessly.

He cleared his throat. "Hey, kids, we don't know if Katherine has other plans." David turned immediately to Katherine. "Do you?"

"Well, no, but I'm not sure your dad—"

"Daddy, can we go have ice cream? Please? Please!" It was a dual request, their voices rising in a nearly simultaneous chorus that repeated the words again and again.

It was a tide even Michael couldn't turn. "If Katherine's sure she doesn't have other plans..."

David and Annie shifted their attention to her. "You don't, do you, Katherine? Do you?"

Gracefully, she laughed. "What other plans could be better than spending the evening with you?"

It was amazing, Michael realized. Somehow, she made both of his children feel important and wanted. It was a rare gift. One his late wife had possessed, one they had fiercely missed.

As they piled into the car, twilight crept about them during their drive to the center of their old-fashioned town. Settled in the mid-1800s, primarily by German and Polish immigrants, Rosewood had been a tiny farming community until oil had been discovered. That phenomenon had propelled the village into a town, but not one so large that it encroached on the charm.

And Rosewood had retained its small town values, along with a main street that looked as though it could have been plucked from the previous century and carefully preserved.

The ice-cream parlor was housed in an ancient building, one that was painstakingly maintained. The swirls and cupolas that decorated the entrance were freshly painted. Inside, an equally well-aged, old-fashioned marble fountain dominated the space. The children clambered up on the stools at the counter.

"Do you mind?" Michael asked, wondering if she would prefer a booth.

"This is great," Katherine replied, claiming a stool for herself.

Michael took the remaining stool—the one beside her.

Pulling a menu from its holder, she glanced at him. "Don't you need to see the selections?"

He shook his head. "Nope."

She smiled. "Chocolate?"

Surprised, he angled his head toward her. "Good guess."

"Stands to reason. Anyone who would prefer straight chocolate over a s'more has to be a devotee."

Even more surprised, he studied her face. Who

was this woman who noticed so much, who fit in so well, who made his children so happy?

"Sprinkles, Daddy," Annie reminded him. "Don't forget the sprinkles."

He smiled tolerantly at his youngest.

"I want strawberry *and* chocolate," David told him.

Michael caught Katherine's gaze. "And you?"

"Hmm. All the flavors look good, but I think I'll try licorice."

"Ick!" David said without hesitation.

"David!" Michael chided him.

But Katherine was laughing. "It's okay. I know I'm probably one of only a handful of people who like that flavor."

"Sort of like me not liking peanut butter?" David asked her.

"Exactly. People tease me all the time."

He nodded. "Me, too. But peanut butter tastes yucky."

"And licorice tastes yummy."

David grinned. "Uh-uh."

Michael watched their exchange. Since Ruth's death, David hadn't opened up to anyone. Yet he seemed at ease with Katherine. Katherine the preacher.

She angled her stool toward his. "I'll call the hospital when I get home, and check on Harmeniah's sister."

Michael stopped short of thumping himself on the head. "I should have thought of that myself." Then another thought struck him. "I wonder if Mrs. Goode will be able to watch the children tomorrow."

Katherine's face was thoughtful. "If you're in a pinch, I could rearrange my morning appointments and push the afternoon ones into early evening."

"Hopefully that won't be necessary, but I appreciate the offer."

"Of course, I might demand sprinkles on *my* ice cream next time," she said with a smile.

But his expression remained sober. "I insist on paying you for your time."

She waved away his words. "Absolutely not. I enjoy the time with Annie and David. I couldn't take money for it."

"I won't ask for your help unless it's absolutely necessary."

She studied him. "I imagine it's difficult for you to take time off from work."

"I own a contracting business, and the buck stops with me. It would almost be easier if I worked for someone else. Then I could take off when necessary. But if the job doesn't get done properly on time, we stand to incur big penalties. And too many people are depending on me for their jobs. I can't forget that. When Ruth was alive, I didn't have to worry about the kids. She knew I was building a life for all of us—and a future. So when I worked late I knew they were in her hands."

Katherine hesitated. "Have you ever considered hiring an assistant—someone who can take your place from time to time?"

He shook his head. "It's not the same thing."

"Agreed. But even when your wife was here to care for the children, they must have missed you when you worked such long hours."

He studied her, wondering if there was any facet of his life she didn't feel comfortable probing into. "I run my business and my family the way I think is best."

"I'm not questioning that, simply voicing a thought. Like you, I prefer doing most everything myself so I'm certain it's done the way I want. In fact, it's been a liability in my work for as long as I can remember. I've had to strive to include others even when I'd feel more confident doing things myself."

"But your work—"

"Daddy, can I have a chocolate-covered cone?" David interrupted.

"I guess so. I don't think you'll be able to eat it all, though."

Katherine laughed. "But you'll have fun trying, won't you, David?"

"Yep. They make the cones here, ya know," David told her. "They have this special machine, and when it's not busy the man lets you watch 'em make the cones."

"I like to smell them baking," she said.

"Me, too," Annie chimed in. "'Specially when they make cinnamon ones." She looked at her father. "Can I have a cinnamon cone, Daddy?"

He sighed. "Why not? With all this sugar, I'll be scraping you two off the walls, anyway."

Katherine grinned. "Me, too. One plus to the sugar, I'll get loads of stuff done tonight when I get home."

The waitress came just then and took their orders. For the next several minutes the kids popped up and down on the stools in anticipation.

Katherine gestured toward them. "It's great seeing them so happy."

Michael nodded in agreement.

"It's also great that you allowed them to come to Sunday School the past two weeks."

"Don't be too happy. It's only a temporary agreement."

She frowned. "I hope not. Annie and David need the interaction with other kids, the positive reinforcement they're receiving."

He stiffened. "I can do that for them."

"You can't do everything," she pointed out gently.

Before he could reply, the waitress brought their ice cream.

After Michael made certain the kids were settled with their cones, he dug into his own. Then he glanced over at Katherine, enjoying the look of pure satisfaction on her face. But he couldn't resist teasing her about the licorice flavor. "You realize you're eating black ice cream."

Her brows lifted as she eyed his chocolate cone. "As opposed to brown. Your point?"

"Hmm. Most women wouldn't refer to chocolate as brown."

She swallowed a lick of her ice cream. "I'm not most women."

He'd noticed, but didn't think it was wise to say so, to let her know how much she appealed to him. "So what kind of woman are you, Katherine Blake?"

She visibly swallowed, her smile leaner, more thoughtful. "I don't have a quick answer for that."

"I don't recall asking for one."

She reached for a napkin, fiddled with her cone. "Well, I'm not a small town girl…at least not originally."

Michael studied her. "Houston?"

Surprise flickered over her face. "Do you have a sideline as a psychic?"

"No. But I work with a lot of people in the oil industry. You fit the profile."

"I didn't realize I was that predictable," she countered.

"You aren't."

She turned her ice-cream cone in her fingers. "You're being very enigmatic."

"I think I'll save that label for you."

She stared at him in surprise. "Me?"

"I hadn't met you a month ago, and now my children think you hung the moon. Yet I still don't know you."

She met his eyes. "I could say the same of you, Michael."

"Daddy, Daddy," Annie called out. "Look, I got pink sprinkles, too!"

He turned to Annie, while David trotted over to Katherine's side. Their chance for a private conversation disappeared. Although Michael was pleased to see his children so happy, he found himself wanting to learn more about Katherine, about what made her tick. Yet he told himself that was a mistake…that she was already intruding too much in his thoughts.

Chapter Seven

❧

Unable to reach Mrs. Goode at home, Katherine stopped by the hospital after she left the Carlsons. She visited with Evelyn, then offered a prayer for her as the woman was prepared for surgery, which was scheduled for the following morning.

Harmeniah followed Katherine out of the patient room into the hallway. "Thanks for seeing Evelyn, Pastor. She says she's okay, but I think she's kind of scared about tomorrow."

Katherine clasped her hand. "You'll both be in my prayers. And I'll be sure to put Evelyn's name on the church prayer roll, as well."

Harmeniah nodded but she still looked disturbed.

"Is something else bothering you?"

The older woman averted her face for a moment. "I hate to ask again, but do you think you could watch the children tomorrow? I really want to be here during Evelyn's surgery."

"Of course you do," Katherine responded. "I can

juggle my morning appointments, do a little shift-ing, and we're set."

"I appreciate it, Pastor. I'll call Mr. Carlson to tell him you'll sit with the children tomorrow. I'm sure he'll be relieved."

Katherine kept her expression benign, not certain she agreed with Harmeniah. "Don't worry about the Carlsons, Harmeniah, and try to get a good night's sleep."

Harmeniah's gaze strayed back to her sister's room. "I'll try, Pastor. I guess you and I will both need some extra energy tomorrow."

But after hours spent with the Carlson children the following day, Katherine was only reenergized. She loved their spontaneity, their fresh outlook on everything.

They were bright, energetic kids who, she was beginning to suspect, were untapped resources. At the slightest suggestion, both were creative and filled with ideas. Katherine believed they would be a joy to care for full time. But then, neither their father nor Mrs. Goode seemed able to do that.

Katherine knew there wasn't a simple solution. Michael clearly loved his children, but his job took much of his time. And it wasn't Mrs. Goode's job to be their mother.

Nor was it hers, Katherine reminded herself. Yet she couldn't repress the pleasure she felt at their least accomplishment. Together they had raked the grass beneath the huge live oak tree in the backyard, pulled weeds along the front path, then swept the area, leaving it tidy and inviting. Even Tessa had enjoyed helping before heading home.

Since the kids loved being outside, Katherine thought it would be fun to eat in the yard. Guessing that all children liked spaghetti, she'd brought over the ingredients. Luckily, she'd been given a huge basket of home-grown tomatoes by one of her church members. And she'd picked fresh basil, oregano and parsley from her own herb garden.

The kids were entranced with the fresh ingredients.

"You have your own garden?" David asked, smelling the soft, fragrant basil.

"Well, it's kind of small, but I love fresh ingredients."

"Could we plant a garden?" Annie asked.

"Well…I think you'll have to ask your dad about that."

"Will you help us make one?" David asked.

She hesitated. Michael Carlson might not be pleased with any long-term plans. "Why don't we talk to your dad first, make sure that he wants a garden."

"Okay," David agreed. "Are you going to be here tomorrow?"

Katherine had made a discreet call to the hospital and learned that Harmeniah's sister had come through surgery all right. She hadn't talked to the sitter, though, and didn't yet know her plans for the following day.

"Perhaps when your dad comes home he can talk to Mrs. Goode, and we'll know."

When everything was ready, they assembled at the table in the yard. The gate creaked as it opened, and the kids jumped to their feet.

"Daddy!"

Annie and David ran toward their father, landing against him with twin thuds. His muscled body didn't flinch. Instead, he scooped them both up, and for a few moments all three voices sounded at once. As Katherine watched them she couldn't completely sort the feelings their tableau evoked...pleasure... warmth... envy.

Before she could wonder further, they converged around the table. In the babble, she greeted Michael, saw the appreciation in his eyes.

"This looks great, Katherine. I'll wash up and be right back."

"Hurry, Daddy!" the children urged.

True to his word, Michael returned quickly, taking the seat across from her, just as though this were their little family. Immediately, a seed of fear sprouted.

Fear that said this all seemed too comfortable, too much like what she'd been dreaming of. And she knew this picture wasn't in her future. No man deserved the kind of wife she was fated to be. Especially not this man who had two such very special children.

More quiet than usual, she allowed the children to chat with their father. They bubbled over, relaying what they'd done that day. He promised to look at their accomplishments as soon as they had eaten.

"I don't want to let dinner get cold," he told them. Then he caught Katherine's attention. "You shouldn't have gone to so much trouble. We're not used to gourmet food."

"Good," she replied. "This is just spaghetti."

"Considering the spaghetti I cook comes in cans, this is gourmet to us."

"It's the fresh tomatoes. It's hard to make anything taste bad when you have home-grown tomatoes in the mix."

Despite her light tone, he said seriously, "Thank you, Katherine. Mrs. Goode's absence could have been really traumatic for the kids. Nothing has been very stable for them since their mother's death. So I appreciate today."

Emotions still stirred, she took a deep breath, repressing any qualms or regrets at what she was about to say. "It sounds like you need a friend, Michael. I could be one…a friend, that is."

A beat of unexpected silence thrummed between them. One that said the tension between them signaled far more than mere friendship.

Finally he nodded. "I suppose I could use a friend."

She ignored a sharp jab of misgiving that proclaimed she wanted to be more than friends, that her words had been a mistake. "Then, it's a deal."

"Daddy." David snagged his father's attention. "Can we make a garden?"

Michael dragged his gaze away from Katherine. "What?"

"A garden, Daddy."

"So we can have fresh stuff," Annie added. "Please?"

"I don't see anything wrong with a garden, but it's an awful lot of work. Where'd you get this idea?"

"Katherine has a garden," David explained.

"She pulls fresh burbs out of it," Annie explained.

"Herbs," Katherine clarified. "I put some in the sauce."

Michael had an odd look on his face, one she couldn't interpret. Then he shrugged. "My grandparents always had a garden, and I don't think it hurt me to work in it."

"Is that yes?" David asked.

"Sure."

Satisfied, the kids turned their attention back to the spaghetti. Katherine, her appetite diminished now that Michael had accepted her offer of friendship, looked toward the house, gently outlined by the fading light. It was the kind of house that seemed to promise happy families…a couple still in love with each other after fifty years of marriage. The kind of happily-ever-after that wasn't in her future.

"I really like your home… It has that 'step inside and stay a while' quality." Immediately embarrassed, she realized the words must have sounded as though she wanted yet another invitation.

But he spoke before she could correct the impression. "You know it's always seemed that way to me, too, real comforting. But Ruth always wanted a new house…in one of those subdivisions they're building outside town."

Katherine thought those houses all looked the same, without the distinction or charm of Michael's home. But most of her contemporaries loved them. They found the new homes modern and sleek. And she'd noticed most were filled with young, happy-looking families. Perhaps she was the one out of step, Katherine realized.

"I planned to get one for her," Michael continued, his voice growing flat. "But I waited too long. Funny. I always thought we had forever. I never guessed we didn't even have tomorrow."

For a brief, insane moment Katherine envied Ruth Carlson, the love she had shared with Michael, their idyllic children. As instantly she was ashamed.

"I suspect she knew your intentions," Katherine murmured. "And sometimes that's almost as good as the reality."

Michael shrugged, an unhappy movement that signaled his pain. "I don't know. I thought she would be cured, as well." Then his expression grew challenging. "At least, that's what I prayed for."

Katherine bent her head for a moment, remembering her own past, the pain of her parents' broken marriage, their fractured family. "Not all prayer is answered in ways we expect."

"It's not answered period." Bitterness flavored the words.

"If you pray for rain and get a monsoon, is that an answer, a solution or a surprise?"

"It's a disaster," he replied flatly.

"Daddy, what are we going to plant?" Annie asked, startling them both.

He took a deep breath. "What do you want to plant, princess?"

She smiled. "What you like, Daddy."

How could he not believe, Katherine wondered, with two such perfect and wonderful children? They alone were proof of everything good.

"Daddy likes those green things," David supplied.

Katherine's and Michael's eyes met, unexpected amusement flowing between them.

Michael cleared his throat. "Any particular green, son?"

"Like on the pizza," David explained.

"You're right!" Michael glanced at Katherine. "I like all kinds of peppers."

"Then we'll plant peppers," Annie told him.

"And sometimes it's nice to put a few flowers in the vegetable garden," Katherine commented. "It adds beauty to the practicality."

Again an unfathomable expression crossed Michael's face.

"I like pink flowers," Annie told her.

"Me, too," Katherine agreed. "Especially roses."

"Not me," David objected.

"I don't know, son. There are few things in this world as incredible as a perfect rose or a beautiful woman, and usually, you'll find the two together."

Something warm curled in Katherine's stomach. She knew Michael Carlson was a special man, but she hadn't expected a soul filled with romance, or for him to possess the words of a poet.

"Okay," David answered with a shrug. "Guess they won't hurt the other stuff."

"Spoken like a diplomat, son."

Katherine looked between father and son. It was more than diplomacy. It was the kind of special relationship this family shared. One she'd always wanted to be part of. One she'd never had, one she could never hope for. Once again Katherine was standing on the outside looking in.

Michael rushed home. Although Katherine had agreed to watch the children, he had insisted it wouldn't be more than a day or so. Now, a week and a half later, she was still helping him. Mrs. Goode's sister was doing well, but she needed care during her recuperation.

Michael didn't know what he would have done without Katherine's help. She was truly becoming a good friend.

And maybe that's what was sticking in his craw.

The fact that she wanted them to be friends, nothing else. Even though he told himself he didn't want anything to do with a minister, he was still immensely attracted to Katherine. There was something about her spontaneity, her fresh approach to life that was incredibly appealing.

He should be grateful, he supposed, that she only

wanted friendship, since he had no intention of returning to the church.

But he couldn't repress an image of her face…the laughter that lurked in her eyes…or her lips parted as she enjoyed a simple ice-cream cone. Katherine's enthusiasm had been as refreshing as a child's; her appeal, however, was completely womanly.

Reaching his house, Michael headed not inside but to the gate that opened to the backyard. He knew where Katherine and his children would be.

Under Katherine's direction, the kids had staked out a garden, tilled the soil and worked like little Trojans to plant a variety of vegetables and flowers. At her suggestion, they had each planted a rosebush in honor of their mother. The gesture had touched him deeply.

Stepping farther into the yard, he saw that Katherine and the kids were all on their hands and knees in the dirt, digging new rows. Yet Michael could see that, in typical fashion, Katherine had managed to infuse the project with fun. They were all laughing over some shared joke.

Katherine spotted him first. Her face changed like the shading of a windswept day. Initially it shone in welcome, then the storm clouds moved in. And he wondered why. Was there something hidden beneath her seeming openness?

Then Annie and David saw him and ran to greet him. He took dirt clumps and kisses with equal aplomb.

"Daddy!" Annie exclaimed. "We're planting corn!"

"Oh?"

"Uh-huh. 'Cause David likes it."

"That's a good reason, princess."

David shuffled, looking pleased but embarrassed. "Not just for me."

"Agreed," Michael told him. "We all like it."

Katherine stood up, dusting the dirt from her bare knees. The late-afternoon sun glinted off her long dark hair, which she had pulled into an impish ponytail. Wearing a sleeveless top and shorts, she could have passed for a teenager.

"Are you about through with the garden for today?" Michael asked.

"Yes. I think we're all ready to get cleaned up."

"Then, why don't we go for dinner?" Michael suggested.

Katherine glanced down at her casual outfit.

"To Casa Boñita in old town," he continued. It was a decidedly casual restaurant that served the best Mexican food for miles.

She nodded. "Sounds great."

Just then, the French doors on the patio opened, and Mrs. Goode stepped out. The kids ran to greet her, and the older woman looked pleased by the welcome. However, once the hellos were aside they showered her with details about the garden Katherine was helping them plant.

Katherine, however, kept the woman from thinking she'd been so easily supplanted. "Your shoes are difficult to fill, Harmeniah. I know the kids are thrilled to see you."

"Well, Pastor, I know they've been in good hands."

"They miss you," Katherine replied graciously.

"Will you be back with us soon?" Michael asked, knowing he couldn't have Katherine caring for his children…for so many reasons.

"I still need to help my sister, but she's on the mend, so I can come back part-time. Of course, if you want to look for another sitter, I'll understand."

As though there were any available. Michael shook his head. "We'll work around it, Mrs. Goode."

She visited with the children a bit more before leaving. Then Michael sent David and Annie inside to wash faces and hands, turning at last to Katherine.

"I appreciate your help, but I don't expect you to continue caring for the kids. It should be easier to find a part-time sitter than a full-time one."

"I'll do whatever I can while you're in a pinch. Luckily summer tends to be slower at church, so I have more time."

"I'm not sure that's a good idea." He knew he sounded reluctant.

For a moment something akin to disappointment blossomed in Katherine's expression, before she composed her features. Still her eyes knowing, her voice strained, she asked, "Because I'm a minister?"

"I've been telling you how much I don't want my children involved in church. And you represent everything I'm opposed to. You're a minister, Katherine, and nothing will change that."

A flicker of pain appeared in her eyes, then was gone. "Which is why I can be a good friend to you. I don't judge, Michael. That's neither my job nor my way of doing things."

"We're at opposite ends of the planet in this matter, Katherine. And I don't believe for a moment that you can't see that, as well."

"I agree that we disagree. But that doesn't mean I can't care about your family."

"And convince my children that I'm wrong, that they shouldn't listen to me?"

Hurt filled her eyes, and for a moment her lips trembled. "Do you really think I would do that? Try to turn children away from their father?"

He passed a hand over his forehead. "I don't know. I guess not. But you have to admit that they can't wait to attend whatever's going on at church."

"That's because they enjoy what's taught there, the interaction with other kids," she pointed out gently. "And since you took them to church before their mother passed away, it comes naturally to them. Children learn by example, not by words. Until the past year, going to church *was* their example."

Logically Michael knew she was right. Yet he was unable to repress the feeling that she couldn't be simply a friend—not when she was a minister. He refused to examine whether there was more to his agitation—that her easy decision to be only friends had been galling him.

Still, the words didn't come easily. "I really do appreciate what you've done for the kids…and me."

Something unfathomable flashed in her eyes. If he didn't know better he would think it was regret.

"That's what friends are for."

Chapter Eight

Katherine took her battered psyche along with her as she continued to help Michael care for his children in Mrs. Goode's absence. The older woman had opted for mornings, and Katherine took over after lunch until their father arrived home.

Michael hadn't been able to find another sitter, even part-time. He couldn't be absent from his current contracting project, and he didn't want to put the kids in day care.

Knowing that, Katherine couldn't allow their strained feelings to affect the children. Innocent, all accepting, they continued to be a joy.

She reminded herself of that when the hurt surfaced. It had been a shock to learn that Michael felt so strongly about her job. She had begun to believe that he had been able to view her differently—as a person...a woman, not a minister.

But maybe that wasn't possible. Not even with a man like Michael. He resented everything she was, everything she represented. There wasn't even a question of his viewing her only as a woman. That debate was over.

Annie and David were a balm to that heartache. Annie, sensing she was down, had drawn her a beautiful red heart. Even David had helped, giving her one of his prized toy soldiers for her own. Realizing how lucky she was to have them even on a temporary basis, she pulled herself out of her funk, vowing to enjoy every moment.

Which was why she had dug out the bicycles in the garage, filling the low tires and making sure they were roadworthy. Together, the three of them rode to the park. They played on the swings, slides and jungle gym. Each moment reinforced what Katherine had guessed all along. Nothing was quite as fulfilling as kids, a family.

Even though she had to shuffle appointments and commitments, Katherine wouldn't have traded a moment of this precious time. Cindy had volunteered to help with sick calls, and she'd also taken on much of Katherine's paperwork and correspondence.

Luckily, her friend was a trust fund baby, thanks to the oil business. Although Cindy volunteered for nearly a dozen organizations and sat on the board of her family's oil company, most of her time was free, allowing her to help Katherine.

"Katherine, do we really hafta go home?" David asked as they pedaled away from the park, interrupting Katherine's thoughts.

"Yes. Your dad may be home soon. You don't want him worrying, do you?"

"No," Annie replied for them both. "Daddy worries lots already."

The comment surprised Katherine. Not because she didn't think the children were perceptive, but because she didn't picture Michael worrying so that it showed.

"Maybe we could bring Daddy back here," David offered, always the negotiator.

"Tell you what. If we get home in time to make a picnic supper, we can ask him. But that's only if he's home early enough; okay?"

"Sometimes he has to work *real* late," Annie told her with a small sigh.

"I know, sweetie. But that's so he can provide a nice home and a good future for you and David. I'm sure he'd rather be at the park with you having a picnic."

David grinned. "Or playing softball."

Katherine glanced at him. "Does he like softball?"

"He was the best player on the team," David replied with pride.

"Doesn't he still play?"

Annie shook her head. "Not since Mommy died."

Apparently Michael had given up everything when he'd lost his wife, even the sport of softball. Although she was deeply touched, Katherine made her voice purposely cheerful. "If we hurry home, we'll probably have time to make that picnic supper."

"I can go kinda fast," Annie offered.

"Not too fast," Katherine cautioned. "We won't save time if we fall and scrape our knees." And the mid-July day was hot.

David grinned. "I can go fast without falling."

Katherine glanced over at Annie. "Well, I'm afraid I can't, so you'll have to hold back a little for me."

Even allowing for the youngest member of their trio, they made good time. Annie and David raced to the front door, burst into the kitchen.

Katherine brought up the rear, teasing them. "First one in the kitchen gets to clean up."

Twin squeaks from their tennis shoes skidding to a halt made her grin. She pushed open the swinging door, walking to stand beside them. "Looks like a three-way tie."

Annie and David both giggled, and soon they were collecting the ingredients for a simple lunch.

"What about Daddy's bike?" David asked.

"Good point. Why don't we check the tires? But in case your Dad's tired, let's give him the option of going by bike or car. *If* he agrees to go," she stressed.

"Okay," David conceded.

Since it looked as though the kids might burst if they waited for their father to come home, Katherine suggested they go into the backyard and jump on the trampoline for a while. But once outside, the kids insisted that she join them. It didn't take much coaxing. Katherine loved bouncing with them, making them shriek. And her attention was focused fully on them, when Michael stepped out the French doors of the patio.

He paused, watching his children frolic with Katherine. It struck Michael again—his disbelief that she could be a minister. It seemed she ought to enjoy more pastoral pursuits, certainly more calm, dignified ones.

But there was nothing dignified about her at the moment. Bouncing alongside his children, her hair was flung out like a dark, silk banner. And her long, tanned legs pumped in unison with David's and Annie's.

Maybe it was a good thing she *was* a minister. It made her far easier to resist, he told himself.

But his resistance was wavering. He wanted nothing more than to take her in his arms, to test his suspicion that she would fit perfectly there.

The children spotted him, waving as they bounced. He walked to the edge of the trampoline. "Looks like everyone's having fun."

Katherine slowed her jumping, her face flushing slightly. "Hi."

"Hey," he replied.

The children scrambled toward him, talking excitedly about the picnic in the park at the same time.

When they'd finished, he studied Katherine's expression.

Her lips edged upward, not her usual grin but a more restrained smile. "We made a simple supper and packed it in the picnic basket, because the kids had such a good time at the park this afternoon."

"Dare I ask what having air in the tires means?"

"We rode bikes to the park, but I reminded Annie and David that you might be tired after working all day and not feel like biking to the park. That is, *if* you feel like having supper at the park."

He was exhausted but he didn't want his kids to know that. Even more, he didn't want them to think his time spent with them was unimportant. "Sounds great. You sure the bikes are really in shape?"

"Katherine knows how to fix 'em," David informed him.

"By necessity," she explained. "As a kid I had to keep my own maintained. And since I still love biking, I kept up the skill."

"Great."

They carried the basket and thermos to the bikes and divided the load between the adult cycles. Briefly Michael remembered the last time the bikes had been taken out. It had been before Ruth had gotten sick…and they'd been abandoned ever since.

Even though the bikes were a painful reminder, he knew he couldn't ignore every activity he'd shared with his late wife. Seeing how excited the children were, Michael was immediately remorseful that he'd put away everything associated with Ruth at their expense.

And David was right—Katherine had checked out the bike, filled the tires, and it was in perfect shape. Only the memories assailing him seemed off kilter.

Then his eyes landed on Annie and David, excitedly pedaling ahead. As Katherine had said, maybe it was time to fold away some of the remembrances, because even though it seemed obscenely unfair, life *did* go on.

Katherine pulled up at his side, her voice quiet. "It occurred to me that it might be difficult for you watching me ride Ruth's bike. I'm happy to put it back in the garage. You don't need me along on this picnic. The kids will understand."

"But I won't," he responded, surprising them both. "You once asked if I trotted out morbid memories for the kids. I didn't think so, but I've attached a kind of hands-off mentality to anything associated with Ruth. And that's not fair to them…or to her, either. She wouldn't have wanted that."

"I didn't know her, but I suspect you're right. I can see a lot of her in your children. They wouldn't be so open and generous without special guidance from an exceptional person."

Michael's throat thickened. How was it that Katherine knew the right thing to say…in fact, seemed to know how he was feeling? Others had tried to talk to him about Ruth but it had been incredibly difficult for him. Each person who'd asked him to open up had simply made him close that much more. It was as though Katherine invited Ruth in, as though there was room for the three of them in their conversation.

Some of his exhaustion fell away with the realization. Together they pedaled toward the park. A light breeze rippled through the evening air, teasing them with the promise of a cooler evening ahead.

Seeing that Michael was staring ahead, Katherine angled her head to study his profile. What was he thinking about? she wondered. Was he immersed in memories of his late wife, or was it possible he had moved past them just a bit?

It was difficult to know. Michael wasn't an open person. She didn't know if he'd been that way always, or just since his wife's death. Katherine also didn't know if she was aggravating the situation by being part of the church he resented so deeply.

Within a short time, they arrived at the park. David and Annie picked a table close to the playground equipment.

"Can we swing, Daddy?" Annie pleaded.

"Please?" David added.

Michael glanced at Katherine. "Can the supper you packed wait a while?"

"Sure."

"Okay," he told them.

They flung their bikes to the ground and scampered toward the swings and slides.

"Think they'll miss us?" Michael asked wryly, leaning his own bike against a nearby tree.

She managed a partial grin as she dismounted. "Probably when they get hungry."

"That's better," he responded.

Katherine looked at him in question.

"The smile. I was wondering where it had disappeared to."

Uncomfortable, she shrugged, parking her bike next to his. "I'm not sure what you mean."

"I think you do."

Since she did, Katherine couldn't argue the point.

Instead, she opened the picnic basket, pulled out a tablecloth.

He took one end, and together they draped the multicolored fabric over the redwood table. As she smoothed the tablecloth in place, Michael retrieved the thermos.

In tacit agreement, Katherine pulled the cups from the basket and he filled them.

"Did you want to swing with the kids?" Michael asked.

She shook her head. "I think I did enough of that earlier today. But you go ahead."

"I'd rather just sit here and talk for a while, if you don't mind."

That elusive feeling of warmth began to curl inside her. "I'd like that, actually."

And for a while they discussed the mundane, the specifics of the day…the light and easy. Which made Katherine that much more unprepared for his next words.

"You've never told me—how did you come to be a minister?"

For a moment she caught her breath. Again the past swirled over her…and between them. "I'm not sure there's one easy answer."

"Then start with part one," he suggested.

"Part one," she mused. For a moment her eyes closed briefly, a defense against memories and also a silent request for strength. "Well, to begin with, I come from a long line of ministers."

"Really?" He looked only slightly surprised. "Your father?"

"Actually," she paused. "My mother."

His eyebrows shot up in shock. "Your *mother?*"

"She was a pioneer in the field. She certainly wasn't the first female minister, but it was a select group. And she was a natural for the job. She possessed a mountain of energy, always taking on more and more projects and stray people. Then and now, she's the strongest woman I've ever known. Her example both inspired and challenged."

"And you wanted to be like her?"

Irony flashed through Katherine's thoughts, but she schooled the impulse to tell him the entire truth. "Actually, I admired that she cared more about her calling than any obstacles she encountered. And she made me care about others more than myself. When most kids were hanging out at the mall, I was volunteering at the soup kitchen. It's something I've never forgotten."

"So you followed in her footsteps."

Katherine flinched inwardly. "In some ways."

"Is that where you learned to balance everything in your life?"

History told her that balance didn't exist for women in strong roles such as her own. "You forget, I don't have a family to add to the equation."

His voice was even. "No, I didn't forget."

She wondered painfully if she'd sprouted the equivalent of a sign across her forehead announcing herself as hopelessly, terminally single. But she pushed away the thought. "I do worry when my job gets between me and friends."

"Is that a not-too-subtle hint?"

"Sort of. My calling should make it easier for me to relate to my friends, rather than be an obstacle."

"It won't be…as long as you don't try to preach to me," he warned.

"Have I done that?" Katherine asked softly, wishing just for the moment that so much baggage didn't exist between them.

"I suppose not," he replied truthfully. "But I expect it to happen."

"That's difficult to fight—expectation."

"Yes…" He hesitated. "I'm very aware of that."

Their eyes met across the table. An unexpected hunger surfaced, crying out to be recognized. In the quiet, repressed need thrummed between them. The need of two wounded people who were afraid to trust, to believe.

And somewhere in the exchange, she felt another nudge of awareness, one that only increased as he sat next to her on the bench.

The ripe smell of full flowering honeysuckle drifted toward them in the lazy evening breeze. It was a hushed twilight disturbed by only the occasional cry of the children at play.

The moment was one she wanted to preserve in time, then keep close on lonely nights. Lonely nights that seemed to stretch out forever in her future.

Michael met her eyes just then, and Katherine wished desperately that that didn't have to be so. That he could share her future and warm all those coming nights.

Chapter Nine

Michael entered his house at the end of the following week, mulling over something that had been bothering him for days. Despite his theological differences with Katherine, he was extremely grateful for her help. Over the past weeks, she had been invaluable in caring for the children.

Not only that, but she had held his family together, suggesting outings, simple dinners, times when they could be together. Times for healing. It was a lot to be grateful for.

Especially since he'd had to work extremely late several evenings—like tonight. And yet he'd done nothing to thank her—to show her the extent of his gratitude. His search for another baby-sitter had been fruitless. His only alternative would be to place them in day care, and Katherine had been adamant about helping rather than place them outside of the home since they were still adjusting to the loss of their mother.

Walking into the kitchen, Michael could smell the remains of dinner. And the house was quiet. Katherine wasn't in sight.

She must be upstairs, Michael decided as he headed in that direction, guessing he would find his children in their rooms. It was a good guess. David was tucked into bed, his hands flung upward on the pillow, his breathing deep. Michael smoothed the blanket, gently kissed David's forehead, and then crept from the room.

Heading down the hall, he was entering Annie's room, when the sound of soft singing halted his steps.

Craning his head, he could view the room more easily. One night-light remained on, illuminating the occupants. Katherine sat beside Annie's bed in the wicker rocker that had once been Ruth's. As his wife had often done, Katherine was singing to young Annie. But there the resemblance ended.

While Ruth's voice had been sweet and melodious, Katherine's was richer—a husky sound that captured him. Standing in the dark hallway, he was supremely aware of her as a woman. Not a minister, not a friend, simply a woman.

Terrified by how drawn he was to her, Michael turned around, exiting the hallway before Katherine could discover him. Downstairs, he occupied his hands by making a fresh pot of coffee. Despite the late hour, he felt the need for a cup of warm, bracing brew.

Scarcely a few minutes later, he heard the light tread of Katherine's footsteps on the stairs.

Spotting him, her face first registered surprise, then pleasure. "You're home."

"At long last. I'm sorry I'm so late. Coffee?"

She shook her head. "Not for me. It would keep me up all night."

He clasped his own mug more firmly, unwilling to let her know that his own sleep would be disturbed, as well. By thoughts of her. He cleared his suddenly constricted throat. "Did you and the children have a good day?"

She smiled, remembering. "It was especially good. The kids are thrilled because the plants in their garden are growing like wildfire. Annie's already planning the meal she wants to cook for you with the crop."

"So it's a *crop* now?"

Katherine grinned. "Absolutely. If we manage even one full-grown pepper and tomato, it will be a smashing success."

"Somehow, I suspect you will."

Then the uneasiness he was feeling spilled out between them, making the silence awkward.

Michael swallowed a sip of coffee. "I've been thinking about something…"

When he hesitated, she filled the gap. "Yes?"

"Actually it's about how much you're doing for Annie and David, for all of us. I honestly don't know how I would have managed without your help."

"I told you I was happy to do it."

"It's more than that," Michael managed to say. "You've been good for them." He stopped short of including himself in the statement. "And I'd like to try to repay you."

"I told you I wouldn't take money—"

"Several times," he replied wryly. "But I want to do *something*. Does your house need anything fixed, maybe some custom shelving, a remodeled bathroom?"

She shook her head. "No, my place is in pretty good shape, but I could use your offer somewhere else."

He met her eyes warily, an uncanny suspicion assailing him. "You don't mean—"

"The church building is old, and there are several things that need fixing, things we can't afford to have done. You already noticed our ancient wiring system."

Michael groaned. "The *church* building?" It was a modest request, but one he didn't think he could grant.

"You did ask," she reminded him. "Of course, you're under no obligation to help. I've told you I'm happy to care for the children."

Michael turned for a moment, staring out the window into the darkness. Everything inside him balked.

Katherine's voice softened. "It's not emotional blackmail, Michael. Forget I said anything."

For a long time only quiet lay between them.

Michael considered his choices, realizing he had

only one. "I don't suppose I have to believe in a client's business to work for them. That can apply to the church, as well."

"I'm beginning to feel bad, Michael. Please forget I said anything."

He sighed. "I'm not built that way, Katherine. I can't simply take without giving back."

"It is a human failing," she agreed. "One most of us share."

He'd made up his mind. "Since tomorrow's Saturday, why don't I plan to meet you there in the morning. I can look over what needs repair and get started."

"Only if you insist," she replied.

However, there was a mischievous glint in her eye. He had a sneaking suspicion he'd just been neatly maneuvered. Yet it *had* been his idea. Hadn't it?

Michael hadn't known it would affect him so to enter the church sanctuary, which he had studiously avoided on previous visits.

It was a race between the clutching of his stomach and the pain in his heart to determine just how he felt. And somewhere in between he stood, flanked by bitterness and sadness.

The hushed quiet was accentuated by the soaring ceiling that swept majestically over the building. Ancient beams anchored the structure. And simple but graceful stained-glass windows filtered the light that dappled over equally old pews.

Michael's throat tightened as he fought the feelings that simply stepping in the building evoked. He had been raised to attend church as naturally as he sat down to dinner each evening. And it was difficult to suppress the memories and emotions that went with that upbringing. Despite his resistance, they were swamping him.

He could easily envision his close friends who had been raised as he had, the activities they had shared. His youth group had been his core of friends, the nucleus of his social life. They were the kind of friends he could still call on today with any problem and know they could be depended upon. They were also friends who wouldn't understand his segregation from the church and who would also, with only good intentions, try to drag him back into the fold.

And if his parents had still been alive they would have been deeply disappointed to learn he'd turned away from the church. In some ways Michael was glad he had moved from his hometown to Rosewood. If he were still there, he would have felt his separation from the church even more keenly.

Michael gazed upward again, imagining all the prayers sent heavenward in this house. Bitterly he wondered how many like his own had gone unanswered. This hadn't been his church, but that didn't change his feelings. God hadn't answered his prayers, or those of his friends and family who had also prayed for Ruth. That door had been relentlessly slammed shut.

Katherine's voice as she spoke was soft, yet it still startled him. "I'm sorry to have kept you waiting."

He suspected the delay on her part had been deliberate, either to give him more time to collect himself, or to encourage him to ponder his faith. He didn't especially want to decide which at the moment.

"No problem."

"As you know, it's a very old building."

"I'd guess mid-to late-nineteenth century."

She smiled. "You guess right. The original stone structure was built in 1853. It's been added on to over the years."

"It's an impressive building."

"I think it was important to the immigrants who settled here to have something so permanent and solid. They were a long way from home." She paused. "I'm sorry. I sound like a tour guide, but this church's history has always fascinated me."

He nodded. "It's okay. Knowing the age of the building can help in making some repairs."

"Why don't I show you around." She led him on a tour of the building, pointing out some cracked plaster, several leaks that had stained the ceiling, and a few other minor repairs. "I hope the roof is stable," she told him. "We really can't afford the cost of a new one."

"I'll go up top, see what kind of shape it's in."

"Great. Oh, and there's one more thing. The lights in the hallway and my office flicker quite a bit."

He remembered the frayed cords he'd seen. "I'll check it out."

She smiled. "I really appreciate this. Although the building is impressive, our budget isn't."

"It's little enough to repay what you've done for my family."

"I'm happy to do it—really. Annie and David add a dimension to my life…" She paused. "A very special dimension."

"I'm glad you think you've gained something from the situation, too, and that it's not all one-sided."

Her voice deepened, a husky contralto. "You needn't worry about that."

Studying her, he wondered if he imagined the faint coloring in her cheeks, the brightening of her eyes. Then she busied herself with the papers in her hands, and he guessed he must have imagined the changes.

"I'll go up on the roof first," he told her.

"Whatever you think best. You're the expert."

He hesitated.

She met his gaze. "Is there something else?"

"Yes. Would you like to go to dinner tonight?"

She froze for a moment. "Dinner?"

"Doing the repairs is one way of saying thank-you, but you've been feeding my kids for weeks. Wouldn't you like a dinner cooked by someone else? Mrs. Goode has agreed to watch David and Annie."

Katherine met his gaze, hers again seeming to brighten. "That would be lovely."

"Eight o'clock all right?"

She nodded. "I'll look forward to it. Um…I live in

the rectory two houses east of the church." Katherine fiddled with the papers in her hands once more, but she didn't look at them. "I suppose I should leave you to the repairs."

He watched as she disappeared in the direction of her office. The dinner invitation had been an impulse. He just hoped it wasn't a mistake, that she wouldn't realize how affected by her he really was.

Then it occurred to him that she probably wouldn't treat it like a real date. He sighed, wondering why his relief was turning to disappointment.

"What do you think?" Katherine asked as she pulled out yet another dress from her closet, holding it up for her friend's inspection.

"Fine, if you're going to a funeral," Cindy told her frankly.

"What's wrong with it?"

"Where should I begin?" Cindy retorted.

"That bad?"

"Absolutely. I know you own pretty clothes. Is there some hidden motive for dressing ugly tonight?"

Katherine held the dress up to her chest and peered into the mirror. "I want to make the right kind of impression."

"That you're matronly and dull?"

Letting the dress slide down, Katherine turned to her friend. "Actually, I want to look like the kind of person who could have a husband and children."

Cindy grabbed her hands. "Oh, Katiecakes! You

are the kind of person who can have the perfect family. But don't you see…you can't pretend to be someone you're not." For a moment the pain of Cindy's own past surfaced in her eyes. "Trust me. That doesn't work. You're not a reserved, stuffed potato. You're you. And that's great. You have style, color, warmth, panache!"

"Panache?" Katherine repeated skeptically.

"You betcha. Don't you see how special you are? I know men might be a little intimidated by the minister thing, but Michael's past that. He's seen how wonderful you are. His late wife may have been the traditional type." Cindy's voice softened; she was awash in her own memories. "That doesn't mean you should try to change who you are."

Katherine looked down at the decidedly drab dress. "I suppose you're right. If I remember correctly, I bought this for a job interview when I was in college." Her voice grew small. "Somehow I thought it might be more suitable for tonight."

Cindy's voice gentled even more, her words guided by the heartbreak of her own experience. "If Michael doesn't like you for who you are, he's not the one for you."

Katherine lifted her eyes. "But I sure hope he is."

"The one?" Cindy asked softly.

"And only." Even as she voiced the words, Katherine felt her heart clutch, remembering her past… and her legacy.

Cindy tried to lighten her mood. "Don't look so

worried. Love's supposed to be about happiness, re-member?"

If only that were so, Katherine thought in despair. If only.

Michael fiddled with his blazer. Although it was freshly pressed from the cleaners, he wasn't certain about his choice. Maybe he should have worn a suit.

Deciding that he was being ridiculous, Michael rang the doorbell. After all, it wasn't a date. Just a thank-you dinner.

Katherine opened the door and those illusions fell away. From head to toe, she was a bright splash of color. Her dazzling red dress was the perfect foil for her long, dark hair, which fell in gentle waves. The overwhelming impression was one of complete femininity, from the earrings that teased with subtle sparkle to her strappy high heels. She looked at once elegant and enticing.

Swallowing, Michael wondered how he had sent such a misguided message. Or had he? The way she looked, he couldn't possibly consider this any less than a full-fledged date. And maybe that's what he'd wanted all along, what he'd denied to himself.

"Michael." She greeted him. "Won't you come in?"

Gingerly he stepped inside, surprise slowing his pace. He wasn't certain what he'd expected. He'd thought she would live in a rather drab house deco-rated primarily with religious art. Which made Kath-erine's house that much more of a shock.

The walls were painted deep peach, a warmly inviting, almost terra-cotta color. And those walls were covered with beautiful works of art, some traditional, some wildly modern. Her furniture was much the same. Antiques coexisted alongside a sleekly contemporary sofa. The room was oddly both invigorating and soothing. Much like Katherine herself.

As he absorbed the surroundings, a small white dog flew toward him.

"And this is Snowy," Katherine told him, "my not terribly ferocious companion."

Michael knelt down to pet the West Highland terrier, who responded by licking his hand. "He's a friendly little guy."

"For the most part. But only if he likes you. He's never mean, but he can be standoffish. You seem to have won him over."

"I like animals, always have."

Katherine cocked her head. "But you don't have any pets."

"I was waiting until Annie was old enough. Then…."

"Of course," she murmured. Then she bent to pet Snowy. "If you don't mind them being around dogs, I could bring Snowy by, see how the kids interact with him."

"Good idea." Michael's gaze traveled over her again, his voice deepening. "You seem to have a lot of them."

Her gaze snapped upward, meeting his. As suddenly, he was certain she realized they weren't talking only about the dog.

But no words passed between them, only an awareness that grew in the silence…that fermented in the glance they shared.

"I made a reservation at the Heidelberg," he finally managed to say, dragging his attention away. "I hope that's okay."

She picked up her purse from a slender hall table, toying with the clasp, her voice overly bright. "Sounds wonderful. It's my favorite."

Once inside Michael's SUV, the dim interior seemed very intimate. Previous times in the vehicle had always included the kids. Now the surroundings seemed very adult, very different. It was a short ride to the restaurant, but the awareness in the car was at a pinnacle.

The Heidelberg had originally been a two-story stone house built by one of Rosewood's more prominent pioneers. It had been converted in the fifties to a restaurant and was considered the nicest one in their small town. The family who operated the business had invested well in period pieces. Some were decorative, but the bulk of their collection consisted of antique tables and chairs. Massive, rustic nineteenth-century chandeliers hung throughout the main dining room and candles lit the individual tables. Ivy wound up the stone walls, spilling over the arched doorways, while fresh flowers filled crystal vases.

Glancing at Katherine as they waited to be seated,

Michael realized she fit in perfectly here. As perfectly as she fit in at backyard barbecues and suppers in the park. It was a rare woman who could.

She met his gaze, her lips tipping upward. "Can you imagine how the original owners would feel knowing their mini mansion was turned into something so *commercial?*"

His own lips twitched. "Mini mansion?"

"Don't you envision them as rather proper, even stuffy, upper-crust pillars of the community? Of course, at that time the entire community probably consisted of half a dozen buildings and maybe one street. Not much to be a pillar of."

His grin turned into a chuckle. "Isn't that a bit irreverent?"

She grinned, looking pleased. "You think so?"

Before he could reply, the hostess approached, then led them to a table across from the huge fireplace. Since it was July, only a small fire had been laid. Still, the flames of the fire echoed those of the candles.

Katherine's face looked incredibly soft in the low light. It wasn't an impression he'd noticed before. She always seemed so strong, so in charge. Now she appeared utterly feminine.

Michael didn't even notice the food as the courses came and went. Instead, the conversation consumed him. Conversation uninterrupted by children. It dawned on him that he hadn't enjoyed an evening so much since…well, in over a year and a half.

Like a breath of fresh air, Katherine continued to

surprise him. And in these surroundings he could almost forget that she was a minister.

Almost.

As they ate, an ensemble music group started playing. The music sounded more American than German, but the diners didn't seem to mind, many taking to the generous dance area.

Michael met Katherine's eyes just as her gaze returned from the dancers, a bit of longing lingering in her expression.

Replacing his coffee cup, he debated his choices. He could ignore her feelings or he could be a gentleman. And, he reasoned, one dance couldn't hurt. "Would you like to dance?"

Her eyes brightened, excitement filling her expression. "Oh, I'd love to."

Once on the smooth stone surface, Michael realized he hadn't thought out his impulsive offer. Putting his arms around her brought them suddenly only inches apart.

Katherine's hand was enclosed within his, her skin enticingly soft. And at the close proximity, he could smell the subtle spring-like aroma of her hair. Flowers and apples, he thought inanely.

Together they moved in unison to the music. For the second time since he'd met her he noticed her height, how it was a perfect complement to his own. For a moment he closed his eyes, briefly remembering the last time he'd danced, holding his petite wife in his arms. Nothing about Katherine reminded him of Ruth. From her irreverent sense of humor that seemed to encompass everything in life, to her physical appearance. It was all different. Very, very different.

But could different possibly be good?

When he'd first acknowledged that he was attracted to her, Michael had assumed it was because she *was* so different from his late wife…that a woman who resembled Ruth only would have been a painful reminder. But had that been a cop-out?

Was it instead because Katherine was Katherine, a tropical flower thriving amidst the native blooms?

She lifted her face, her brown eyes impossibly dark. And something in them pulled at him so strongly that it was almost a physical pain. Her lips were a gentle curve, one he wanted to explore.

And still the music swirled around them, romantically soft, evocative. When the song ended, neither of them pulled away.

As the second song started, Michael questioned his sanity. They began to dance again. His emotions were running high and it was neither comfort nor friendship he felt.

Katherine didn't exude a sense of homecoming… rather one of new exploration. And it had been a long time since he'd taken the first steps of such a journey.

Even if he were ready to start that journey, though, it couldn't be with a minister. He had convinced himself that he could reconcile his own beliefs to work on the church building. But he couldn't compromise his feelings to include dating someone who represented the source of his betrayal.

And this time when the music ended, he did pull back.

Surprise, followed by a flash of disappointment, crossed Katherine's face. Michael took her elbow, guiding her back to the table.

"I thought you might like some dessert," he attempted to explain, picking up his coffee cup, then replacing it in the saucer without drinking.

Her smile wasn't as broad as it had been. "I don't really feel like any, but you go ahead."

His stomach suddenly felt full of lead. "I think I'll just have coffee."

"Mmm," she murmured. But she didn't reach for her cup.

"Are you sure you don't want dessert? They're supposed to have a killer chocolate torte, and this *is* a thank-you dinner."

Her eyes flew up to meet his.

"For the—"

"Children," she completed his sentence flatly.

He started to correct her, to say it was for everything...for all of them, but the words wouldn't come. They couldn't. Because he was already too far over the line he'd drawn.

Chapter Ten

The stars truly were big and bright in Texas. At least, they seemed that way to Katherine. Despite the subdued ending to her dinner with Michael on Saturday night, she had put on her best smile and returned late on Monday afternoon to watch the children, allowing Mrs. Goode the time she still needed. Luckily, the older woman was able to spend a bit more time each day at the Carlson home. Her days freed, Katherine could still devote most evenings to David and Annie.

After all, Michael had made it clear that the dinner was only a thank-you between friends. Nothing more.

And the pain still fractured her.

Despite knowing she wasn't suited to be his wife, that she played too strong a role to fit in his traditional family, she had still held hidden hopes.

And now those were shattered.

Michael was late coming home, and she doubted

it was a coincidence that he had managed to avoid dinner. She probably should have put the children to bed, but she had been drawn to the night sky as she often was when troubled. After a few tales of her own stargazing times with her father, Annie and David had become intrigued, begging to stay up.

They had carried two quilts out into the backyard, snuggling on either side of her as they lay on their backs, staring upward.

"I see more and more and more!" David exclaimed.

"They're all popping out!" Annie cried.

"I used to imagine that I could see them coming out one at a time," Katherine confided.

"Can we count them?" David asked.

Katherine laughed. "You can try."

"I wish we could put them in a basket," Annie told her. "It would be all shiny!"

"And that would be a beautiful basket, sweetie."

"You can't put stars in a basket," David scoffed.

"You're only as limited as your imagination," Katherine told him. "That's what opens up new vistas, changes our world, makes it better."

"Do I have 'magnation?" Annie asked.

"Yes, you both do."

"Does Daddy have 'magnation?" Annie persisted.

Katherine swallowed her hurt. She had once thought so.

"Of course." Michael's voice coming from the dark surprised them all.

As Katherine sat up, the children scrambled to their feet. "Daddy!"

"How are my stargazers?" he asked, after hugs were exchanged.

"There's milk dippers in the sky," Annie told him.

"Big ones and little ones," David said with authority.

"I see," he replied seriously.

"And we're going to count all the stars," David told him.

"That should take a while," Michael responded with a mild smile.

"Katherine says with 'magnation we can do anything," Annie reported.

His gaze strayed to meet Katherine's. "Is that so?"

She lifted her head. "It's been my experience."

He sat down on the quilt next to Katherine's, and the children piled around them. "Then, I guess we ought to check out the sky, see what we can see."

"It's better if we lay down," David said, flinging himself on the quilt.

Obligingly Michael lay back. "It's funny. The stars are up there every night, but I can't remember when I looked at them last. When I was kid, we did this all the time."

"Katherine did, too!" David told him.

Michael angled his head, studying her. "Really?"

"I still do. It reminds me how infinite life is." She stopped short of saying *eternal,* but the unspoken inference lingered between them.

Michael spoke after a few moments. "My grandfather was somewhat of a naturalist, maybe the term is *environmentalist*. He made me aware of how we have to live in sync with nature, how important it is to conserve, that we have only one planet to experiment with. If we fail, it does too."

"That's why Daddy uses 'cycled stuff," Annie told her. "Even if it costs more."

"It's a good investment," Katherine replied. "One for *your* future, I'm sure."

"And well worth it," Michael agreed.

For a time they simply studied the stars, watching one errant cloud pass over the moon. When it cleared again, the children oohed at the sight.

But Katherine had lost her sense of comfort at the diversion. She was too aware of Michael's proximity…their last encounter. The deep dark of the night, the soft glow of the stars—all seemed to intensify the feelings.

So when Michael tapped her arm, she nearly bolted.

"Jumpy?" he asked.

Controlling her breathing with an effort, she tried to make her voice calm, her answer equally believable. "No. I was lulled by the exceptional quiet out here."

"Hmm." He didn't sound particularly believing as he continued. "So…which is your favorite constellation?"

"I like them all. Especially when they seem close enough to practically reach out and touch."

"Daddy, *they* think you can put stars in a basket," David told him in a loud whisper.

"Son, women are surprising creatures, with surprising abilities."

Startled, Katherine tried to hide her reaction. Just what did *that* mean?

But he didn't enlighten her further. Instead, they continued to study the stars, the crickets providing a nocturnal accompaniment. Shadows danced off the leaves that were caught in the glow of the outdoor lantern, and lush gardenias sweetened the air.

Katherine and Michael didn't speak. Instead, they longed for what could never be.

Her chest constricting, Katherine forced away the threat of uncharacteristic tears. When she had offered to be only his friend, she hadn't realized what a difficult task that would be. Nor had she guessed how much Michael's rejection would hurt. It was for the best, she told herself, since she couldn't be the kind of wife he needed.

Yet the hurt resonated in the deep Texas night. And for the briefest moment she wondered why the Lord had led her to this path. But digging deep for strength, she knew He had never led her astray. And she had to trust He wasn't doing so now.

The following week was an emotionally difficult one for Michael, yet on Saturday he returned to the church to work on the repairs he'd promised to do. He needed the physical labor to clear his muddled thoughts.

His feelings for Katherine had progressed beyond his control. Yet he couldn't cross this final line. He couldn't embrace his faith…which was necessary to have a relationship with her. And he couldn't help wondering how she really felt. The night he'd held her in his arms as they danced, he'd suspected she might be feeling much as he did.

But her behavior since then hadn't indicated reciprocated emotions. Of course, he'd bungled the end of the evening terribly. Even though her smile had been back in place, it had never fully reached her eyes. Yet, if she didn't want to be anything more than friends, why was that so?

Wishing he had the answer, Michael searched for Katherine in her office, but it was vacant. Without her presence the room seemed dimmer somehow.

Reluctantly he entered the sanctuary, again feeling the wash of conflicting emotions. How was it that the church offered such a sense of returning home after a lengthy and painful journey? Deep inside, he longed for that familiarity and anchor. Yet, in other ways, he still felt like a stranger, one who had been turned away. And although he stamped down the feelings, a persistent kernel inside longed for that haven.

Someone began playing the piano, an old-time spiritual he remembered from his childhood. And the lump in his throat told Michael the music of his youth could still move him. Unexpectedly, a voice added words to the song, a husky voice that tripped over him, evoking familiarity.

Walking slowly up the side aisle, he passed the pews without seeing them. The piano was angled so that the pianist was scarcely visible. Yet Michael knew who was singing. Katherine's distinctive voice was as recognizable as her wide grin and her refreshing sense of fun.

Her voice rose, echoing over the empty area. And he moved forward again. Katherine's head was bent over the music, her expression unfathomable. She was dressed simply, but the bright yellow of her T-shirt stood out against the subdued ivory walls.

The song drew to a close and the notes faded away.

"That was beautiful," he told her in a quiet voice.

Katherine's head jerked up, her expression unguarded, vulnerable. "I didn't know you were here."

He gestured to the tool belt secured around his waist. "I'm only halfway down your list of repairs."

"I shouldn't have asked you to do so many."

"Yes, you should have."

She didn't seem to have an answer, and the silence pulsed between them.

"I didn't know you sang," he said finally.

"Most of us have a few secrets," she replied.

Michael wasn't certain why, but he didn't believe she was referring to her musical talent. "Deep dark secrets?"

But her expression closed. "Not terribly."

Again he didn't believe her; however, her manner didn't invite speculation. "Oh."

When she didn't reply, another uncomfortable silence grew between them.

He couldn't quash the feeling that she was upset about something. "Are you okay, Katherine?"

"Any reason I shouldn't be?"

He swallowed, wondering at the cryptic reply. "If I've said something—"

"Of course not."

Sensing she would appreciate a change of topic, he reached for the handiest one. "I'm going to take a closer look at the wiring. Last week I was only able to make a cursory inspection. I'm a little worried since it's an old system."

Still looking distracted and somehow incredibly sad, she nodded. "It's been a source of concern in the past. But we haven't had the funds to bring in a contractor for evaluation."

"One of the advantages of having a contractor in your personal debt."

Another cloud passed over her face, then she smiled. "So it is."

Michael searched her expression for a moment before turning to walk away.

Katherine watched him, feeling her heart lodge in her throat. How had she allowed herself to be so completely swept up by this man and his life? Why hadn't she listened to logic? Why had she begun to hope that she might somehow escape her destiny?

Plagued by doubts, Katherine had been pondering whether she had irretrievably tangled the lines between her profession and her emotions. She should have been considering Michael's spiritual needs rather than her own personal ones, her role as his minister. Even though he kept insisting that she was *not* his minister, that he neither wanted nor needed a minister.

Debt had brought him to church today, but she could only hope that a return to faith would convince him to remain.

It had taken much prayer and soul-searching, but Katherine had come to the decision that she was ready to be the Lord's instrument. As much as it would hurt, she was willing to step away emotionally if it meant that Michael could find his way again.

Immediately, a picture of her parents' distressing breakup flashed through her thoughts. She could see her father's agony, the irreparable break in their family circle that had never healed. It was for the best, she told herself, that she wouldn't inflict the same fate on Michael, Annie and David.

Yet her heart wouldn't be still. Michael had crept inside, securing a foothold on emotions she had tried to contain. She admired that he didn't fit the mold of other men who had been intimidated by her job. Perhaps it was all the pain Michael had suffered in losing his wife, but intimidation wasn't his problem.

The gap that separated them, however, was far worse than intimidation. And far more impossible to bridge.

* * *

Frowning, Michael closed the church's fuse box. The repairs he'd made had only reinforced his earlier suspicions. Walking up the short half flight of stairs, he crossed the hall toward Katherine's office. She sat at her desk, absorbed by whatever she was writing on her computer. Still unaware of his presence, she wrinkled her brow, then smiled as she typed rapidly.

Although he didn't want to admit it, she took his breath away. Her long hair was loose, draping over her shoulders. Late-afternoon sun glinted on the dark waves, a teasing play of light. Even sitting at her desk, she radiated energy. She had fire, Michael realized, fire in her soul. And despite the contradiction, he realized that was what attracted him to her, drew him as no other woman had.

She glanced up just then, her mahogany-colored eyes deepening to an even darker hue. Again he sensed a wealth of hidden secrets, and now, even more strongly, wondered why.

"Hi." She greeted him.

"You looked glued to that screen. Something interesting?"

She met his gaze. "I hope so. It's tomorrow's sermon. Come and listen. Then you can judge its quality for yourself."

Immediately his defenses leaped to attention. "I'll take your word for it."

"Actually," she countered, "Annie has a part in the program tomorrow. I'm sure she'd love to see you there supporting her."

At a Sunday morning service. No…he couldn't.

"She's singing with the other young Sunday School classes, and her teacher tells me Annie has a solo."

He groaned inwardly. What a choice. Enter the source of his betrayal or fail to support his daughter. Why was it Katherine kept pushing? Couldn't she just leave well enough alone, let him deal with his beliefs in his own way? "Should I ask whose idea it was for the solo?"

Katherine shrugged but met his gaze evenly. "I wasn't part of the selection process, if that's what you mean. But if I have to venture a guess, I'd say it was because she has a remarkably sweet voice. Surely you've noticed."

Had he lately? Michael wondered. It seemed he spent every waking moment keeping home and body together.

When he didn't answer, she seemed to sense his quandary. "So, how are the repairs going?"

"I've had time to thoroughly examine the church building."

"And?"

"I'm afraid the repairs I've made are only a stop-gap measure. The roof must be replaced. And the building itself needs major structural renovation and restoration."

Although her brows drew together, she nodded.

"Worse, the antiquated wiring is a serious threat. You've been fortunate that the church hasn't suffered any damage, but you can't be lucky forever. Frankly, the wiring's downright scary."

Again she nodded. "Then, we'll have to take care of the problems."

He realized she probably knew little about construction or repair costs. A new wiring system didn't come cheap. "Katherine, I don't think you understand the scope of what I'm talking about. It's going to be extremely expensive."

Her expression was unruffled. "God will provide."

Michael cleared his throat rather than make a harsh comment. He knew from experience that wasn't true. "In the meantime, you'd better check out all your fire extinguishers—make sure they're all in tiptop shape."

She frowned. "Is the problem that serious?"

"I don't want to scare you. The building's been around for a lot of years and chances are it will survive for many more. But don't get complacent. You need to start on the repairs as soon as possible."

"I'll meet with the church board on Monday. I'm sure they'll share your concern."

"Good." For a moment he hesitated, wondering if he dared ask her to another dinner. After the last one, he wasn't too confident of a different outcome.

But Katherine spoke before he could. "In the meantime, I hope you'll reconsider attending church tomorrow. I'm sure your presence would mean the world to Annie."

Her words hit him like a bucket of cold water.

Dinner was a foolhardy idea, as was any time spent alone with Katherine. "Why don't you let me worry about that?"

But she didn't try to cajole him; her expression remained sober. "You have to face it sometime, Michael."

Maybe so, but Katherine wasn't going to call the shots. A picture of his daughter's trusting face flashed through his thoughts. And Michael wished he didn't have to call the shots, either.

Chapter Eleven

The following morning the church was hushed. Only the sound of lowered voices broke the quiet. The service would begin in a few minutes, yet Michael shifted for the dozenth time on the well-padded pew. He still couldn't believe he was sitting in the sanctuary. It had been different coming in to do repairs. He had been able to reason that it was simply work, nothing to do with the Lord. But now, sitting in His house, the rationale wasn't easy to maintain.

Annie's pleas had worn him down. He couldn't find an answer when she'd asked him why he didn't care about her song. The expression on her sweet face told him she was brokenhearted. And he'd crumbled. Late the previous evening he had reasoned that he could simply attend, keep his distance and not allow his surroundings to affect him.

But that wasn't the case. Thousands of memories assailed him. Good ones—like the many times he had sat beside his parents, confident in the belief that all was right with the world.

And then there were the dark memories. Ones of betrayed trust, pain and disbelief. Disbelief that something he believed in so strongly had failed him.

As the service progressed, Michael tried to shove away the memories. But the minutes ticked by slowly. And the memories, both good and bad, continued to assault him.

Finally the Sunday School classes rose from the front rows to stand on the steps at the front of the pulpit. Despite his resistance, Michael swelled with pride when he gazed at his son and daughter. Young voices blended together as they sang "Jesus Loves Me."

Consulting his program, Michael knew that the second selection, "Gladly the Cross I Bear," was Annie's solo. It was only one verse, but Michael had spent most of the previous evening helping her practice. She thought the words were "Gladly the Cross-Eyed Bear."

While Michael expected that rendition would produce a ripple of laughter in the congregation, he didn't want Annie hurt. She had told him that her teacher had instructed her to rely on the Lord for help when she needed it. And in her usual caring way, Annie had told him not to worry, that she would remember the right words.

With her teacher prompting her, Annie stepped forward. Her high, sweet voice began delivering the verse. Michael's pride multiplied. At the same time, his heart was touched and he tried to tell himself it had nothing to do with the Lord.

But the thought was fading as Annie sang, sweet and true. Love and pride mixing, Michael's throat worked as he was flooded by emotions.

The song drew to a close, and the children filed off the podium. Michael had planned to leave as soon as that portion of the service concluded, but he saw Annie heading directly toward him. David was only a few steps behind.

Trapped, he waited as his children slipped in to sit beside him. He squeezed Annie's shoulder, signaling his pleasure at her solo. Her answering smile was instant and huge.

Katherine stepped behind the pulpit, and he stiffened.

After a few preliminary words, she glanced at him. Was it his imagination that she was singling him out?

"I would like to extend a warm Rosewood welcome to those of you who have chosen to visit with us for the first time today."

His irritation ignited, and Michael knew his imagination was not overacting.

"I encourage our members to stand and greet both our visitors and one another," she continued.

It took a few seconds, but Michael realized that although her words *were* directed at him, it was a personal welcome, one he didn't have to share with the rest of the congregation.

As he remained seated, several people offered congenial welcomes. It wasn't nearly as painful as standing alone to be gawked at.

His irritation receded but he couldn't quite put a name to the emotion that followed when her sermon began. Her topic was on forgiveness and trust...trust in the Lord even when we don't understand His purpose.

Neither her design nor the irony escaped him. Even though he resented the choice of topics, he couldn't suppress his admiration at her style and delivery. The enthusiasm she gave to everyday events absolutely poured from the pulpit. Again he realized what she gave the congregation—her fire.

After the service ended, Michael shepherded the children toward the exit. Katherine greeted each member by name, clearly enjoying this aspect of her job.

When she met his gaze she hesitated for only a moment. "I'm pleased you joined us, Michael."

He nodded, his gaze cutting to his children, letting her know he wouldn't say anything disparaging in front of them.

"How did you judge the sermon?" she continued.

One lip curled. "It's not my place to judge—however, I'd be extremely interested in knowing when you chose the subject."

Her lip twitched, as well. "I think that comes under pastoral discretion." Then she bent to greet the children.

Annie impulsively flung her arms around Katherine's neck. "Did you like my song?"

"It was wonderful, sweetie." Her glance moved to include David. "You both did a spectacular job."

"You, too," the forthright boy replied. "Guess we all did."

Katherine chuckled. "Thanks! I guess we did." Her gaze lifted to meet Michael's. "So, what fun things are you doing this afternoon?"

Annie and David both shrugged. Michael, however, stiffened. He didn't want to be put into the position of refusing an invitation to the church picnic. "We don't have any specific plans."

"Sometimes a lazy day is best," Katherine replied, surprising him.

"Daddy reads us the comics," David told her. "There's lots on Sundays."

"One of the many benefits of the Lord's day," she replied easily.

Cautiously Michael nodded, ready to end the exchange.

"Oh, there is one thing," she said, as he took a step to move away.

He knew it! If she thought she would push him into another picnic he couldn't refuse—

"The kids told me that you used to play softball."

Thrown, he tried to guess her new motive. "Yes. It's been a while, though."

"We play on Tuesday evenings, and we're short a player. We could really use you this week. We're playing the church from Schlumberg, and they have a killer team."

"You could play, Daddy!" Annie exclaimed.

"Yeah. You could show 'em how good you are," David added.

"Please!" they cried in unison.

Helplessly he glanced between his children and Katherine. Was her smile a tad *too* beatific?

"I'm not sure," he tried to protest. "I'll have the kids and—"

"They're welcome, too. And we'll have hot dogs and lemonade."

"Please, Daddy!" they cried again.

"You'd really be helping us," Katherine added to the mix.

He knew it was time to gracefully acquiesce. After all, softball wasn't played inside the church. "I suppose it won't kill me *this once*."

She acknowledged his emphasis, then smiled. "Probably not. But I guess we'll see on Tuesday."

Startled, his gaze flew to hers. Then he spotted the laughter lurking in her eyes. Despite his resistance, he couldn't help grinning. "Wouldn't do much for your church's reputation if you knocked off your players."

Her answering smile was uncomfortably captivating. "You got me there."

He didn't, but it worried him that the prospect was so appealing.

Sunshine warmed the late August afternoon. Bright glinting light bounced between both softball teams. Katherine adjusted her ball cap, allowing her ponytail to escape through the back opening.

She hated to admit how much she'd looked forward to the game. Mrs. Goode had switched mornings for afternoons the previous week, and Katherine hadn't seen much of Michael other than at church when he worked on the repairs, and for those brief moments on Sunday. And that time hadn't lent itself to private conversation.

She closed her eyes now, remembering her resolution. Remembering that she couldn't hope to be any more to him than a friend.

Then he sauntered onto the field, and the resolution fled her thoughts, scattered her emotions.

"Hello, Coach," he greeted her.

"I'm just one of the players," she corrected him. "I'm not good enough to be the coach."

"Don't listen to her." Tom Sanders spoke up from behind her. A sandy-haired, perpetually smiling man, he was the coach of their team. "She's better than any other two players we have."

"Better not let your team overhear," Michael responded with a grin, "or you'll be more than one player short."

Tom extended his hand. "You must be our pinch hitter."

"And you must be overly optimistic," Michael responded.

Tom chuckled. "You'll fit in just fine on our team." His gaze cut over to Katherine. "She said you would."

Katherine smiled at Michael, hoping he didn't think she'd rattled on about his private life. Out of the corner of her eye she spotted Cindy, and her hopes sank. As much as she loved her best friend,

Cindy could chatter, and was capable of revealing far more than Katherine wished. Her only hope was that Cindy would keep on walking past them.

Instead, her friend veered in their direction, heading straight toward the team.

"Hi, all!" Cindy greeted them. Her gaze immediately zeroed in on Michael. "I know everybody here except you. Anyone want to correct that?"

Katherine cleared her throat, but Michael was already extending his hand. "Michael Carlson."

"Cindy Thompson," she replied, dragging her eyes from Michael over to Katherine and then back again. "So, have you come to play with us?"

Katherine sent her friend a pleading glance.

Cindy smiled in return, her brows rising in appreciation as she studied Michael.

"Do you want us to take our positions to warm up, Tom?" Katherine asked desperately.

Tom shrugged. "I'm not sure that'll help. I've watched Schlumberg's team play before. Unless they're all incapacitated with the flu, I'm afraid we're doomed."

Katherine tried again. "You haven't seen Michael play yet."

"Whoa," Michael protested. "No expectations, please."

Cindy casually linked her arm with Michael's. "If Katherine and Tom want to practice, let them. I'll keep you company."

Michael glanced toward the hot dog stand. "I need to keep an eye on my kids."

"I'm sure Katherine will do that," Cindy replied breezily, guiding him toward the bleachers. As she left, she looked back over her shoulder, winking at Katherine.

It was clear what Cindy was up to. She wanted time to push Michael and Katherine together. Katherine nearly groaned aloud, wondering how she could convince her friend to stop.

"Katherine," Tom repeated, sounding concerned.

She pulled her attention back. "I'm sorry. I'm kind of distracted. What did you say?"

"I was suggesting that if you want to warm up, we need to get out on the field."

"If you think we must."

Tom's usually smiling face was a bit exasperated. "It was *your* idea."

So it was.

She took one last longing glance toward the bleachers, then sighed. She could hardly tell Tom she wanted to rescue Michael from Cindy's too, too helpful clutches.

Annie and David, loaded with hot dogs and drinks, waved to her. She ran over and made sure they were seated near one of the women in the church who had promised to keep an eye on them.

The pre-game warm-up crawled by with excruciating slowness. When Cindy and Michael finally strolled back to the field, Katherine's anxiety level was topped out.

Michael, however, seemed at ease, as he began tossing the ball back and forth with Tom.

Katherine tried not to stare but it was difficult. How was it that Michael looked so handsome in shorts and a simple T-shirt? And how was it that it had become so difficult to focus on anything other than him?

One of the other players had run out on the field, and was talking excitedly with Tom. Curious, Katherine joined them. She was just in time to hear Tom's woeful words.

"Great. No pitcher. We won't just lose, we'll be smeared."

"Is anything seriously wrong with Gregg?" she questioned, concerned.

"No. Emergency business trip. Gregg's sorry, but he can't make the game."

"So, who's going to pitch?" Katherine asked.

Tom shrugged. "I suppose I can give it try." Then his gaze sharpened. "Unless our new recruit has had some pitching experience."

Michael demurred. "Hey, I haven't pitched in a long time. I'm sure you can find someone more qualified."

"Afraid not. Gregg was our only pitcher."

Michael glanced at Katherine, and she wondered if he thought she'd dreamed up this scenario to push him into becoming more involved with the team. "I can give it a try. But don't expect much."

Both teams got into position. Katherine tried not to stare at Michael, but then reasoned she should be paying attention to her team's pitcher. Somehow, the excuse sounded weak even to her.

Play began. Michael threw two balls, and inwardly Katherine groaned. She didn't want him embarrassed after being roped in first to play, then to substitute as pitcher. But his third pitch was a strike. As were the following two.

Excitement began to stir on the Rosewood team. But was the accomplishment a fluke?

The next batter was up. Michael's first pitch was a ball. Then a strike. And another. A ball followed, but so did another strike.

New life infused the Rosewood team. Katherine found herself grinning. Since she played first base, she was in direct line with Michael and she could see that he was pleased. She hoped he felt a sense of camaraderie with the team. She suspected fellowship was only one of many things he missed about church.

As the game progressed, Rosewood stayed ahead of the competition. Katherine made several base hits, and Michael struck gold with two home runs.

By the end of the ninth inning, their team had won, and was giddy with unaccustomed success. Surrounding Michael, they insisted on taking him and his children out for pizza. He couldn't refuse without offending them. And in seconds Michael was swept into their good cheer.

Watching him, Katherine's heart was warmed by the fellowship her friends were offering.

At the pizza place, Annie and David sought her out, each catching one of her hands. So it was natural for her to sit beside Michael at the tables the team had pushed together. She and Michael were at the core of the group, and she couldn't help thinking this was much the way life would be if they could overcome their barriers.

It made the moment bittersweet…the wondering, the wishing…the wanting.

As that instant, Michael raised his eyes, meeting hers.

Did she imagine the longing she glimpsed there?

"Michael, you're drafted," Tom announced, breaking the connection. "We definitely want you on our team."

It looked for a second as though Michael wouldn't address the comment, then reluctantly he turned his attention to the other man. "I have a pretty full schedule already."

"But you're first rate. You've got to allow some time for softball."

Michael's gaze drifted again toward Katherine. "I'm not sure I can commit right now."

She swallowed, a thousand questions stirring in her mind.

"You'll find we don't give up easily," Tom persisted.

Again Michael's gaze nailed Katherine's. "So I've learned."

Something inexplicable gripped her. And again she felt the sharp thrust of connection. A tenuous one perhaps, but one that seemed to single them out from the crowd.

Tom clapped Michael's shoulder. "We have another game on Friday. If you don't show up, we'll come collect you."

Since the words were delivered with admiration, Michael was able to grin in response.

Then Tom's face screwed up in concentration. "Say, are you the Michael who's been doing the repairs at the church?"

"That would be me."

"Ah."

Katherine saw the questions on Michael's face and spoke quickly, again not wanting him to think she'd spoken out of turn about him. "Tom's on the board. We met yesterday to discuss the repairs."

"Sounds like it'll cost a lot of money," Tom mused.

"It will," Michael responded. "The necessary repairs are extensive."

"Unfortunately, our funds aren't—" Tom bemoaned.

"Which is why we've applied for a bank loan," Katherine broke in.

"I thought you said the Lord would provide," Michael replied quietly, as Tom turned his attention to the man on his other side.

"He has many ways of providing," she responded.

"You're so sure?"

She met his eyes. "As sure as I am that the sun will set each night and rise again in the morning."

"And what if it doesn't?"

Immediately she recognized the meaning of Michael's seemingly unreasonable question. "Even on the darkest days, it's there. Sometimes it's hiding deep behind the thickest clouds as though it's been vanquished, but it's still giving life."

The pain in his eyes deepened. "I've stood in the cold, waiting for the warmth, but it never came."

She wanted so much to lend her strength, even a fraction of her faith. "That's when it's hardest to believe."

"You're wrong, Katherine. That's when it's easiest to believe."

There was no answer, no explanation, no comforting words. Nothing she could think of to remove the anguish in his eyes. And she knew the anguish was far deeper than the loss of his wife. It was the loss of his faith.

Chapter Twelve

A week later Tom frowned as he read the bank's preliminary report. Absently he passed the cream to Katherine, then pushed back his chair a fraction. "Sounds like we're going to have to spend a mint for a structural report before we even know if the bank's going to give us the loan."

Katherine's brows drew together as she placed the creamer on the table without adding any to her coffee. "Maybe not."

Tom lifted his gaze from the papers. "You have an idea?"

"I'm not sure. I'm hoping perhaps we can get one for a reasonable amount."

Tom's gaze narrowed. "From our star pitcher?"

Flustered, she tried to think of a reply.

Tom saved her the effort. "Relax, Katherine, you told me he was doing the repairs at the church." Then his eyes softened. "Hey, it's okay for the preacher to have someone special in her life."

Troubled, she couldn't quite meet his gaze. "It's not that simple."

"You know, I've been on the church board for a lot of years, and I've seen quite a few preachers at our pulpit. In fact, I was one of the diehards who thought only a man should have that particular position. Then I met you, Katherine. And you've changed my mind about that and more. But I'm still certain about one aspect—things are only as complicated as you make them. For laypeople *and* preachers."

Katherine thought about his words as they completed their meeting, then as the afternoon wore on. Could he be right? Had she made things more complicated than they needed to be? And hadn't she once made the same observation to Michael?

The afternoon turned to evening. Michael phoned to say he wouldn't be able to make the softball game. So Katherine had taken David and Annie along to watch her play. They had happily stuffed themselves with hot dogs and lemonade. To her delight, Pastor James McPherson and his wife had stopped by on their return to Houston from a trip for seminary business. The McPhersons and the Carlson children had taken to one another instantly.

In fact, James had commented that Katherine was a natural with the kids. His remark pleased her, but she couldn't dismiss the belief that baby-sitting was far different than motherhood. Still, she was unable to shake the image of James's wise and knowing expression. Could there be any truth to his words?

She had replayed them as she spent the evening with Annie and David. Now, despite their protests, the kids were finally asleep upstairs. And still Katherine was mulling over James's words. Combined with Tom's advice, it was quite a lot to think about.

Hearing the back door open, Katherine stood and crossed to the kitchen, relieved Michael was home safe. She had begun to worry.

"Sorry I'm so late," he began. "We had some serious complications at the site today. For a while I thought we might have been set back irreparably."

"Did you solve the problems?"

He pulled off his cap, crossed to the sink and began washing his hands. "I think so. We'll know tomorrow when we find out if we got approval from the zoning commission."

"Good."

Wiping his hands, Michael glanced at his watch. "It's really late. You sure you're not ready to bail?"

She shook her head. "It's not in my makeup."

He paused. "No. I don't suppose it is." He moved a few steps closer. "But I feel terrible about keeping you here so late. Is there anything I can do to make it up to you?"

Katherine clasped her hands together. "Funny you should ask."

He raised his eyebrows. "What is it?"

"Actually we need a structural report before the bank will consider our improvement loan."

"You got it."

Surprised, she studied his face. "Just like that? Don't you want to discuss the price?"

"Nope. There won't be a price. I can't ever repay you for taking care of the kids. Even with the report, I'll still be in your debt."

"But I understand these reports cost thousands. I was only hoping for a price break."

"Nope," he repeated. "I don't think you grasp how much it means to me to know my children are safe and well cared for. You can't put a price on that. Just like I won't put a price on your report."

"But—"

"No arguments. I'll start on it tomorrow."

She bit her lip.

"Are you worried about what I'll find?"

"Somewhat."

"I thought you said the Lord would provide."

"I've no doubt He will," she replied quietly. "That's never a question for me."

"Then, you're lucky," he responded, unable to hide his bitterness.

"No. I'm blessed. And that's far better than luck."

Blessed. The following afternoon Michael still doubted that. Unless being blessed meant that your historical church building failed its structural report. Strangely, being right didn't please him. In fact, he hated to pass on this news to Katherine. He'd learned that the church funds were sparse. And without the bank loan, they were sunk.

Katherine was at home with his children. He

called, asking her to set the backyard table for dinner, knowing the kids would be easily distracted by the trampoline. He also told her he was bringing pizza, a surefire way to keep David occupied.

He had to break the news to Katherine gently. Michael wasn't certain why that was so important to him, but he didn't want to examine his reasons. He only knew that he didn't want to hurt this very special woman.

Katherine and the kids were weeding in the garden, when he stepped into the yard. Vibrant yellow and green peppers, their glossy skins shining in the late-afternoon sun, flourished next to ripening tomatoes and tall stalks of corn. Marigolds, petunias, daisies and moss roses flanked the vegetables, lending more hues to the colorful display. The once sadly neglected corner now pulsed with new life and purpose. Much as he and his family had since Katherine had entered their lives, Michael realized.

"Pizza man," he called out, not wanting to dwell on that last thought.

The kids came running. After hugs were exchanged, they were happy to carry the pizza to the table.

Michael snagged Katherine's arm, pulling her out of earshot.

"Is something wrong?" she asked, concern filling her expression.

He wished suddenly for better news. "It's the structural report."

"Have you finished it already?"

He hesitated.

"You have, haven't you?"

"I'm afraid so."

"What is it, Michael?"

"It's not good. Based on what I've found, I doubt the bank will grant the loan."

Her expression sagged. "Are you sure?"

"There's no question. And I can't cut corners on the report. Structural integrity—rather the loss of it—could cost lives."

"I agree." Her eyes lightened. "Don't worry. During the services tomorrow, we'll pray for assistance. I know God will provide."

Her insistence amazed him. She was facing losing the church, yet she didn't budge an inch in her faith. For a fleeting moment, he yearned for the security of faith, one he'd once worn like a protective blanket. One that even now beckoned to him. "You're so sure?"

She laid her hand on his arm, her eyes imploring. "As sure as I am that you'll find your way again."

Bitter yearning clogged his emotions. "And if I don't?"

Something unfathomable deepened in her eyes, something resembling love, but then it was quickly masked. And he supposed he'd imagined that fleeting glimpse. Had he wanted to see into her heart so much that he'd conjured up the look in her eyes? Given substance to something that existed only in his dreams?

But she didn't linger to allow him to confirm or

deny his suspicions, instead walking quickly to the table, shuttering her thoughts.

The following Wednesday, Katherine sat beside Tom in the bank manager's office.

Loren Johnson glanced from one to the other sympathetically. "I'm really sorry, but based on the structural report, we can't extend the financing."

Katherine swallowed, trying to make her smile bright. "It's not like we're going to run out on the loan."

"I know you aren't. But I answer to my board, Katherine. And based on this report, you don't have enough collateral to secure a repair loan."

"But surely the building itself is collateral," Katherine argued.

Loren's face was sympathetic. "According to the structural evaluation, the entire building may be a loss."

Not expecting that, Katherine sucked in a deep breath of disbelief.

Tom patted her arm reassuringly, but he, too, looked shocked. "Are you sure, Loren?"

The manager nodded. "I'm afraid so. In fact I've gone over the report several times, looking for another answer. Unfortunately, there's no way we can grant the loan."

Dismayed, Katherine managed to thank the man. Then she and Tom left the bank.

"This is worse news than I expected," Tom said, still reeling.

"I needed some fresh air," Katherine murmured, sinking back against the brick exterior.

"We need more than that," Tom muttered, still looking shell-shocked.

"The Lord will provide," Katherine assured him.

"I know. I just hope it's before the building falls down."

Michael noticed that Katherine had been uncharacteristically quiet. It was something that had been happening frequently over the past few days.

"Did you hear from the bank?"

"We met with the manager today."

"Bad news?"

"They aren't going to give us the loan."

"I thought you said the Lord would provide."

"I said the Lord would provide, not the bank," she pointed out gently. "And He will."

Amazed, Michael stared at her. "And you still believe that?"

"Absolutely. My faith hasn't wavered. My prayers may not have been answered as I thought they would, but I know they were heard."

"Maybe they'll be answered as mine were," he replied ironically, not wishing that fate on her but knowing how likely it was.

"Perhaps." She met his gaze. "But that won't affect my faith. I haven't always received the answer I hoped for, but I can't imagine how empty my life would be without Him."

As empty as mine, Michael acknowledged. Yet he couldn't let go of the bitterness...the betrayal.

Katherine laid a tentative hand on his arm. "You may not believe this but I've been disappointed, too, about some of my own answers. I think most everyone has. It's awfully hard for us mere mortals to understand the entire scope of the heavens and our place in it."

Meeting her eyes, he glimpsed traces of pain she couldn't quite hide. He wasn't certain why, but he didn't believe the sorrow was related to the loss of the bank loan. "Katherine, what has hurt you?"

For a moment her eyes shimmered and her lips trembled ever so slightly. Then she averted her face. "My mind's just full right now. As you pointed out, we don't have a bank loan or much hope of getting one."

"You don't believe that," he replied, startling himself.

"What I do believe is that the Lord is always with me," she replied. Then she stood. "But I'd better get home and start thinking about some fund-raisers."

"Don't go," he protested. "It's still early."

Her still saddened gaze traveled toward Annie and David, who were playing in the fading twilight. "Without me, you'll be able to spend some family time together...the most valuable time."

Turning, she fled.

Although he stood to object, Katherine didn't glance back, instead disappearing into the dusk. And as he tried to figure out what had just gone wrong,

Michael realized just how much he'd come to count on her presence. And how much he would miss her if she continued to pull away.

The swings and slide weren't the only attractions in the park. At least, not for Michael. In the park the kids were occupied by the amusements, allowing Michael time alone with Katherine. And it was time he desperately needed. More than a week had passed, and Michael still didn't know why Katherine was so quiet, why she continued to withdraw. Each day in so many small ways she was distancing herself. And he neither knew why…nor knew how he could stop it.

"You haven't told me. How's the fund-raising coming for the repairs?"

Distracted, she frowned slightly. "Kind of slow."

Immediately he thought of the precarious wiring system. He wouldn't want Katherine to be working in her office if it failed. And he refused to examine the rightness of that thought. "Katherine, the repairs really can't wait. It's only a matter of time, and maybe not much of it, until the wiring shorts out and starts a fire."

Worry creased her expression. "But if it's lasted all this time, won't it hang together until we get the money?"

He wished he could reassure her. "I'm afraid not. It's nothing short of a miracle that the whole place hasn't gone up like a stack of dry kindling."

She dissected his words. "At least you admit there *are* miracles."

"It's just an expression."

But she waved away his explanation. "No. It's not. The Lord's protecting us and that *is* a miracle."

"For your sake, I hope that lasts. But on a practical basis, you're literally playing with fire. Just a routine test of the fuse box causes more sparks than you'd need for it to combust."

"We could stop testing it," she suggested.

"Won't do any good to hide your head in the sand," he rebuked her gently.

"Did you know ostriches really don't do that?" she questioned, blatantly changing the subject. "It's a misconception. It's simply a defensive stance they take near their nests to camouflage and protect the eggs."

"Katherine, avoiding the issue won't make it go away."

She sighed. "I don't suppose I really want it to go away. We just haven't come up with a good solution to find the money. We've organized a bake sale, and our carnival's scheduled for the beginning of September. They'll be a start, and even if they only bring in a small amount, the Lord will show us the way."

"And what if He doesn't?"

Her smile was tender yet knowing. "My faith isn't a pick-and-choose proposition. It's there no matter what."

As his used to be. Unable to still the motion, he

reached out, catching her hand. "Katherine, you might not be safe there."

She stared at their joined hands, slowly raising her eyes to meet his. "That's where you're wrong. It's the only place I *am* safe."

It seemed her words left far more unsaid than expressed, and he wondered why that was. Also, why her huge eyes were filled with a knowing pain. From sensation in the pit of his stomach, he guessed she would withdraw even farther. And there wasn't a solitary thing he could do to prevent it.

Small towns like Rosewood seemed made for carnivals. Old oak trees thrived because they didn't have to be cut down to make room for new buildings. And those trees provided a natural canopy for the booths and games that lined the perimeter of the church parking lot. A cotton-candy machine whirled nonstop, adding the sweet smell of scorched sugar to the aroma of hot dogs and popcorn. The fragrance of grilled knockwurst and bratwurst tantalized taste buds for blocks.

Dominating the center of the carnival, the haunted house was a huge draw, eliciting delighted screams and groans. It was designed to appeal to kids and teens alike, so it wasn't too scary. But scary enough that David and Annie asked to go through twice.

Michael kept searching the crowd for Katherine, but there were more people in attendance than he'd expected. He had thought it would be a quiet, intimate affair, one at which he could talk to Katherine. To his surprise, apparently most of the town had turned out for the annual event.

Then he felt a familiar touch on his arm. Turning, he met Katherine's grin.

"So what do you think of our little carnival?"

He laughed, enjoying the mischievous look on her face. "You could have told me it was the biggest draw in town."

"And ruin the surprise?" She glanced around. "Where are David and Annie?"

He pointed to a game close by. "Playing ring toss for the sixth or seventh time."

"I hope everyone will. It'll help fill the repair coffers."

"Do you think you'll make enough from the carnival to get started on the restoration?"

She shrugged. "It's a good fund-raiser, but we don't usually make a huge amount. We keep the prices low so everyone can afford to attend. For big families, especially, it's one of the few events they can truly afford."

"Admirable, but it won't get you a new wiring system."

"I believe you're more worried about that than I am."

"*I* saw the system," he pointed out. "Which makes me glad the carnival's running on a generator."

She looked puzzled. "Does that make a difference?"

"It keeps from overloading your already overloaded circuits."

She bit her lip.

Wary, he met her gaze. "Katherine?"

"Well, we don't actually have a generator."

"What?"

"There wasn't enough money in our budget. We're running extension cords."

Appalled, he stared at her. "Katherine! That's dangerous!"

She fidgeted. "Now that you've pointed out the generator issue, I can see that."

"You need to shut everything down, *now!*"

"Oh, we can't! Everyone has worked so hard and looked forward to the carnival!" Her voice grew coaxing. "Besides, we've had this same carnival every year. We haven't had a problem before."

"You haven't had a leak directly into the wiring system before, either!" he retorted. "Water from your leaky roof has exacerbated the problem."

Shifting uncomfortably, Katherine looked apologetic. "I appreciate your expertise and concern, but I really think everything will be all right. I'll keep a close watch on things."

"Better do it with a fire extinguisher in hand," he replied in exasperation.

"I will," she promised. "Actually, I bought a new extinguisher after we talked the first time."

"It's a step, Katherine, but only a small one."

"Sometimes those are the only kind of steps we *can* take." She reached out, laying her hand on his arm. "Please don't worry, Michael. Everything will be fine."

He paused, but guessed nothing he could say would convince her. Instead he sighed. "If I can't convince you, then how about coming with me to the booths?"

Her hesitation was barely perceptible. "Fine. Should we collect the kids?"

"Sure. They should be tiring of ring toss by now."

With Annie and David flanking them, they visited the stalls that boasted everything from fine art to toys made from yarn and wood. But it was at one of the last booths that Michael's eyes lit up.

Distracting Katherine, he sent her with the kids to buy snow cones. His idea might seem a silly gesture, but he guessed she would like it.

His purchase complete, Michael caught up with them. Katherine's hand was filled with a large snow cone, and a bit of the strawberry syrup had found its way onto her cheek. Somehow, it looked perfect there. Just as she did.

She looked up, met his eyes, and he felt something deep inside solidify. Refusing to dwell on the feeling, he held out his gift.

Katherine blinked, stared, then blinked again. "A giant bubble blower?"

"You said you blew killer bubbles." He couldn't voice the reason behind the impulsive gesture, his desire to see the pleasure in her expression. "Now you can prove it."

For a moment her eyes glistened suspiciously. "You remembered," she murmured. Then a wide, if tremulous, smile reached across her face as she held up the two-foot hoop. "Thank you."

Annie and David were immediately entranced with the huge bubble blower. "Can we help?"

She glanced at them fondly. "I was hoping you'd offer."

Michael glanced at the trio, thinking again how right they seemed together.

And Katherine *could* blow killer bubbles. Enormous, iridescent rings of soap that took on mystical proportions as they floated skyward.

David and Annie teamed together to blow through the large hoop, thrilling as a mammoth bubble burst forth.

"We did it!" David exclaimed.

"I knew you could!" Katherine exulted, giving him a hug.

"That's the bestest present," Annie told her.

Katherine's eyes lifted toward Michael. "Yes. It is. The bestest one I ever got."

Again something warmed inside, and Michael realized it felt right. All of it. Himself, Katherine and his children. Unbelievably right.

Chapter Thirteen

Katherine wasn't sure what woke her. It could have been the blanket of smoke that crept insidiously through the windows she had opened to allow the sweet autumn air to enter. Or possibly the frantic barking of her dog. Or it could have been the *clang* of the fire engine sirens breaking the quiet of the night.

Bolting upright, Katherine's heartbeat stampeded out of control. She threw on clothes, grabbing the nearest ones she could find. Dashing through the house, she flung open her front door, not bothering to close it as she ran outside. Snowy was at her side, barking furiously, nipping at her heels, urging her to flee.

For a moment she stood paralyzed, watching as the flames leaped up the steeple, greedily consuming the dry, aged timber. Flames from the chapel shot up in the air like a grotesque bonfire, singeing the ancient oaks and smothered the surrounding buildings.

She wasn't certain when the tears came. It could have been as she found her feet and tore off toward the church. Or later when it was clear all hope to save the building was gone.

Hours after it began, fire trucks remained sprawled across the street, the hoses a giant jumble. Firemen covered each portion of the church property, spraying water on the ruined building. Persistent embers stirred despite the massive onslaught.

A television crew from a larger nearby town stayed long enough to record some quick and shocking images to fill the morning news hour. But Katherine couldn't be persuaded to give a comment. The loss was too personal to be reduced to a sound bite.

Irrespective of the damage beneath it, the sun rose, clear strong beams that illuminated the smoke-blackened stone, the soggy ash debris...the complete devastation.

As they had all night, people remained grouped around the church. It was a sober gathering.

"Such a shame," one person sympathized. "That building's been here as long as the town."

"Yes," Katherine agreed, to this stranger to whom the loss was nothing more than historical interest.

Members of the church felt compelled to share their tears and sorrow, though, looking to her even now for leadership. And all Katherine could think of were Michael's words—his warning.

Then someone was pulling her into a hug. But it couldn't be, could it?

"Michael?" she whispered against his shoulder, craving the solace of his embrace.

"I heard about it on the news." He pulled back slightly, offering her an encouraging smile. "Before I had my coffee. It was enough to wake me up."

"It is that," she agreed almost tonelessly.

"I'm sorry, Katherine."

"Me, too. I should have listened to you."

He stared at her in disbelief. "You're not blaming yourself for this, are you?"

"You told me what could happen, and I didn't listen."

"God failed you, Katherine. Don't you see that?"

"It's not His fault. It's mine."

"How can you say that? Everything you've trusted in is in rubble at your feet!"

Pain scissored across her face, but she didn't waver. "Faith can't be rubble. And I'm sorry you don't see that. I had a responsibility that I didn't live up to. I'm not going to blame God for my mistakes."

"Are you suggesting I'm to blame for what went wrong in *my* life?" Michael demanded.

"Of course not. But I don't know how you've survived without the Lord since then. That's what keeps me going. What will keep me going now."

He gestured at the ruins of the building. "In spite of this?"

"Perhaps *because* of this."

Her answer overwhelmed him. It was something he'd once believed, as well. The loss of his belief was suddenly an agony, as though he'd severed a limb.

Even though it was being offered back to him, he couldn't accept, couldn't undertake that level of pain again.

"So what will you do now?" Michael managed to ask.

"I'll meet with the board."

"And?"

"And I'm not sure. We'll discuss the options..."

Michael knew there couldn't be many options, yet his strongest desire was to comfort Katherine, not add to her pain.

Somehow his arm was around her shoulders again. Together they watched as the rest of the neighborhood awoke. They listened to the sounds of surprise and dismay. And they both knew they needed a miracle...a multitude of miracles.

Meeting the next day, the board didn't exhibit the same degree of optimism Katherine did. The mood was dark, their confidence as destroyed as the church building.

Tom met Katherine's gaze, his own filled with both sympathy and despair. "I don't think we have many choices."

"We could try for a loan," she suggested.

"The bank has already demonstrated their unwillingness to extend credit," Roger Dalton replied.

"And we don't have enough money to consider repair or rebuilding," Don Westien added. "Even the carnival proceeds went up with the building."

Katherine grimaced, remembering again Michael's warning.

"We should have gotten fire insurance years ago," Tom fretted guiltily. "Right now, the large premiums don't seem so bad."

"We couldn't have afforded the premiums," Don pointed out. "So there's no point in wondering 'what if.'"

"I'm sure our congregation will rally to the cause." Katherine tried to buoy the group.

"If they don't, I'm afraid we'll have to disband," Tom replied solemnly.

"Oh, no!" Katherine protested.

"Without a miracle, I don't think we'll have a choice," Tom asserted.

"Then, pray for one." She glanced around to include the other members of the board. "All of you."

Discussion withered and died as they realized the gravity of the situation. One by one they left, until Katherine was alone.

Funny, her house had once been simply an auxiliary part of the church property. Now it was the only usable building they had left. But the tiny cottage wasn't big enough to accommodate a church meeting that involved more than a dozen people. Sadly, it wasn't an option for holding church services.

The idea of losing the church was unbearable. This pulpit had been very special to her. Almost from the first instant, she had felt Rosewood was the place she was meant to be, the place she would likely stay forever. It didn't seem possible that that could be taken away.

The doorbell rang, and Katherine wondered who it might be. Members, feeling a sense of disconnection and loss, had been dropping by nonstop since the fire.

But to her surprise it wasn't a member.

Michael filled her doorway. In his hands he held fresh daisies. "I thought you might be feeling down."

Nodding, she opened the door farther. "Come in." Accepting the flowers, she clutched them close, touched by his gesture.

After she sat on the smallish sofa, he took the place beside her. "How'd the board meeting go?"

She quickly filled him in on the details, trying to make them sound painless but not succeeding terribly well.

"I'm sorry. I know how much the church means to you."

"Oh, I'm not giving up. I know the Lord will provide."

"How can you say that? It will take a miracle."

"The Lord is capable of more miracles than we can imagine." She glanced out the window, and together they stared out at the charred remains of the church. "Far more."

Something deep inside cracked, a slow thawing fissure that Michael tried to hold back. But the feelings refused to be stilled. Feelings that told him he had to do something to help…for more reasons than he dared examine.

Of equal importance, Michael knew he couldn't allow Katherine this ultimate sacrifice. "I could help you rebuild," he blurted. "The bank would probably be willing to lend the money for materials, using the land for collateral."

Her eyes widened and filled with gratitude. "But it will take far more than materials, won't it?"

"I can talk to my employees, see if any of the men will volunteer a portion of their time or offer to reduce their wages."

"Do you really think they might?" Jumping up, she didn't wait for his reply. "We can call on the congregation for donations!"

He rose as well. "And for volunteers. Didn't you tell me you have a plumber on the church roster?"

"I did!" she exclaimed.

"Surely you have more skilled or even unskilled who will volunteer."

Katherine's eyes blurred, knowing that the Lord had provided the miracle she had prayed for. And not only in rebuilding the church. This was the first step in Michael's recovery of faith. He wouldn't offer to help if he didn't believe the church *should* be rebuilt. If he didn't feel the pull of the path he'd strayed from—if he didn't want to believe again.

Given a challenge, Michael was formidable. Several men in his crew volunteered their time. A few others offered to work and then wait to get paid until the church had the funds. As Michael had predicted, volunteers literally sprang from the church roster.

Among them, Michael and Katherine were surprised but pleased to find, were several skilled workers. The work wasn't going as quickly as it would with a full-time, paid crew, but it was coming along.

And the bank, pressured by public opinion, had granted the loan for the materials.

Katherine restrained herself from reminding Michael that the Lord had indeed provided. She wanted him to see that for himself, to believe himself.

When she thought about the possibility of Michael regaining his faith, she was elated. But then Katherine would remember they were one miracle short. She still didn't have what it took to be a wife and mother.

And now, since that last concern had occupied her thoughts for weeks, she found herself crawling through the attic to drag down a trunk filled with old letters, diaries and pictures.

Back downstairs with the mounds of paper and pictures surrounding her, Katherine prepared to take one of her infrequent trips to the past. But the doorbell interrupted her reverie.

Opening the door, she blinked in surprise. Michael, Annie and David stood on her porch. She recovered quickly and ushered them inside. "What a nice surprise!" Then she glanced at Michael in sudden apprehension; Mrs. Goode was back to watching the kids when they returned from school. Katherine only watched them on the evenings Michael worked late. "I thought Mrs. Goode was going to stay late tonight."

"She did. We thought maybe you could use some company."

David wandered near the sofa. "Can we look at your pictures?"

Katherine glanced at the boy helplessly. It would seem cruel not to share her pictures with the children. But she knew from past experience that it could be difficult viewing the photos alone. With company, it might be downright unbearable.

Annie joined her brother, pointing at one of the pictures. "Is that you when you were little?"

Recovering, Katherine nodded. "Yes, it is."

Michael studied her face, seeming to sense her reluctance. "The kids don't have to look at your photos."

Her past wasn't something she could hide any longer. It was part of her, part of who she was, something she couldn't deny. "They can look. I'm afraid the pictures aren't very interesting, though."

Crossing to the sofa, she handed David and Annie each a shoe box containing photographs. "Can you guys carry these to the table, while I clear the couch?"

"Sure!"

As they scampered to follow orders, Michael stepped close, lowering his voice. "I'm sorry. I should have called to see if you had plans."

"I wouldn't consider sifting through the past as 'plans' exactly." Although it was strained, she managed a smile.

"Still—"

"No. I'm *very* glad to see you. It'll make going through the pictures more tolerable."

He looked puzzled, but glanced at the kids and didn't question her words.

Soon they were all around her circular oak table. Annie and David were fascinated by the most mundane photo.

"What are you doing here—?" David asked, holding up a picture.

She glanced at it, remembering. "My dad and I were fishing."

Annie peered at the picture. "Your daddy's looking at you like our daddy looks at us, when we're making him happy."

"Which is all the time," Michael told his youngest.

Katherine picked up the picture, studying it in a way she never had before. Could she have been making her father happy? The thought had never occurred to her before. All her family memories seemed a quagmire. Katherine hadn't believed it possible to make anyone in her family happy. Had she been wrong?

Glancing up, she saw Michael's gaze on her. Embarrassed, she put the picture down.

For the next few hours they sifted through the photos, evoking in Katherine more than memories. Strangely, she found she didn't mind sharing the experience with Michael and the children. Somehow it was comforting. And that was something she never expected.

"Do you feel like taking a walk?" Michael asked after they'd looked at many of the pictures. "It's a perfect night."

"The stars are waked up now," Annie informed her.

"Oh?"

"Uh-huh. Daddy says the stars sleep during the day so that they can shine so bright at night."

Katherine found herself smiling, appreciating this warm and thoughtful man who made everything so special for his children. "Then, we'd better go see them."

"Can we look at the rest of your pictures some other time?" David asked.

"I can't imagine anyone I'd rather share them with," she replied truthfully.

"I think I hear the moon calling us," Michael told them.

"Can the moon *talk?*" Annie asked, suddenly intrigued.

"Only if you listen *very* carefully," Michael replied.

"To the man in the moon," David added with authority.

Smiling again, Katherine grabbed a light cotton sweater from the hall tree. "I'm ready when you are."

"Let's go, then."

The kids ran across the porch and down the steps, the sound of their footfalls echoing over the ancient wood.

"Don't get too far ahead," Michael called out.

Then he lowered his voice. "I think we've disturbed your evening."

"On the contrary, you've saved my evening."

He reached for her hand, folding it in his own. "If I'm treading where I don't belong, tell me. But I have the feeling you're troubled about something."

She shrugged. "Not all family memories are happy ones."

"Are you referring to your own family?"

Katherine hesitated, her face pensive in the silver shadows of the moon. "I'm afraid so. Just because my mother was a minister doesn't mean we were a model family."

"I imagine it's more difficult with a minister mom than most others."

Surprised, she stared at him. "How did you know?"

"I didn't. But it's a fair assumption. That sort of career takes a lot of time and attention."

"Which didn't leave much for her family," Katherine admitted in a choked voice. "I admired what she did for the community, for the members of the congregation, but there was never any time for my father or me."

"Yet you turned out pretty well. You even followed in her footsteps."

Katherine shrugged. "Yes. But unlike my mother, I know my limitations."

"You? I find it hard to believe you have any."

Katherine couldn't make her smile more than perfunctory. "The same ones my mother had. Only, she was determined to have a husband and family even though she knew she couldn't give them what they needed."

"What happened?"

"Eventually my father could no longer be merely a shadow, a prop for my mother's career."

"Divorced?"

Closing her eyes, she could remember the pain as clearly as if it had happened yesterday. "Yes. Their marriage was irreparably damaged from lack of care on my mother's part. I think my father stayed around as long as he did because of me. They don't speak anymore. And it's not out of anger, but lack of anything to say. There's no desire to exchange civilities at the holidays, no wish to resurrect a relationship that never should have happened."

"You sound bitter," he reflected in a neutral tone.

"I think a part of me always longed for a different resolution, certainly a different sort of childhood."

"Do you blame them?"

She considered this. "I suppose not. They were who they were. And it was in no way my father's fault. He married my mother, expecting a traditional wife. And she could never have been that. It simply wasn't in her. I guess the kindest way to put it is that theirs was a terrible mismatch."

"And so it makes you sad to look at your family photos, to remember how things were?"

She met his glance, a wealth of pain in her eyes. "Even more so knowing that's how they'll always be."

Puzzled, he angled his head. "With your parents?"

"No…with me. I'm the product of my upbringing, of the example I learned…and the profession I chose."

"You think your mother's failing in her marriage was strictly because she was a minister?"

Katherine thought for a moment. "I suppose it was her personality—she was strong, independent and opinionated."

"Is that bad?" he asked mildly.

"I suppose not…unless you want a successful marriage."

"And you think you have to be meek and mild to be happily married?"

Katherine paused. "I don't know. But I am certain my mother's formula was a disaster. Which means I would be a disaster."

"Isn't that a pretty big assumption?"

"Remember, I lived it."

"From a child's viewpoint. It's not the same."

"It taught me my limitations. I wish my mother had been so lucky."

"So you would have traded for different parents?"

Startled, she snapped her face upward. "I didn't say that!"

"Essentially. You can't have it both ways."

She considered this, then met his gaze, her own unbearably sad. "You're right. And neither could my mother. Which means I can't, either."

Michael pulled her closer, his arm a protective shelter. It was a comforting gesture. One that spoke more eloquently than any words he could offer. They continued walking, letting the quiet and dark soothe age-old wounds.

Having circled the block, now they were coming up to the site of the church. Even though it was late, some men were still working.

"The response has been wonderful," Katherine murmured.

"It's what you expected, isn't it?"

She nodded, still staring at the activity. "All of the members have offered to help—even if it's just sweeping up, helping the professionals. And we've gotten donations from the hardware store, the lumberyard, and even the paint store. Yesterday the owner of the antique shop over near the highway called and offered us some old church pews. He said he'd rather see them in our church than in some New York loft."

"It's amazing what can be accomplished when people pull together."

She turned, her face brushing his shoulder. "Especially you. I know you're working a killing pace between your job and coming here in the evenings and on weekends."

He shrugged. "As general contractor of your project, I'm bound by law to keep an eye on things."

Her eyes darkened with appreciation. "You've saved us a fortune by taking on that responsibility."

"On the downside, it may take forever to finish the project."

She brightened. "We've gotten permission from

the owners of the old school outside of town to use their facilities for services. They've been trying to sell the building for years without success. The owners think it might help for prospective buyers to see it used as something other than a school. They aren't charging us any rent—just the cost of utilities. But it'll be wonderful to come back to the old building once it's repaired."

As they watched, the moon broke free from surrounding, slow-moving clouds. It seemed to shine directly on the church, as though in approval of the restoration.

"Even damaged, the church retains its dignity," Michael observed.

She glanced at him, wondering if this was a step closer for him. "Is it getting easier?"

But Michael couldn't yet voice his shifting feelings. He sensed the welcoming arms of the church. But in other ways, he still felt himself a stranger, one who had been turned away once again from a safe haven. And he wasn't certain that would ever change.

Katherine's hand curled in his. Michael suspected she thought the darkness concealed the vulnerability on her face. However, the same moon that illuminated the church also exposed her feelings.

The admissions about her childhood stunned him. No wonder she continued to withdraw. But now that he knew the cause behind her withdrawal, he was even further from guessing a solution.

One thing was clear. It wasn't only his lack of

faith that stood between them. Katherine's past loomed large and unmoving. What were the chances of two miracles?

Glancing down at her unguarded face, his own was somber. That was about two more miracles than they were due.

Chapter Fourteen

"Our clothes are best!" Annie whispered, slipping one hand into Katherine's, the small fingers curling trustingly.

Katherine smiled. Learning that the other mothers and daughters would be wearing matching outfits, Katherine had sewn identical sundresses for herself and Annie for the Sunshine Girls mother-daughter luncheon. When Annie had invited her, Katherine had hesitated, not wanting to step on Michael's feelings by assuming the mother's role at the event, but Annie had pleaded. And when Michael agreed that Katherine should go, Annie was thrilled. He had planned an all boys' day with David so his son wouldn't feel left out.

"Did your mother sew matching dresses for you and her?" Annie asked.

Katherine laughed ruefully, remembering. "She could barely sew on a button."

"Then, how'd you learn?"

"In Home Ec—that's a class I took in school." Katherine also remembered the award she'd been so proud of, the one her mother had dismissed.

"Will you teach me?" Annie asked.

"If you'd like to learn."

"Uh-huh. I want to make us more matching stuff."

Touched, Katherine hugged her. Then she straightened Annie's locket. Struck by a sentimental impulse, she had purchased matching gold heart lockets for herself and Annie.

Knowing that her role in helping the Carlson family would eventually be completed when Michael no longer needed her, she wanted Annie to have something to remember her by. She'd also bought a watch for David, ostensibly because she hadn't wanted him to feel slighted, but actually as a keepsake, as well. In her own locket, she had placed pictures of David and Annie. She hoped they would think of her once she was no longer a part of their lives. Katherine didn't know if she had a day, a month. When Michael found someone else to watch the children on occasional evenings, she guessed that would be the end of their association. Katherine knew the children would be in her thoughts often. They had relentlessly crept into her heart.

The children had been thrilled over their presents, not because their father wasn't generous, but because they were remarkably unspoiled. Michael believed in fairness, discipline and lots of love. In Katherine's opinion the formula was a smashing success.

Even now Annie was reaching to stroke the locket, thrilled by the pretty trinket.

The luncheon went well. Everyone was presented with a single rose, and Annie kept hers close. They sang the Sunshine Girls song, and then the fashion show began. Teenagers and adults modeled the latest clothes from the local department store to the *ooh*s and *aah*s of the appreciative audience.

Annie leaned close to Katherine, whispering, "You're prettier than all the other ladies."

Touched, Katherine hugged her lightly. "Thanks, sweetie. I needed that." And she couldn't help wishing Michael shared his daughter's opinion.

After the fashion show, they strolled around the craft booths that had been set up around the park. A portion of the proceeds went to fund the Sunshine Girls. When Annie fell in love with a small wooden doll cradle, Katherine bought it. "We'll have to find something for David, too."

Annie nodded. "Okay. Maybe they have some soldiers."

There weren't any soldiers, but together they found the perfect thing: a framed picture of David's sports idol, Michael Jordan.

By the end of the afternoon, Annie was sated and happy. After they loaded their purchases into Katherine's car, the child reached up to hug her.

"Thanks for being my mommy today."

Katherine's heart flooded with love and her eyes filled with unexpected tears as she returned the hug.

"I loved every minute, Annie." And every minute would be preserved forever as a treasured memory.

When they returned home, Michael and David were in the backyard, the barbecue blazing. To her surprise, the table was laid for four.

"Your world-famous hamburgers?" she asked Michael.

He grinned. "Proper macho food for our male-only day."

"But you have to stay and eat with us," David insisted.

She tried to demur.

"No excuses," Michael replied. "You wouldn't want to disappoint Annie and David, would you?"

Only the children? Not him? "Of course not."

"So what did you do on your all-guys day?" Katherine asked.

"We worked at the church," David told her proudly. "I helped doing sweeping and stuff."

Touched, Katherine gave him a hug. "I thought you were going to do fun things."

"It's what we wanted to do," Michael replied quietly.

Katherine met his gaze, just as Annie tugged at his sleeve.

"Daddy, look what Katherine bought me!" Annie told her father, showing him the cradle.

As he admired her new toy, Katherine handed David the picture she'd bought for him.

"This is way cool," David exclaimed. "Jordan's my favorite."

"Annie told me." Katherine smiled, pleased by his reaction.

Then Annie held up her rose, touching it to Katherine's. "And we got flowers, too."

"I see," Michael replied.

"I'm going to put mine in water," Annie declared, pivoting to run into the house.

"You don't have to buy them gifts," Michael said, as the kids scattered.

Katherine kept her tone even. "I know. I did it because I wanted to."

She waited for him to challenge the statement, but he didn't, instead studying her face.

Katherine wanted to turn away, to have him stop probing her expression, but she couldn't move. She was drawn into his gaze, the darkness of his eyes.

He stepped a bit closer.

Katherine swallowed.

Michael reached out to touch her rose, his hand barely grazing hers.

Feeling as fragile as the delicate petals of the flower, Katherine caught her breath.

"I was right. Beautiful women and perfect roses *are* found together."

Katherine felt something deep inside melt. Struggling against the feelings, she wished suddenly that the problems between them didn't exist. That they were simply a man and a woman. A man of faith who was ready for love and a woman who could accept that love without the constraints that now bound her.

But as much as that temporal wish filled her, Katherine knew it was not a solution...not even a consideration. Painfully, she stepped back.

Disappointment flashed across his face. Then he withdrew his hand. Immediately she felt a deep sense of loss. One she guessed would be with her for a long time. An incredibly and painfully long time.

A few days later Katherine's feelings were much the same. Despite her distraction, she brought her telescope to the Carlson home that evening since Michael was working late again. Mrs. Goode had been eager to leave. Annie and David were immediately entranced. Katherine had owned it since she was a child; remembering how much she'd enjoyed using it to study the night sky, she had decided to share it with the children.

"You can see stuff real far away!" David exclaimed.

"It looks like we can touch the moon," Annie murmured.

"I used to think I could," Katherine confessed. "And then my father told me about shooting stars."

"Shooting stars?" They spoke simultaneously in voices full of wonder.

Katherine smiled. "They leave a path in the sky that looks like a roadway to heaven." She paused, remembering. "My father would drive me around at night, and we would search the sky for them."

"Did you find any?" David asked.

"Sometimes." She smiled, thinking it was one of the better memories of her childhood, one she had preserved, one of only a scant handful.

"Could we do that?" Annie asked.

"Please?" David enjoined.

"Oh, I don't know. It has to be completely dark…"

"It's dark now," David protested.

"I know, but your father isn't home from work yet and I'm not sure—"

"Actually, I am home." Michael flicked on the lantern, illuminating the area. "I just got here."

"I didn't see you, Daddy!" Annie cried.

"Me, either," David echoed.

"I came in from the house through the patio, but you guys were focused on the telescope."

"You can see the moon and stars real close up," David told him.

"Hmm."

"And maybe we can touch them," Annie added.

He smiled. "Looks that way, doesn't it, princess."

"Katherine used to go looking for shooty stars," Annie replied.

Michael met Katherine's gaze over Annie's head. "I heard."

"And if you say it's okay, we could go look for some," David pleaded.

Katherine shrugged an apology, not wanting Michael to feel obligated. "It's late. Your father's had a long day at work—"

"But not too long," Michael interrupted. "We're going to look for shooting stars. Right, guys?"

Jumping up and down, they shouted with pleasure.

"So, how does this work?" Michael asked her. "We just point the car in the direction of the nearest star?"

But Katherine couldn't abandon her doubts. The more time she spent with Michael, the more difficult it would be to bid him goodbye. "You three go ahead."

"And who would navigate?"

Refusing to let her out of the excursion, Michael collected blankets and quilts, then put the seats down in the back of the SUV. When he was done, his gaze roved over her, his eyes full of questions he wasn't asking. "Is this how you did it?"

She swallowed the sudden nervousness that had erupted with just his look. "Well, it was a station wagon when I was a kid, but otherwise pretty much the same."

For a moment neither of them spoke, the silence stretching the night. Then the kids were surrounding them, small hands pulling at theirs.

Katherine tucked the blankets around David and Annie, and they snuggled into the makeshift beds. Unable to resist the gesture, she passed a hand over their heads, smoothing the hair from their foreheads. Their trusting sweetness caused a maternal pang so intense it was nearly unbearable. It also played havoc with her belief that she didn't possess any maternal urgings or abilities. Quickly she drew back, knowing she didn't dare grow any more attached to David and Annie.

Or their father, Katherine thought, once in the front seat beside Michael. The proximity seemed very intimate, very sheltered. Darkness enveloped them, as did the quiet of the evening. The children's voices were hushed as though noise might scare away the shooting stars.

Unable to still the motion, Katherine glanced at Michael. He turned his head just then, his gaze meeting hers. Was it the shadowy night that made it seem as though he, too, sought answers beyond their control?

He reached out just then, shifting into cruising gear. His hand brushed hers, and her breath caught. Swallowing, she couldn't tear her eyes away, as he reached over a bit farther, his hand taking hers. It wasn't an accidental touch, a bumping of fingers to be snatched back. Instead, her hand curled within his, the warmth reaching far beyond the simple touch.

Ever so slowly, she raised her gaze from their joined hands. His eyes acknowledged the connection. Beyond that, she glimpsed only mystery.

They continued driving, moving out of the neighborhood, past Main Street, until they reached the open fields at the outskirts of town. Without the lights from town to blend into the sky, the stars seemed clearer, even more enticing.

As the minutes passed, Annie and David remained entranced, whispering to each other.

Katherine was equally entranced.

With Michael.

It seemed they drove for miles, but no one suggested ending the evening. The stars, the sky, the darkness—all conspired to make the atmosphere nearly magical. They were moments too good to end, too fragile to disturb.

Katherine wished desperately that she could ignore her past…that she could hope for more tomorrows just like today, with the man now beside her.

The days passed. And although Michael was tired, it was a good tired. His current contracting job was going well, allowing him to spend more time working on the church repairs. He was pleased, but not especially surprised to find that the congregation continued to volunteer selflessly. Everyone from youngest to oldest had contributed in some way. Many of the elderly women had undertaken the task of preparing meals for the workers, freeing the younger women to act as construction helpers. And even the children swept and raked in the safe areas.

And something deep inside Michael continued thawing. He wasn't yet ready to put a name to what he was beginning to feel. Nor was he ready to name how he felt about Katherine.

Once again, she had been quiet all during dinner. And now, as the kids jumped on the trampoline, she continued to be uncharacteristically still.

"Problems?" Michael asked, wanting to get past the barriers she had erected.

For a moment her gaze locked with his, and again he thought he glimpsed that inexplicable expression, one he'd spotted a few days earlier—one that had haunted his dreams. However, she shook her head.

"Not really."

He didn't believe her, but just then Annie ran up to them, her hair flying behind her, her grin wide and open.

"Daddy! Katherine! Guess what?"

"What?"

"I jumped higher than David!"

Studying his daughter, Michael smiled indulgently. No doubt his son had let her win. David was a protective big brother, always looking out for his younger sister.

As though thoughts of David conjured him up, his son sprinted toward them, skidding to a halt. "Annie! You forgot this!"

Annie whipped around, reaching for the flowers her brother held. Then she extended the small bouquet. "For you, Katherine."

To Michael's surprise, he thought he detected a glimmer of tears in her eyes as Katherine accepted the flowers the kids had picked from the garden. She acted as though she'd received a precious gift. Then she hugged both children.

"Thank you. They're lovely. Just as you are."

Annie smiled, and David scooted his foot across the grass, embarrassed but pleased.

"How about ice cream?" Michael asked them, sensing Katherine needed an emotional break. He wasn't certain what had caused her to be so sensitive tonight. She claimed nothing was wrong, but he didn't believe her. She seemed more vulnerable than he'd ever seen her.

"Yea!" they both shouted.

"Yea?" he asked Katherine.

She clutched the flowers a bit closer and nodded.

It didn't take long for the kids to clamber into the SUV or for them to drive to town. And once they'd consumed their ice-cream cones, Michael suggested a walk.

The kids skipped ahead, but Michael purposely trailed behind.

"Is something wrong, Katherine?"

She shook her head. "My mind's just full."

"Worried about the money for the repairs?"

"Not really. Of course I'm concerned, but I have faith that the Lord will see us through this."

"Then, what is it?"

Her smile was at once sad yet mysterious. "It's funny how our past is so part of the present."

He angled his head toward her, wondering if he'd misread her expression, the reason for her quiet behavior. "Are you talking about me?"

For a moment surprise flitted across her expression. "No. If I wanted to talk about your spiritual needs, I'd be more direct."

"Your past, then?"

"It's not checkered," she responded, but her comment couldn't lighten the somber mood.

"I didn't think it was. But something's bothering you."

"Do you think you can overcome your past, the way you've been raised?"

Again suspicious, he closely studied her face. "Like in the church?"

She shook her head. "I mean relationship-wise. Or is our mold permanently set by the way we're raised?"

Not certain where she was going with this line of questioning, he was cautious with his reply. "My parents had a happy marriage. Hopefully I learned something from their example. I didn't really have a chance to find out."

She touched his arm. "I didn't mean to stir up sad memories."

"You didn't. Actually, it's getting easier to talk about. Ruth was part of my life…" Michael's next thought surprised him and the words came slowly. "Part of my past." He rubbed the bare spot on his ring finger where he'd removed his wedding band some weeks before.

Katherine looked surprised, as well. He could almost guess her thoughts. Was she, too, wondering if his broken faith was also part of his past?

Wordlessly, she extended her hand. Taking it,

he wasn't sure if she was offering a lifeline or, impossibly, accepting one.

As the weeks passed, Michael tried to deal with his escalating feelings for Katherine. He could no longer deny that attraction had developed into something deeper…something enthralling…something terrifying.

Because to be with Katherine meant putting everything on the line. Not only his heart, but his faith, as well.

And while he searched for the miracle that could allow them to think of a life together, he couldn't take the steps that would make it so.

At the same time Katherine continued to withdraw. It wasn't anything he could verbalize. In fact, she was even more tender with the children, always there for David and Annie as she continued to care for them some evenings.

But when she didn't know he was watching, Michael saw the pain in her eyes. When he'd tried to question her, she'd closed up completely. And his gut instinct told him more questions would simply drive her away.

Yet everything in him wanted to ask, to learn why she was distancing herself. So he'd tried to think of someplace where he could be alone with her, a place where she might relax and open up.

The roller-skating rink hadn't been his idea. And it was hardly an inspired choice. However, he'd promised Annie and David he would take them. He had thought of a quiet dinner with Katherine, even an intimate walk. Instead, they were surrounded by children, noise and a PA system that alternated between blaring announcements and teen idol music.

Annie and David skated like pros, zooming past them on their inline skates, leaving Michael alone with Katherine. Side by side, they maneuvered around the rink. Never a timid soul, Katherine took to the activity as though she skated every day.

Michael couldn't repress a grin. As usual, there was nothing restrained about Katherine. However, in spite of their skill they continued to bump into each other as they avoided younger, less adept skaters. But he couldn't complain, enjoying the proximity.

A bunny-hop gone wrong sent Katherine reeling. It was only natural for him to reach out and steady her. He didn't drop her arm, though, instead snagging her hand with his own.

She met his gaze. Although the tension sparked between them in a nearly visible fashion, she didn't remove her hand. But he detected nerves when she bit her lower lip.

The younger set groaned when a strobe light came on and the music changed. The PA system spit out a golden oldie, and the song filled the rink—a romantic tune that seemed in keeping with the lovely woman at his side.

Their movements slowed in sync to the beat.

"How is it that music is like magic?" Michael contemplated aloud.

"I think it takes us to other times in our lives,

hopefully to happy times," she replied softly. "They played this song at my prom."

"I bet you were the prettiest girl there."

She shook her head. "Hardly. I was at least a foot taller than all the boys in my class. And skinny. Not a teenage boy's ideal."

"They didn't know what they were missing."

"That's gallant of you to say so."

"Nothing gallant about it." He was amazed that she didn't realize it. But then, that was part of Katherine's appeal: lack of artifice.

She smiled, a curving of her lips that lit her entire face. "Too bad you weren't in my senior class."

"I don't know. I think you came into my life at just the right time."

A bit of alarm surfaced in her expression.

He reached for her hand again, to take advantage of the slow pace of the song that was playing. But the music changed again, a fast, loud tune that eliminated the possibility of conversation. Although Michael continued trying, he couldn't reach Katherine and he didn't know the cause of the sadness in her eyes. And even though he tried to tell himself it wasn't any of his concern, Michael wanted to know. He wanted to erase that hurt. And the reason he did so scared him to death.

Chapter Fifteen

"It's looking good," Tom said.

Michael turned away from his blueprints, then glanced at the structure that was slowly but carefully being erected. He couldn't stifle his pride at what he and the volunteers were accomplishing. "It's because of all your hardworking members."

"They have a stake in the outcome. We all do."

Michael wondered if the other man knew how Michael felt about Katherine, if the casual comment related to her.

But Tom continued easily. "Our biggest thanks goes to you. If you hadn't taken on the contractor's role, we couldn't even have gotten started."

Michael shrugged. "The church is important to Katherine."

Tom searched his expression but kept his own counsel. "That it is. I never imagined a woman preacher before meeting Katherine. Now I can't imagine Rosewood without her."

Again Michael nodded. He'd come to respect and like Tom, knowing he was the kind of friend who could be depended upon. But he wasn't ready to share his feelings about Katherine or the church. "She's not going to rest until the church is completely rebuilt."

Tom chuckled. "Or you, from what I've seen. I hope you know how much we all appreciate this. We're all indebted to you."

"I'm here because I want to be."

It was Tom's turn to nod acceptingly. "I understand that."

Michael glanced at the kindly man but didn't see any double meaning. Then it struck him. Tom was simply acting like the church members he'd known all his life. He was offering fellowship, and Michael realized how much he'd missed that.

Relieved, he gestured over to the refreshment tables. "How 'bout some coffee and a sandwich?"

Tom ruefully patted his roundish stomach. "Never met a sandwich I didn't like."

Michael grinned, but before he could reply, Cindy sauntered over to them.

"Hey fellas. How's the Rosewood building team?"

"Almost as good as our softball team," Tom replied.

"So you're pitching again?" she asked Michael.

"Looks like it."

Her smile was wide and genuine. "Then we're sure to win this one, too. I'm going to grab some coffee, then I'm yours to command." Giving him a thumbs up, she strolled across the room.

Michael shook his head. "Yesterday she was climbing the scaffolding like a seasoned ten story man."

Tom smiled. "She gives the impression of glitz and fluff, but that's not the real Cindy. She'll work harder than most laborers and not complain once that she's ruining her manicure."

"Good. We've got plenty of manicure-breaking jobs."

He glanced at his watch as they walked over to collect their sandwiches. "It's later than I thought. I hate to keep everyone here so long."

"You know you can't even chase them away. You've tried that before. They simply won't go."

"True. You'd think they were being paid double overtime."

Tom nodded. "In a way they are. No greater reward than doing the Lord's work."

Something inside Michael acknowledged the statement, but he was still struggling.

One of the women manning the refreshment table smiled at them as they approached. She was seventy if she was a day, but her smile was as perky as a youngster's. "You boys must be hungry."

It had been quite a while since Michael had been referred to as a "boy." He couldn't repress a smile. "Yes, ma'am, we are."

Her gaze sharpened. "You're the nice young man who's in charge of the rebuilding."

"Guilty."

Her smile was at once sweet and huge. "Welcome to our family."

Taken aback, Michael wasn't certain how to answer.

"It's a good one, our church family," Tom said, smoothing over the moment.

Again the woman smiled. "We're thankful the Lord brought you to us."

Swallowing a sudden lump in his throat, Michael managed to nod. "That's very kind of you."

"Nothing of the sort. Just the truth." Then she picked up a platter of sandwiches. "I'm Ruth. Ruth Stanton."

Michael's outstretched hand trembled a bit. And the lump in his throat grew. A woman named Ruth saying the Lord had sent him to this church?

"We have ham and cheese, turkey, tuna salad, roast beef, egg salad. And the soup today is vegetable beef."

Still rattled, Michael picked a turkey sandwich. "This looks good." After thanking her, Michael and Tom carried their food to a makeshift eating area. People had brought their own tables and chairs from home. It was an eclectic collection of everything from folding chairs to a few rockers.

Companionably they ate the tasty meal, but Michael couldn't shake the woman's words or the coincidence of her name.

Tom unwrapped his second sandwich. "Something wrong, Michael?"

Michael started to demur, then hesitated. Maybe he needed a sounding board. It was one of the things he sorely missed—the fellowship. "It's something she said just now."

"Ruth?"

Michael nodded, again struck by the depth her simple words had struck. "My late wife's name was Ruth."

"Oh," Tom replied in a quiet voice.

"That in itself isn't so remarkable, but then her words about the Lord guiding me to this church…"

Tom hesitated. "A crisis of faith?"

Shocked, Michael stared at him. "Did Katherine—"

"Absolutely not. You should know her well enough by now. She's loyal to a fault. It's just something I've sensed. Probably because I was in the same place not so long ago."

"You?"

"Don't sound so surprised. You're not a minority of one. My loss wasn't as significant as yours, but at the time I thought it was. The company my family had owned for generations was taken over by a corporate raider. Employees who had been with us their entire lives were let go, many losing their homes. Others had no other option but to leave town in order to find new jobs. I poured in every penny I had, to try to save the business, but it didn't work. And I was left with nothing. My wife was furious, and she filed for divorce. I thought the Lord had betrayed not only me, but everyone in our company who was counting on Him."

"But you've rebuilt the business?"

Tom snorted. "Nope. Not that I didn't try, but my credit was ruined, and I couldn't get enough capital to start a lemonade stand. So I took a job in sales."

"And your wife?"

Tom's laugh was brittle. "Long gone."

"Yet you're back, deeply involved in the church."

"God gives us free will for a reason. He didn't choose my wife. I did. And deep down I always knew she loved my money more than me."

"What about the corporate takeover?"

Tom shrugged. "I have to believe that His plan is greater than I can understand."

"And that's enough?"

Soberly Tom met his gaze. "I've never felt so alone as when I didn't have the Lord to count on. I may not understand the whys, but that's okay."

"Have you had doubts since then?" Michael asked, knowing his own crisis wasn't as easily solved.

"Not about my faith. It's hard to understand at times. Like now. A few years ago I'd have had enough money to donate a new wiring system to the church so the building wouldn't have caught fire. But apparently that's part of the plan, even if we can't understand it."

Michael blinked at the enormity of the possibilities. Without the fire, he wouldn't be standing in the church building, devoting so much of his time and feeling some of his doubts crumble. But surely… In an instant he pictured Katherine's face, and the longing that still lingered between them.

"There's a lot to understand," Michael finally managed to say.

Tom nodded. "Faith isn't static. It's only when we believe it is that we get in trouble."

"I never thought about it that way."

"I've had a while to think about it, to find my path again." Tom hesitated. "I haven't known you long, but if you need a friend who understands, you can call on me anytime."

Touched, Michael nodded. "I may just do that."

Only a few weeks had passed when Katherine glanced at the skeleton structure of the sanctuary, remembering when it had been aflame. Then it had seemed nearly impossible to believe it would rise again. She had always trusted they would find a way. But she'd never guessed it would be in the form of Michael Carlson.

He had come to be part of the congregation even if he couldn't yet acknowledge it. He was known by name and greeted warmly by all the members. He was even pitching for the softball team. Offers to care for his children while he worked on the church had poured in by the dozen. And three members who had construction work planned for the future told him the jobs were his. One, a new restaurant, was a sizable job. Katherine had been gratified, but not surprised, by the generous treatment.

"Does it meet your approval?" Michael asked, surprising her.

"I didn't know you were here!"

"It's my home away from home," he replied.

Her eyes flew up to meet his, and the air vibrated with the tension his casual response evoked.

Regardless of the consequences, she reached up to stroke his jaw. Even though she was hopelessly in love with him, he still surprised her with his generosity and spirit.

"Katherine?" he said quietly.

Her hand lingered another moment before she drew it away. "I've been hearing a lot about you lately."

"I guess I could take that a couple of ways."

"Nope. It was all glowing."

He shrugged. "Just helping a good cause."

One that was pulling at him? "I agree."

For a moment the unspoken thrummed between them.

Then he glanced upward where the spire had once reached toward the sky. "So much in life is fragile."

Katherine's throat thickened; she knew he was right. "Which makes me appreciate it even more."

Again their gazes met, the emotion undisguised.

The breeze picked up slightly, ruffling Katherine's hair. She reached to smooth it, but Michael's hand was swifter. His touch, light but strong, lingered in her hair, its effect reached to her toes.

So much needed to be said, but neither could break the silence or disturb the precarious balance.

Michael's gaze flickered over Katherine again, and she sensed his frustration. But she couldn't continue their conversation. Their feelings were frighteningly close to the surface, and she didn't dare allow them to spiral out of control. Too much was at stake for Michael and his children. Too much for all of them.

For the first time in her adult life, Katherine felt helpless. And that she couldn't bear.

Chapter Sixteen

The following afternoon in the park was exquisite. Trees, decked in their October finery, practically strutted beneath their layers of changing leaves. And the sky was the blue lovers dream of. Even the pristine white clouds drifted by in lazy abandon. Mrs. Goode had needed the afternoon off—the kids had a half day at school. Fortunately, Katherine's schedule was clear.

She and the kids were resting on the swings. They had exhausted the slides, carousel and monkey bars. Usually about now Annie would plead for another round of all three. But she was unusually quiet. Though always a gentle child, Annie was typically filled with energy.

"Annie, is anything wrong?"

"I'm kinda tired," she responded, looking lackluster.

Katherine caught David's eye. "Then, let's head home."

Glad that she'd brought the car instead of biking, she tucked Annie into the front seat. David didn't protest when he was assigned to the back.

By the time they arrived home, Annie's head sagged and she dragged wearily inside, collapsing on the couch. Katherine carried her the rest of the way upstairs to her room and then searched for a thermometer.

Usually healthy, the kids hadn't required any nursing while she had taken care of them. Katherine tried to remember now, what she could about her own childhood illnesses. Her mother's advice had been to buck up and get on with things. Her father had been more sympathetic, tucking her beneath a comforter, preparing soup, Jell-O and toast. And a humidifier had entered the equation a few times.

After helping Annie into her jammies, Katherine tucked the child into bed, covering her with a favorite, soft coverlet. Unable to find a thermometer, she placed her hand against Annie's forehead and cheeks. Flushed, they did seem warm. But Katherine wasn't experienced enough to know if the child was warm enough to warrant concern. After giving Annie some cool apple juice, Katherine phoned Michael.

He wasn't worried. "It's probably nothing to be concerned about. Kids get colds, and usually there's at least one in the fall or winter."

Not certain why, Katherine didn't feel completely reassured. "What if it's more than a cold?"

"If it's the flu, you do basically the same things," he responded.

"Should I call her pediatrician?"

"I really don't think it's necessary," Michael assured her.

"Do you know where the thermometer is?"

He groaned. "I broke it when I used it last on David. I meant to buy a new one, and I completely forgot about it. I'll stop on the way home and get one."

"She seems awfully warm," Katherine fretted.

"Don't worry. I'll cut it short and get home as soon as possible. Usually juice helps."

"I've done that."

"Good. Sounds like you have everything under control."

Katherine wasn't certain. After ending her conversation with Michael, she quickly dialed Cindy. Her friend's advice was to calm down, but she did suggest looking for the humidifier in the laundry room.

"Why?" Katherine asked.

"I'm not sure. Just that my mother kept hers there."

After ringing off, Katherine did find the humidifier in the laundry room. Not questioning her good fortune, she filled it and carried it into Annie's room. She wasn't certain it would help, but she doubted it would hurt. And doing something, anything, made her feel better.

"Would you like some toast?"

Annie shook her head weakly.

"A Popsicle?"

Again Annie declined.

Worried, Katherine pulled the wicker rocker from across the room, angling it beside the bed. "How about a story? Your favorite about the princess?"

"Okay."

As she read, Katherine stroked the child's hair, keeping her touch gentle. When the story ended, Annie latched her fingers onto Katherine's.

"You don't feel good, do you, sweetie?"

"No. Will you stay with me?"

"Of course. Do you want some more juice?"

Annie shook her head. "Just you."

Something deep inside melted, and Katherine knew that these children would forever be in her heart. Neither time nor distance could sever the feelings.

The minutes seemed to crawl by as she waited for Michael to come home. Katherine wasn't sure why, but some instinct kept clawing to be heard. She couldn't put a name to her feeling, but she was terribly worried. Perhaps she was overly concerned because she hadn't had children of her own, but the change in Annie seemed to warrant more attention than would a cold or the flu.

David was remarkably helpful, pouring more juice for Annie so that Katherine could stay by her side, then preparing his own sandwich.

"What would I do without you?" Katherine said,

giving him a one-armed hug as she continued to hold Annie's hand. "You're so grown-up and responsible."

Pleased, he shrugged. "Do you want me to do something else?"

"Yes. Can you listen for your dad and let me know as soon as you hear his car?"

David nodded seriously. "Is Annie going to be okay?"

"Of course. It's probably a cold or the flu." Then it struck her. The last major illness in this house had been when David had lost his mother. She reached out again, snagging him in another hug. "She'll be just fine. You've had the flu before. It's really rough the first day or so. Then you get better."

"I guess so."

"No doubt about it," she reassured him. But inside, a yawning spasm of worry gripped her. Annie's breathing seemed a bit more shallow, her color a little worse. "David, could you bring me the phone?"

"Sure."

Annie appeared to be sleeping, and Katherine's nagging feeling had grown to mammoth proportions. She needed to know that Michael would soon be home.

As soon as David brought the phone and scampered back downstairs, she called Michael. But he didn't answer his cell phone, and she guessed he might have left the phone in his car when he'd gone in the store. She didn't leave a message on his voice mail, not wanting to add to his worry.

"Daddy's home!" David shouted from downstairs a few minutes later.

Worried, Katherine looked at Annie, but she hadn't even stirred at the noise.

Michael hurried up the stairs at David's insistence. His easy manner faded into concern when he saw his daughter's listless state. "Hey, princess."

But she was groggy, unresponsive. Quickly he used the thermometer he'd purchased. It read 104 degrees.

He met Katherine's concerned glance. "You were right. We should have called the doctor. Let's get her to the ER."

Within minutes, Michael carried Annie to the SUV, having already laid the seats down to make a bed. David insisted on coming along rather than being left with a neighbor, and Katherine backed him up. It would be more frightening for him to be left out of the picture than to accompany them to the hospital. Katherine used Michael's cell phone, however, to call Cindy. Her friend agreed to meet them at the hospital and to divert David if necessary.

The ER doctor took Annie's condition seriously, immediately calling for a pediatric specialist.

"It's probably the flu, isn't it, Doctor?" Michael asked. "We wanted to be sure, but it can't be anything serious, can it?"

The doctor wasn't quick to reassure them. "Why don't we run some tests, Mr. Carlson. Then we'll know what we're dealing with."

Quickly the medical staff whisked Annie away,

her body seeming incredibly tiny on the stretcher. And then Katherine and Michael were guided into the outer waiting room.

Cindy sat in one of the charmless vinyl chairs. Spotting them, she stood up, immediately making her connection with David.

Which was good because Michael looked as though he'd been sucker punched. Katherine took his arm, guiding him to a window.

"This can't be happening," he murmured.

"Michael, we don't know what's wrong yet. And you have to remain strong for David…and for Annie."

But he didn't reply at once, instead staring out the window. When he did speak, his voice was tormented. "This is how it started with Ruth. At first they said tests, just routine. Everyone reassured me things would be all right."

"This isn't Ruth," Katherine reminded him. "Annie's a young, healthy girl."

"It wasn't supposed to happen with her mother, either. She was strong, healthy. And then…"

Katherine touched his shoulder, meeting his gaze straight on. "You have to believe that Annie will be all right."

"Have faith?" he asked in a tortured voice.

Although tears blurred her vision, Katherine nodded. "If not for yourself, then for Annie."

He bowed his head. "It's not a matter of pride, Katherine."

"It's a matter of faith, Michael. And you're the only one who can decide that."

Still agonized, he clenched his jaw. "I'll see what the doctors say."

However, over two hours later, the news wasn't good. Annie's fever was escalating, and she was having more difficulty breathing.

"Mr. Carlson, we're admitting Annie," the pediatric specialist, Dr. Thomas, told him.

"What is it?" Michael asked desperately. "What's wrong with her?"

"We don't know yet."

Michael gripped Katherine's hand. "You must have some idea."

"She's in respiratory distress, and we've ordered a comprehensive panel of tests." Dr. Thomas removed his glasses. "I won't tell you not to worry, because frankly her condition is serious. However, until we know what we're dealing with, I'd rather not speculate and have you worry needlessly. I will keep you informed every step of the way." He met Michael's gaze squarely. "And I'd like to take samples from your son, as well."

"You don't think—"

"Just as a precaution. We'll also check him over."

Michael nodded, but strain creased his face. Clearly he was reeling. Katherine felt his shock and pain, her heart absorbing an equal share. She could only imagine how alone he must feel without his faith to turn to. But she kept her hand firmly in his, emotionally shoring him up, incorporating him, as well as Annie, in her prayers.

For the next hour, they simply tried to deal with the shock. David finally returned and Michael hugged him fiercely. But then his attention splintered, obviously thinking about his youngest child. Cindy tried to engage David, but he had eyes only for his father.

"Michael, I think David needs you," Katherine whispered.

He nodded, releasing her hand. In moments he was at his son's side, looking collected and strong. "Davey, they're going to keep Annie here tonight."

Katherine watched, knowing how difficult the words were for him.

"Is she going to be okay?" David asked, his young face pulled into lines of worry.

Michael swallowed. No doubt he was remembering when he'd told David that his mother, too, would be all right. "We have to wait and see, son."

Katherine met her friend's eyes and saw the tacit agreement in Cindy's gaze. So she knelt down beside David and Michael. "If it's all right with your father, Miss Cindy can take you home for the night. Then you can come back and see Annie tomorrow."

"I have four kinds of ice cream in my freezer," Cindy told him. "And tons of video games. And you can sleep in a bed shaped like a sports car." She met Michael's surprised glance. "I'm lucky enough to have foster children on occasion. I keep the place stocked with kid-friendly stuff."

David looked between Cindy and his father, obviously torn.

Michael put his arms around David. "You'd be helping me, son, if I knew I didn't have to worry about you. And right now I can't think of anything I need more."

David took in the information with a thoughtful expression. Hesitating only a short while, he nodded before hugging his father fiercely. Still hanging on to Michael, David glanced up at Katherine. "But I don't think I should have fun while Annie's sick."

Katherine's heart caught at the love between these children, this family. She smoothed back the hair on his forehead. "Oh, I think Annie wants you to have fun. Actually, twice as much fun, for her and you."

David drew his brows together. "You sure?"

She nodded, the emotions clogging her throat.

Releasing his father, David clung to Katherine, hugging her equally hard.

Tactfully, Cindy stood, her gaze connecting with Michael's.

"Should we talk about school later?"

Michael nodded.

Holding Michael's and Katherine's hands, David glanced up at them. "You're *sure* I can come back and see Annie?"

Katherine glanced at Michael, silently pleading for him to agree. "Yes, David."

After the boy left with Cindy, Michael frowned. "I'm not sure it was a good idea to let him think he can come back to the hospital."

Katherine took his arm. "I know this is difficult to hear, but the last time someone in his family was put in the hospital, he was shunted off and told everything would be okay. And he lost his mother. Even if it's only for a short while, I think he needs to be here, to feel he's part of the solution."

Michael's throat worked. "What if there's no solution?"

Katherine felt her own heart breaking—for Michael's pain, for her own love of his children, for the agony they'd all shared. But hand in hand with the pain was her conviction, her certainty, that the Lord would help this family. Still, a solitary tear rolled down her cheek as she took his hand.

"We do the only thing we can, Michael. We pray."

For a moment their gazes locked, the unspoken love thrumming between them, the promise of hope calling out to them, as well.

The nurse broke the moment, coming in to tell them that Annie was being transferred to the intensive care unit. She gave them directions to the unit's special waiting room. "However," she concluded. "Annie won't be back in the unit for some time. She's undergoing tests. If there's any change, we'll page you."

"Intensive care?" Michael whispered. "That's the last stop before—"

"No!" Katherine insisted. "I won't listen to that. It just means she needs more care than they can give her in the ER."

Michael covered his eyes with his hands, and she knew he was concealing his anguish.

She felt compelled to act. "Michael," she pleaded gently, "let's do something for Annie."

Slowly he raised his head. "What?"

Knowing where the chapel was, Katherine guided Michael through the hallways. Once at the doorway of the small room, he balked, his torment clear.

A pair of tears slipped down Katherine's face as she held out her hand, knowing she couldn't decide this for him. Knowing she could only offer her support and guidance.

The pain in her chest multiplied as the moment lengthened. Just when she thought he was going to turn away, Michael took her hand. Closing her eyes, she silently thanked the Lord.

The chapel comprised a small altar and six equally abbreviated rows of pews. It was a place intended for prayer and meditation, and was usually attended only by visiting clergy and the family members of seriously ill patients.

Once seated, they bowed their heads. Katherine prayed not only for Annie's recovery, but for Michael's, as well. One physical, one spiritual—both equally important.

More than an hour later, Michael lifted his head and broke the silence. "I want to go and check on Annie now."

Sensing he needed to do this on his own, she nodded. "I'll either be here or in the waiting room."

She remained in the chapel, wanting to make sure he had enough time alone.

Then, needing to check on Annie herself, she returned to the waiting room. Michael stood alone by the window.

Hesitantly she approached. "Michael?"

He turned, meeting her eyes. "They've downgraded her condition. The doctor says it's touch and go."

Katherine's throat closed. They *couldn't* lose Annie. They just couldn't. "Did the doctor suggest anything?"

Michael's voice was even. "To wait."

"We can do that, Michael."

He met her gaze, his own revealing. "I don't think I could do this alone."

"You're never really alone," she reminded him gently.

He gripped her hand. "So you keep telling me."

As the hours passed, they waited for news. News that wasn't forthcoming. Alternately, Michael sat beside her, paced the small waiting room, and walked the corridors of the hospital. Katherine wondered if he'd sought out the chapel, but she didn't ask, sensing he was very close to the edge.

By dawn, they both were.

So when the doctor approached, Michael and Katherine stood with a mixture of relief and trepidation.

The doctor's face was somber. "I'm afraid I don't have good news. Her condition continues to slip.

We're working to avoid lung failure, convulsions or a coma."

"Do you know yet what she has?" Michael demanded in a hoarse voice.

Katherine wanted to echo the request. It was incredibly difficult fighting this nameless, phantom illness.

The doctor shook his head. "Unfortunately, all I can say for certain is that it's a viral infection. We're treating it with antibiotics."

"Will that cure her?" Michael asked desperately.

"We can't be certain. To be perfectly honest, all we can do at this point is treat the symptoms, not the cause."

Again Michael looked tortured. "But how could she get so sick so fast?"

"It happens this way," Dr. Thomas replied. "I've seen a few other cases in the last two weeks. Comes on suddenly without warning and can reach the critical stage in a matter of hours."

"I should have done something sooner," Katherine murmured, guilt and worry consuming her.

The doctor allowed a flicker of sympathy to enter his expression. "You couldn't possibly have known. To be frank, in many of these cases the parents treat it like the flu, put the child to bed, and by the following morning it's too late. So, there's absolutely no reason to feel guilty, Mrs. Carlson. At least you brought her in as soon as you did."

Katherine gulped in relief. Only then did she react

to his form of address. She opened her mouth to correct him, but Michael spoke first.

"What are her chances?"

The doctor hesitated. "We're facing a life-and-death situation. I've notified the school. They're checking to see if she's come in contact with any other children who have shown similar symptoms."

Michael took that blow, yet managed another question. "And if she makes it, will there be any permanent damage?"

Again the doctor hesitated, but sensing Michael wanted the truth, he met his gaze steadily. "Convulsions can result in brain damage. And comas are unpredictable. At the moment, our pressing concern is to fight the possibility of lung failure." He paused, his gaze flicking between them. "You can't do anything for her right now. Get something to eat. We'll locate you in the event of change."

Although they thanked the doctor, neither Katherine nor Michael could face the idea of breakfast.

And by lunchtime, food still held no appeal. Cindy brought David for a brief visit, but he couldn't see his sister.

"She may be contagious," Katherine explained. "Do you know what that means?"

"I can catch it," David answered solemnly.

"Exactly. And your father and I couldn't bear it if you were sick, too."

"Cindy let me have pizza twice," he confessed. "Is that okay?"

Katherine reached out to hug him. "It's perfect."

Michael's hug was even longer, more intense. "Will you stay safe for me, Davey?"

"You haven't called me Davey since I was little," the sturdy seven-year-old told him. "Except for last night."

"I guess I forgot for a minute how grown-up you are," Michael replied. "That's such a help to me."

"That's what Katherine said, too."

Michael smiled, holding him close for a moment. "And she's right."

The waiting room seemed very empty once David left with Cindy. And the hours passed with excruciating slowness. However, Katherine and Michael couldn't ignore the approaching darkness that eventually cloaked the windows in the waiting room. It signaled the length of their wait, one that still showed no end. They couldn't be certain if the duration of Annie's stay indicated hope...or a lack of it.

Michael stood, then glanced at his watch. "It's been twenty-four hours since we brought her in."

To Katherine it seemed like years since the previous evening.

"Do you think that's a good sign?" he persisted.

She rose to join him. "I'm sure it is." It had to be.

Michael looked out the wide bank of windows, even though nothing was visible in the darkness. It was as though the world beyond the shrouded confines of the hospital had ceased to exist. Then he turned to face Katherine.

"I've had time to do a lot of thinking."

Wearily she smiled. That was all they'd been able to do throughout the long hours. That and pray.

Michael met her gaze. "I've made a decision."

Katherine waited, suddenly sensing the importance of his words. As suddenly, hope and trepidation crowded her heart.

"Whichever way this goes, I know I can't live any longer without faith…" Michael's voice deepened to a near raspy sound. "I need the Lord to lean upon…"

Katherine felt the tears escape and knew she hadn't cried so much since she was a child. Gratitude and love poured through her, too. It was the miracle she'd prayed for. "Michael!"

Somehow she was in his embrace, their arms providing a mutual shelter. It seemed so right, so lasting.

When they finally pulled apart, he gently pushed back the tousled hair at her forehead. "I don't think I could have made my decision without you."

"It was inside you all along. You just had to work it out."

"Mr. Carlson?" The nurse startled them both, filling them with dread. "The doctor suggests that you see Annie now."

Terrified, they hurried after her into the hushed critical care unit. Here, no flowers relieved the sterile atmosphere and no laughter eased the tense surroundings. It was undeniably serious, unrelentingly terrifying.

The doctor met them as they approached. "I believe your daughter may slip into a coma. And I subscribe to the school of thought that insists this progression can be halted by the voices of loved ones. So, talk to her. It doesn't matter what you say, just that she knows you're here."

Annie looked so incredibly small in the bed. More frightening were all the machines and tubes hooked into her.

For the first time, Katherine wondered if Michael would crumble. It was a sight no one should have to endure, one that would destroy the strongest of the strong.

Katherine wanted to rush forward, to envelop this precious child, to hold her and keep her safe, to protect her from anything that might ever hurt her. As the parent, Michael must feel that a thousand times over. But something deep inside denied that thought. She couldn't love or care more for Annie if the child were hers by blood.

Michael took his daughter's hand. "Hello, baby. Daddy's here." He bowed his head briefly. "And Jesus is watching over you," he told her, ending the words in a strangulated sob.

Katherine put her hand on his shoulder, then leaned close to Annie's bed. "Hey, sweetie. It's Katherine." For a moment her throat closed and she wondered if she could go on. But she called on strength she wasn't sure she possessed. "You have to hurry and get well. Your daddy and I need to see your sweet smile. And David misses you. He's eating pizza and ice cream and wants you to catch up with him." Even though she willed them away, tears blurred her vision, and she gripped Michael's shoulder so hard her fingers made indents in his jacket.

"You're my princess, you know that, don't you, Annie?" Michael told her softly. "And we need you more than you can ever know."

"You have to get better," Katherine said through her tears, her voice choking. "I need to hear you sing 'The Cross-Eyed Bear' again."

Michael gripped Katherine's hand as the doctor approached, reading the data on her machines. "No change. But that's not bad. The readings were steadily declining until now. You can stay with her a few more minutes, then we'll let her rest. In a few hours, you can come in again."

Somehow Katherine and Michael made their way back to the waiting room. Losing track of time, they no longer knew how many hours passed.

A phone call from Cindy assured them David was fine. She also let them know that Annie's name had been placed on the prayer roll and that the entire congregation was praying for her. It was what they needed—a chorus of voices to heaven.

Tessa and her mother brought flowers that couldn't be taken into the intensive care unit. The child's large eyes were filled with worry for her best friend. Young Tessa had also brought her own favorite teddy bear for Annie. Promising to take the bear in to Annie when it was allowed, Michael clutched the stuffed toy, trying not to despair.

An anxious Mrs. Goode came by, as well, offering to watch David, to do anything she could. But there was nothing anyone physically could do. However, they gratefully accepted her offer of prayer, knowing it was added to the many other voices praying for their precious child.

The doctors changed Annie's antibiotics again in hopes they could fight whatever was gripping her. Michael and Katherine spoke to Annie two more times, yet there was no change. As evening approached, their worry intensified, obliterating everything else.

It was a situation that would try the most devout believer. And Katherine wondered if Michael would denounce his newly recovered faith. To her relief, although anguished, he suggested another visit to the chapel, drawing strength from prayer.

After counting the minutes until their next visit with Annie, Michael and Katherine practically bolted into the intensive care unit when the time arrived.

Annie was still lying quietly. Again they talked for some time. Michael held Annie's hand in his, willing her to live, begging the Lord to help her.

Katherine watched them, her heart lodged in her throat. As she did, Michael suddenly lifted his head, his eyes disbelieving. Katherine followed his gaze, her breath catching.

Annie's fingers curled slightly in Michael's hand.

"Baby?" he whispered in a plea of mixed disbelief and hope.

Although she didn't speak, Annie's fingers continued to gently move.

"That's right," Michael encouraged, his voice nearly cracking. "You have to stay with us."

Katherine couldn't believe it possible to feel the threat of tears yet again, but they filled her eyes, choking her.

The doctor approached. Katherine could only manage to point, unable to speak. Dr. Thomas spotted the movement Annie was making. Instantly, he checked the readings on Annie's machines. For the first time, light entered his expression.

"Does this mean she's getting better?" Michael asked.

Dr. Thomas glanced at them. "It's a cautious improvement," he said before leaving the room.

Katherine met Michael's gaze, hope flooding her own.

Michael's eyes deepened with another equally intense emotion. "I couldn't have handled this emergency without you either, Katherine. I couldn't have believed that Annie would make it. And I wouldn't have believed I could deal with it if she doesn't…" He paused, his throat working. "And I don't want to manage anything else without you in the future."

"Oh, Michael…"

His fingers were tender as they bracketed her face. "This may not seem like an appropriate time…" Briefly he closed his eyes, his fear for his child written across his features. Then his gaze met hers again. "But I never believed I could feel this way. And then there was you, changing my life, filling it in ways I never dreamed possible. I love you,

Katherine, and I want you in my life—" his voice broke for a moment "—and my children's lives... forever."

Wordlessly she stared at him. It was what she'd hoped for, what she'd wanted from the moment she had grown to know what a wonderful man he was.

But she couldn't compromise his family's happiness with her inadequacies. They deserved so much more than she could give.

The nurse didn't chase them out when their time ended, so Michael continued to hold his daughter's hand. Katherine stood beside him, gently stroking Annie's hair. More than two hours passed. They watched her so intently that it seemed impossible their sheer will alone didn't awaken her.

Annie's fingers had stilled some time ago. When they began to move again, Michael jerked forward. Katherine's own hand flew to her mouth.

As they watched, Annie's eyelids fluttered.

Breath held, hope beckoning, they stared at her.

"Daddy?" she whispered.

Katherine's lips trembled, her face crumpling. This time she didn't even try to halt the tears sliding down her cheeks. Blindly, she turned to try to find the doctor. But Michael snagged her arm, pulling her close.

Annie's eyes opened fully. "Katherine?"

Katherine wondered that her heart didn't explode with love, relief and gratitude. Unchecked, the tears salted her lips, traced her face. "Yes, sweetie?"

"Do you want me to sing?" Annie whispered.

Katherine's muffled sob echoed against Michael's shoulder.

"Do you want to sing, princess?" Michael asked her, his own eyes full.

Annie's sweet smile surfaced. "For you and Katherine."

In a few minutes, the doctor formalized her prognosis. "She's on the road to recovery. Just as we don't know what caused the viral infection, we'll probably never know what cured her." He scratched his head. "It's nothing short of a miracle."

Katherine met Michael's gaze. It seemed impossible to believe. They'd been granted two miracles. Could they possibly hope for a third?

Chapter Seventeen

By morning Annie was remarkably improved. The doctor, believing the danger had passed, had allowed David to visit his sister briefly. Michael behaved as though he had a new lease on life.

Only Katherine was still wrestling with a problem.

She kept replaying Michael's words in her mind. For a moment she wondered if they had just been an impulse. But Katherine knew better. He wasn't the sort of man to make a proposal on a whim.

Michael had left for a few minutes to fetch coffee and make a few calls. But Katherine didn't mind. Not when she could spend the time in Annie's room while the child slept. It was such a joy to know Annie was improving, that she would be whole and well soon.

The door opened. Expecting one of the hospital staff, Katherine was surprised to see her mentor, Pastor James McPherson.

"Katherine." He greeted her in a hushed voice.

"James! What are you doing here?"

"I came to offer solace on the fire at your church. The note I'd written didn't seem enough."

"Oh," she murmured, realizing she hadn't given the fire or the subsequent repairs a thought.

"I was able to reach Cindy, and she told me you were here."

Katherine stroked Annie's hair. "This little one was awfully sick—" Her voice stumbled. "In fact, we almost lost her." Brightening, Katherine looked at him. "But she's going to be fine."

"That's wonderful." James searched her expression. "But something else is wrong. What is it?"

Her smile was tremulous. "You've always known me too well." She hesitated, again looking at Annie. "I'm afraid I've grown too close to her, and her brother…" Katherine glanced up at him. "And her father."

James's gaze was kind and understanding. "Why don't you tell me about it."

And so she did, pouring out what had happened, her own feelings, and Michael's proposal. Then haltingly she explained her background as well and the disastrous result of her parents' failed marriage.

"So you see," Katherine concluded, wiping away her tears, "why Michael and I can't have a future."

But his answer wasn't what she expected. "I'm afraid I don't. You've just told me you love Michael and his children. Not having an ideal childhood doesn't preclude you from being a good mother."

"How can you say that?" she demanded, expecting him to be the one person to understand.

But James's voice was gentle. "Katherine, I wish you could see what I do. A woman who has stayed beside the man and children she loves, one who even now can't take her glance from that child for a moment. You have fussed over her since I arrived. I don't think even a blind man would view that as indifference or inability. Whatever maternal urges your mother lacked have been given to you two-fold. You forget, I saw you with the children before. You're wonderful with them, and they're obviously crazy about you. Katherine, your love for Michael and his children all but consumes you."

Could he be right? Hope that had been nearly extinguished fluttered to life. "But what if you're wrong?"

James placed one hand on her shoulder. "I don't think that's the question. Search your heart, Katherine. I'll come back and visit you in a few hours. In the meantime, I'll be praying for you. For all of you."

Katherine nodded, her gaze still on Annie. She heard the door close, and James was gone.

But that left Katherine with only her thoughts. Thoughts that whirled relentlessly.

What if James was right? Could she be the kind of mother Annie and David deserved? She'd never considered the possibility. Her past kept remorselessly slamming back into her thoughts. She'd seen others who had tried to outrun their pasts, but it seldom worked. Instead, marriages crumbled and families split. True, she loved Michael and his children, but was that enough?

The door opened again, and Michael tiptoed inside. "How is she?"

"About the same. She fell asleep shortly after you went for the coffee."

Michael handed her one of the foam cups of steaming brew.

She accepted it gratefully, latching on to the warmth it provided.

"You really should eat something," he told her.

She met his gaze, her own ironic. "So should you."

"When Annie's out of here, I'm going to buy us all the best meal in town."

Katherine's gaze flickered over Annie again. "I almost couldn't believe it when the doctor said it wouldn't be long till she can go home." Her lips trembled. "We have so much to be grateful for."

Michael placed his cup on the bedside table, then reached for her hand. "That we do. Katherine, I can't believe it took me so long to see the truth. I meant what I said last night. I don't ever want to lose you. I love you and I want you to be my wife."

It was everything she'd dreamed of, but what if she was wrong for him? He couldn't survive another blow like the loss of his wife. Katherine knew it was too much of a gamble. Michael deserved so much more...so much more than she could give.

Helplessly she stared at him in silence.

"Katherine?"

"Oh, Michael…I want only the best for you and for your children. And that's not me."

His voice deepened. "You don't love me?"

She bent her head. "There's more to consider—"

"What's more important than our love for each other?"

Again she stared at him, her own heart breaking. "It's more complicated than that…" Tears welled in her eyes, one escaping to slip down her cheek.

He reached up to wipe it away, his fingers as tender as his words. "What can possibly mean more than our feelings?"

Just then Annie stirred, her voice weak. "Daddy?"

Michael tore his gaze from Katherine and leaned over his daughter's bed. "I'm here, princess."

"I dreamed we were at the park."

"We'll go there as soon as you're better," he told her, before raising his head to meet Katherine's gaze, his own both probing and promising.

"Good," Annie murmured. "I want to go on the swings."

"Then, swings it'll be," he replied.

His pager beeped, and Michael glanced at it, scanning the digital readout. "Looks like we have a problem at the site."

"Go ahead and check on it, Michael. Annie and I will be fine."

He smoothed the hair from his daughter's forehead. "That okay with you, princess?"

"As long as Katherine stays with me," she replied, slipping her hand into Katherine's.

Michael gazed at them both, finally nodding. But before he left, he leaned forward, his soft whisper reaching only Katherine. "I'll go, but we're not done talking."

She watched him leave, the hole in her heart threatening to choke her.

"Katherine?"

"Yes, sweetie."

"Will you go to the park with us to swing?"

The innocent words tore at her. How many more promises could she make to these children, knowing they weren't to share a future? "Why don't we see how soon you get better?"

"Okay. Can you tell me the pixie story?"

So Katherine did, relating the tale of the tiny pixie who fell in love with a leprechaun. Their love seemed impossible, yet in the magic forest the impossible became possible.

Katherine couldn't help wishing for a touch of that magic.

As she spoke, Annie's eyelids drooped and soon she was asleep. Katherine's heart filled with gratitude that their prayers had been answered, that this precious child had been saved.

A few hours passed. Michael phoned to make sure everything was all right, and she assured him he could take care of his crisis without worrying. The doctor had been by, again confirming that Annie was dramatically improving. Still, Michael promised to be gone only a short while longer.

But James McPherson arrived first.

"How's she doing?"

"Great, actually. The doctor thinks she'll be able to go home soon."

"Then, your prayers have been answered."

She nodded even though her lips trembled with emotion.

James met her gaze. "Perhaps not all of them?"

Katherine bent her head. "I'm so confused."

"So you've been thinking about what we discussed?"

"Truthfully, that's all I've thought about. But I can't dismiss my concerns."

"Do you love Michael?" he asked quietly.

She bit her lip. "With all my heart."

"Do you want him to be happy?"

Katherine nodded.

"And his children?"

"They mean the world to me," she admitted.

"And you feel that you and Michael are equally yoked?"

She knew that was now true.

"Then, all that's holding you back is your own lack of faith."

"Mine?" she uttered in amazement.

"You have to trust the Lord to guide you," James replied. "Just as you've advised Michael and many others."

"But…" Her protests died. In that instant she

knew James was right. The same counsel she'd given applied to herself, as well. She had to trust the Lord. He would not have given her this wonderful man and his children to love if that was not to be her path. Gratefully she looked at her mentor and friend.

"How could I have been so blind?"

James took her hand. "Not so blind that you didn't finally see. I expect an invitation to the wedding."

The door opened. Michael entered, pausing when he saw her hand in James's.

But her mentor didn't falter. "You must be Michael."

Nodding cautiously, Michael drew closer. "Yes."

James smiled at them both, placing Katherine's hand gently in Michael's. "Then, this must be yours."

James left as quietly as he'd entered.

Michael met her gaze. "Should I ask who that was?"

Her eyes were bright, but this time the tears were born of joy. "A very wise man."

"Oh?"

"One who agrees with you."

Michael looked wary but he didn't speak.

She swallowed, her heart so full it nearly crowded out the words. "He said you were right...that I should marry you."

Michael's expression was sober. "And what do you say?"

"Yes," she replied, unable to believe so much happiness was to be hers. "Definitely, positively, unchangeably yes."

His hands moved to frame her face. "I'll make you happy," he promised.

"You already do." Her heart hitched. "I love you so much, Michael."

His fingers traced the contours of her face, finally cupping behind her neck. "And I you, Katherine Blake, with all my heart."

Gently his lips touched hers.

Insistent light pushed past the undraped window, enveloping them, creating a golden, sun-stained silhouette of their embrace.

In the halls, the usual bustle of the busy hospital continued. Outside, people laughed and played in the park while traffic continued to fill the streets. But for Katherine and Michael, the moment was suspended in time. A moment only for them. One that only their love could achieve, and only their faith could sustain.

And one only their hearts could believe.

Epilogue

"Are you sure his outfit looks all right?" Katherine fretted, leaning over the carriage, fussing with the baby's clothes. It was still hard for her to believe that she and Michael had been married nearly a year and a half.

Michael smiled indulgently. "It's perfect. You made it stitch by stitch yourself. You *know* it's perfect."

"He looks pretty," Annie told her, skipping beside the buggy, her cheeks flushed with healthy color. Not a trace of her illness remained. She was radiantly, blessedly well.

"Boys don't look *pretty*," David told her, his hand possessively resting on the side of the carriage.

"I don't know," Katherine demurred. "I think he's absolutely beautiful, just like you and Annie."

David toed the sidewalk with his Sunday shoes, hiding his embarrassed pleasure.

"If we don't stop mooning over him, church will

be over by the time we get there," Michael told his family. Yet, he, too, reached to smooth the baby's blanket.

"They can't start without us," Annie protested with a sidelong glance at Katherine. "We have the minister with us."

"It's a perfect day to christen both a church and a baby," Katherine mused.

The new building had risen from the ashes of the old. It possessed all the modern conveniences, yet they'd salvaged the original stone, the remnants of its beginnings, a sign of its history. Now the church was truly the best of old and new.

As was her family, Katherine acknowledged. Together, they blended as one. Her heart had never been so full, nor her gratitude so overflowing.

Katherine remembered the beautiful autumn day of their wedding. Michael had been impatient, insisting they not prolong the date. Although she'd had only four weeks to plan the wedding, Katherine was certain she'd never seen one more beautiful. Her dress had been a magical creation, and her long hair had been laced with fresh flowers and ribbons.

James McPherson had officiated. Cindy, as maid of honor, had beamed at her, eyes bright with joyous tears. Tom was both pleased and proud to be the best man. David, as their ring bearer, and Annie, as flower girl, nearly stole the show.

But Katherine couldn't contain her radiance when her gaze connected with her groom's. Remembering, she guessed the love they shared had been evident to all the guests.

In a gesture of peace and to symbolize the beginning of her new life, she had invited her parents to the ceremony. Her father, incredibly touched, had proudly given her away. But it was her mother's reaction that had shocked Katherine. Victoria had wept while the vows were exchanged.

And during the reception, Edward and Victoria had taken a stumbling start toward ending their silence. Her parents would never reunite, Katherine knew, but it signaled a better future for them all.

Annie tugged at her dress. "Are we really going to be late, Mommy?"

Katherine glanced down at her precious daughter, knowing a day would never pass that she didn't give thanks for her very life.

Almost as soon as she and Michael married, Annie had asked to call her Mommy. David had soon followed suit. And some days Katherine could scarcely remember a time when they hadn't been her children.

"I think we'll make it, sweetie." Katherine straightened the bow in Annie's hair, her hand lingering a moment. Then she draped it over David's shoulder. "You've already met Pastor McPherson and his wife. You remember their boys. One is your age and the other is just a bit older."

"Are they still coming to lunch?" Annie asked.

"Absolutely," Michael answered. He had become friends with Katherine's mentor, and would always be deeply grateful for James's words—the ones that had convinced Katherine to venture into marriage. And to finally have a family all her own.

Katherine paused as the church came into sight. Her breath caught when she thought of the love that Michael had poured into its rebuilding. He hadn't experienced a reluctant return to faith. Instead, he had embraced it, weaving his belief back into the fabric of his life. And he'd also pondered her earlier words about the long hours he worked. Michael had hired a competent assistant, which freed him to spend more time with his family.

With Michael and the children hurrying her, they entered the sanctuary. A pew near the front had been reserved for them.

It was a new experience for most of the congregation—having a woman minister with a brand-new baby. *Ooh*s and *aah*s rippled through the rows of people. The entire congregation seemed to feel this was *their* baby, their family.

James McPherson and Jean greeted them with wide smiles, clearly pleased to be special visitors. At Katherine's request, James was performing the baby's christening. Together, James and Katherine would bless the new sanctuary.

Regardless of custom, Katherine insisted that Annie and David stand beside their brother during the christening. Both beamed with pride and love.

Young Danny, whose name was chosen because it was a combination of David and Annie, opened his eyes, seeking those he loved: his mother, his father and his very special siblings.

"We named him," David whispered to Pastor McPherson.

"After us," Annie added.

"Wise choice," James whispered back.

Then he blessed the youngest member of the Carlson family. Katherine tried to blink back the tears, but her joy was too great. Again she gave thanks for her incredible husband, their children, their abundance of gifts.

Meeting Michael's eyes, she found the reflection of her own feelings. He held their son, his large, strong hands incredibly gentle as they dwarfed the small head and body.

And somehow, Katherine fell in love with Michael all over again.

The music swelled, filling the sanctuary. Sunlight pierced the stained-glass windows, casting the most beautiful of shadows, prisms of shattered color that laced the pews.

Katherine's gaze locked with Michael's. Love bound them, a love so consuming that even now it made her breathless. To her wonder, his glance alone could reach out and touch her, conveying all the emotions she'd once despaired of knowing.

The tender look between them lingered.

Hearts filled beyond expectation, they celebrated this newest miracle, knowing they had received miracles without measure. And they'd only just begun.

* * * * *

Dear Reader,

This book was a joy to write because I could connect so deeply with the characters and their struggles, struggles only an abiding faith can weather. As a child and then young person, I was extremely fortunate to grow up in a close-knit, warm and loving church family. In writing this story, my heart swelled with memories of the great fellowship, the friendships that endure over time and distance. Like the hero of this story, Michael Carlson, I lost someone very special, someone who grew up with me in that same home church. But it's our faith that carries us through, that buoys us in both the best and worst times.

From writer to reader, thank you for allowing me to share part of my experience, for this is the connection we share. God bless.

Bonnie K. Winn

P.S. I'll always miss you, Caren McCurdy, even though I know your sweet voice sings with the angels.

CHILD OF MINE

And God gave Solomon wisdom and
understanding exceeding much, and largeness
of heart, even as the sand that is on the seashore.
—1 *Kings* 4:29

For Donna Hobbs, friend, sister, keeper of secrets, guardian of memories. You've been there for me through everything. We've shared weddings, babies, dreams and everything in between. I think often of the days we tunneled to lunch, walked to Sam Houston Park, the library. Our connection transcends the miles, but I miss you, dear friend.

Prologue

Los Angeles, California

The carton was small. But it was all Kyle had left behind when he'd disappeared eight years ago, taking their precious baby, stealing her hope.

Sitting cross-legged on the floor in the attic of her parents' Brentwood home, Leah Hunter dug through the contents of the carton as she had hundreds of times before. She'd tried to leave it behind when she moved to her own apartment. But she couldn't. She was searching for a clue, *any* clue that could tell her where Kyle had gone.

She had been nineteen when she'd married him. A naive nineteen, she realized now, because she'd believed Kyle's lies. But she'd never believed he would kidnap baby Danny.

Leah picked up the only unique item in the carton, a hand-carved box. It was so simple it was elegant. She opened the hinged lid and smoothed her fingers over the sleek wood interior, searching for a hidden panel—yet again. But she still couldn't find anything. Like everything else Kyle had left, it was a dead end.

She had been as dazzled by him as he'd been by her parents' money. It was all he'd ever wanted from her. But when they wouldn't hand out the money, he'd taken Danny.

Frustrated, Leah tapped on the side of the box fiercely. A small drawer, the same size as the base of the box, slid open.

Her heart skipped a beat. Shaking, she lifted it to the light.

The drawer was empty, but engraved on one side was a name: *Matt Whitaker.* And a place: *Rosewood, Texas.*

It could just be the name of the person who'd carved the box, Leah realized. But it was the first clue in eight years. And nothing would keep her from trying to find her son. Nothing.

Chapter One

Rosewood, Texas

*W*hitaker Woods. Like the box Leah clutched in her hand, the native pine storefront was simple. Pushing open the door, she expected to find small, similar pieces inside. She was surprised instead by the array of large furniture. Dramatic armoires, one-of-a-kind chairs, trunks, chests.

"Can I help you?" An older woman emerged from the back, the wood floor creaking beneath her.

"Yes." Hope crowding her throat, Leah showed her the box. "I'm trying to locate the sales record for this."

The woman wiped her freckled hands on the industrial apron she wore. "That I can't do."

Leah fought her disappointment.

"Matt only makes these for friends or family," she continued, picking up the box. "He doesn't sell them."

"Oh?"

She turned the box over. "Yes. They're special."

Leah seized the new information as if were gold. "Do you by chance know Kyle Johnson?"

"Kyle? No."

Leah hadn't really expected that she would. Still… "Could I speak to Mr. Whitaker?"

"Matt's not here right now. He'll probably be back in a few hours. I could have him call you."

"That would be great." Leah handed her a card. "This has my cell number. I'm staying at Borbey House just down the street."

"Annie's place. I know it."

Leah smiled. "Thanks for your help."

"Welcome to Rosewood."

Matt whistled as he unloaded the pickup truck. He was especially pleased with the custom hall tree he'd just finished. The concept was Victorian. The contemporary design, however, was all his own. He loved working with his hands. Always had. Bringing the wood from one life to another.

Easing the hall tree through the back door of the store, Matt was careful not to scratch the multiple layers of varnish.

"Boss, that you?"

"Yeah."

Nan walked through the swinging doors that separated the display area from the back room and spotted the hall tree. "Oh, that's nice!"

He stood back, surveying the piece. "I'm happy with it."

"Bet it doesn't last long. And you'll have a dozen requests for more."

"You're better than an ad in the *Houston Chronicle*."

Nan grinned. "Glad you noticed."

"How's the day been?"

"Steady. Cindy Mallory wants to talk to you about ordering some new furniture for the triplets. Sounds like a pretty big commission. And I sold that rocking chair I've had my eye on for my youngest daughter. Should have bought it myself when I had the chance."

He chuckled. "I told you to put it aside."

"Sold it to a tourist for full price, Matt."

"Not everything's about the bottom line."

"Good thing I take care of the books," she chided. "Oh, and a pretty young woman came by to see you."

"Ah...wish I'd been here."

"She had one of those special little boxes you make, wanted to see if I could trace it." Nan handed him Leah's card. "And she wanted to know if I knew a Kyle Johnson."

Matt froze.

"Told her that you just made them for special friends. She's staying over at Annie's place. Card has her cell number on it, too. Seemed nice enough. Funny though. Her having the box and not knowing they're special. But I told her I'd ask you to call." Nan paused. "Matt? You okay?"

"Yeah...sure."

"You never used to sell the little boxes, did you?"

"No. Uh...I'd better get back to the house."

"Well, okay. You sure everything's all right?"

"Yeah. Just been a long day."

Nan glanced at her watch. "It's just after two. You want some coffee?"

"No. You go ahead."

Back in his truck Matt studied the card. And eight years crashed away.

Sitting in an overstuffed chair that was so comfortable it should have lulled her into a nap, Leah stared at the phone in her room. A few hours, the clerk had said, before Matt Whitaker would return to the store. She'd unpacked and tried to fiddle away as much time as she could but she still had too much left on her hands. It would be a while before he called. She pictured her mother back in L.A., anxiously waiting to hear if she had any news. Might as well let her know not to sit by the phone.

Rhonda picked up on the first ring. "Leah?"

"Hi, Mom."

"Have you found out anything?"

"Not yet, but I'm working on it."

"Maybe you should have let the investigators—"

"Not this time, Mom." Leah's jaw tensed. "I have to do this one on my own."

There was a pause. "Maybe you're right. The detectives never found out anything despite all their searching."

No. And though Leah had believed Kyle would bring Danny back, he hadn't. She sighed.

"We could contact the FBI again," Rhonda reminded her.

"It didn't work the last time."

Rhonda's silence told Leah her mother didn't appreciate the comeback. But the silence was short-lived. "How you could have been married to a man who left absolutely no record of his name…and for you to not have his social security number…"

Leah didn't have an answer. Kyle hadn't held a job while they were married and her mother knew it. And the FBI found that the background he'd told her was fiction—a fairy tale to make a gullible girl fall in love. Which gave them nothing to trace. "What do you want me to say?"

Rhonda must've tapped her rings against her desk, the sound coming clearly through the phone. "I don't suppose there's any point in going over old wounds."

What did it matter now? They'd already been scraped open. Leah rolled her eyes. She knew her mother was just anxious about Danny. But the woman was cranking her own anxiety level even higher. She struggled to keep her voice calm. "Is everything okay at work, Mom?" Hunter Design was a thriving L.A.-based design firm with an international clientele. Kyle had seen only dollar signs in the family-operated business. Her parents had been willing to hire him, but he hadn't wanted to work. He just wanted the money.

"Jennifer's keeping an eye on your jobs. She's competent, even if she doesn't have your touch."

Jennifer was Leah's assistant. "She'll be fine."

"Leah? Don't be too disappointed if this doesn't… well, turn into the lead you're hoping for."

"I won't, Mom."

Once she'd said goodbye to her mother, Leah glanced around the storybook room in the quaint bed-and-breakfast. She had been on hyper-speed since she'd found the secret compartment in the box and decided to pursue this long shot at finding Danny. On edge, she'd flown to Houston, rented a car and driven more than three hours to this small town, hidden in the heart of the Texas hill country. She'd heard it was a beautiful region, but she'd barely seen anything she'd driven past.

The thought of just sitting, without anything to do, was making her crazy. Maybe she could walk off some of her nervous energy.

Stopping at the antique breakfront that served as a desk, Leah rang the bell. Annie, the B and B owner, popped out of the adjoining kitchen, wiping her hands on a cloth. She was more than happy to forward any messages to Leah's cell phone.

The air was clear, delivering early spring's promise of new life, as Leah walked down the old-fashioned boardwalk. Tall elm trees shaded the street. The buildings belonged to a different era, she realized. Enchanting Victorian structures, which all housed working businesses.

She passed a quaint drugstore, hardware store,

costume shop and newspaper office before reaching Whitakers Woods. She lingered in front of the wide-paned window, but didn't see a man inside. The door opened and a customer stepped out.

The woman Leah had met earlier called out to her. "Hi, there!"

Leah walked inside. "Hello…"

"I'm Nan," she said with a smile. "Should have introduced myself earlier. Matt was here sooner than I thought and I gave him your card."

"Great! Then I guess I'll be hearing from him soon."

Nan nodded. "Oh, my, yes. Matt's real good about getting back to people."

Relieved, Leah smiled. "That's wonderful. Thanks for your help."

"Glad to do it. You settling in at Annie's?"

"Yes. It's a charming place. Like the town."

"Thing is, it's a real town, not put on for tourists like some places. No T-shirt and souvenir shops. Not that we don't welcome visitors, but this is our home."

"I got that sense right away."

"Good. Hope you have a nice stay."

Leah crossed her fingers. "I'm counting on it."

Matt sat at his kitchen table staring at Leah's card. It had to be her. It all fit. L.A. The box John had taken from him…along with Matt's savings.

"Kyle" she'd called him. Kyle Johnson.

His half brother had always hated his real name.

John Litchkyl Johnson. Litchkyl, their mother's maiden name. He'd been John all his life in Rosewood. His hick life, he'd called it. He must have gone by Kyle once he'd gotten to California and married Leah.

But why was she here now?

She'd abandoned John and their baby when Danny was only six weeks old. What kind of woman did that? Only the lowest kind.

And she had money, John had said. Enough to have hired nannies, people to help out, to make raising her child as easy as possible. Instead she'd left. Said she didn't want the responsibility of a kid.

Matt could still feel the weight of that tiny bundle in his arms the first time he'd held Danny, the clutch of little fingers around his own. The promise he'd made.

He knew John had his faults. His half brother had been immature, irresponsible. But he also knew that a child belonged with his parents. At least the one who cared enough to stay with him. John had abandoned his own dreams of making it in California to come back to Rosewood where his only family remained. Their mother had passed on when John was sixteen, and John's father had died years before. Matt was all he had left.

And though he'd never expected to be part of raising a baby, Matt had fallen in love with Danny at first sight. That had never changed.

But the family dynamics *had* changed almost immediately. While Matt was still learning how to clean up diapers and mix formula, there was the car accident.

And then it was just the two of them. An ill-prepared bachelor and a motherless child. That's when Matt made the promise he never intended to break.

And he'd built two cradles. One for the house, one for the shop. So he could watch over Danny, protect him. That wasn't going to stop. He would do anything, give anything to keep his boy safe. Even if it meant taking over as the only father Danny would ever remember. Oh, he'd tell Danny the truth when he was old enough to understand. And he knew none of his neighbors would dare bring up the sensitive subject. Yes, he would keep Danny safe. Even if that meant keeping him from his own mother.

Chapter Two

"Are you sure there aren't any messages for me?" Leah asked.

Annie shook her head. "I'm sorry. I double-checked. If I'm out, I have an answering machine. Locals are usually pretty good about leaving messages. I can't be as sure about out-of-towners…"

"It's local. Whitaker Woods."

"Oh, they're really good about getting back to you." Annie smiled. "Matt's stuff is special, isn't it? People find out about his furniture, drive up here from all over. Usually Nan is at the store most of the time, though."

"Actually, I need to speak to Mr. Whitaker."

"I'm surprised he hasn't followed up with you since yesterday." Annie glanced at the clock. It was after seven. "Wow. It's been a day and a half. That's really not like him. Have you talked to Nan?"

"Repeatedly. Seems he's out on a commission job."

Annie nodded sympathetically. "Matt works like

an artist, gets all caught up in what he does." She pointed across the room. "See that bench? He recreated it from some fuzzy old photos for my grandfather. Took great care with every detail. The original was lost in a fire. It was a wedding present to Gramps from my great-grandparents. And it meant so much to him when Matt was able to make another one. He said it brought Granny closer to him those last years." Annie cleared her throat. "Anyway, like I said, Matt becomes really caught up in his projects."

Leah understood, but it wasn't getting her any closer to talking with him. "Thanks anyway."

Climbing the stairs back to her room, she couldn't help but wonder. Matt usually got back to people quickly. So, why wasn't he getting back to her?

At breakfast the next morning, Leah dawdled over her French toast.

"Do you want another slice?" Annie offered.

"No, thanks. It's delicious, but I shouldn't be eating anything this rich for breakfast."

Annie chuckled. "The guests usually say that. But they rarely order anything else after they try it. It was my grandmother's recipe."

"I'm guessing you were close to your grandparents."

"This was their place. The one that *didn't* burn down." Annie lifted the coffeepot. "More coffee?"

"Since I'm the last one in the dining room, why don't you join me, unless I'm keeping you from something?"

"Best offer I've had all morning."

Leah added more cream to her cup. "Do you ever get tired of having your house full of people?"

Annie hesitated. "You'd think so, wouldn't you?"

"Actually, I've been considering combining work and home spaces—I'm a designer."

"Really? That must be interesting."

"I like it. But then I kind of fell into it. It's my family's business. A third-generation business."

"Like mine. This was a bakery during my grandparents' time."

"So you know what I mean. I grew up playing with fabric and paint. I thought sample books were toys."

Annie grinned. "I'd have loved that. I've always wanted to do something more with this place."

"It's beautiful. Fits perfectly with the period of the building, of the town actually."

"Thanks. For the most part, these were my grandparents' furnishings. They used this room for the display area so it was a natural for the dining room. But I'd like to put my stamp on another room."

"It's the woman in us," Leah commiserated.

"True."

Leah sipped her coffee. "Do you know if Whitaker's combines its workshop and retail space?"

"Hmm? Oh, there's a work space at the store, but Matt does most of his work at the shop behind his house."

"Did you have a particular room in mind to redo, Annie?" Leah asked, picking up on her earlier comment.

"One the public doesn't have access to, I think," she mused. "Maybe my bedroom."

For a few minutes they talked about Annie's decorating wish list. Leah didn't want to rush the conversation, but at some point she intended to ask Annie just where the Whitaker house was.

If Matt Whitaker wouldn't call her, she would have to call on him.

The rambling two-story house was old, well kept and surprisingly cozy-looking. It also appeared to be empty.

First, Leah rang the bell at the front door. Then waited. Then rang it again. And again.

She tried knocking.

She tried the back door.

Not thwarted, she searched out the shop. A tall, wide double door stood open. Apparently theft wasn't an issue in this part of the world.

She found nothing but wood and tools in the orderly, pine-scented shop. She breathed in the smell of newly cut timber and wood dust, but they didn't tell her if Whitaker had been there that day or even that week. She suspected the shop always smelled of freshly cut wood.

Going back to the house, she took out a card, scribbled a message on the back—explaining that she urgently needed to speak to him—and tucked it in the space by the front door.

Leah considered camping out until Matt Whitaker returned, but who knew when that would be?

So she checked again at the store. Nan was apologetic, assuring her that Matt would be in touch at some point.

She waited at Borbey House until after five o'clock and drove out to the Whitaker house again. No one was home.

Frustrated, she returned to the bed-and-breakfast.

Annie was tidying the parlor. "Any luck?"

"None." Disheartened, she started climbing the stairs.

"Wait." Annie put down her feather duster. "I know it's exasperating, I mean, you driving all this way, not being able to get in touch with Matt. Why don't you come with me this evening to the church supper? It's always fun. We have games afterward."

Leah was about to refuse. "And Matt might be there."

That clinched it for her. "Oh? Are you sure I won't be in the way?"

"At our church? Never. It's a potluck and we always have plenty of food and then some."

Annie was about Leah's age, and her lively dark eyes were warm and inviting. But Leah didn't want to take advantage. "Then, can I make a donation?"

"It's not necessary. Really, everyone's welcome."

"Hmm. I couldn't help noticing that you make a lot of extra pies."

"This *is* Borbey House—Hungarian for 'baker.' Selling the pies is a holdover tradition from the days when my grandparents ran the bakery."

"Good. I'd like to buy two, please."

Annie grinned. "Hungry, are we?"

"I'll let you pick the flavors." Leah glanced down at her jeans and frowned. "I didn't bring a dress."

"You look about the same size as me. I'll loan you something."

"Really?"

"It won't be a designer label, but if that doesn't bother you…"

"Annie, you redefine hospitality."

Rosewood Community Church was located in a beautiful old building. Annie explained that the structure had sustained an electrical fire that had nearly wiped it out a few years earlier. But the membership had come together to rebuild. By using some of the original stones, they had maintained the best of the past, while making sure they had a future.

Leah listened as she clenched and unclenched her sweaty hands, studying the people around them. She leaned close to Annie. "What does Matt Whitaker look like?"

"Um…tall, early thirties, dark brown hair that's kind of sun-streaked…" She paused. "You know he works with lots of wood and tools, so he's fit, muscular. Casual dresser. What did I leave out?"

Leah shook her head. "Not much." But she couldn't stop staring at every man who passed by.

She didn't pay much attention to the tables of food, although she followed Annie's lead and filled her plate, then took a seat. The people were friendly, introducing themselves. She was surprised by their welcome. It was so different than being in the city.

"There's Matt. About two tables over on the left." Annie pointed tactfully. "See? Next to that family?"

Leah was relieved to finally see him. She'd begun to think that even in such a small town she wasn't going to catch up to him. Although she wanted to pin him down now, manners kept her from bothering him until he finished his dinner.

A man and woman sitting at the table between hers and his stood up, clearing her view. It was then she saw the young boy at Matt's side. A boy that looked to be about the same age Danny would be. Leah swallowed.

She always noticed young boys, wondering how her own son had turned out. Still… She watched father and son together. Their postures were nearly identical. Their gestures similar. Matt paid careful attention to the boy.

"Dessert, Leah?" Annie asked.

"No, thanks."

"There's a cheesecake over there calling out to me. I don't want to be rude, so I think I'll go answer."

"Mmm."

Annie shrugged and walked over to the dessert table.

Leah watched Matt Whitaker and the child. Although she couldn't hear what they were saying, the two heads were bent together and she could see the boy's grin, Matt's quick smile.

They were close. It was evident in the easy body language, the looks they exchanged.

Surely a man who loved his son this much would understand her quest.

As Leah watched, the boy jumped up from the table, hugged Matt and then ran to join the other kids his age in the games that were beginning. Leah found it difficult to take her gaze from him, watching until he and the other children left the fellowship hall with a basketball, probably to go to the gymnasium.

Annie had returned with her cheesecake, extra happy that she'd found chocolate sauce to go with it. She urged Leah to go over to see Matt.

He was still at the table, finishing his meal, when she approached.

"Mr. Whitaker?"

He glanced up.

"I'm Leah Hunter."

His expression turned wary. "Yes?"

"I've been trying to reach you at your store. Sorry to ambush you here." Leah smiled, trying to take the businesslike edge from her words. "I'm with Annie. I mean, she invited me to the church supper, being a stranger in town and all."

Not a word from him.

"And me being at loose ends," Leah continued, filling in the awkward silence. "I wasn't planning to be in Rosewood long. I just came to talk to you. I think Nan gave you my card."

The silence was so protracted she wondered if he would speak.

When he finally did, his voice was deep, somber. "She gave it to me."

Which told her nothing. "So…" Leah studied his unblinking gaze. "I'm trying to trace down a box I have—"

"Nan told you we don't keep records on the boxes."

"She said you only make the boxes for family or special friends—"

"Miss Hunter, my friends don't sell their boxes."

"I didn't say I'd bought it."

"You've come a long way for nothing then." He stood, stepping aside and pushing his chair up to the table.

"No, Mr. Whitaker, I haven't." She pulled the box from her purse. "This is the first clue I've had to finding my son in eight years and you're not going to just dismiss me." She held it up. "This belonged to Kyle Johnson. Did you know him?"

His expression was at first startled, then guarded. His lips thin, pressed tightly together. One word finally emerged, as though it were painful to say. "Yes."

Her hope, thready at best, flared. She bit her lower lip to stave off tears. "Oh, Mr. Whitaker, you don't know what this means to me." Despite her effort, one tear slipped down her cheek and she wiped it away. "Where can I find him? I know he's difficult to pin down."

"Not anymore."

"No?"

"He's dead."

Chapter Three

Reeling, Leah stared at Matt's back as he walked away. She'd never let herself believe Kyle could be dead. Because if he were, that meant…

But the investigators had never found Kyle's death certificate. Whitaker had to be wrong.

"Wait! Please!" She ran to catch up to him. "When did Kyle die?"

He stopped and turned to her, his words clipped. "Eight years ago."

She gasped. Shaking, she felt the last remnants of her self-control slip away. "That can't be. We've been checking for years and never found a death certificate."

"His first name was John. Kyle was part of his middle name—Litchkyl."

All of Kyle's lies. Even his name. He'd signed their marriage certificate as Kyle Johnson. He'd cheapened every single thing about their marriage.

She closed her eyes, afraid to ask. Hope and despair warred in her heart. Swallowing, she lifted her chin. "And the baby? The boy?"

He hesitated.

And her heart nearly stopped.

"Is safe."

"Where is he?"

Matt stared at her.

"Please, if you know anything." She took a deep breath. "I'm sorry. I haven't explained myself very well. I was married to Kyle. The baby, the boy, I mean, is mine. I've been looking for him. That's why I'm here, why I'm trying to trace the box. So, if you can tell me anything…"

"It's too late. You made your choice."

She gaped at him. *Where did he get off…?* "I understand loyalty to a deceased friend, but you don't understand the circumstances—"

"I understand plenty."

There was derision in his tone, but she had no idea why. "I don't know what Kyle told you—"

"The truth."

She shook her head. "His version. Despite what he may have said, I need to find my son. You're a father. You must understand that."

"I understand you walked away once. Do the best thing for your son again. Walk away now."

Stunned, Leah watched as Matt Whitaker crossed the room and headed out the door.

Back at the bed-and-breakfast, Leah sat in one of the overstuffed chairs near her bedroom window.

She still couldn't believe Matt Whitaker's reaction. And she never would have imagined that Kyle could elicit such loyalty.

Kyle dead. For all her anger, it wasn't something she would have wished. He'd been so young.

Who was raising her son? Had he been legally adopted?

Throat dry, she considered the possibilities—along with Matt Whitaker's harsh response. Getting his help wasn't going to be easy. But she would really need it to find Danny, especially if there'd been a private adoption. That wasn't something that could be simply traced.

Staring out at the quiet street, she knew she wouldn't sleep that night. Her mind was filled with too many questions.

Leah watched for Whitaker's truck. From her vantage point at the parlor window in the bed-and-breakfast, she could see the traffic going down Main Street.

Persistence paid off by midafternoon. As soon as he parked in front of his store, Leah bounded outside and down the boardwalk.

Matt was alone in the display area, his back to her. "Be with you in a minute."

"Fine."

He stiffened and turned around slowly.

"Mr. Whitaker…Matt, please, let me tell you about my relationship with Kyle…John."

"I know all I need to."

"Obviously not, or you wouldn't be shutting me out. I was nineteen years old when we got married. I believed everything he told me—"

The bell over the door clanged as it opened. A group of young boys piled in, talking and laughing. The one she recognized as Whitaker's son ran up to him.

"Dad! Billy's dad's gonna take everybody for pizza after soccer practice. Can I go?"

Distracted, Matt glanced down at him. "Who's driving?"

"Billy's and Dustin's dads. Is it okay?"

Leah watched the boy, able to see him close-up for the first time. He was animated, eager. Then he turned and she could see his face more clearly. As she studied his features, she saw that his eyes were a unique shade of green, like her own. Even their shape was similar to hers. So was his mouth. He looked up at her and the impact of recognition hit her.

Matt glanced at her, then down at his son. "It's all right, but home right after the pizza. And mind Billy's and Dustin's dads."

"Okay," the boy agreed. "Thanks, Dad."

"Come on, Danny," the others called.

Leah shivered as she watched him dash out with his friends. She'd been almost certain when she saw his eyes. The name confirmed it.

No wonder Matt had been avoiding her, putting her off. It all made sense. Perfect, horrible sense.

Anger, hot and raw, clawed through her. "How could you?" She turned on Matt with every bit of righteous pain and accusation she could muster. "I've heard of slime like you. How could you steal my child and then have the gall to pretend that you didn't know where he was?"

"Steal? Just how is it a person *steals* an abandoned baby? You're a real piece of work. What? Did you decide after eight years that it might be fun to play mommy? Forget it. Danny's done just fine without you until now. Go with your original instincts. Pretend he doesn't exist."

"Abandoned?" Leah shrieked. "Abandoned?"

"Boss, is everything okay in here?" Nan rushed in from the rear entrance. "I just got back from the post office and it sounds like someone's plucking live turkeys. You can hear it all the way outside."

Breathing hard, Leah and Matt paused.

"Yeah," Matt said in the awkward silence. Then he slammed out the door, got in his truck and roared away.

Leah was left in the heavy silence.

Embarrassed, Nan cleared her throat. "Sorry to interrupt."

"No. If anyone should apologize, it's me, I was the one yelling." Leah tried to calm her breathing. "Will you tell me one thing?"

"If I can."

"Did you know a John Johnson?"

"John? Sure. He was Matt's younger brother. Half brother, really. Matt was always looking out for him."

And still was, apparently.

* * *

Leah allowed enough time to collect herself before driving to Matt's house. His truck was parked out front. He didn't answer the door, so she walked around back to the shop.

He was sitting at his work bench, a piece of alder wood in his hands. Although she was sure he heard her, he didn't stir.

And she didn't bother with greetings. "You could have told me about Kyle being your brother."

"It didn't take you long to figure it out."

"I shouldn't have had to."

Matt put the wood down on the bench. "Why would you want to come back now? You're a stranger to Danny."

That stung. Badly. "Through no fault of my own. Kyle wanted money from my parents. They expected him to work for it. That wasn't in his plans, so he took Danny. Then he called and asked for half a million dollars. He said it was to set him up in his own business. He wanted to be a big-time real estate mogul just when the market was hitting bottom. My parents refused. I thought he'd give up and bring Danny home, but he didn't."

"I don't believe you."

"Danny was an infant! Barely six weeks old."

Matt met her gaze. "I'm the one who fed him. Changed his diapers. Rocked him to sleep. Held him when he cried."

Leah's chest constricted. "You think I didn't want to?"

"No."

"Because Kyle, who lied about everything, told you so?"

Matt stood. "You knew him, what? A year? I knew him all his life."

"Then you should have known he was chasing one half-baked idea after another. He didn't care about family, about establishing a real life together. All he wanted was a great big handout from my parents, and when that didn't happen he stole my son."

"He was pursuing his dreams, which he gave up to raise his son when you abandoned him."

She shook her head. "You can't really believe that."

"Because you say it isn't true?"

"I'm his mother."

"Which hasn't meant squat."

"This isn't going to end with your say-so. Danny is my son. That means legally, no matter what steps you may have taken."

"So you'll just rip him away from everything and everyone he knows and loves without a qualm."

Leah swallowed. "I know my rights."

"Kyle said that money ruled your conscience."

She gasped. "That isn't true."

"Then think about Danny instead of yourself." He walked toward her.

Automatically, Leah took a step backward.

Matt continued advancing. "He's not a baby anymore. He'll ask questions. About where you were."

"I'll tell him the truth."

Matt scoffed. "And he'll believe *you?* Why?"

"Because I'm his mother." Even as she spoke, Leah recognized the futility of the words. Danny didn't feel any connection to her. He would believe Matt. "You're not going to dissuade me." She could feel the pressure, the tightening in her chest, the ache against the back of her throat. But she wouldn't give into tears in front of this man. "I'll be back."

Trying to look as though she were still in control, she fled before her emotions exploded. Back in the car, she drove only a short distance from his house before she pulled off the road onto a deserted cattle crossing. Then she let the tears flow. Ugly, painful sobs clutched her chest and scraped her throat.

Her baby.

He didn't know her. He thought she'd tossed him aside. How was she going to fix that? And how was she going to explain that she had to take him away from the only parent he'd ever known?

Chapter Four

Leah picked at her oatmeal the following morning. She'd considered calling her parents' attorney, but Matt Whitaker's words echoed through her mind.

Then it occurred to her that she had only his version of how Danny had arrived in Rosewood.

"More coffee?" Annie asked.

"Thanks."

"You're awfully quiet. Everything okay?"

Leah glanced around the dining room and saw that the only other guests remaining, an older couple, were gathering their things to leave for the day. "Not really."

"I'm sorry. Anything I can do?"

"Do you have a minute?"

"Sure."

Annie put the coffeepot on the sideboard, waved goodbye to the other guests and joined her.

Leah twisted the linen napkin, wondering how to begin.

Annie waited patiently.

"I need to know something."

"I'll tell you if I can."

"Did you know John Johnson?"

Annie nodded. "Yes. It's been a long time. He died…I'm not sure…seems like almost ten years ago."

"Do you know anything about his child?"

She sighed. "Saddest thing. John met a girl in California. They got married and had a baby, but she ran out on him when the baby was just tiny. So John brought the baby back here, but he got killed in a car crash not long after he came home. His brother raised the boy like he was his own. He's Matt Whitaker— the man you came here to talk to." Her eyes widened.

Leah lowered her chin. "Is that what the whole town believes?"

Annie nodded slowly. "Leah?"

"Yes. I'm the girl. But it's not true." She looked into Annie's honest eyes. "I need someone to trust."

"I can keep your confidences…but, Leah, you have to know…the town feels really strongly about this. Everyone backs Matt. They admire how he took in the baby."

"But they don't know the truth."

"It's the truth everyone's lived with for nearly a decade," Annie reminded her gently. "Even if it wasn't true to begin with, it's going to be hard to convince people otherwise, especially after seeing a big strong guy like Matt with a baby. He's raised Danny by himself…. He never married."

Leah's heart caught as she thought of all the time she'd missed, all the firsts, all the accomplishments.

"Do you want to tell me about it?"

So Leah told her.

"John wasn't exactly wild," Annie remembered. "But he didn't run with my kind of crowd. He was a year ahead in school, but I remember he was different. Actually, I can see him taking off for California. So, if you didn't abandon Danny, that means you have legal rights."

"Yes."

"But if you take him away from everything he knows…"

Leah sighed heavily.

"If it helps," Annie said, "Matt seems to be a great father."

"I'm not sure it does. Of course, I wouldn't want to know Danny had been miserable. But his relationship with Matt complicates everything. I've always known that if I found him, it wouldn't be simple. But the reality is a lot harder than I ever imagined." And Leah was longing to put her arms around her little boy, to hug him close, to tell him that he was hers… to let him know how much she loved him. Instead, she sat drinking coffee, not even sure where he went to school.

Annie plucked the petals from one of the daisies on the table. "There's another way."

Leah met her gaze.

"Stay here in Rosewood. Get to know Danny. Establish some trust before you tell him who you are."

"Do you think Matt would let that happen?"

"I've seen Matt with him. I don't think he could hurt Danny by telling him the truth right now."

For all the other objections Leah might have about Matt, she couldn't deny his love for Danny.

She would do what it took to restore her maternal rights to her son, to convince Danny that she loved him. "Thank you, Annie. You've got a full-time guest."

Leah learned that Danny attended the Community Church's elementary school. No wonder his name had never appeared in public school records. Then she found out that he went by Danny Whitaker. In a small-town private school, a birth certificate hadn't been necessary, she guessed.

Or maybe Matt had taken the legal steps and adopted him.

She didn't have the heart to find that out just yet.

Instead, she decided to put her design skills to their best use. She made an appointment with the principal, explained that she was taking a break from her stressful job in L.A. but would love to volunteer at the school to give herself something to do while in Rosewood.

"Miss Hunter, we'd be delighted to have you," Principal Gunderland said after their meeting. She was taking Leah to see the lounge she had agreed to work on.

"Leah. And I'm pleased that I can be of help."

"An actual designer to help redecorate our teachers' lounge. The last time we tried to do anything with the room, we wound up painting it ghastly pink. No one liked it, so we repainted it institutional green, which is just as awful, maybe worse."

"I'll try for something a little more aesthetically pleasing," Leah murmured, struggling not to be obvious as she peeked into the classrooms they were passing.

"Don't take this the wrong way, but we'll be thrilled with anything."

Leah spotted a room full of children who looked to be about the right age, but she didn't see Danny among them. She needed to know what grade he was in. "Um…anything?"

"As long as it's in keeping with the church school."

Leah glanced into another classroom. "Of course. Tasteful, I understand."

"Mr. Whitaker!" the principal said in a delighted voice.

"Whitaker?" Leah echoed, jerking her gaze back to see Matt stalking down the hall toward them.

"Yes, he's one of our best supporters and volunteers."

Of course.

And he was glowering at her.

"Mr. Whitaker, is something wrong?" Principal Gunderland asked. "I saw the new bookcase in the library. It looks wonderful."

"Good."

The principal seemed surprised by his curt reply.

"Oh, this is Miss Hunter. She's a new volunteer, and you won't believe it—she's a professional designer!"

Leah smiled sweetly.

"We've met," he muttered.

"Then you know how lucky we are to have her," she exclaimed.

"Yeah, lucky."

"Miss Hunter, you'll be working quite a bit with Mr. Whitaker since he coordinates most of our re-decorating."

The school secretary came hurrying up to them. There was an important call for the principal.

"Mr. Whitaker, would you mind escorting Miss Hunter to the teachers' lounge?" Mrs. Gunderland asked. "I'll meet you there in a few minutes."

He could hardly leave her there like a lump of hot coal, Leah realized, but she could tell he was seeth-ing as the two women walked away.

"What are you doing here?" Matt asked as he led her into the lounge.

"Checking out my son's school."

"How did you find out this is Danny's school?"

"It was hardly rocket science. Rosewood's a pretty small town. There aren't too many choices."

Matt wasn't satisfied. "Did you bring investiga-tors to town?"

"Professionals wouldn't have stumbled around for two days to find out about Danny."

"I don't want you here."

"You don't have any choice."

"I could pull Danny out of this school."

"From everything he knows and enjoys?" she replied evenly.

"So, what? You're going to play at this until you get bored again?"

Leah wanted to shake him. "No. I'm going to stay in Rosewood until I get to know my son better."

"You won't last a week. This isn't L.A. We don't have fancy boutiques or clubs."

"You don't know me, Whitaker. Not everyone from L.A. is a party girl."

He snorted.

"I don't spend my days shopping and playing tennis," she informed him. "I have a job."

"Don't you need to get back to it?"

"I'm on a leave of absence."

Matt looked at her suspiciously. "Just like that?"

"It was easier because my parents own the firm," she admitted. "But that doesn't make my work any less of a real job."

"Sure."

"Look. I don't have to prove anything to you. You're the one who didn't bother to check out Kyle's story." She saw the principal heading back toward them. "This isn't the place for this discussion."

"This isn't the place for *you.*"

Leah kept a grip on her temper.

"So, what do you think of our teachers' lounge?" the principal asked, huffing a bit as she hurried toward them.

Leah hadn't even glanced at the room. Now that

she did, she realized the principal was right. The lounge was ghastly.

"It could use some tender loving care."

Mrs. Gunderland laughed. "Said diplomatically. Don't you think so, Mr. Whitaker?"

Leah gave him her attention, too, just to needle him.

He noticed.

"We haven't done anything to the lounge since it was painted," he replied.

Avoiding the question, she noticed.

"We don't have much of a budget for redecorating," Mrs. Gunderland apologized.

"I have access to overrun materials through my work. Most I can get just for shipping costs." Leah thought of all the extra stock in the warehouse. Her parents would be happy to donate what was needed for a good cause. "There shouldn't be a problem."

The principal brightened. "Wow, you truly are an answer to prayer."

Leah thought of all her searching, all the years of wondering if she'd ever find Danny. "Thanks. That's how I feel about being here, too."

The following day Leah stretched out her time at the school, making different sketches of the teachers' lounge until recess. When the bell rang and the classes were dismissed, she watched eagerly until she finally spotted Danny filing out of his classroom.

Although he stayed in line as he was instructed,

she could see the restrained energy, the animation she'd noticed before. She absorbed every detail. His hair was dark brown like Kyle's had been, but with the same sun streaks as Matt's. And he had freckles.

She swallowed. Silly. Freckles shouldn't make her come unglued.

But they were so precious.

And his eyes. They'd been so easy to recognize because they were like hers and like her father's.

Leah smiled, imagining Leland Hunter as a child, imagining him with his grandson.

Danny was a beautiful child, just as she'd known he would be. And he seemed so happy, easily smiling, laughing. Matt was right about one thing. She couldn't take him away.

But he was wrong about her commitment.

She would last far more than a week.

She would last as long as it took.

Chapter Five

"Dad? Where's Timbuktu?" Danny asked, sitting at the kitchen table, doing his homework.

Matt chuckled. "Where'd you hear about Timbuktu?"

"At school. Miss Randolph said that's where she's gonna go on her next vacation."

"I think Miss Randolph was joking. How many more reading questions do you have?"

"Two."

Miss Randolph must have been having a bad day, but kids could drive the most patient adult batty. Matt remembered when Danny was about three, an age when he was questioning everything. He went through a period of asking about everyone he saw. Everyone they passed on the street, walking or driving. And even though Rosewood was a small town, that was a lot of "who's that?" Matt smiled to himself. But the little guy had been so excited to see every new face.

Every stage had been a revelation to Matt. He'd seen the world through new eyes.

Danny put his books and notebook into his backpack, then hung it on the hook near the door.

In the adjoining great room, Matt sat on a thick rug that was anchored by a heavy coffee table. On it, he and Danny had assembled an elaborate dinosaur settlement. Danny joined him, but seemed preoccupied as he adjusted the volcano.

Matt hoped Leah hadn't said anything. "Something bothering you, pal?"

Danny shrugged. "Billy's gonna have a baby brother or sister."

Matt could hear the dejected note in his son's voice. "You don't sound very excited."

"Billy was my only friend like me. You know, who didn't have any brothers or sisters."

Matt sighed. "I see." In the past he'd told Danny that it took both a mother and father in a marriage for siblings. He had impressed upon him the value of family, the sanctity of marriage. But he didn't want to bring up the subject of Danny's mother right now. He'd always told Danny that he didn't know where she was. "Billy's always been a good friend to you, hasn't he?"

"Uh-huh."

"And he's happy about having a new brother or sister?"

Danny pushed a toy brontosaurus close to a tall, plastic palm tree. "Uh-huh."

"Then, how should a good friend feel for him?"

Danny was quiet for a while. "Happy?"

"Yes, even though that's not very easy. But, what do we know about the right thing to do?"

"That it's not always easy."

Matt leaned over to hug him, his heart tightening. He believed everything he'd taught his son and what he was telling him now. But he also believed everything he'd told Leah Hunter. He couldn't let her snatch Danny away from everything he knew and loved until she tired of whatever she was playing at. For all John's failings, Matt couldn't accept that he would have lied about something so important.

John's father had been a weak man, but Matt and John's mother had been a woman of deep faith and strong values. And Matt was convinced that John would have matured into a responsible man had he lived.

"Dad, do you think you might get married sometime?"

Matt cleared his throat. There hadn't been much time for anyone in his life except Danny. And now… "I don't know," he replied honestly. "But I can't get married just so you'll have a little brother or sister. It has to be someone I love."

Danny's eyes were so serious. "Do you love anyone?"

"You betcha." Matt tousled his dark hair. "I love you, buddy."

Danny giggled. "I know *that!*"

"Gǫod." Matt reached across the table, adjusting one of the toy dinosaurs. "Your tyrannosaurus rex is about to eat that palm tree."

"Nah! A rex doesn't eat trees!"

Soon they were engrossed in the dinosaur valley and remained so until bath and bedtime. After a story and prayers, Matt tucked Danny in.

He looked so young as his eyelids grew heavy and he fought the last surrender to sleep. So young and innocent. How would it affect his son if he and Leah waged a legal battle over him?

Sighing, Matt smoothed the hair back on Danny's forehead. He straightened the blanket, then turned the lamp off. But he left a small night-light on as he'd always done.

Back in the kitchen, he reached in the refrigerator for a Coke when he heard a quiet knock on the back door. Opening it, he was glad to see his old friend. "Hey, Roger."

"It's not story or bath time, is it?"

"Nope, Danny just got to sleep."

"Wish I hadn't missed seeing him, but I'm glad I'm not interrupting. Can I borrow your router?"

"Sure." Matt held up his can of cola. "Want something to drink?"

"Sounds good."

Matt pulled out another Coke and handed it to his friend. "I'm sorry I didn't bring that bookcase over today."

Roger shrugged as he straddled one of the bar stools. "I figured you got busy."

"I got paranoid."

Pausing midway in opening the soft drink, Roger glanced at his friend. "That doesn't sound like you."

"Danny's mother's in town."

"What?"

Matt took the stool across the counter. "No warning. Just showed up."

"What does she want?"

"Danny."

Roger reared back. "Just like that?"

Matt recounted Leah's story. "And now, showing up at the school…"

"That's not exactly sinister. If she's on the level, it'd make sense that she'd want to see where and how he's being educated."

"Or how she can get to him," Matt replied darkly.

"You think she's planning to snatch him?"

"I don't know," he admitted. "It's what I've been asking myself ever since she showed up."

"But then she'd be opening herself up to a legal nightmare." Roger shook his head. "Unless she's completely stupid, that wouldn't make any sense."

"Hmm."

"Have you considered that she could be good for Danny?"

"In what possible way?"

"Every kid wants a mother, Matt. She may not be perfect, but she is his mother."

"Not perfect? What if she gets to know him, gets bored and walks away again? No. I'm not going to let Danny get hurt like that. He deserves the best, and up till now that's what I've tried to give him. She could tear all that down, make him doubt the foundation he's always trusted."

"Are you sure she's really as bad as all that? I mean, you said she just got into town. How do you know what kind of person she is? It's been eight years. She could have changed. Sounds like she was just a kid herself when she had him."

"She's going to say all the right things," Matt protested.

"Have you got a choice? At least here, it's on your turf. If you get into lawyers, she could win. Mothers always have the edge in custody cases, even when they shouldn't. Think about it. What better place is there to learn who the real Leah is?"

Matt didn't want to learn who the real Leah was. He kept picturing his brother when he'd returned home, shaky, almost frightened.

But Roger was right. He had a better chance of uncovering the real Leah here in Rosewood than anywhere else.

Within a few days, Leah had discovered which classroom Danny was in and had met his teacher. One of the younger teachers, Miss Randolph was open and friendly. But then Leah had found that the entire staff was pretty much that way. As part of the Community Church, the school reflected the church's attitude, Annie had explained.

When Leah volunteered to help out in the class, Miss Randolph was happy to have her. Nervous about her first day, Leah brought cupcakes to smooth the way. Annie, now her staunch supporter, had offered both the use of her kitchen and her grandmother's cake recipe. But Leah had painted the faces on the cupcakes herself with layers of multicolored icing. Tigers, lions, giraffes, bears.

Now that the time had come to offer them to the children, Miss Randolph clapped her hands together. "Okay, let's line up for treats."

Accustomed to the routine, the kids got into an orderly line. As prearranged, Leah held the large platter of cupcakes. The kids were used to treats, but eyes widened when they saw the elaborate animal faces with realistic whiskers and expressions.

Pleased, Leah relaxed somewhat. But it was difficult to pull her focus from Danny. She wanted to watch his every move. Knowing she couldn't single out one child for her attention, she tried to be casual, tried not to stare.

But he was so lively. And interested in everything.

All of the children were intrigued by the unusual treats and took care choosing just which animal they wanted. When it was Danny's turn, he scrunched his face into concentrated lines, then picked the lion.

"Thanks," he said politely with an upturned grin. "These are cool."

"You're welcome."

"Did you make 'em?"

"Yes," she replied, wanting to say more, but knowing she couldn't. Especially since she felt the sting of tears. The cupcake was the first thing she'd given him…the first thing he'd been able to thank her for. Such a simple, ordinary occurrence.

And it meant the world.

She kept it together as she handed out the rest of the treats and then did cleanup duty. But her gaze continued to stray until the teacher divided the children into reading groups. Leah was supposed to help anyone who needed it.

Since the class, like all the others in the school, was small, so were the individual groups. Leah rotated between them as Miss Randolph had instructed, but she was drawn to Danny's.

Danny read his section aloud without error.

It was a little girl named Lily's turn. She was obviously much shyer. "The water hit the wall with a big…" She paused, trying to decipher the word.

"Splash," Danny whispered.

Lily smiled. "Splash," she said aloud, then continued reading.

Leah was pleased to see that he was kind to the children who didn't work at his level. That behavior could come naturally.

Or from what he'd been taught.

She had to acknowledge the truth. Danny's upbringing had been a good one. And that was because of Matt.

Beneath the man's glower and glare, there must be something else. Something that had shaped Danny.

By late evening most of the guests at the bed-and-breakfast were either upstairs in their rooms or relaxing in the main parlor. The spacious old house had a small rear parlor off the kitchen that was Annie's private space, one that she invited Leah to share.

"These old Victorian houses are great," Leah said, relaxing in a bentwood rocking chair.

"Some people are put off because they're too big. I think they're cozy. Especially here by the kitchen."

Leah smiled. "I always thought it would be nice to have a sturdy table right in the middle of the kitchen, the family gathering around for meals."

"That not what you're used to?"

"Oh, my mother likes things more formal, dinner in the dining room, using the china and crystal." Leah shrugged, her eyes softening. "This just seems warmer, homier."

"Do you have a very big family?"

"No. I'm an only child. My parents had me kind of late, when they were in their forties. And when I didn't come along in the expected time line, I think they gave up. So I was a surprise. And by then they were used to giving dinner parties, entertaining clientele."

"Sounds lonely."

"I didn't mean it to. They doted on me. Because they were older, their friends were, too, so I had lots of attention. We traveled, which was great. It's just that, sometimes, I wondered about places, well, like Rosewood. Elegant is beautiful, but I wondered about simpler places where rustic is okay, too." Embarrassed, Leah laughed. "Listen to me."

"I'm enjoying it. I don't have many friends from outside of Rosewood and I know practically nothing about city living."

"How about you? How did you come to be the one who inherited your grandparents' house? No siblings to share it with?"

Annie's dark eyes saddened. "When I was a baby, my parents and older brother and sister were killed in a car accident. I was here with my grandparents."

Horrified, Leah stopped rocking and laid one hand over Annie's. "I'm sorry. I shouldn't have pried."

"It's part of who I am." Annie's face was drawn. "Part of the family curse."

"Curse?"

"I don't know what else to call it. I told you my grandparents' first home burned. Their other child, my mother's only brother, died in the fire."

"That doesn't mean your family's cursed, Annie."

"When I was twenty-one I met…the most wonderful man in the world." Annie's voice thickened. "He wasn't from here. He was a tourist just passing through. But after we met…well, anyway, we fell in love. And we got engaged. The day after, I was waiting for him so we could call his parents. When he didn't show up, I got worried and went over to the hotel. He didn't answer when I knocked on his door. The manager finally got the key, and when he opened the door, David was inside. At first I couldn't understand how he could sleep through both of us banging on the door." Annie paused, remembering. "He had died in the night. His heart. The doctor said he must have had a preexisting condition. He was twenty-five years old. I knew then what the preexisting condition was—my family curse."

"Oh, Annie, no! It was a terrible thing to happen, but it wasn't your fault."

"If he'd just kept driving, hadn't met me—"

"You can't believe that!"

Annie leaned back in her chair. "I keep praying it isn't true. But it isn't safe for anyone to become part of my family. Look what happens."

"So you intend to live alone the rest of your life?"

"No. I turned the bakery into a bed-and-breakfast so I have company." Annie smiled, trying, but still not hiding her pain. "And sometimes, when I'm lucky, guests are as good as family."

"I don't believe in curses, and I've always wanted a sister. So, I'll sign on."

Annie's smile faltered. "Don't even joke."

"I'm not. I took a huge leap of faith by trusting you with the most important secret I have. You proved that was the right thing to do. Let me prove this to you."

"Oh, I don't know, Leah. You haven't lived with this fear."

"I've lived with the fear of thinking I might not find my son alive every day of the last eight years. There isn't a greater fear."

Annie's lips trembled. "I've prayed that this curse isn't real."

Leah held out her hand. "Sisters?"

Annie hesitated, then reached out, as well. "Sisters."

Chapter Six

For the next few weeks, work on the teachers' lounge was progressing to Leah's satisfaction. The walls were freshly painted the color of sunwashed sand, and she'd done the trim in bright, clean white, with sections stained a deep mahogany for contrast. It was a drastic change from the dreary institutional green.

An ugly column stood in the middle of the room, and rather than trying to blend it in, Leah decided to make it a focal point. Using a trompe l'oeil technique, she turned it into a graceful willow tree, with a trunk, branches and leaves that reached around all four sides.

Continuing the theme, she used the same method to paint willow trees that faded in to the corners of the room, as well. The windowless, odd-shaped room was now open and inviting. The teachers were thrilled and there wasn't a stick of furniture inside yet. That required Matt's involvement.

He was the furniture man. She didn't want to delay finishing the job, but she didn't want to speak to him.

Problem.

She'd hoped to tiptoe around him by dealing with Nan at the store. But the older woman had cheerfully offered to have her boss get back to Leah.

Leah had come to the school that morning to complete a few touch-ups. The lounge door was propped open to allow the paint to dry, and she could hear footsteps, sure and distinctive, approaching from down the hall.

Instinctively, Leah knew it was him. She braced herself before facing him.

He wasn't smiling. He never did around her. Not that she expected him to.

For an instant she wondered how it felt to be in his shoes. To have raised Danny, to have had him at his side all this time. To wonder if he would be taken away.

Something in her softened. "Thanks for coming," she said as he walked in to the room

"I was close by. Nan gave me your message." He glanced around. "The place looks a lot different."

"Better, I hope."

He cocked his head, examining the center column. "Yeah."

More pleased than she would have expected, Leah smiled. "I was hoping we could replace the rectangular tables with some round ones, if that's possible. Hopefully in varied sizes."

"The school doesn't keep a huge inventory of furniture in stock."

She pursed her lips. "It's just that a few round tables would be better for the teachers, especially if they need privacy to work on a project. And with the odd angles in this room, well… But I know they like to sit together, too…."

"I can see if we could do some switching around," he said grudgingly. "Maybe with the library—"

"That would be great!"

"I didn't say for sure," he warned her.

"I understand." Leah proffered a sketch pad with a drawing of the room featuring assorted round tables. "I've got some great red chenille that I want to recover the chairs in."

"You don't think that's too ambitious?"

Leah felt a flash of temper. "You're doubting me?"

"It's a lot of work."

"Give me some credit, Matt. I'm a designer. I'm used to hard work. Do you think these walls painted themselves?"

"Give *me* some credit. When you're at your fancy design firm, you're not painting walls and recovering chairs yourself. You have people who do all of that."

"I learned from the ground up. We don't send jobbers out to do anything we don't know how to do ourselves, except electrical and plumbing. Maybe you ought to stop making assumptions and start learning about me, Matt. That's what I decided to do about you. Even if I don't like everything I find out." The last admission cost her, but she didn't back down.

He searched her eyes, then sighed. "Yeah. I can't do less than I expect of Danny."

"What?"

"I just reminded him that the easiest route isn't always the right one."

"Does that mean—"

"No assumptions, that's all, Leah."

It wasn't much. But it was a start.

The Sunday morning service at Rosewood Community Church was packed. Afterward, as the members dispersed, Annie began introducing Leah to some of her friends.

Leah sensed a kindred spirit in Emma McAllister, owner of the local costume shop.

"Welcome to Rosewood. You'll find we're a caring community. I was a stranger a few years back myself." Emma's arm rested on the shoulders of her son, Toby, who held the hand of his younger sister, just a toddler. Her handsome husband, Seth, had been equally friendly. "But it's difficult to stay a stranger long."

"Annie's convinced me of that."

Emma smiled. "Please stop by the shop so we can talk. The kids will keep things lively, but I'd like you to meet my partner, Tina."

Leah was touched by her openness. "That's very kind of you."

"It's not easy to be new, but you couldn't have chosen a better place for it." Toby tugged on her hand. "Now, I'd better catch up with my husband, but I'll be watching for you at the shop, okay?"

"Okay."

Annie nudged her. "I told you not to be nervous about today."

"You were right."

"And there are more people I want you to meet, too." When Leah started to protest, she held up a hand. "Okay. Not all at once."

Leah smiled, then spotted Matt and Danny walking in her direction. They were dressed in matching suits—the tall man, the small boy. Matt held Danny's hand securely in his own. Their bond was deep. So deep.

Danny saw her at about the same time. And smiled.

Her heart melted.

"Dad! It's the cupcake lady!"

Matt didn't have enough warning to avoid her.

"From my school! The animal cupcakes."

Matt cleared his throat. "Danny told me all about the cupcakes. They must have been something."

Impossibly touched, Leah shrugged. "I had fun making them."

"And she doesn't even have a kid in the class," Danny told Matt.

Leah's smile faltered, but she tried to hide the pain.

"Danny said the whiskers looked real," Matt told

her in a quiet voice. "He had a hard time deciding between the lion and tiger. He said he picked the lion because the mane was so thick, but he wanted both."

Leah met Matt's eyes, silently thanking him for the time to recover.

"Yeah, I liked all of them!"

"Tell you what. How about if I make you one of each? And you share them with your Dad?"

Danny's eyes widened. "Really? Wow!" Then he glanced up at Matt. "Would that be okay?"

Matt put a hand on Danny's shoulders. "That would be nice of Leah."

Danny grinned. "Are you comin' back to my class?"

"Yes. Would you like that?"

"Uh-huh." Then he frowned. "But you can't give me special cupcakes in front of the other kids. It wouldn't be fair." He brightened. "But you could come to our house." He glanced up again at Matt. "Couldn't she, Dad?"

It was evident he wanted to say no. An emphatic no. "Well—"

"And we could all share the cupcakes!" Danny's excitement grew.

Just what Matt wanted. But Danny was nearly dancing in his freshly shined shoes.

"Leah's probably too busy—"

"No," she replied, unwilling to relinquish any opportunity to spend time with her son. "I have plenty of time. Just tell me when."

Matt edged a step backward. "I'll have to check my calendar."

"There's nothin' on it for Thursday," Danny piped up helpfully. "I know 'cause I filled in the squares for soccer and softball practice nights."

Trapped, Matt forced out the invitation. "So, Thursday?"

"Thursday," she agreed. Cupcakes with her son. It was one of the fantasies she'd dreamed of a thousand times. To share the simple moments.

Try It On design and costume shop was located right in the middle of Main Street. When it opened, it had been a tiny place, and it was during the remodeling that Emma had fallen in love with her contractor, Seth McAllister.

In the witness protection program at the time, she couldn't tell him the truth about herself. It was a situation that didn't change until it was nearly too late.

Emma and Seth had each lost a child. Remarkably, Toby had come into their lives and they were able to adopt him. And now, the Lord had blessed them with another child, Ashley.

As a result, Emma had made her longtime associate and friend, Tina, her business partner. Still single, Tina had more hours to put in than Emma did these days. But Emma had installed a playpen in her office, making the business a family-friendly establishment.

It was crazy at times, especially when they were planning a big event like a wedding. Designs, fabric and people crowded the shop, and keeping an eye on her little one was a challenge. But Emma didn't want to miss a single moment of her daughter's life.

Nor did she want to miss out on new friends, which was why she was glad to see Leah Hunter pausing outside the shop's front door.

"Tina! Company!"

"The woman you told me about?" Tina called out from the back room.

"Yep."

The bell tinkled over the door as Leah pushed it open.

"Come on in," Emma invited, walking toward her. "I'm so glad you decided to come by."

"I hope I didn't pick a busy time."

"Not at all. Tina's just making some tea. Tuesdays are rarely busy, and we just finished one of the biggest weddings we've ever done. We've had a little breather, but now the elementary school...actually, the one at the community church, is gearing up for a play."

"And you're doing costumes as well as wedding parties?" Leah asked, impressed.

Emma grinned. "I love it."

"I can imagine why. The play must be the most fun. I'm already picturing the kids dressed up—they must look so cute!"

"Especially when they're little frogs or butterflies or daisies. The more inventive, the better for me."

Leah leaned over to touch the bolts of fabric

lined up against one wall. "You have some beautiful materials."

"Thanks. I don't know how they look to a real professional."

Leah pulled her mouth down on one side. "You're joking, of course."

"No. This is my second career. My first was the law."

"It certainly doesn't show." Leah walked over to one of the costumes hanging on the wall. "Is this an original design?"

"Yes."

"It's exquisite."

"Thank you," Emma replied.

"I was supposed to make tea," Tina announced, carrying in baby Ashley on her hip. "But someone wasn't asleep."

The child, newly awakened, had that rosy glow only children and pregnant women possessed, one that automatically stirred smiles. Shyly, Ashley laid her face against Tina's shoulder when she spotted Leah.

"Oh, now you don't want to hide," Emma coaxed gently.

"Mama," Ashley replied.

"And Mama's new friend, Leah."

Ashley lifted her head slowly, looking over Leah carefully. When she was satisfied, she wriggled a bit and Tina put her down. She toddled her way over to Leah.

Seeing that she was coming her way, Leah knelt down. "Hey there."

Ashley thrust her plump hands out and Leah caught them.

"What a pretty girl you are," Leah cooed.

"You're a natural with her," Emma said quietly.

Leah tipped her head to one side, smiling at the baby. "She's so sweet."

Emma smiled, too. "I think so. But we're easily charmed."

"True," Tina agreed.

Leah's face had softened. "Oh, I can see why."

Perhaps it was the loss of her own child, or a gift the Lord had bestowed on her because of it, but Emma could now sense a similar loss in others, and she felt it now in Leah Hunter. Emma wondered if that was why He had led Leah to Rosewood.

There was still pain in her eyes. Emma had seen it when they met on Sunday. Oh, it was carefully hidden. But her own had been, too. Before Seth, before the Lord had helped her through it, had made her whole again.

Watching Leah with her latest blessing, Emma silently promised the Lord she would help Leah as much as everyone in Rosewood had helped her. To be one of the friends she sensed Leah would need.

"I'm so glad I came by today." Leah inhaled the sweet baby fragrance as Ashley allowed a hug. It was as if she couldn't get enough of that precious unmistakable scent.

"Me, too."

"And now I can get that tea," Tina called over her shoulder, heading into the back room.

"Whatever." Leah smiled at Ashley, who smiled back. "I have everything I need right here to entertain me."

Chapter Seven

By Thursday, Matt was examining his sanity. He'd had one weak moment Sunday when Leah had looked so vulnerable and hurt. But to invite her here…

He groaned. History was full of tales of strong men destroyed by allowing their enemies to get too close.

Okay, enemy might be a little harsh. But he and Leah weren't far from that. They both wanted Danny. And only one of them could have him.

He poured cream into his mother's old earthenware pitcher and put it on the table. He'd avoided Leah over the past week, but he'd seen the work she'd done. She'd finished the teachers' lounge. It looked good.

No.

He had to admit it looked great. He wouldn't have believed it could be done. That misshapen room had been an eyesore. Now it was the buzz of the whole school. Of course, most of it was trompe l'oeil. Like Leah, real on the surface, but no substance.

He wasn't sure how the teachers were going to like the round tables she'd cajoled him into giving her. She was good at that. The cajoling. It worried him. Would she be able to sway Danny the same way? First volunteering in the school, now cupcakes…what was next? She had talked his brother into marriage before John was ready. Could she convince Danny he would be happier somewhere else? With her?

Taking the sugar bowl from the cupboard, he plunked it on the table. Of course, she probably used some fake sugar he didn't have. Not that he was running a Starbucks.

She probably thought a hick from Rosewood hadn't even heard of Starbucks. His mother's gentle yet firm voice twigged his conscience, reminding him that a guest should always be treated well.

That shouldn't be a concern. Danny had been running around all afternoon on hyperspeed. He'd insisted on buying ice cream, two flavors, to go with the cupcakes. And he'd volunteered to clean his room, in case Leah wanted to see it.

Matt had never seen him so excited about a guest. And it worried him more than he wanted to admit.

"Dad, do you think I oughta go wait by the mailbox so she won't miss our house?"

"No. She'll find it."

"What time did you tell her to come?"

"Seven o'clock."

"It's almost seven o'clock now. Maybe she's lost."

"Maybe she's almost here," Matt replied patiently. "Put the napkins on the table."

Danny complied, but it only took a few moments to lay out three napkins. "I could wait on the porch."

Matt mentally counted to three. "If you want to."

Danny was off like a shot, the screen door banging behind him. The wide porch was like another room with its chairs, glider and tables. In the summer they used it as living and dining room. Shaded by tall oak trees, it was quiet and cool. When Matt was a kid, his parents used to crank homemade ice cream here, then spend long evening after the last of it had melted, holding hands even after he had dozed off. He knew because sometimes he would wake briefly to see them sitting with their fingers intertwined, their voices low.

He missed them both. His dad had been gone so long now. Matt had been only six when he died of cancer. And his mother had married John's father a year and a half year later. But Tom Johnson hadn't been the man his mother thought he was. Not bad, just weak. Too weak to give John the grounding he needed.

Matt wondered what his mother would think of the situation now. Of Leah coming back, claiming to want Danny. His mother had been a wise, strong woman. Her one weak decision might have been in choosing her second husband, but Matt knew she'd done it for the right reasons—for him, so they'd have a whole family again, so he wouldn't grow up without a father.

His mother's life had been all about sacrifice. Everything she'd done had been for her sons, her family. And she'd always made him feel that she was exactly where she wanted to be…that he and John were loved, wanted.

One of his biggest regrets was that his mother hadn't lived to know Danny. She would have devoted herself to her grandson just as she had her sons.

And she would have been able to discern the truth about Leah.

He heard the spin of gravel in the driveway, the rush of Danny's feet as he ran to meet her, then the garble of voices, Danny's chatter in a high, excited voice.

As Matt went to join them, he just couldn't get over the way his son had taken to her. Biology, nature, whatever, she was still a stranger.

Leah walked up the path, the late sun striking her long, wavy red-blond hair. Danny's hair was dark like his own, but the shape of their eyes and mouths…those were a match. And when they reached the bottom of the wide steps and looked up at him, more than the shape of their eyes matched. The color, the unusual green that hadn't belonged to anyone in his family, was there in duplicate.

Matt swallowed hard.

"Hey, Dad, it's Leah."

She held up a plastic container. "The cupcake lady."

"Come in. I just made fresh coffee."

"And we have milk," Danny told her. "Sometimes, we even get to have chocolate milk."

Leah smiled. "That sounds good. Guess what? Some of these cupcakes are chocolate."

Danny grinned. "Yay!"

"We eat in the kitchen here, nothing fancy." Matt gestured toward the big table when they reached it. Probably didn't compare with what she was used to in the city.

Leah put the container on the table. "Looks good." She ran her hand over the smooth, sturdy surface. "Is this one of your pieces?"

"One of my first. I made it for my mother…."

She looked as though she wanted to ask about her. "I like how solid it is."

His designs had evolved since those early days. They were more sophisticated, far more developed, but he wasn't ashamed of this table, or anything else in his house. He hadn't given Danny elegance. He'd given him something better, something long lasting.

Leah lifted out the cupcakes, placing them on a large square platter Matt had set out. "I added a dog and cat to the circus animals. Hope you like pets, too."

"Uh-huh." Danny climbed onto one of the chairs. "We had a dog, Roxie, but she died."

"I'm sorry. It's hard to lose someone you love. You must miss her."

"Uh-huh. But she's in heaven now."

Leah's eyes misted. "Then she's happy."

Matt suspected she was just saying what she thought they expected to hear. She had her act down good.

Danny's eyes were roving over the cupcakes. Clearly he was having a hard time trying to decide between them.

"Gentlemen, I'm leaving all the extras here, so don't strain yourselves making your first-round picks."

Her words seemed to make Danny decide, and he chose the puppy.

She'd made long floppy ears on the pup, her favorite, as well.

Matt took two mugs from the cabinet. "Coffee?"

"Please."

Danny reached into the freezer and removed the ice cream, holding up the cartons. "We have chocolate and vanilla."

She smiled. "I like both, so I'll have whatever you're having."

"You get to pick."

He looked so serious Leah suspected this was important. Chin in hand, she concentrated. "If it's okay with your dad, we could have a scoop of each."

"Yay! That's what we get to do on special days."

Relieved that she'd gotten it right, Leah smiled back. "Can I help with the scooping?"

"Okay. Sometimes it gets kind of stuck, you know."

"Absolutely." But that was okay, because it gave her an opportunity to cover his small hand with hers.

Matt glanced at the bowls. "*Small* scoops, Danny."

"Okay, Dad."

She had so much to learn about being a good parent. It *didn't* all come naturally. Left to her own devices, she'd have let him eat too much and he'd probably have ended up with a stomachache.

Subdued, Leah accepted a mug of coffee and watched Danny.

He carefully peeled the wrapper off one cupcake and took a bite. "Tastes real good."

"I'm glad."

Danny swallowed another bite. "Do you have to cook a lot?"

She tilted her head. "No. I hardly ever cook, actually."

"Is that on account of you don't have a husband?"

Leah almost choked on her coffee. "Uh, no, I don't."

Matt drew his eyebrows together in an admonishing glare, but Danny missed it.

"Or a boyfriend?"

"Danny!"

Leah swallowed the hot liquid in her mouth. "It's okay. No, Danny, I don't have a boyfriend. Why?"

His shoulders bunched upward. "I just wondered."

"I wonder about lots of things, too." She scrunched her eyebrows together. "Tell me about you."

"I got into Scouts this year. You have to be eight."

"That's great."

"Me and Dad go campin' and fishin'. And that's

gonna help get me some of my badges." He wriggled in his chair. "And we make furniture. Dad showed me how. I use real tools, not baby ones, but you gotta be careful and use safety goggles and stuff 'cause they're not toys."

"Of course not. Wow, that keeps you pretty busy."

"We play soccer. Dad's the coach. And I play Little League."

They did so much together. "Thank you for having me over tonight. I can tell you don't have much free time."

"It's okay," Danny answered candidly. "I like you."

"I like you, too."

Danny finished his cupcake and ice cream. "You wanna see my room?"

"If it's all right with your dad." She glanced at Matt.

"It's not exactly a highlight on the Rosewood tour...."

"Aw, Dad!"

Matt's designs spoke from every corner of the bedroom. Furniture of soft native pine had been built so there were no square edges. With any other designer the pieces might seem too safe to be creative. But there was creativity in each stroke. Leah recognized the inspiration. It came from carvings made by the Black Forest artisans of the eighteenth century. Matt must have painstakingly formed the thickly roped furniture out of singular pieces of wood. Leah ran her hand over the surface. It was as smooth as fine silk.

"These are my fish," Danny told her proudly, leading her over to a tank at his eye level. "And Dudley, my turtle."

"I had a turtle," she remembered. But she'd wanted a dog. A dog that would shed, her mother had explained regretfully.

"What was your turtle's name?" Danny asked.

"Shelley."

"That sounds like a girl's name."

"I think she was a girl turtle," Leah explained. It wasn't a fact she would have wanted put to the test. They all looked the same to her.

"Oh."

"This is a super room. You know, my job is decorating rooms, and I've never seen a kid's room with furniture this special before."

"Really?"

"Really."

"My dad made it."

"I thought so."

"He can make anything."

She swallowed. *Matt was his hero.* "That's great." *She wouldn't cry.* "Really great."

"Do you like my dad?"

She kept her eyes on Danny, refusing to look at Matt. "Sure."

"Good. 'Cause he's the best dad in the world."

Matt cleared his throat. "I thought you wanted to show Leah around the garden."

"Oh, yeah. Do you like flowers 'n' stuff? We plant stuff every year. I like watermelon best. But Billy—he's my best friend—he likes cantaloupe best. And Dad likes the tomatoes. He says you can smell the sunshine in 'em. We don't plant yucky vegetables like spinach." He made a face. "But Dad puts some of the stuff we grow on the grill and it tastes real good. You wanna come have supper with us and see?"

She darted a glance toward Matt. "That would be nice sometime."

"We don't have a lot of company for dinner 'cept maybe Billy or Roger," Danny continued.

Leah guessed that Matt probably wasn't thrilled with having the details of his life spilled out like the seeds in his garden had been. "Did you help plant everything?" she asked Danny as they headed outside.

"Dad showed me how." They walked beside the neat rows in the vegetable garden, then moved on to the older, mature flower gardens that twined around and beside the house.

"My grandma planted the rose bushes," Danny explained. "When they grow flowers, they'll be yellow."

"Yellow roses of Texas," she murmured.

"My mother's favorite," Matt said quietly.

Hearing the traces of pain that lingered in his voice, she turned to him. "I'm sure they're beautiful."

He reached out, cupping the tender leaves in his hand. "She gave them lots of TLC. Like she did her family. All of us." His gaze challenged her on the issue of Kyle.

But she wouldn't pursue it in front of Danny. "How long has she been gone?"

"She died about ten years ago—heart attack."

Danny looked up at her. "I didn't know my grandma. Dad says I missed a lot."

"I'm sure you did, sweetie."

"I didn't know my mother, either."

Leah caught her breath.

"But I could get a new mother. If my dad gets married."

Chapter Eight

The upcoming play by the elementary grades was the buzz of the entire Community Church and school. The production was a favorite of teachers, parents and the community. Whether the smallest actors remembered their parts was of little consequence when they looked so adorable in their costumes.

Leah offered to help Emma McAllister with the outfits. She and Annie both. It was slow at Borbey House, so the two of them had volunteered to spend the morning at Emma's costume shop.

"I appreciate your help—I can use all the extra hands I can recruit." Emma lifted a bolt of shimmery yellow fabric. "How would this look as an overlay for our littlest ears of corn?"

"Perfect," Leah murmured. The play was about the Lord's bounty. The youngest children were going to portray nature's elements while the major speaking parts would go to kids in the older grades.

Annie picked up a roll of grass-colored fringe.

"I heard it's an original play, written by one of the teachers."

"Apparently they've done Noah's Ark to death and they wanted something more meaningful than *Alice in Wonderland.* And the choices narrow when you want enough parts for everyone to participate." Emma shifted the fabric to her cutting table.

"The school's lucky to have a playwright on staff." Leah slid a bit of the material between her thumb and forefinger. "Which teacher is it?"

"Ethan Warren. Wrote it in his spare time. He's single and says he has lots of that available."

Leah glanced meaningfully at Annie, who ignored her with equal resolve. "Is he an old, graying bachelor who's done this all his life?"

Emma laughed. "Early thirties, a thick head of dark hair, not a gray straggler among them. Are you interested?"

"Hmm. I'll have to think about it. I signed up to help build sets, too. Will you be in charge of those?"

Emma shook her head. "This is all I can handle. Matt Whitaker heads that group."

Of course. She should have seen that coming.

Focusing on her work, Emma cut the material in a straight line. "And he doesn't have any gray stragglers that I've noticed, either."

Startled, Leah jerked her head up, her eyes round, her mouth open.

Emma shrugged. "In case you wondered," she added, her tone mild.

Was that an innocent remark? Leah couldn't tell.

There was a twinkle in Emma's eyes and she was certain Tina had grinned.

"I have enough chicken salad in the fridge in the back room to make a decent lunch," Tina announced. "I can run across the street and get some croissants, we have tea…"

"If you're waiting for objections, you won't get one from me," Leah told her.

"Me, either," Annie chimed in.

"You know my vote," Emma added. "The baby's asleep in her crib, which won't happen in a restaurant."

"This really is the ideal setup, isn't it?" Leah mused.

"I'm blessed." Emma moved a stack of sketches. "A few years ago I thought I was destined to live out the rest of my life alone. Now I don't take a single day for granted."

"You're wise," Leah said. "Little Ashley will grow up quickly…more quickly than you can imagine." She paused. "Let me go to the bakery and pick up the croissants."

"And I can pop home and pick up a fresh pie for dessert," Annie suggested.

Tina rubbed her hands together. "This meal is really shaping up."

A light breeze skipped leaves across the sidewalk and tossed them into the street.

Leah dug in her purse for her wallet. "Ethan

Warren sounds like just the perk you deserve for volunteering to help on this project."

"Thanks for not blurting that out in front of Emma and Tina."

"I sensed that. Annie, remember you agreed we'd take on this curse thing together."

Annie shook her head. "But Ethan Warren didn't volunteer to be a guinea pig."

"Do you hear yourself? Did you volunteer to lose your family members? Of course not. And I didn't volunteer to lose Danny when he was a baby. But we can't just stand back and accept it, Annie. We're sisters now, remember? And I don't give up on family."

"I don't know…."

"It'll only sting a little at first. You'll see."

"Sounds like an inoculation."

Smiling, Leah shrugged. "I *could* say something cheesy like you get a passport to romance with these inoculations…."

Annie groaned.

"I said I *could* say it…."

"Tell me this was the part that stings."

"Okay, right." Leah laughed. "Definitely the part that stings."

Set building brought out hammers, wood, paint and more opinions than a school play warranted. Being the new kid on the block, Leah decided she probably ought to keep hers to herself.

But when she saw *nature* being portrayed in

colors nature didn't possess, she was hard-pressed to keep silent.

Several helpful parents had donated leftover cans of paint. She wondered why so many of them owned lime, orange, pink and lemon, all in neon, but it was pointed out that they were extremely popular colors with the kids. Leah flipped open her cell phone, made an urgent call to L.A., checked the warehouse, found there was plenty of paint in the overrun materials section in more natural colors and arranged to have it shipped.

"We're not used to high-powered intervention," Matt told her, obviously having overheard the conversation.

Crestfallen, she stared at him. "Having seen your work, I'd have thought you'd want nature to look more, well...natural. Besides, it's not high-powered. These are overrun materials. Paint that sits too long gets thick, then gets thrown away. Why not use it here?"

"That's not the point. This is a production the parents, children and teachers put on."

Chastised, Leah felt once again the outsider. "I was only trying to help. Can't the neon paints be used for other projects?"

"I don't know. But you can't ship all the materials for the sets from L.A. The parents look forward to this. It's something they want to be part of, and for some of them, especially ones without a lot of money, that means donating the props. And they won't be perfect. This is *Rosewood.* Simple, uncomplicated, no frills Rosewood."

"Then *Nature's Bounty* shouldn't be neon," she retorted, keeping her voice quiet so none of the parents would overhear.

"Is this how you plan to fit in? By turning Rosewood into a mini L.A.?"

"Hardly," she muttered.

"John said you and your family had to have everything your way."

"Which gave him carte blanche to steal my child, I suppose!"

"So you admit it?"

"I admit no such thing. Just because I had a good idea—"

"Problem?" Ethan asked, coming up behind them.

Leah cringed, then turned to the writer/director of the play. "Apparently I overstepped my bounds when I sent for some paint that's not in the neon palette."

"Do we have to pay for it?"

"No."

"Good deal!" Ethan grinned. "We don't have enough money in the budget for all we need, and I wasn't sure I could talk the hardware store into donating that many gallons. Neon lime grass wasn't quite the look I imagined for the play."

Leah met Matt's cryptic gaze. "My thoughts exactly. Mr. Whitaker was concerned that the parents who donated the paints would be offended if they aren't used. I thought they could be used for other projects."

Ethan nodded. "Or we can use them for the signs to advertise the play. The kids are going to make those in art class."

"What a *great* idea!" Leah laid it on so thick, it was a wonder her voice didn't clog.

"I'm excited to have a volunteer with your enthusiasm," Ethan assured her. "Feel free to share your ideas. Even though we want to consider the parents' feelings, we can always use some new blood to stir things up."

She smiled. "I'll keep that in mind."

"Mr. Warren!" A harried teacher approached, gripping a stack of scripts.

"Duty calls. Thanks for getting the paint, Mrs.—"

"Miss. Hunter. Leah. And you're welcome." He was nice. And if he was unattached, he might be just right for Annie. She broadened her smile, but it disappeared as she turned to Matt. He looked even sterner than usual. "What now?"

"Nothing."

"You mentioned props. With this nature theme, are you going to be building a lot of them?"

"Probably."

"I haven't seen any sketches, but I can make the padded scenery."

Matt stared at her, then reluctantly opened a slim leather portfolio. "These are still kind of rough."

But his talent was obvious. The same talent that she'd seen in the extraordinary pieces of furniture he designed, even the small box that had brought her to Rosewood. But he hadn't made these too complicated. The sets were simple enough to showcase the children. "They're good."

He glanced at her. "You wouldn't change anything?"

"No. And even though you don't want to hear it, they deserve better than neon paint."

"You're worse than a dog with a bone."

"That's a flattering picture." To fill the awkward moment, she studied the designs again. "Have you thought about using real wheat for motion and dimension?"

"No."

"Maybe some potted field grass and thistle? Wouldn't cost anything. I've seen the thistle growing wild here in the ditches. And, if they wanted to, those parents you mentioned who help with props could pick some."

"Danny has a speaking part."

Scenery forgotten, she stared at him. "I thought only the older kids did."

"It's only one line actually."

"Still…" Ridiculously touched and proud, Leah grinned. "He'll be the best one in the whole play."

Matt seemed to forget their animosity for a moment. "Yeah. He will."

Annie's clogs clacked as she approached. "Leah!" Her voice rose on the second syllable, causing it to sound like an accusation. Both Leah and Matt turned to her.

Annie pointed at Leah. "I need to talk to you." Taking her arm, Annie dragged Leah away. "How could you? We've barely started working on the play, and now Ethan thinks I'm after him. This is too humiliating. I'll have to quit. And it's not as though Rosewood's big enough to lose myself in. Why couldn't you leave it alone and—"

"Hold it! I haven't done anything."

"Right. He just started talking to me for no reason."

Leah smiled gently at her new friend, noticing the pretty blouse she'd worn, the extra care she'd taken with her makeup, the earrings that brought out the dark glow of her eyes, her softly brushed hair. "He had plenty of reason. Take a look in the mirror."

Annie narrowed disbelieving eyes. "You really didn't say anything?"

"Cross my heart." Leah clapped her hands. "But I couldn't have planned it better if I *had* intervened. He seems really nice, don't you think? And he goes to your church, all information courtesy of Emma. And married women are the best source."

Annie's pretty face paled. "How do I tell him he's going to be a guinea pig?"

"Oh, Annie! Do you really think you're meant to be alone?"

Her friend's mouth opened, then closed.

"I don't think so, either. Even better, it looks as though Ethan Warren's a *very* smart man."

Chapter Nine

The following week, the set builders and the costume crew shared the auditorium. As Matt worked, he could watch the comings and goings.

Parents had warmed to Leah's suggestions for gathering thistles and other wild grasses that grew in the ditch banks and fields, free for the taking.

It was that knack of hers, he realized, for drawing people in, convincing them of her ideas. The same quality that worried him when it came to Danny. She'd already ingratiated herself with the teachers in the school. How could an eight-year-old resist such strong appeal?

Danny talked about her all the time, the *cupcake* lady. How she could draw and paint, how she was the best volunteer his class had *ever* had. How nice she was. How her treats were the kids' favorites.

Matt couldn't tell Danny that it was probably all an act. Or at best, a temporary situation. That Leah would soon get tired of baking treats and volunteering in an elementary school.

He doubted he could convince any of the parents, either. She was winning them over, as well.

Roger handed him a sheet of plywood. "You look like you've been chewing on rusty nails."

Matt grunted. "Just thinking."

"Then think about something more cheerful." He shrugged. "Picture the kids when this is done. Danny's told me his line at least a hundred times already. The kid's so hyped, you'd think he was starring in his own Disney flick." Roger glanced across the auditorium at Leah, who was waist deep in piles of fabric. "You've been awfully quiet about her. Is that because she's changed?"

"Changed?"

"Volunteering, making costumes. Danny says she brought over cupcakes."

"Danny sounds like the Rosewood grapevine. He tell you anything else?"

"Touchy, touchy. Anything else to tell?"

"No. Just that she's making sure she's part of everything, so I can't keep her away from Danny."

Roger pushed his cap back and scratched his head. "Let me see if I've got this straight. You were afraid that she was just here for a little while till she got bored. Now you're afraid she's making herself a part of everything, which means she could be around for a good while."

"I thought you were here to help, not talk."

Roger reached for a clamp. "Yeah, yeah."

Leah climbed the wide, shallow steps that curved around the stage. She smiled at Roger, then held out some soft white fabric for Matt to examine. "How do you like this for padding the clouds? It's not a pure white, so I think it looks more realistic. What do you think?"

"It's fine," he muttered.

"Try to hold down your enthusiasm."

Roger chuckled.

She grinned at him. "I'm Leah Hunter."

"Roger O'Brien. Good to meet you. And I think the fabric looks like a cloud should."

"Thanks. I know it's not Broadway, but…"

"It's for the kids and that's what counts."

"Exactly. I want it to be perfect." She held up the fabric. "I'd better get back to work."

"Sure." Roger waited until she was out of earshot. "I wouldn't mind having her stick around."

Matt grunted.

"You still have that thorn in your paw? She's nice, and in case something's wrong with your eyesight, she's also pretty. Wouldn't be a hardship for me to be around her."

"Just like that?"

Roger thumped the side of his head with his middle finger. "*If* she treats Danny right, of course. But I wouldn't be setting up the roadblocks you are."

His friend had always seen the easier side of life, Matt thought. He hadn't heard all the terrible things

Leah had said about his brother, things Matt knew couldn't be true.

Although she was worming her way into the community, it didn't mean she intended to stick around. It could be her way of making him relax his guard. Even now she could have attorneys preparing papers to back up her threats.

And he wasn't blind, either. He'd noticed how pretty she was.

But he *was* scared.

She was insinuating herself into every aspect of Danny's life that she could. Danny had just told him that she was one of the volunteers for tomorrow's field trip to the zoo in San Antonio. Danny wanted to sit beside her on the bus, and also at lunch.

Matt felt as though he was fighting to keep his son's attention. And he couldn't compete with her flashy projects. His was a steadier attention, one that didn't impress little boys.

The clouds darkened briefly in the dawn sky, but as the bus rolled toward San Antonio, the weather cleared. The kids, primed for a day in the city, sang and cheered as they drove first on the small farm-to-market roads, then reached the main highway.

Danny got his wish and sat next to Leah. Although there were plenty of chaperones for the group of eight to ten year olds, they were still far outnumbered by the kids.

Matt sat across the aisle from Danny and Leah. As she leaned forward in her seat, Leah's long, strawberry-blond hair was ruffled by the breeze. The wind didn't seem to bother her as she sang along with the kids, laughing aloud at the silly hand movements, then clapping in unison with Danny.

Usually the bus ride seemed to be the longest part of these field trips for Matt, but he was so absorbed by his son's interaction with Leah, he was startled when he realized they were already in San Antonio, pulling up in front of the zoo.

As soon as they got off the bus, the kids started calling out their favorite animals: elephants, monkeys, tigers, lions. Miss Randolph had their route already planned out, including breaks and lunch.

"I love the giraffes," Leah confided as she and Danny migrated next to him. "I hope they're on the list."

Giraffes were an unusual favorite. "Any special reason?"

"They're so gentle. And how can anyone resist their huge eyes with those incredible lashes?"

He looked into her unusual eyes as she glanced up at him. And he saw something different. Something that had nothing to do with his son. Nothing to do with their differences.

"We're starting with Amazonia," Miss Randolph told the children. "What do we know about this part of the zoo?"

The kids jumped up and down. "Those are animals that live in the Amazon!"

"Guess that leaves out the giraffes," Leah murmured. Then she smiled. "But I bet we make it to Africa."

"And the aquarium," Danny told her. "That's what I wanna see. Zillions of fish, and this zoo's 'posed to have 'em all."

One of the largest in the country, the San Antonio zoo had more than thirty-five hundred animals—seven hundred and fifty species, from white and black rhino to snow leopard to whooping cranes. The premier facility also put conservation at the top of its priorities, along with educating children.

As they left Amazonia and strolled to the African plains, they saw many of the kids' favorites: elephants, zebras and, as they neared the valley that led to the treetop lookouts, the giraffes.

"Ooh!" Leah squealed, sounding as young as Danny. A family of giraffes moved gracefully together, their long legs taller than the trunks of the nearby trees. Close up, their strength was evident in their thick limbs and muscled bodies.

Both the mother and father kept their large eyes trained on the youngster. Not typical in the animal kingdom, Matt thought. But they were an unusual species.

It was time to take a break. Even though the kids claimed they could keep going, eager to see the lions and then head on to the Australian Walkabout, they were happy with their cold drinks and burgers.

"We're gonna see the aquarium, aren't we, Leah?" Danny asked as he finished his burger.

"Sure! I got to see my giraffes, didn't I?"

"I think the bird house is after the walkabout, pal," Matt told him. "There's a lot to see here in one day."

"But Leah said we'd get to see the aquarium!"

Matt cleared his throat. "We'll try to fit everything in, but Miss Randolph has a tight schedule to keep. All the kids have special things they want to see and we have to be fair."

Danny kicked the concrete table.

"Don't we?" Matt insisted.

"I still wanna see the aquarium."

Leah looked pleadingly at Matt. "Maybe there'll be enough time."

But there were a lot of exhibits left on Miss Randolph's schedule. And the teachers wanted to get back to Rosewood before nightfall. Neither Matt nor the bus driver had liked the look of the skies that morning. As beautiful as the hill country was, its weather could be equally treacherous, especially in March.

"Danny, we have to stick to Miss Randolph's schedule, do you understand?"

Danny stared at the table, then nodded. "Yes, sir."

"So, no unplanned trips to the aquarium."

"Yes, sir."

As Danny ran to join Billy and some other friends, Leah tried to lighten the mood. "At least he's not obsessed with the snake house." She shuddered. "I'm with Danny on this one. I'd rather look at fish, too."

"If all of the kids demanded their own agenda, think of the mess we'd have."

"Well, yes, but—"

"It's not always easy to say no, but sometimes it's necessary."

Leah frowned. "And there's no room to be flexible?"

"I know the routine. This isn't my first field trip."

Her lips thinned and he saw the pleasure she'd been having dim. "But it's mine. Thanks for the reminder."

Didn't she see they had to set the boundaries? That they had to be the *parents?* At least he did. He could have explained, but what was the point? This was just a temporary gig for her.

Refreshed by the break, the kids were excited to see the Australian animals. By the time they'd visited the wetlands exhibit, they were running behind schedule and the weather was shifting. The snake house was still left to see, but Matt recommended skipping it.

As he conferred with Miss Randolph, she was at first reluctant, then agreed.

They stopped at the restrooms for the last time before heading home, then made their way back to the bus for a head count. Two short. It took Matt only a few moments to realize Danny and Leah were the ones missing.

Matt and a couple other parents agreed to search for them. The other two started with the restrooms. Matt glanced toward the aquarium. No. Danny wouldn't disobey a direct order. Instead, backtracking to the last exhibit, Matt searched the area, but they weren't anywhere in sight. Danny had said something about wanting an ice cream, but they weren't in the snack area, either.

Matt checked his watch. He'd already wasted nearly an hour. He flipped open his cell phone, wishing he had Leah's number. He hadn't thought to get it. But then the chaperones weren't supposed to wander away. He'd gotten numbers for the other searchers and called them, but they hadn't found Leah and Danny yet. They agreed to look in the snake house.

Danny had grumbled about passing by the water fowl too quickly, but they weren't there when Matt looked, nor were they in the bird house.

The aquarium.

Leah wouldn't have ignored his instructions.... Making his way over there, Matt felt a mix of disbelief, anger and relief when he spotted Danny inside, standing next to Leah as they ogled the fish. He could have appreciated the fascinating display of underwater creatures if he hadn't wanted to choke both of them.

Fighting to control his anger, Matt phoned the other chaperones and called off the search. He stalked up behind the two of them. Oblivious to his presence, they continued to stare at the display.

He latched one firm hand on Danny's shoulder.

The boy turned around, his expression suddenly guilty. "Dad."

Leah turned, too. "Matt! Did you decide to come and see the aquarium, too?"

"No. I've been searching the grounds for you and Danny."

She glanced at her watch. "Oh! I guess we've been in here longer than I realized."

"That's not the point. We came here as a group. Everyone else is waiting for you on the bus."

Danny hung his head.

Leah rushed to explain. "I thought we could come in here while everyone else was in the snake house since Danny wanted so badly to see the aquarium."

"We skipped the snake house because the weather's turning. Now we've wasted more than an hour searching for you two."

"I didn't think it would hurt anything," Leah tried to explain.

"You didn't *think*." Matt glanced down at Danny, who avoided his eyes. "And, Danny, who knows better, went along with you. Talking him into disobeying *does* hurt."

She swallowed. "Matt, I—"

"Let's get going.

The mood was tense as they made their way to the bus and headed home. The sky was now muddy gray and deep navy, streaked with bright flashes of lightning.

The bolder children saw the coming storm as an adventure. The more timid ones curled up on the bench seats of the bus, some with quivering lips, some holding hands, many wanting their mothers.

Leah's guilt was immense. While she'd been in the warm, comfortable aquarium, the storm had been gathering. And although the number of chaperones had seemed adequate during the day, now there seemed too few to comfort the scared children. What had she been thinking? She'd only wanted to please Danny. It had seemed like such a small thing at the time. But she hadn't thought through the consequences.

Danny was visibly miserable. Disappointing Matt, upsetting his friends and teacher hadn't been worth the side trip to the aquarium. As the adult, she should have known that.

The rain began before they left San Antonio, slowing the traffic down even more.

By the time they reached the highway, the rain sluiced over the bus in drenching sheets.

Even though it was a few hours before nightfall, darkness had already descended, stealing the last of the daylight. The children, dressed in T-shirts and shorts, shivered in the cooler temperatures. Fortunately, they'd all been instructed to bring outerwear.

Leah, along with the other chaperones, bundled the kids into their jackets. There were a few blankets in the first-aid kit, but not nearly enough to go around. She used her own jacket to spread over the legs of two little girls who were shivering.

If the group hadn't been delayed by her actions, they'd nearly be in Rosewood by now, instead of just leaving San Antonio. Leah gulped as she thought of what lay ahead—dusty, steep-shouldered washes that could fill with water and overflow.

This was so much worse than giving a child a

stomachache. Had missing all the years since Danny's birth blunted her intuition about children? Stolen her instincts?

She wondered how the driver could even see through the thick rain and murky gloom. There were no streetlights on the highway as they left the city, and the situation was even worse when they turned off onto the smaller roads.

Matt stayed in the front of the bus, helping the driver by watching road markings and signs.

Leah, who was circulating among the children, slipped in place beside Danny. He still looked miserable.

"Are you scared?" she asked.

He shook his head.

"Danny, I want to apologize. Your dad was right. I wasn't thinking when I suggested going to the aquarium. I honestly didn't think I was causing you to disobey your…dad, but in retrospect… I mean, now that I've thought about it, that's exactly what I did. Which was wrong. And I'm sorry. I would never purposely want you to disobey him or cause you to break your promise."

Danny thought about her words for a minute. "It's okay. I shoulda said no."

Oh, he was a good kid. "You're letting me off easy. I *am* the grown-up. I should have known better."

"My dad taught me to do the right thing." Danny shrugged. "So I shoulda known, too."

She wanted to hug him to pieces. She settled for ruffling his hair. "You warm enough?"

"Yeah. I'm not a *girl*."

She bit back her smile. "What was I thinking?"

Feeling somewhat relieved, Leah settled back in the seat and stared out the rain-streaked windows. There was nothing to see but darkness, though. Not much traffic was on the road, just the occasional flash of headlights. Matt and the driver had the radio turned on the weather station, but they kept the volume low. Leah wondered if there were any flood warnings in place. The other chaperones occasionally walked up to the front of the bus, spoke with Matt and returned to their seats, looking tense and worried.

Leah didn't want to worry Danny, and she guessed he would be too curious to be put off with a vague answer, so she didn't go check the radio.

As they bumped along, Leah thought about her next apology, guessing it wouldn't be as easy, or as easily accepted.

The unexpected light from flashing strobes atop emergency vehicles split the night. Everyone on the bus leaned toward the windows, peering outside. The bus slowed, then stopped. The driver opened the door. Immediately, the fierce rain pelted inside as a highway patrolman entered, his rain gear dripping puddles on the steps.

"Bridge ahead is near washout," he told them. "Road's closed."

"How long?" the driver asked.

"Don't know. At least till morning. Flood warning's in place until six a.m. Best to get turned around. I'm not sure how stable this road is. It could wash out, too."

"Thanks, officer."

"Be careful, folks. There's enough room to get the bus turned around—just barely, without getting it stuck. I'll watch for you out here, signal with my flashlight if you get too close to the drop-off."

"Thanks."

A flash of lightning lit the bus and Leah caught Matt glancing back at her. She could read the blame in it all the way from where she sat.

It was tight turning around on the two-lane road. And as the driver retraced their route, there was nowhere close and dry to wait out the storm.

Miss Randolph motioned from the front of the bus for all the chaperones to come speak to her. "We're going to have to try to contact the parents. I don't know what kind of signals we'll get out here—we may be out of range, and what with the storm…but we need to try. If you get through to *anyone,* have them contact Principal Gunderland. She'll have a list of the kids who are on the bus and she can start a phoning relay."

"What do we tell them?" Leah asked. "About where we're going to stay tonight?"

"That's a tough one. We don't know yet. Just that we'll find someplace dry and safe. Emphasize that the kids are all right."

Leah looked at the circle of worried faces. "I'm sorry that I delayed our return. If Danny and I had been back on the bus—"

Miss Randolph clasped her hand. "Don't give that another thought. The storm would have happened regardless."

Leah avoided looking at Matt.

"Now," the teacher continued, "we have to call on our strengths. Let's pray." She bowed her head. "Lord, please be with us, guard us and watch over us, help us to be strong for these precious children in our care, keep us always mindful that we are in Your sight and in Your hands. Amen."

Feeling calmer, Leah walked back and took her seat beside Danny.

"What's going on?"

"We're going back the way we came until we find a place to spend the night."

"Like a motel?"

"I guess so." Leah couldn't remember passing one in quite some time. The logistics of bedding down this many children was boggling. They'd need a dormitory to do it properly.

But first she needed to follow Miss Randolph's instructions and try her cell phone. The one number she called frequently in Rosewood was Annie. She turned on her cell but there wasn't any signal. Not surprising. They were in the middle of nowhere surrounded by a lashing storm that sounded like it was peeling the paint off the bus.

The rain pelted down even harder as they drove into the darkness. There was a lonely feel to driving in the night away from home, toward the unknown.

It seemed they drove along the deserted road for

miles and miles. Locals, listening to weather reports and their own good sense, were probably secure in their homes.

At last the bus approached a bypass just off the main highway. The driver turned in at the only building they'd seen, a large truck stop. The covered parking lot was filled with eighteen-wheelers whose drivers had hunkered down to ride out the storm.

Miss Randolph consulted with Matt and the bus driver, then motioned to her volunteers. "Looks like we can park here for the night," she said when they gathered around her.

So much for my notion of a motel, Leah thought.

"Mr. Whitaker's going to check on hot meals."

"I'd like to pay for those," Leah offered. She met Matt's gaze. "On my credit card—it'll be the easiest way."

"That's very generous," Miss Randolph said. "We'll sort it out when we get back and repay you from school funds. I'm going inside with Mr. Whitaker to check on the phone."

The kids watched out the windows, silent, until Matt and their teacher reappeared.

"Looks like they can handle us," Matt said. "Plenty of empty booths and tables."

After phoning the principal, Miss Randolph and the chaperones lined the kids up and took them inside. The storm didn't seem as scary once they'd had a warm meal, milk and hot peach cobbler.

As the children finished eating, Leah searched

the aisles of the shop in the truck stop, collecting all the souvenir T-shirts the store had in children's and adult sizes, along with jackets and ballcaps. She found some soft stadium seats emblazoned with "San Antonio Spurs" that could be used for pillows.

Returning to the group, she told Miss Randolph about her purchase. Delighted, the teacher asked a few other chaperones to help her carry the bounty to the bus. "Don't forget to save the receipt so we can reimburse you, Leah. We can pass out the T-shirts and jackets and see how far they'll stretch. Already an answer to prayer."

Leah and another mother cut off tags, then sorted the clothing. The other parents watched the kids as they stretched their legs in the store and used the restrooms.

By the time they were ready to board the bus, word of their situation had gotten around to the truckers. As the children climbed back onto the bus and received a T-shirt or jacket, drivers of the big rigs started bringing them blankets. Most said they were extras, all insisted on donating them for the kids.

Between the T-shirts, jackets and blankets, all the kids were warmly covered as they settled in for the night.

Danny still insisted that Leah sit beside him. Matt didn't want to make a scene, but he was deeply disappointed in his son's behavior. It wasn't like Danny to bend under a bad influence. But Leah was an adult, which was a completely new experience. The adults in his life, up until now, had provided good role models.

Since he and the bus driver were the only men on the trip, Matt kept watch so the others could sleep. They should be safe, parked in the truck stop, but the bus had no locks on its doors.

Tired after the long day, the children quickly succumbed to sleep, many of them slumped against one another. Even Miss Randolph and the chaperones gave in to their exhaustion.

As the soft sounds of slumber filled the bus, Matt moved down the center aisle to check on Danny. He had fallen asleep, stretched out on Leah's lap. To his surprise, she was still awake.

"I thought everyone was asleep."

She shook her head. "I keep thinking about what I did today, how wrong it was…in so many ways." She bit her lip. "I've apologized to Danny. But there hasn't been an opportunity to apologize to you. I'm so sorry. You were right. I *didn't* think. I not only did something wrong, I caused Danny to do something wrong, something he knew was wrong."

"You don't have to—"

"It didn't seem such a big thing at the time. I just thought if everyone else was going to the snake house, it wouldn't hurt if we went to the aquarium. The truth is, I wanted to give him something he wanted. I hated to see him disappointed. And look what happened. I caused Danny to break his word to you. I stranded an entire busload of children. No credit card is going to fix this, is it? All the parents are going to be worried sick until they see their children tomorrow. I've disrupted all those families." She leaned her head back against the seat, and he could see the trembling in her throat. Her eyelids flickered rapidly as she clamped down hard on her lip and he realized she was trying not to cry.

"What you did was wrong. There's no two ways about it."

She nodded.

"But if you're smart, you'll learn from today."

Leah glanced down at Danny. "There's one thing you'll never have to doubt—how much I love him, how I would never hurt him. No matter how many years or miles separated us, he has always been in my heart. Like you, I would die for him." She stroked the hair on Danny's forehead, her touch gentle. "Children are so vulnerable. I used to think about all the things I would do with him when I found him…ironically, the zoo was on my list. But I didn't dwell on the challenge of teaching him the lessons of life, the important things. The things you've been teaching him. He feels terrible, you know, about disappointing you. Which means you've done all that part right."

Matt was silent. He couldn't imagine the last eight years of his life without his son, especially after having held Danny in his arms the first time. To have had him taken away…

But then he pictured his younger brother. For all his reckless impatience, there wasn't that kind of evil or anger in him. John wouldn't have stolen his own child from its mother. He just wouldn't. And the way she'd acted today…reckless, immature. It was all she'd accused John of being. How could he begin to know what to believe?

Chapter Ten

By morning the storm had passed and the road had held. Water had poured past the banks of the gullies and over the bridge during the night. But now, by midmorning, it was draining down the washes, a benign reminder of what could have been killer flash floods.

After a hearty breakfast, the chaperones assisted the children back onto the bus for the return journey to Rosewood. As soon as the bus pulled up in front of the school, Leah could hear the cheers go up from the group of anxious parents gathered there.

The kids cheered back, pounding their tennis shoes against the floor of the bus, and the minute the driver opened the door, they all piled out in a rush.

Miss Randolph made a token effort at order, but it was hopeless.

Leah smiled as she watched the children and parents hug one another. There was an awful lot of happiness in Rosewood that morning. Matt stood with his hands on Danny's shoulders.

Leah tried not to feel as though she was the only singleton on the ark. Parents shook her hand and thanked her, as they did the other chaperones. Leah couldn't help thinking they wouldn't be so grateful if they knew she was the one who'd caused them to be stranded overnight.

Miss Randolph kindly thanked her for volunteering, as though she'd done nothing wrong. Suddenly exhausted and feeling terribly lonely, Leah walked away from the noisy crowd, unwilling to stand there until she was left completely alone.

"Dad?"

"Yes, son?"

"I'm sorry. About goin' to the aquarium."

"I know."

"Leah said it was her fault, but I knew better."

Matt digested this information. "Yes, you did."

Danny kicked at the loose gravel by the curb. "I wanted to see that aquarium awful bad."

"Was it worth all the trouble you caused and the way you've felt since?"

"No." They walked almost the length of the block before Danny spoke again. "Dad?"

"Yes?"

"How come Leah didn't know that? She's a grown-up."

Matt battled with his conscience. What he said would influence how Danny felt about his mother. But she was no role model. "Grown-ups make mistakes, too."

"That's what she said. She said it was wrong for her to make me make 'em, too."

Matt sighed. In some ways, it seemed as though Leah was beating herself up enough about the incident.

"Do you still like her, Dad?"

Oh, the brutal honesty of children. "Do you?"

"Yeah. Jesus doesn't stop lovin' us when we do somethin' wrong."

No, He doesn't.

"Right, Dad?"

Matt pulled Danny into a hug. "Very right."

Annie brought in a tray with a teapot and cups. "This is a local chamomile blend. Guaranteed to put some color back in your face."

"I'm fine," Leah insisted, glad to be back at the bed-and-breakfast with her *sister,* but still feeling the exhaustion of the entire ordeal.

"Hmm." Annie poured the tea and handed her a cup. "That's why you're so pale, you look like you've been dusted in flour."

Leah grimaced. "A baker's joke?"

"Drink your tea."

She smiled half-heartedly. "You're a bossy land-lady."

"I feel responsible, suggesting you make a good impression on the town."

"Don't." Leah took a sip of the soothing tea.

Annie offered a plate of small, plain cookies.

"They're kind of like gingersnaps. They'll settle your stomach."

"My stomach's fine," Leah insisted, but she gratefully took a cookie.

Annie poured a cup of tea for herself and took a gingersnap. "I'm not sure mine is."

"I really let Danny down. I always thought that given a chance I'd be a great mother, and instead..."

"Give yourself a break. For eight years you've wanted to do things for Danny. No wonder the dam burst. I think you should get an award for your restraint up until now."

"Not if Matt Whitaker's on the awards committee."

"Even he's got to see that you didn't plan what happened. Besides, the important thing to remember is everything worked out okay. The children are all fine, including Danny. And, as you work on the school play together, he'll get to know you, see what kind of person you are."

Leah groaned. She'd forgotten about the play. And facing Matt.

Ethan Warren had a way with the kids. They listened to his direction. The older ones came to rehearsal early and stayed late. The younger ones gained a sense of confidence on the stage, little ears of corn mingling with farmers and fishermen.

Danny was excited by every rehearsal, reciting his single line to anyone who would listen.

Matt grinned, watching him. He glanced toward

the volunteers rushing around backstage. Leah was fitting costumes amid the madness, but she looked unperturbed.

The sets were nearly finished. Roger had helped him with all the large pieces. Except for some touch-ups, the only pieces left to be mounted were the clouds. He'd expected Leah to be right in the middle of set construction, but she'd distanced herself. In the week since the field trip she'd been making costumes. And quietly encouraging Danny. But she'd avoided him.

So, had she folded under the first bit of pressure as a parent? And did that mean she was about to run again? If so, he needed to know, before Danny became too attached. Picking up one of the cloud cutouts, he crossed the space between them.

Leah kept her attention on the pair of overalls she was adjusting. "Hi."

"Are you going to have time to work on these clouds," he asked, "or should I plan on padding them?"

"Oh." Her expression skipped from looking trapped to guilty. "I'll do them. I have all the materials."

"Ethan wants everything in place for the dress rehearsal. If you're behind, I can take care of them."

She stuck a pin in the pin cushion. "I said I'll do them."

"Costumes coming along okay?"

"Yes. I'm just helping. Emma's in charge of them. Her store looks like Santa's workshop."

He leaned against the doorjamb. "You say that as though it's a given Santa's workshop exists."

She sighed.

"And that you've seen it."

She glanced up, a smile reluctantly edging the corners of her mouth. "Yeah. It's one of my regular stops every Christmas."

"You really *do* have connections then."

That made her laugh. "I try not to brag."

"I won't spread it around." He shifted the wood cutouts in his hands. "You really plan on sticking around until the play opens?"

Her smile dissolved. "What's that supposed to mean?"

"If you're planning to take off, I'd like to know. It'll give me time to come up with a plausible story for Danny."

She stiffened. "Your family's real good at making up stories, but it won't be necessary. This time you're not dealing with a teenager. And trust me, there's not a place on the planet you can hide Danny. Not this time."

By the evening of the play, not only the children were brimming with excitement. The community gave its usual support, filling the auditorium, along with parents and families of the junior thespians.

Principal Gunderland welcomed everyone to the *worldwide* debut of Ethan Warren's original play, *Nature's Bounty.*

Everyone oohed and aahed as the youngest members of the cast, dressed in Emma's imaginative costumes as seeds, grain, ears of corns, leaves, birds and butterflies, filled the stage. Then the older actors, portraying farmers, dairy processors and ranchers, joined them.

Leah held her breath as the play progressed and the time came for Danny's part. He was one of the leaves. Their costumes were green in the front, with yellow sides and reddish orange backs.

Matt was situated off to one side of the stage. Shortly after Danny's line he would have to change the scenery. But instinctively, despite the anger she was still nursing toward him, Leah knew he must be on pins and needles, too.

Then it was time for Danny's line. Confident and sure, he spoke in a clear, high voice. "When I change color, it's time for fall!"

In unison, all the green leaves turned around, revealing their reddish orange backs. The audience, delighted, broke into applause.

Smiling widely, Leah looked across the stage, meeting Matt's gaze. For that single instant they shared the parental bond of sheer pride. Of joy in their child's accomplishment.

Then it was time for Matt to shift the backdrop. Leah's heart beat faster. In pride, she told herself. Just pride.

After the play was over, Leah was still smiling. It was another milestone for her. So many memories in such a short time; she felt she was making a scrap-book in her heart.

Milling around the auditorium with other parents, she started toward the exit, when Danny ran up to her, tugging her hand.

"Leah, wait!"

"Hey, there," she greeted him. "Great job, Danny! You were the best leaf in the play!"

"Thanks! You wanna come get ice cream with us?"

Matt was a few feet behind Danny and she glanced at him to see if he was in agreement.

He looked uncomfortable.

But Danny wasn't to be stopped. "We're going to the drugstore on Main Street. They make the best ice cream in the world!"

"This side of the Mississippi," Matt corrected.

"And the fountain is made of marbles."

"Really?"

"It's one of the oldest marble ice-cream fountains left in the country," Matt muttered.

"How can I resist? Especially with such a hand-some young man for an escort?"

Danny giggled.

"I haven't had a banana split in…well, so long I can't remember when," Leah mused. "So, does this ice-cream *fountain* have banana splits?"

"Sure. Haven't you been to an ice-cream fountain before?"

Matt smothered an unexpected laugh with a cough.

"Yes, but not the best one this side of the Mississippi. You'll have to show me what's what."

"They have booths, but we sit at the counter," Danny told her.

She nodded, realizing this was important information.

"That way you get to see 'em make everything. And sometimes they give you extra cherries, especially if Clyde's working."

Obviously, *very* important information.

"But you're not supposed to ask for them," he continued.

"I see."

"It's not polite." He was so serious she wanted to smile, but she didn't.

"I understand."

"Did you drive?" Matt asked.

She shook her head. "No. I rode over with Emma, but I told her I'd walk home."

"Then you can come with us," Danny invited. "We got lots of room."

Lots was relative, Leah realized, as she sat next to Matt in the pickup truck. Danny, using the manners Matt had taught him, insisted that she get in first.

She'd known Matt was tall, but sitting beside him, her shoulder wedged against him, she realized that hers only came to the middle of his arm.

As he shifted the gears, she could see the easy play of his muscles. He was a man who worked with his hands, and she'd been aware that he was strong and fit. But somehow it hadn't hit her with the punch that it did now.

Swallowing, she tried to sit still and straight, not to take more than her allotted space, or sway when the truck turned. She didn't need this complication. This unwanted, unwarranted attraction to her son's father. A man who was more irritating than a scratchy wool sweater in the dead of summer.

Still, she was almost painfully aware of him as they drove to the drugstore. While nothing was far in Rosewood, the blocks seemed like miles.

Other families had had the same idea and the drugstore was crowded. The booths filled fast but there were three empty stools at the counter. The old-fashioned soda fountain was wide and deep, a thick slab of marble covering the counter. Tall, long handled levers dispensed soda, and deep refrigerated wells held the ice cream. An incredible assortment of sauces, sprinkles, candies, nuts and sliced fruit was lined up along the back of the counter, with an array of specially shaped dishes and glasses.

"I get to order whatever I want," Danny told her.

"That's because you're a star."

He laughed. "Uh-uh."

"Ask your dad."

"You were great, pal."

Danny grinned. "Billy said I'd forget what to say."

"But you didn't," Leah and Matt replied in unison. Surprised that they had, their voices trailed off.

"Jinx," Danny announced. Then he lowered his voice to a whisper. "I hope I get extra cherries."

Leah couldn't contain her grin. "Me, too."

They watched with fascination as the young man making the sodas for other customers "jerked" the levers with precise movements so the glasses were filled just to the top and didn't overflow. Danny told Leah he wanted to be a soda jerk, too, when he was older. Leah guessed that Rosewood might be one of the few places left in the country with the kind of soda fountain that would need one.

The banana split was loaded with everything wonderful, but it wasn't the foot-long, foot-high variety that novelty ice-cream stores in the cities had begun serving. Leah wasn't certain who those appealed to—possibly small nations or large families, but certainly not single women. But this, this was a real banana split. Warm, homemade hot fudge bathed the smooth ice cream and melted it just enough to drown the bananas. Yum.

Matt dipped into his own ice cream. "From the look on your face, I'd say you like it."

"I can't believe I've been staying only a block away from this place and haven't tried the ice cream."

"I'd eat ice cream here every day if I lived on Main Street," Danny said between bites.

Their server had placed four extra cherries on Danny's double caramel and hot fudge sundae. "I can see why. They obviously like you here."

"They know I like cherries," Danny confided.

She looked at him with such longing she felt her

heart expanding even more. Oh, this child of hers. Yes, hers. How could anyone not want to spoil him?

"We've been coming here since Danny was a toddler," Matt explained. "They know him pretty well."

"One of the advantages of a small town," she acknowledged.

"Yes."

"Big cities have stuff we don't." Danny plucked one of the cherries from his sundae.

"I come from a big city, you know. Los Angeles."

"Do you like it?"

"Yes."

"Do you like it better'n Rosewood?"

She hesitated. "Not better, just different."

"How's it different?" He scooped up a spoonful of ice cream drenched in hot fudge.

She thought for a moment. "Like you said, big cities have things small towns don't, like museums."

"We have a museum. It's gotta two-headed calf and a civil war uniform in it."

Matt met her gaze. His seemed to say *top that.*

"There are different kinds of museums. We have the Getty with all kinds of wonderful paintings and sculptures."

"Oh."

"And the Huntington. It has real Japanese gardens."

"Uh-huh." He swallowed his ice cream.

Sensing she was drowning fast, she grasped for a lifeline. "And museums of natural science with dinosaurs."

"Dinosaurs are cool," Danny replied. "The museum in Houston has this really huge dinosaur that goes all the way to the roof."

And Houston was in reasonable driving distance from Rosewood.

Was that a smirk she saw on Matt's face? She wanted to tell him not to gloat yet. She'd barely begun on the advantages L.A. could offer. But tonight wasn't the time to list them. Not when they were having such a good time in one of Danny's favorite places in Rosewood.

However, she would begin. Because Rosewood didn't have the one crucial thing Danny did need. A mother.

Chapter Eleven

Warm currents of air carried the scent of freshly cut wood from Matt's shop. Sawdust littered the floor, the shavings curling beneath their feet.

"Hey, Dad."

"Son."

"I been thinkin'."

"Anything special?"

"Kinda."

Matt put down the sander and waited.

"You know how Billy's gonna have a new brother or sister?"

Matt nodded.

"Well, I was thinkin'. Maybe we could make it a cradle. People give the new baby presents, don't they?"

Matt knew how hard it was for Danny to accept that Billy would have a new sibling when there wasn't one on the horizon for him. "Yes, son, they do. And I think a cradle would be a fine present. We could start on it this afternoon, if you'd like."

"Yeah. That'd be good."

They picked out the wood, settling on a native pine. And for a while they worked on the cradle's design in relative quiet.

But Matt couldn't contain his pleasure at Danny's gesture. "It's tough, Billy getting a new brother or sister when you're not, and I'm proud of you for being a good friend."

"It's okay. Besides, I'm prayin'."

"We've discussed this. First I have to meet someone and get married—"

"I know, Dad, that's what I'm prayin' for. That you'll have somebody to love. So we can have a brother or sister like Billy."

Matt swallowed. He couldn't honestly tell Danny his prayer was wrong.

"You should have somebody else to love besides me 'cause I'll grow up," Danny continued earnestly. "And the other grown-ups all have somebody."

Matt's heart caught.

"Like the other kids have mothers," Danny continued.

There it was. The bittersweet truth he couldn't pretend didn't exist.

"Do you miss having a mother?"

Danny shrugged. Then he kicked his tennis shoe against the toeboard beneath the main workbench. "Billy's mom's nice. And she smells good."

Of course he missed having a mother. Matt remembered how important his own mother had been to him, how she'd nursed him through his illnesses and childhood wounds, both physical and emotional. His father had been a strong and wonderful presence in his life but his mother had provided the tenderness. He'd thought he could do it all…but obviously he couldn't.

He thought of his daily prayers, asking the Lord to let him keep Danny. Swallowing, he realized he should have been asking Him to do what was best for his son. Even if that meant letting him go.

Annie had polished the parlor furniture until the old rosewood pieces shone as brightly as the waxed floors. The scent of lemon oil and beeswax pervaded the entire bed-and-breakfast, blending with the aromas of today's pies—blackberry and apple crumb.

She'd been up since dawn, cleaning the life out of the already immaculate house. Now she was carefully removing each crystal teardrop from the elaborate chandelier in the dining room, wiping them individually.

"I didn't know we were having the president for dinner," Leah mused, watching her friend.

Annie flushed. "The school's artistic committee is holding their meeting here tonight."

"Oh. Ooh…! Isn't that Ethan Warren's committee?"

"Yes, I believe it is." Annie tried to look nonchalant. She failed miserably.

"Why didn't you tell me? What do you want me to do? Not that the house doesn't already look spotless. But I can clean. And cook. You need to primp for tonight, not work on the house." Leah reached for one of Annie's hands. "You've ruined your manicure doing all this cleaning. First, we have to do your nails. Can we get you in somewhere today? And is the place in town good? If not, I can do a decent manicure. And your hair, hmm…"

Annie's hands flew to her hair. "What's wrong with my hair?"

"Nothing. Just, how do you plan to wear it tonight?"

"I haven't given it any thought."

Leah took the dust cloth out of Annie's hands. "Okay. You're through. *I'm* in charge of cleaning from this minute on. *You're* in charge of looking gorgeous. I bet you haven't even decided what to wear."

"I'm not sure…."

"Have you thought about something new?"

Annie shook her head.

"Think about it. Also, you can borrow anything of mine you want. You like that melon outfit. And it would look great with your coloring."

"I wouldn't feel right—"

"Hey, we're sisters, remember? From what I've heard, that's what sisters do. Now, scoot. Start the beauty regime while I finish here."

Annie looked both terrified and thrilled. "You're sure?"

"Absolutely."

Annie hugged her, then ran up the stairs.

Leah picked up one of the crystal teardrops, then

glanced at the chandelier, trying to figure out just how it was supposed to be attached. "Oh, you and I are *not* going to be friends," she muttered.

By that night, Annie had primped until there was nothing left to primp. Her hands, given over to the care of Rosewood's capable manicurist, were soft and her nails elegant. After she'd darted into her favorite clothes shop and found nothing she liked, she'd agreed to borrow Leah's melon dress, which not only set off her dark hair and eyes, but also brought a certain degree of sophistication that updated her look.

Leah refused to let Annie in the kitchen, and finished the appetizers and pasta salads that her friend had already started. She'd also taken care of any last-minute tidying, and managed to wheedle the reason the committee meeting was being held at Borbey House out of Annie.

"I volunteered," she confessed. "Ethan was saying something about how there never seemed to be enough meeting rooms at the school for all the committees, so I said, why not use the B and B. We usually have an empty spot."

"Good for you!"

"It's a small committee, and apparently there was room on it for at least another person. And it doesn't have to be a teacher...."

"You!" Leah was so pleased for her friend.

Annie bit down on her lower lip. "You really

think so? All I've done is volunteer to help for the one play."

Leah smiled knowingly. "Annie, do you think Ethan would have agreed to hold the meeting here tonight if he weren't interested in you?"

"I'm nervous and scared and excited and, and…"

"Those are good things, you know."

"But what if he really did just want a quiet meeting room?"

"Doesn't the public library have those?"

Annie's big doelike eyes considered this. "I suppose. But they don't allow food in their meeting rooms."

Delighted by her friend's total lack of artifice, Leah laughed. "That's it. He's smitten by your food."

Annie laughed, too. "Well, this is hardly a date. Remember the committee?"

"Sometimes the path to love has company. I'll serve though, so you can hostess."

"This seems all backward," Annie worried. "You're a paying guest and here you're doing all this work—"

"We're sisters, Annie. That's what sisters do, right?"

Annie nodded, her smile suddenly wobbly.

"Don't you dare," Leah warned, struck by what a good friend Annie had become. "You'll ruin your makeup."

The bell over the front door jingled.

"That must be them. Go, go!" Leah urged, feeling more like a mother hen than a friend or sister.

Annie was back in the kitchen within a short time. "Leah, Matt's here."

"Um." Leah looked at the egg salad she still had to assemble. "Ask him to come in here, I guess."

"I can take over."

"Oh, no, you can't."

She had her hands in the mixing bowl when Matt appeared. He seemed startled to see her covered by a baker's apron. "Come on in. I can't really stop what I'm doing."

"Will you be done soon?"

"With this? Yes. Then I'll stuff it in the minicroissants. Why?"

"I need to talk to you."

She paused, hearing the serious note in his voice. "Is something wrong? Is Danny okay?"

"Danny's fine."

Her heartbeat settled back down.

"But I do need to talk to you."

She glanced pointedly at the food on the counters. "Actually we've got something special going on tonight. Ethan Warren's coming here and I'm pretty committed to—"

"Can we talk afterward?"

"Well…okay. And you're sure Danny's all right?"

"Yes. He's fine."

Matt left as abruptly as he'd arrived, but Leah didn't have time to worry about him. The bell jangled again, signaling the arrival of Ethan and the rest of the committee. Annie's nerves went into overdrive.

But Leah was used to entertaining. It had been

such a part of her life since she was a toddler, and she tried to let her calm confidence rub off on Annie. After a while, when it was clear that the roof wasn't going to fall in, Annie began to relax.

It was immediately evident to Leah that Ethan Warren hadn't come knocking on Borbey House's door solely for a convenient meeting place. He watched Annie's smile and delighted in her laughter. And by the end of the evening, she was voted to fill the vacant spot on his committee. Since Annie wasn't a particularly artistic person, that said it all. Leah had done so much talking, she'd gotten herself on the committee, too.

Ethan was the last member to leave the B and B, lingering until the table was cleared and until Leah discreetly withdrew to the kitchen.

It seemed he'd barely had time to drive away when the bell over the door jangled again.

"I don't recall being this busy since the train derailed and I had people sleeping in the halls," Annie declared.

Matt entered the front door.

Spotting him, Leah thumped her forehead. "I completely forgot. I'm so sorry. But we really just finished the meeting."

"That's okay. Do you have some time now?"

"Sure." She glanced around. "Do you want to sit outside?" Although the B and B fronted Main Street, the wraparound porch led into the backyard, a surprisingly private place. A glider provided a quiet retreat for a talk.

Once they were seated, Leah took a few deep breaths, falling into the calmer rhythm of the night. "I've been running all day. It's good to be still."

"Yes."

When Matt fell silent again, Leah realized he must have something serious to tell her. There was no point putting it off. She needed to know. "You might as well spill it."

"I never filed any legal papers for Danny."

His admission stunned her.

"I never thought I had any need to. I was sure you weren't ever going to come around. I was John's next of kin, his only family."

"So..." she ventured unsurely. "Is this your notice that you're planning to now?"

He sighed, a deep sound from a big man. "No. I've been thinking about what you said...that Los Angeles has a lot to offer that Rosewood doesn't. I know it's more than just museums with dinosaurs. It's a whole life that I can't begin to offer him."

"Are...are you—" she stuttered, unable to form the words.

"Danny wants a mother. You're his mother."

"But...what made you change your mind?"

"I've been thinking about what a strong woman my mother was. She would have given up any and everything for us. And I've been thinking about what you said—that you'd give your life for Danny. Only his mother would do that."

The sudden knot in her throat made it difficult

to swallow. "But you said it would be cruel to take Danny away from everything he loves."

Matt bent his head, his voice raw. "I've prayed for an answer, Leah. Don't make me regret telling you the truth."

"And you got this…this answer?"

There was such pain in his eyes, it tore at her to witness it. "Yes."

"You have that much faith?"

"It's how I've always lived my life…how I've raised Danny. It's what I have to put my trust in now."

Chapter Twelve

Songbirds chirped outside her bedroom window, but they didn't waken Leah. She'd been fighting her sheets and light coverlet all night. Giving up the battle for sleep with the birdsong, she padded to the closet and pulled out a T-shirt and cotton pants. She dressed quickly, slipping into her tennis shoes in case her wandering took her farther than she planned.

Freshly baked cinnamon rolls and yeasty bread sent out signals from the bakery that she wasn't the only early riser. But most of the other businesses she passed were closed, and thankfully, no traffic disturbed the silence of the sleepy lanes and shaded neighborhoods.

Leaving Main Street, Leah walked briskly for several blocks until she left the business district behind.

She hoped the morning air would clear her head, bring some sense to her muddled thoughts. Instead she felt the weight of Matt's words as solidly as she had through the night.

Danny wants a mother. You're his mother.

Matt Whitaker hadn't struck her as someone who would have given up easily. But he was a man of truth. And one of faith. And he was laying out both for her to see.

She could take Danny and run to L.A. as fast as she could. Legally, she had the right. Morally... morally she should feel vindicated. Instead, just the thought left a bad taste in her mouth. She'd feel like a thief in the night. This was what she'd come for, what she'd hoped would happen after more time had passed, after she'd convinced Matt what a wonderful mother she was.

What a joke. With her instincts, it was a wonder she didn't need a keeper of her own. Clearly she needed a strong parenting partner like...well, Matt. Someone who instinctively knew the right path for Danny, who made good decisions, and who could help shape and guide him.

Yet Matt had prayed, and based on the answer he felt he'd received, he was willing to trust her with the child he loved with all his heart. Humbled, she wondered what it must be like to have such faith. For all that she had prayed for Danny's return, she'd never had Matt's sure, unwavering belief.

Slowing her pace, measuring her breath, Leah passed beneath century-old magnolias, equally ancient hickory trees, thinking about the solidity of this town. Annie had told her about its history. The settlement was established in the mid 1800s, and neighbor had helped neighbor ever since. Being off the beaten track had not led to the town's demise but had strengthened its sense of community. In a shifting world where she, like most people she knew, found little to depend on, the people of Rosewood had come to depend on each other.

Leah had already met many members of the Community Church and felt their welcome, their kindness. It spilled over into the school, into social events. And into everything Danny had ever known.

Not that L.A. didn't offer things that Rosewood couldn't. Grandparents for a start. But an entire community of support? A community that embraced the values that had shaped Danny into the loving child he was?

It was truth time now. She was alone with just the sky and the sleeping town.

No. A life in L.A. wasn't the same as growing up in this community. Her own upbringing was evidence.

So. What was the answer? She looked heavenward. She hadn't prayed so much as pleaded with God all those years Danny had been missing. Perhaps she had to learn now how to listen.

The waiting was interminable. A week had passed and Matt hated going to the mailbox, expecting to withdraw an envelope from some fancy L.A. law firm. He hadn't told Leah to pursue the legal options open to them, but he'd given her the go-ahead.

With each phone call, each ring of the doorbell, his blood stilled, then his heart raced. And he questioned his sanity, his good sense, everything but the Lord.

Because the answer had come clear in the still and quiet. He'd given the problem over to Him and He'd answered. And although Matt felt anguished, his heart broken, he couldn't disobey.

Leah must have changed, Matt realized. While he still didn't believe that John had done anything evil, Leah must have changed. The Lord alone would know what was in her heart.

But how to tell Danny?

Of course, he would be excited to have a mother since he wanted one so badly. Matt flipped the calendar pages on the refrigerator. He would complete the cradle they'd started for Billy's new baby brother or sister. Maybe he and Danny could work on it that afternoon. It was Saturday and they didn't have anything planned.

The doorbell rang.

And his bad feeling returned.

He opened the door. Leah stood there, looking expectant. "Hello."

"Morning," she greeted him.

He took a deep breath. He hadn't really thought out the details, but then maybe that was why she was here, to iron them out. "Come in."

"Actually, I was wondering if you could come out. You and Danny that is. Just as far as my car."

"Danny's in his room. Just a minute." He went

back inside, calling up the stairs. "Danny! Come on down. Leah's here."

It didn't take long for Danny's running footsteps to sound on the wooden stairs.

"Hey!" Danny greeted her.

"Hey yourself! I've got a surprise."

Matt's stomach had sunk so far it was hovering near his knees.

"Neat!" Danny exclaimed.

They followed her to her car. Leah opened the passenger door and lifted out a cardboard box.

Danny's eyes grew round as something in it wriggled.

Kneeling, Leah lowered the box to Danny's level. A golden retriever puppy immediately tried to climb into his arms.

"A puppy!" Danny shouted.

"A puppy," Matt echoed in disbelief.

"A puppy," Leah agreed, grinning. "Since yours died."

The silky-haired pup licked Danny's face.

"Is it really for me?" Danny asked.

"Yes," Leah replied. "That is, if your dad agrees."

Three heads turned in Matt's direction, the puppy seeming to guess his was the vote that counted. It occurred to Matt that he should say something about a puppy being a huge decision, one that should be discussed first. But wasn't there a much larger decision looming on the horizon, one that took all precedence? "Sure."

"Yay!" Danny and Leah chorused.

Danny threw his arms around Leah's neck and

hugged her. She held on, obviously cherishing this first hug.

"Thanks, Leah."

"You're welcome, sweetie."

He turned back to the puppy, who latched on and started chewing on his ear. Laughing, Danny carried the dog to the grass beneath the oak tree where they could play.

Her hand shaky, Leah took a paper from her pocket. "He's already started his puppy shots—they're all written down here. But he has to have more in four weeks."

"Just like a baby." Matt couldn't stop the response.

Her expression was soft. "Pretty much. But then you've been through the long nights, the getting into everything stage."

From a distance, Danny and the puppy rolled in the grass, Danny's giggles drifting in the morning air.

Matt took her hand, surprising both of them. "Why? Unless..."

"No. The puppy means I think Danny's where he belongs. But, Matt... It doesn't mean I'm ready to let go of him. You were right. I'm his mother. And I want him to know that. When it's time. When he's ready."

Matt felt the peace in his heart that had eluded him since he'd had the answer to his prayer.

He still held Leah's hand. "I'm not sure what to say."

"I guess we have to figure out where to go from here."

He looked at her hand just as she did. Releasing his hold, he stepped back a fraction. Just as quickly she pulled her hand back. This was a truce for Danny's sake, not theirs.

The church social was one of those cake and homemade ice cream affairs that brought out everyone from babies to grandparents, especially since all the women tried to outdo each other with the cakes they brought. Not that anyone ever dared voice that aspect of the tradition. But the two-layer cakes grew to three and then were topped one year by a four-layer. After that, there was no stopping the ladies.

It was the one time of year Annie bypassed her pie-baking skills and poured all her energy into a German chocolate torte that was so rich she suspected it could set off a sugar coma.

Leah wasn't concerned about impressing other women with her domestic skills, but she did have one particular eight-year-old in mind. While Annie slaved over her secret family recipe, Leah kept her butter cake batter simple. But the shape was challenging. A puppy. A fat, rollicking-looking retriever puppy. It took her a while to shape the cake, but it was worth every moment. Frosting and decorating it was relatively easy. Her only moment of panic came when she arrived at the church hall. What if someone cut into the cake before Danny saw it?

But luck was with her. Danny was trailing his father, talking with his friends when she arrived.

"Hey, Leah!" he hollered.

Matt turned at the sound of Danny's voice.

Leah held out the cake a bit self-consciously. "Hi!"

"Cool!" Danny and Billy said together, skidding toward her.

"Jinx!"

"Did you *make* that?" Danny asked in awe.

"Yes," Matt repeated, arriving a few moments behind them. "Did you?"

"Guilty."

"Looks just like Hunter, huh, Dad?"

"Yes, it does."

"Hunter?" Leah echoed.

Matt cleared his throat. "Danny decided to name him after you."

Touched, she nearly wobbled the cake.

Matt reached out and steadied the plate. "Would you like some help carrying that?"

"Thanks." She relinquished it to him.

"Can we go on ahead and see the rest of the cakes, Dad?"

"Okay."

The kids scooted around the slower moving adults, anxious to see the display of mouth-watering goodies.

"He usually comes home from this ready to burst," Matt told her.

She frowned. "What do you do about that?"

"Resign myself to it."

She blinked. "Oh."

"Not everything's black and white. Some gray days we all overindulge."

"This parenting thing is a lot harder than movies and sitcoms would have a person believe."

"It doesn't come with a how-to manual."

"The most important job in the world—it should."

They made their way toward the cake tables, Matt keeping a strong grip on his cargo. "You have to trust your instincts."

She groaned. "I was afraid you were going to say that."

Matt found space on one of the tables for Leah's dog-shaped cake. It was unique among the towering displays of elaborate confections. Self-conscious, Leah was aware of a few speculative glances toward her creation.

"I think you may have started something," Matt murmured.

"As long as Danny likes it."

The men had cranked the tubs of homemade ice cream and many were as proud of their creations as their wives were of their cakes. Peach was a perennial favorite, but Leah was drawn to a vanilla that had been made with real vanilla bean.

"I guess I'm just a plain Jane, but this one gets my vote," she declared, enthralled with the creamy treat.

"Plain Jane?" Matt shook his head. "I don't think so."

Never shy, Leah found herself suddenly possessing two heads with at least as many tongues. Shuffling her feet—did she really only have two?—she struggled to balance her purse and the ice cream, hoping she didn't stumble into Matt. Good grief, what was wrong with her? All he'd said, basically, was that she wasn't ugly as a post.

Deciding to take refuge in the ice cream, she gobbled it down too quickly. The frozen treat hit her head like the proverbial brick, and she tried to pretend it hadn't just made the headache worse.

"Would you like some punch?" Matt asked.

Was that sympathy in his voice? "That would be nice."

He'd barely stepped away when she put down her ice-cream dish and pressed her hand to her forehead.

She felt someone tugging on her hand.

"Leah? You okay?"

"Danny!" She opened her eyes. "Yes. My head hurts, that's all."

He put his small hand on her forehead, looking intent. Absorbed by the gesture, by his matching green eyes and face so close to hers, she simply watched.

After awhile he removed his hand. "You don't have a fever."

"Actually, my head doesn't hurt anymore."

He drew his brows together. "Really?"

"Really." And it was true.

When he smiled, she started to reach out, to hug him. But she stopped as he said, "Hey, Dad. Leah's head hurt, but she doesn't have a fever."

"That's good."

"Yeah."

Leah accepted the cup of punch Matt offered. "Thanks."

"Me and Billy counted. There's more chocolate'n anything else. Mrs. Carruthers put Snickers bars on hers."

"Pace yourself, pal."

"Okay, Dad." And he was off, running to catch up with Billy.

A small handful of musicians were playing old tunes while the crowd milled, breaking into smaller groups, laughing and socializing. There was an awkward silence between the two.

Matt finally cleared his throat. "Veterans of this social. Like I told Danny, you have to pace yourself. Only amateurs try to take it all in at once."

She took a sip of her punch, then smiled.

"What?"

"Just thinking. This is kind of like my old school days. The parties. Only better, you know. Not all that worry and tension."

"What did you worry about?"

Her nerves returned in force. "You know...well, I guess you don't. You were a boy." She took a deep breath. "Worrying about ending up alone. Nobody to talk to."

He stared at her as though in disbelief.

Now thoroughly uncomfortable, she looked off in the opposite direction, toward the exit doors.

"I find it difficult to believe you could ever end up alone, Leah."

"I didn't mean…"

"Not tonight, anyway. I'm not going anywhere…. I mean, if that's all right with you…?"

She was wrong. This didn't remind her of a school party. Those naive days when she'd thought flash was attractive in a guy, which was why John had won her heart.

This was…different. She felt secure beside Matt. And aware. Aware that he was more than Danny's dad.

What did he see when he looked at her? Danny's mother? The woman who'd run out on the most important person in his life?

The music swirled around them, rising up to the rafters of the old church hall. Standing together in the middle of the crowd, Leah tried to hold back her shifting feelings. But the gate had already been unlatched.

Chapter Thirteen

Matt sat in the back room of the store that also served as his office. With all the turmoil in his personal life, he'd gotten behind on his paperwork. Although Nan helped with the books, the correspondence was his responsibility.

A discreet ivory, linen-weave envelope caught his attention. It was the sort of stationery he'd expected when he thought Leah would confirm her intentions to take Danny to L.A.

With a caution he wasn't certain he understood, Matt slit open the envelope. The engraved letterhead was impressive. And as he read, he learned the offer was, too.

Barrington Industries was proposing a buyout of Whitaker Woods. His designs, actually. Their plan was to merchandise his pieces all over the country in their high-end furniture stores.

He was amazed.

Granted, Whitaker Woods had been written up

in the *Houston Chronicle* and featured on morning shows in Dallas, Austin and San Antonio, as well. And people had been coming from all parts of the country to buy Matt's furniture. But he'd never imagined an offer of this scope. Barrington... How had they come across him?

His eyes strayed to the return address.

Los Angeles.

Coincidence?

Leah's family probably had considerable influence. Their design firm was a big deal in L.A. Had they brokered a deal with Barrington so that he would have a reason to relocate? Not that the letter specifically mentioned relocation, but it seemed probable.

He thought of Leah's wide smile when she presented the puppy and told him that Danny was where he should be.

He thought of holding her hand at the ice-cream social. The reaction she'd stirred. Then he thought of what he'd known all along, what John had told him about her.

As he laid the letter down on the desk, a card slid from the envelope.

Leonard Jenkins, Vice President, Acquisitions. Handwritten on the card was a simple note: *We can discuss options in person. Call me to set up a meeting at your office.*

Matt was unfamiliar with the ways of big business, but he was pretty sure that it should be the other way around, that he should have to hoof it to L.A. if he wanted this deal. He believed in his own

talent, but he knew he wasn't the only furniture designer in the country. Barrington could afford to sit
in L.A., send out their letters and wait for designers
to come running.

Disappointment churned in waves of such pro-
portion he felt flattened. For himself. For Danny.
Because despite everything, part of him wanted to
believe in her. To believe his son had a good mother,
who would love him as much as Matt did. Not one
who used deceit to get what she wanted.

But he'd been directed in prayer about his decision. And that he didn't question. But how did he
reconcile that with what he'd just learned? He had
no choice but to wait and see when she would reveal
her plans.

The unmatched smell of freshly carved wood
drifted together with that of lemon oil and beeswax.
He couldn't imagine leaving all that was familiar.
Rosewood was more than just a town. It was roots,
church, friends, neighbors, support.

But Danny was his son. And if leaving Rosewood
was what it took to be near him, he would do it. Still,
the disappointment was bitter as he thought of Leah.

The Scout spaghetti dinner was a big fund-raiser
for the troop. The proceeds went to buy new camping equipment. Danny was going to be one of the
many Scouts who helped serve the garlic bread,
punch and plates of spaghetti.

Leah had bought tickets for herself, Annie and,
so as not to be obvious, the four other members of

the school's artistic committee. At only five dollars a ticket it was a bargain to set up her friend with a really nice guy. Shamelessly, she suggested that Ethan meet Annie and her at the B and B so the singles could ride together. The other committee members were married and Leah hoped to meet up with them at the church hall where the dinner was being held.

Again she fussed over Annie, this time pulling out all the clothes she'd packed, along with the last box she'd had her assistant send. She was rapidly filling her room in the bed-and-breakfast. This wasn't the first shipment from her apartment. The antique chifforobe was stuffed, as were the bureau and vanity table. Leah knew she couldn't continue living in one room indefinitely, but there was comfort in the old Victorian home, in having Annie just down the hall. And in not having to make a long-term decision.

Her parents had been pressing her more and more in phone conversations about what she was going to do. She hadn't gotten up the courage to tell them that Danny would be staying in Rosewood. She knew how disappointed they would be. And since she hadn't figured out just what she would do yet, she couldn't see upsetting them. She wanted to be close to Danny. That she was sure of. When she'd first come to Rosewood, she couldn't have imagined giving up her life and career in L.A., but now... Fortunately, she had her trust fund, which would allow her to live in Rosewood indefinitely if she chose to.

But could she and Matt coexist as parents when...

well, when she didn't see him as just Danny's father anymore?

A lot of people she knew co-parented from opposite ends of the country. There were holidays, summer vacations. Danny could be in Rosewood the bulk of the time and she could have him those other times.

Leah swallowed hard. That wasn't what she wanted. It wasn't what she wanted for Danny. She thought of what Matt had said about his mother. Sacrifice. She'd sacrificed everything for her sons.

Crushing a linen skirt in her hands, Leah wondered what she was willing to sacrifice for Danny. It wasn't a popular concept these days, giving up everything, especially a career like hers, for family. But did that compare to the sacrifice of a child being shuttled across the country? Not every single parent had a choice. She did. When it was the right time to let Danny know who she was, she could tell him that she would be staying right here in Rosewood.

She relaxed her hands. When would it be the right time to tell him, she wondered? Would he be glad? Had he imagined a certain kind of mother? She thought of Emma McAllister and her effortless mothering techniques. Maybe that was the kind of mom Danny had dreamed of. Sighing, she knew she wasn't anything like Emma.

"Leah?" Annie called from the stairs.

Releasing the now mangled skirt, Leah stood. "Yes?"

"A box just came for you."

"Great!" It was the other box she'd asked Jennifer to send. She scrambled down the stairs. "Annie, help me get this open."

"What is it?"

"I went shopping just before I left L.A. This stuff was still in the bags."

"Oh, Leah! You don't mean…"

"What are sisters for? You can go shopping via UPS."

"But you haven't even worn the things yourself!"

Leah shrugged. "So? Now let's get this open." Tackling the box with a letter opener from the antique breakfront, she slit open the tape.

As Leah pulled out the first garment, Annie gasped. "I love the color."

The cut and material of the dress were simple, perfect for the evening, and Leah held it up to Annie. "I think it loves you, too." A deep topaz, the dress would look beautiful with Annie's dark hair and eyes. "I hate to say it, but we might have hit gold with the first one out of the box."

They combed through everything else, but the prize was right on top. After several reassurances that it was really all right to wear the brand-new dress, Annie clutched it close, ran upstairs and changed.

Leah gathered the remainder of the clothes and took them to her room. In the box was a blouse that she'd bought because it was the same hue as her eyes. Wistfully, she held it up to her chest and peered in the mirror. But who would be there to notice?

Telling herself not to be a big baby, she clipped

the tags from the blouse. There. She would wear it for herself, and because it was a special occasion for Danny.

In minutes she was dressed. She slipped on a pair of delicate gold filigree earrings that dangled from her earlobes to swing lightly beside her long, slender neck. A quick glance in the mirror told her the blouse, paired with a slender skirt and sandals, was perfect.

Leah noticed that Ethan's eyes nearly popped out when he saw Annie. Pleased and feeling very much the mother hen, she managed to scramble into the backseat of the car before Annie could so that the pair could sit together on the drive to the church.

After presenting their tickets at the door, the maître d', known to them as Billy's dad, checked the seating chart for three available seats. The Scouts had set up the long banquet tables end to end, filling the room. Since most of the town usually turned out for the annual event, the Scouts had come up with the seating plan so they could accommodate as many people at one time as possible.

"Table eighteen," Billy's dad told the hostess.

Smiling, the volunteer den mother led them over to a table where they picked up their salads and chose the dressing they wanted. Then, she directed them to their table, which had three empty spots.

Laughing and talking about the cute way the Scouts had come up with for seating them—"a table for three"—Leah didn't immediately notice the fourth person at their section of the banquet table.

It was Matt. She was so startled, she forgot her role of mother hen.

Ethan pulled out a chair for her, and luckily she remembered how to sit.

Annie sat two seats down from her, Ethan in between them. Fortunately Leah hadn't needed to push them together.

"Hello," she greeted Matt, smoothing her skirt, conscious that she was more dressed up than usual.

"Evening."

She craned her head, searching. "Danny's excited, isn't he?"

"Yes."

"Is he serving this table?"

He glanced over at Ethan. "Nope."

Monosyllabic answers. "Are you okay?"

"Just came from work. Had a lot of correspondence to deal with."

She tilted her head toward Ethan and Annie slightly, then leaned close to Matt and lowered her voice. "They make a great couple, don't they?"

He stared at her in surprise. "I suppose."

She noted he was still on his salad, so he hadn't been there long, either. "So, what happens next?"

"One of the Scouts will come and ask what you want to drink and bring garlic cheese bread."

"I don't suppose there's a drink menu." She laughed, trying to break the tension she sensed in him.

"This isn't L.A. You remember L.A.? Land of big deals? Your family specializes in them, don't they?"

Her smile faded. For some reason his words hurt more than they should have. He hadn't snapped, but there had been an undercurrent, barely perceptible, in his tone. Glancing around, she looked for someone she recognized, someone else she could talk to besides him. She didn't know anyone else at their table other than Annie and Ethan, and she didn't want to interrupt them.

A young Scout approached. "Hi. Do you want something to drink?"

"That'd be great."

"Um. Water or punch?"

"Punch, please."

"Okay." He started to leave, then turned back. "Um. Do you want cheese bread?"

She smiled at the earnest youngster. "That sounds really good."

"Okay."

He left and she busied herself with the paper napkin in her lap.

Matt was still silent. Self-consciously, she ate her salad, scanning the crowd, wishing she could spot Danny. The room was noisy, especially since it seemed that most of Rosewood was packed inside. There was a lot of chatter, neighbors catching up with each other. Leah was glad to see that Ethan and Annie were caught up in conversation. She wouldn't interrupt even if no one spoke to her the rest of the evening. Which seemed highly possible with Matt seated next to her.

The Cub Scout returned with garlic cheese bread for her and Matt. An older Scout carried their punch.

"Ma'am, do you want your spaghetti with or without meat?" the older boy asked.

"What do you recommend?"

"I like the one with meat best."

"Then that's what I'll have." She smiled at the pair of boys.

"Mr. Whitaker?" the Scout asked.

"With meat, Randy."

Naturally Matt knew the boy's name. Leah straightened in the folding chair and tried to look comfortable.

"The cheese bread's the best part." Matt's voice was quiet. Still, it startled her.

"Oh… Um, I haven't tried it yet." She opened the packet of aluminum foil and pulled a bit of the warm bread out and tasted it. "You're right. It's really good." She was so relieved he'd broken his silence. Even if the bread had tasted like cardboard, she'd have replied positively. Not that she appreciated the subtle sarcasm about her family's deal making. For just one evening she'd hoped there would be no tension between them. She'd thought things had improved since she'd told him Danny should stay in Rosewood, but maybe it was still too soon. She had no interest in fighting with Matt, though, so she kept to a neutral topic. "Looks like the Scouts will raise plenty of money for their equipment."

"They need a new trailer."

"Trailer?" She began picturing an open bed trailer, then a horse trailer…

"One to haul the camping equipment. The old one's too small and rusting out."

"I didn't know they needed a trailer, but then I've never been camping."

"It's for the long campouts when they carry a lot of supplies." He looked at her skeptically. "You've never been camping?"

She shook her head. "Nope. My dad's not really the camping type. We had all sorts of great weekends together but not camping. Does Danny enjoy it?"

"That's an understatement."

"I'd love to go on a campout with him."

"Hmm."

"What's that supposed to mean?"

"Nothing."

"You don't think I could handle it, do you?"

"People who haven't camped don't always have a realistic picture of what's involved."

"People?" Realizing she was raising her voice, she forced herself to speak more quietly. "You don't mean people, you mean me."

"You *are* a city person—"

Leah forgot about her resolve not to be baited. "I'm getting tired of hearing that. When's your next available weekend?"

"Why?"

"I want to take Danny camping."

He raised his eyebrows.

"And you're invited," she continued.

"Big of you."

"I'm serious. I want to be more than a visitor in his life."

Matt glanced down the table.

Leah followed his gaze, reminded of her friends' presence, but they were absorbed in their own conversation. "Well?"

"And if you hate camping?"

"Then I'll stick it out."

"It could be miserable."

If he made it that way. So they were back to his favorite subject, what she was made of. "Like I said, I'll stick it out."

"Next weekend then."

Chapter Fourteen

Danny was so excited that Matt didn't have the heart to say anything negative about the trip. They'd taken other kids camping with them, but this was the first time they'd brought a lady along.

The cupcake lady as Danny still sometimes referred to her.

They left on Friday as soon as school was out. Matt had put the camper shell on his truck and it was already packed. He'd stopped earlier at the B and B for Leah's things. She'd bought her own tent and sleeping bag, along with a few other items he'd suggested on a list, but Matt had the rest of the equipment they'd need. They'd agreed that he would be in charge of the food supplies, even though she insisted on paying for half. She'd baked brownies and cookies, but otherwise he was surprised to see she'd packed light.

As they headed toward one of their favorite spots,

Danny talked nonstop about the lake, fishing, hiking and telling campfire stories.

Unlike the mountains that ridged western Texas, the hill country rolled gently. Tucked away amid the clustered trees and open fields was the small lake they sought.

Once they arrived at their destination, Leah insisted on helping to unload the equipment. After securing Hunter, Matt and Danny went to work setting up camp. They always brought a large main tent that could be used for meals and recreation if the weather turned bad, plus a smaller tent to sleep in.

He glanced over at Leah, who was taking her brand-new tent out of its box. "You need help pitching your tent?"

"Um. No." She was reading the instruction booklet.

"Okay."

He and Danny pounded in stakes, securing the main tent.

"Maybe we should help her," Danny whispered.

"Give her a chance first," Matt replied quietly.

They pitched their second tent, put in the air mattresses and sleeping bags. Then they set up the camp tables and stove. Matt glanced at Leah occasionally as he unloaded the rest of the gear. She had the rear of the small tent erected, but it was sagging. Of course, it wasn't easy to pitch a tent while trying to read the directions.

Danny came to her rescue, showing her how to place the middle pole.

"The man at the hardware store said this tent was an easy one to put up," she said.

Danny shrugged. "Yeah, it is sorta. But it's not the kind that just pops open."

"Oh." She looked over at Matt and his tent. "Yours isn't, either, is it?"

"No. But we've done it bunches of times before." Danny helped her finish putting up the tent, then staked it.

"Thanks."

"S'okay. You'll do better next time."

She smiled ruefully. "I'll certainly try."

Danny put an air mattress in her tent.

"I didn't bring that."

"Dad packed it for you."

Matt dumped firewood next to a pit lined with the remains of old ashes, then dusted his hands. "The ground gets awfully hard."

Her expression lightened.

He didn't want to dwell on the difference her smile made to his mood as he squatted to build the fire.

"What can I do?" she asked.

"Hang out with Danny."

"Really?"

"We're set until supper, and it just has to cook once I get the fire going."

"Shouldn't I help prepare the food?"

"First night's easy. Dinner in foil packets in the campfire. And you already made dessert."

Her delight was as simple to read as a first-grade primer. "If you're sure…"

"Yes." Danny knew to stay within the parameters of the camp, not to wander too far. Still… "It'll start to get dark in about an hour, so—"

"Don't go too far." She pulled a compass from one pocket and pedometer from the other. "I came prepared to make sure we don't."

After he built the fire and put the foil packets of food at its base to cook, he settled back. Once the fire was established, he felt camp was set. The meat and vegetables in the packets would roast, giving them a hearty meal.

The skies were clear, and the weather forecast promised good weather. Should be nothing to worry about. But it seemed strange for Danny to be in someone else's care for the moment. Especially Leah's.

Well before the sun torched a path toward the horizon, they returned, their canvas bags filled with sticks for tomorrow's fire.

Relaxed, laughing, happy. It amazed Matt how natural they were together, as though the birth connection had somehow remained alive, strong.

"Something smells wonderful," Leah declared, pulling off the backpack of wood. "And the fire looks great. I insist on doing all the cleanup tonight."

Danny began giggling all over again.

"What?"

"There isn't any cleanup the first night," Matt

explained. "We just crumple up the foil and put it in the garbage. But I'll keep your offer in mind for breakfast."

Leah reached over and tickled Danny. "Smart guy."

He just laughed even harder.

Matt watched them together throughout dinner. As darkness settled over the land, their campsite seemed a more intimate space. Fallen logs made good seating around the fire as they toasted marshmallows and told scary stories.

As the appointed storyteller, he was amused to see that Leah's eyes were nearly as wide as Danny's when the story came to its climax. And when he reached out to spook Danny at the end, she jumped, as well, almost falling off the log. Then they both dissolved into laughter. Danny, not content to leave Matt out, tickled him, as well, and even Hunter joined in, barking at everyone.

"You're supposed to be scared," Matt gasped, moving out of reach.

"We were!" Leah scrambled to her feet. "But now we're paying you back," she teased.

"Truce!" He held up his hands. "I know where the hot cocoa is."

She looked at Danny. "Think we should let him off?"

"Yeah. I want cocoa."

Grinning to himself, Matt uncovered the packets that were in the food box. The tin coffeepot, filled with water, was already on the Coleman stove.

Leah located mugs and spoons and started snipping marshmallows into small pieces.

"I guess this doesn't exactly seem like roughing it." Looking sheepish, she held up a pair of tiny, folding scissors. "But I don't travel anywhere without these."

"Relax. The written test isn't until the *end* of the trip."

She grinned back at him.

Danny's eyelids started drooping before his cocoa was gone.

Matt draped an arm on his shoulders. "Hey, pal, how 'bout tucking in for the night?"

Danny struggled to stay awake, not wanting to miss anything. "It's not late."

"We've got the whole weekend ahead of us. You don't want to be too tired to enjoy it."

The little boy took one half-hearted sip of cocoa. "Okay."

Leah gently took his mug. "Good night, Danny."

"'Night."

Matt tucked him in, securing him in his sleeping bag. He smoothed back the hair on his forehead, knowing the boy was exhausted from the big day.

"Bless Daddy," Danny mumbled.

Matt knew he was almost asleep, that evening prayers wouldn't be complete tonight.

"An' bless Leah. Thanks for givin' Daddy somebody to love."

The fire snapped outside the tent, the sound sharp

in the silence Matt felt in his heart. *Was this what his son had been praying for?*

Hunter whined, butting his head at the sleeping bag so that he could lie next to Danny.

Matt stayed in the tent as long as he could—when he finally went back outside, Leah looked up at him. Her face, illuminated by the glow of the fire, was anxious.

"Is he okay?"

Matt nodded, then cleared his throat. "Just tired. Big day for him."

"Right. And me, I'm so wound up I'm sure I won't be able to go to sleep."

"Oh?"

"Afraid so." She hugged her knees. "To be able to spend so much time with Danny…" She glanced toward the tent, lowering her voice. "Is he asleep?"

Matt nodded.

"I can't explain how much this means to me… how much hope I have… I know this campout wasn't your idea, but I really appreciate being able to share this experience with Danny. I…" Woodsmoke floated between them. "Before…before I found Danny, I used to imagine how he'd turned out. I thought about sports and boy things and all that. I wondered what he liked, what he didn't like. But I never imagined…" She looked at him earnestly. "He's so…perfect."

Matt thought so, too. He also remembered the prayer he'd just heard. "No one's perfect."

She shook her head. "Maybe I'm not explaining

it right. I feel like I did after I counted all his fingers and toes when he was born and saw that he was healthy. It wouldn't have mattered if he hadn't been beautiful, or if he'd been born with flaws or a handicap—to me he was perfect. And that's how he is now, how he's turned out…how he's been raised."

Speechless, he stared into the fire, then held out his hand.

She accepted it.

The words were hard for him to say, especially since he still had so many doubts about her. Ones he wasn't certain he could ever overcome. "This is a partnership that I never expected, that I'm still not sure about."

Her fingers curled within his hand. "Then let me prove to you it's one that will work."

Leah dreamed of the spa in Beverly Hills that gave the best facials in Southern California. Mudpacks, wraps, salt rubs that had their clientele begging just to be put on waiting lists. But she had reached the top of that list. Her facial was exquisite. Fingers were massaging her skin, moistening it, sanding it, licking it…

Licking it?

Giggles made her open one eye and squint into the light. What in the world?

Hunter, deciding she was free game, lapped at her face, lavishing her with doggie kisses.

"Are you awake?" Danny asked in a mock whisper that could have been heard at least two tents away.

"Oh, yeah." She struggled to sit up in her sleeping bag while the determined dog kept licking her face.

"Breakfast is ready."

"Oh, no!" She had planned to be up early, to make the meal, or at the least to help.

"Dad probably won't make you eat all of yours."

She grinned. What a wonderful way to wake up.

Matt stood at the stove piling eggs onto plates. "'Morning."

"'Morning. Sorry I'm a slug."

"It's okay. You're on KP anyway."

She headed toward the aroma of coffee, although the fresh air was more than enough of a wake-up. Grabbing a mug, she filled it and then joined the males at the table.

"What's on the agenda for today?"

"Hiking. Up for that?"

"I'm up for anything." She felt like she could climb mountains, swim oceans. But a hike was good. She'd checked out every book in the Rosewood library on camping and hiking, including both the Girl and Boy Scout Handbooks. She'd bought the right shoes for hiking. And socks. They'd also been on Matt's list. She'd been cramming for this trip from the moment Matt had agreed to it. She'd even selected the tent based on what she'd seen in the books. Apparently she should have gone with the one that just popped into place—the one the man in the hardware store had suggested—if she'd wanted to impress Matt. But something told her it would take far more than that to impress him.

Eager to begin their hike, Leah whizzed through the cleanup. With all the food, coolers and garbage secured in the truck's camper shell, they headed out.

Danny and Matt both had well-used walking sticks that Matt had carved. She was surprised when Matt handed her one, obviously new. She suspected that in his shop it would sell for a high price. One of the books she'd consulted had said to cut a stick in the woods. "Thank you. I didn't expect—"

"I know. But you'll find it makes the hike a lot easier."

The wood was smooth beneath her fingers as they walked, and it warmed under the persistent sun. Accustomed to an hour at the gym every day in L.A., she wasn't winded when they took their first break on an outcropping of rocks shaded by trees that grew farther up the hill.

Taking off her hat, Leah bathed her face with some of her drinking water. The curse of fair skin was that she flushed so quickly. But her energy was still high.

The wildflowers that covered the hillsides were breathtaking. Some delicate in color. Some, like the orange paintbrush, as bold as the state itself. They stayed on the trails where possible so they wouldn't crush the unspoiled blooms.

"Everything's so vast," Leah wondered aloud, seeing the miles of virgin land that stretched out before them. "That no one else has been on this path yet this spring, stepped among these flowers…it's amazing."

"The world is a big place," Matt replied.

And yet she'd found Danny.

The trail steepened and Matt held out a hand to help her climb. She didn't really need his help, yet she took it. And she didn't question why. Nor did she release his hand too quickly.

Or his gaze when it touched on hers longer than it had to. It wasn't thirst that dried her throat.

Nearly an hour later they came to a fork. Matt turned toward her. Then he frowned. "Where's your hat?"

Automatically, she reached toward the top of her head, but the hat was gone. All she felt was her hair pulled back into a ponytail. "I had it."

"Did you take it off?"

"I don't think so…I… Yes! I took it off when we had our break."

His frown deepened. "You're getting sunburned. We'd better turn back."

Danny let out a cry of distress.

"Danny," Matt cautioned.

"We don't have to go back!" Leah thought quickly. "I'll just keep putting on sunscreen."

"Do you have some with you? I didn't bring any because we're wearing hats and long-sleeved shirts."

"Sure. No reason to turn back." She smiled brightly despite the fib, remembering plenty of hikes when she was younger. She hadn't had a hat or sunscreen and she'd been fine. And she wasn't going to spoil this outing for Danny.

Matt looked at her closely. "I guess so."

"Goody!" Danny was already turning back to the trail, Hunter bouncing along beside him on his leash.

The climb to the crest where they were eating lunch was strenuous but the view was worth it. White-tailed deer scattered as they entered a clearing, but they were close enough to see a wide-eyed doe and her fawn before they took flight.

Matt shrugged out of his backpack, the one containing most of the food. Leah's pack, like Danny's, was much lighter. Again she used her drinking water to bathe her face, hoping to cool down.

When she turned around, Matt was frowning again. "Are you sure your sunscreen's working? You look pretty red."

"I always flush from the heat. It's my Irish ancestry showing. Nothing to worry about."

But she could feel the sting in her cheeks and hoped that some of it might really be caused by exertion. That morning she'd been in such a rush to get going that she'd forgotten to put on any sunscreen at all. And there hadn't been any point in wearing makeup. But she wasn't going to wimp out and let Danny down.

During lunch she forgot about the heat, revitalized by granola bars, dried fruit and jerky.

"Not far now to the caves." Matt put on his backpack. "Just over the ridge."

She had mixed feelings about the caves. They would be cool and dark inside, but there might also be bats. Ugh.

Danny, on the other hand, was thrilled. "The caves are way cool, Leah."

"I'll bet," she said, trying to sound enthused.

The caves were worse than she'd expected, dark and narrow, with barely enough room for her and Matt to stand up straight. Leah was afraid she'd scrape her head against the ceiling, getting bats' wings or something equally unappealing in her hair. Shuddering, she fell into line behind Matt as he and Danny led the way, side by side, into the cave, Hunter following quietly, subdued by this strange new place.

The beams from their flashlights bounced off walls so dark they were beyond black. The cavern gradually widened, the stone ceiling sloping upward, growing higher. Water dripped down on them. At least Leah hoped it was water. She couldn't see anything in the gloom.

She licked her lips, remembering she was thirsty. Momentarily distracted, she forgot about following Matt's exact steps. She couldn't have deviated much, but suddenly she felt something brush against her forehead, her face.

She screamed as bats flew past, their furry bodies and wings whipping around her head.

Matt turned and she lurched toward him. He stretched out his arms and she jumped into them, hanging on tight. A split second later she screamed for Danny and pulled him into their circle. While she hung on for dear life, she felt them shaking—not with fear, she finally realized, but laughter. Hunter barked furiously, running in circles, tangling his leash around their legs.

When the bats had passed them, Leah disentangled herself. She shone her flashlight from face to face. Matt was doing a better job of containing his amusement than Danny. One part of her wanted to hang on to her dignity, the other to blast them. But they'd almost been swarmed by bats. Gross, nasty bats.

Matt cleared his throat. "Are you okay?"

"What do you think?"

"Uh, I think you've never had that particular experience before."

She looked down at Danny.

"You can really jump *fast!*" he said with admiration.

She could stay mad, but instead she hooted with laughter. "I guess I can. But any more bats and I'm outta here."

Although they didn't have any further encounters, Leah was relieved when they finished exploring and made it back to the bright sunshine. They'd only been inside the cave a short time, but it was way too long for her.

"You'll get used to it," Danny told her. "First time's always hardest."

What a good boy he was. And he spoke with such assurance that there would be more of these outings with her.

"Time to head back," Matt announced.

"Aw, Dad."

Matt turned to Leah. "He'd say that if we hiked to San Antonio."

The sun was still high and hot as they headed down. The trail was a challenging one, but Leah didn't have any trouble, thanks to the sturdy hiking shoes and thick socks Matt had specified. She had wondered if he would try to sabotage her on this trip. It would have been easy enough to do. Instead, he'd made sure she had all the proper equipment, even offering to provide her tent and sleeping bag. It was the kindness in him, she realized, and the goodness. Even though he believed that she hadn't told the truth about Kyle, he wouldn't do anything to harm her.

She stumbled and Matt turned back, holding his hand out. She took it, steadying herself.

"Tired?"

"No, just thinking."

"About?"

"Ironically, what great hiking shoes I'm wearing."

"They don't leap tall buildings or sticks in the trail, though."

"Nice way of saying I need to pay attention."

"You've done fine."

"Just *fine?*"

"No whining, no asking for special treatment. No real girly stuff."

She laughed. "Except for screaming and jumping into your arms in the cave. But I still contend bats go way beyond just girly." She shuddered. "Yuck, gross."

"No more caves for you?"

"I didn't say that."

"You've got pluck, Leah." He shook his head. "That's what my mother called it."

Touched, she swallowed. "That's the nicest thing you've ever said to me."

He drew his eyebrows together. There was surprise in his eyes. And doubt. She wondered at its cause.

"Dad, Leah! Look, foxes!"

They both turned to see. Dainty, graceful and strong. And then the animals were gone.

And so was the moment.

The day was uncommonly hot, and her water was nearly gone. Bathing her face with it had used up her supply. By the last break she was so thirsty she sucked her lips in to hide their cracked appearance.

But Matt noticed. "Your sunscreen's no good." He pulled off his hat. "Wear this."

"No. I'm the one who lost my hat." And they hadn't found it on the way back. The wind or an animal must have knocked it from the trail.

He plopped it on her head. "No arguments. You're red as a late summer tomato."

Since even her eyeballs felt hot and her head was beginning to throb, she complied. At least the trail was getting easier, flattening out more.

The last hour Leah's face and neck seemed to be on fire. Her energy was sapping, but she concentrated on Danny's happy voice. She had to admit that the camp looked decidedly wonderful when they reached it, though.

Shrugging off her backpack, she collapsed on the log near the blackened fire pit. If not for Danny, she would have crawled into her tent and closed her eyes until morning.

Miraculously, he and Matt were puttering around camp, starting a new fire, preparing for dinner, acting as though they hadn't hiked a zillion miles. She knew she should stir, but her legs felt like rubber.

Matt tapped on her hat. Well, his hat.

"You under there?"

She nodded.

He added wood to the pit to rekindle the fire he'd carefully banked that morning. "You're awfully quiet."

She nodded again.

"Something wrong?"

Leah started to shake her head, but the motion sent the throbbing behind her eyes into full gear and she reached up to grab the sides of her head, encumbered by the hat.

"Leah?" Concerned, he tipped the hat back from her forehead. "Leah!"

She knew her face must look half-cooked by the day in the sun. Her lips, swollen and cracked, were difficult to move. "What?"

"You're burned to bits. What kind of sunscreen were you using?"

She closed her eyes, the movement painful. "I didn't actually have any."

"What?"

"I was afraid you'd make us turn back if you knew I didn't have any sunscreen after I went and left my hat on a rock."

"But...why?"

"I didn't want to disappoint Danny."

"He'd have gotten over it," Matt said in exasperation.

Her vision was swimming. She wasn't certain if it was tears or light-headedness. Her throat felt so dry. "But this was so special to me."

"You beat all." He laid the back of his hand on her forehead.

A tear slipped from her eyes. "I read all the books."

"What books?"

"From the library. On camping and hiking. And the Scout manuals. I wanted to do everything right."

He smoothed the tears from her cheeks, his touch gentle. "It's not worth crying over."

"I didn't think I'd lose my hat."

"Can't really tell if you have a fever," he muttered. "Your whole face is burned. So's your neck." He picked up her pack and shook her water bottle. "Empty. You probably used more of it cooling down your face than drinking it. I don't know what to make of you. All so Danny wouldn't be disappointed. What if you'd had a heat stroke? That can be fatal, you know."

"But Danny—"

"Would be disappointed, I know." He dipped his bandanna in cool water and laid it on her forehead. "I imagine he'd be pretty disappointed if you dropped dead out here, too."

She groaned.

He sighed. "That's not going to happen. You need to fill up on fluids." He reached for her arm. "Come on. Rest for you tonight."

"No," she pleaded. "I want to stay up with Danny."

"But—"

"Please. I don't want him to know I messed up again."

He wavered. Retrieving the water jug, he poured her a full cup. "Sip slow, but steady."

Another tear escaped, trickling down her burned cheek. "I feel so stupid."

He relented. "You're just a little too enthusiastic, sometimes."

Matt left her with the water. The first-aid kit contained burn medication, but he searched for a native plant that would work better. Finding an aloe vera, he cut off a stalk, slit off the thorny edges, then peeled back the outer layer to reveal the gooey pulp.

"Okay, Leah, this will feel kind of slimy but cool." She braced as though the cure would be worse than the burn. He was careful as he applied the transparent gel to her forehead. Her eyes were nearly level with his and she watched as his fingers moved over her cheeks, then eased down to her cracked lips. "There, that ought to do it." He kept his hand on her face a moment, reluctant to break the contact. Her eyes kept searching his. In them he saw questions and a vulnerability at odds with the strength she was always bent on proving. "I'd better get that fire started."

She was so close he could see her swallow. "Right." Her voice was husky. "Thanks."

"I'll cut some more aloe vera so you'll have plenty for tonight." He fumbled with the piece in his hand. "Now I'll get to that fire."

Danny and Hunter loped toward them, both arriving breathless. "You're awful red!"

"Too much sun today," she admitted.

"Your hat," he remembered.

"Yes. I shouldn't have left it on the trail. Pretty dumb, huh?"

"It's okay."

"You're very forgiving."

"Jesus forgives us so we're supposed to forgive others." He shrugged. "Even yourself."

She reached out and hugged him, sunburn and all.

Matt turned away, the clutch of emotion as powerful as a home run hit miles out of the park.

By morning Leah felt better. Matt's care was responsible. He'd kept applying the pulp of the aloe vera plant on her face and neck, all the while insisting that she keep drinking water. As she rehydrated, her headache faded and her body began to feel normal again. He was even sensitive to the fact that the campfire would hurt her sunburn, so they sat around the table instead.

And he'd insisted on cooking breakfast without her help, cleaning up the same way. So she sat now at the table, watching as he and Danny put away the cooking gear.

"Leah, we have our own kind of service on Sundays when we camp, nothing formal, just our own thing. Do you feel up to walking down to the lake?"

She waved her hands. "I'm no wilting buttercup. And the lake's within sight. Besides, I feel much better this morning."

"Okay." He picked up his Bible, handing her his hat to wear. Together, along with Hunter, they strolled to the shore of the small lake. The morning was cool and trees shaded the grassy area they stood on.

Matt opened with a prayer, then Danny sang in a sweet clear voice the well-known verses of "Jesus Loves Me."

Matt hesitated a moment. "Would you like to read the Bible passage for us, Leah?"

She trembled from nerves, then nodded. "Yes." She accepted the outstretched Bible and turned to the one passage that she remembered well, that she had read often when Danny was missing.

"This is from Luke 18— *'And they brought unto him also infants, that he would touch them; but when his disciples saw it, they rebuked them. But Jesus called them unto him, and said, Suffer little children*

*to come unto me, and forbid them not: for of such is
the kingdom of God.'"*

When she finished, she looked at Matt to see if she
had done all right. Was that approval in his gaze?

"Now we tell what we've had to be thankful for,"
Matt explained. "Danny, do you want to begin?"

He nodded. "I'm thankful for Hunter....

Leah and Matt smiled.

"And my dad and Leah...."

She swallowed.

"And all my friends, especially Billy and his new
brother or sister."

Matt looked at Leah.

"I have so many things to be grateful for," she
said, struggling to steady her voice. "My parents,
their love and support. Good friends. The special
people who've come into my life here in Rosewood."
She drew another calming breath. "Danny and his
father, my friend Annie." She didn't meet Matt's
gaze.

The gentle breeze stirred the leaves.

"I'm thankful for my son," Matt began. "For all
he brings to my life, for the joy he gives me. And
I'm thankful to the Lord for His blessings. They're
constant, never failing."

Surrounded by the beauty of the countryside,
Leah considered the source of Matt's unwavering
faith. Faith so great it baffled and humbled her.

Chapter Fifteen

"Sounds like the trip was a huge success." Annie refilled their orange juice glasses. Her other guests had already left for the day, wanting an early start on the nearby wildflower trails that filled the hill country and drew visitors to Rosewood.

Leah felt the warmth that had stayed with her since Matt and Danny had dropped her off the previous evening. "It was good. Really good. How about you? Did you see Ethan?"

"At church. Oh, Leah, I like him so much. I just never hoped…"

The nudging was paying off.

"I almost forgot. Your mother called twice."

Leah frowned. Her mother was becoming more and more insistent. "What did you tell her?"

"That you were out looking at wildflowers. I felt funny not coming clean. I mean, it wasn't *exactly* a lie. I knew you were bound to be looking at wildflowers at some point on the campout, but…"

"It wasn't squeaky clean, either. I'm sorry. I didn't mean to stick you in the middle, but I'm not ready to tell my parents what I've decided."

"What *have* you decided?"

Leah gazed out the large window that overlooked the peaceful backyard. Songbirds perched on the sturdy limbs of the old magnolia tree, hopping over to the well-stocked feeder. "Annie, have you ever thought of leaving here? Starting over somewhere completely new?"

"Sure. I thought maybe if I left, I could put this— whatever it is that makes such bad things happen in my family—behind me. But this is all I know. Rosewood is where my friends are. It takes courage to start somewhere new, more than I've got. Even though I understand why you had to come here, I don't think I could do what you have. Jumping right in at the school, volunteering…not knowing anybody."

"It's not courage, Annie, it's…Danny's mine, even though I'm the worst mother on the planet—"

"That's not true!"

Touched by her friend's loyalty, Leah patted Annie's hand. "It's not just what I've done, it's what I haven't done."

Perplexed, Annie waited.

"I haven't figured out how to tell Danny who I am."

"Well, it'll take time."

"But will the news get any easier to take?" she wondered aloud. "I mean…it's going to be a shock no matter when he hears it. Will it be worse now or when he knows me better?"

"When he *likes* you better, you mean."

Leah ducked her head. "Is that wrong?"

"I don't know. He's *your* child. What do you think?"

"He likes me now." She felt the warmth of his hug, the joy of his laughter, the promise in his eyes. "That I'm fairly certain of. And I think his feelings for me are growing. But I also think it's too early to test them."

Annie fiddled with the handle on the juice pitcher. "So, what are you going to tell your parents when they call again?"

"I told them I'd be home well before my birthday."

"Is that soon?"

"Next week." Leah sighed. "Which isn't any big deal, except that I made it into one. I told them I was determined to have Danny home with me by then."

"Still planning to be in L.A. for the festivities?"

"No. I'll find a way to explain to my parents."

"So what day next week?"

"Saturday. Why?"

"Just wondering."

"Don't make a fuss, Annie."

"I think we have all the fuss going on we need already, thank you."

"Good. Because this is the birthday nobody believes—my twenty-ninth. Everybody's always twenty-nine! I'd sooner skip the groans of disbelief."

"That you're twenty-nine not twenty-one."

Annie's smile was so genuine that Leah rolled her eyes. "Fine, cake. You and me. But that's it!"

Leah managed to avoid her mother's phone calls for more than a week, but she was squeezing Annie into a corner. And her friend was running out of excuses for why Leah wasn't returning messages from the inn or on her cell phone.

And with her birthday only days away, her time of grace was just about up. So when her cell phone rang as she walked down Main Street, she gritted her teeth and answered the call.

"At last! I thought you'd gone underground! If that's possible in the middle of nowhere."

"Only if you're a prairie dog, Mother."

"Is that some sort of Texas humor?"

"I suppose. So, how are you?"

"Getting frantic to be truthful. Not being able to contact my only child for more than a week…"

Oh, this was high drama. "Now, Mother, you know I left messages on your voice mail."

"When you knew I wouldn't be there! It's as though you deliberately didn't want to talk to me." The pouting came through, loud and clear.

"Mother, I have decisions to make—"

"So what are you planning to do? Hang around in that little town until you reach an agreement with this man?"

She hedged. "Something like that."

"Leah, how can you possibly expect that to work?

The boy needs to know how his life is going to be structured so he can adjust. If you're confused, he'll feel it."

She took a deep breath. "Mother, I'm working things out, but nothing's settled yet. And it won't be for a while."

"How long a while?" Rhonda's voice gathered suspicion.

"I don't really know. But don't make any plans with me in them, starting with my birthday."

"Starting?"

"Like I said, it's going to take a while."

"I don't like the sound of this, Leah."

"You'll probably want to shift my client base to Edward."

"Leah!"

"For now, Mother. Some of the accounts need more personal attention than Jennifer can give them. Until I make a permanent decision, I think that's best."

"It sounds like you've already made one, and it doesn't bode well."

"No, I'm trying to make one. It's…difficult."

"To bring home your child? How can that be?"

"It's complicated, Mother."

"You have the best lawyers at your disposal. Use them."

How could she explain it wasn't a legal issue? "Mother—"

"You said you could fight this on your own. But your father and I can be on the next plane out—"

"No!"

"Really, Leah, this is the time for family to stick together."

"I can handle it, Mother. I don't need a show of Hunter power."

"Why not bring the boy's uncle back to L.A., too?"

Leah sighed. That would be like uprooting a hickory tree and expecting it to flourish on one of L.A.'s freeways. "I don't think so."

"Are you trying to make it impossible to come home?"

"Of course not. I'm just trying to explain why it's difficult, complicated, why it's going to take longer than I thought."

"We could help make it easier, Leah."

She clutched the phone closer. "I know you want to help. But let me do this."

"Your birthday, sweetheart. All alone in a strange town…"

"Hardly. I've made friends. Annie, who runs the B and B, is making a cake from an old family recipe, my favorite. She's great. You'd like her."

"You have friends here," Rhonda reminded her.

"I have room in my life for both."

"I thought this trip was about Danny."

"It is. Annie's an unexpected blessing."

"Blessing?" Surprise coated the word. But then it hadn't been in Leah's vocabulary before.

"I've discovered quite a few in Rosewood."

"I see."

Leah wondered what exactly her mother was picturing at the moment—what her daughter had gotten involved in. "It'll be okay, Mother. Trust me."

Rhonda sighed. "It sounds like I'll have to."

It wasn't a vote of confidence, but it would do.

Leah didn't mind helping Emma with inventory at the costume shop. In fact, usually it was a lot of fun, but trying on half a dozen costumes wasn't her favorite thing. And this last one…Cinderella. Leah felt like she ought to be climbing into a pumpkin any minute. Emma had insisted she put on the whole getup, and then she'd rushed over to the B and B to meet with her client, the one who was going to sponsor the costumes for the school's next play. She planned to bring him over to the shop for a preview.

The phone rang and Tina answered. "Are you sure? Well, why can't you come over here? You want me to wear *what?* I guess so. But you owe me big."

"What's wrong?"

Tina clicked off, looking disgusted. "Our sponsor has a sprained ankle and wants us to trot over to the B and B wearing our costumes."

"Our?"

Tina grimaced. "She expects me to put on that blasted Tinker Bell outfit."

Leah barely covered her laugh with a cough that came out sounding more like a croak.

"Go ahead and laugh," Tina muttered, grabbing the offending costume and heading into the dressing room. She continued grumbling but was out in a remarkably short time. "Might as well get this over with. Ready, Cinders?"

"Ready, Tinker."

Feeling a little ridiculous in a ballgown, not to mention tiara, wand and silver shoes, Leah walked the short distance down Main Street with Tina. This same sponsor apparently donated a small fortune to the local theater so it was well worth the temporary discomfort for the school coffers. But the two of them collected a few odd looks.

"We should have taken the pumpkin," Leah muttered. "Less conspicuous."

"I hate to hitch up the mice for these short jaunts," Tina replied.

"True." Leah pushed in the latch to open the front door of Borbey House.

"Surprise!"

Truly, completely surprised, Leah stood stock still, her mouth ajar. Streamers, balloons and crepe paper decorated the entryway.

"Happy birthday!" The wishes came at her from all sides as people dressed in costumes popped out of their hiding places, then drew her into the room.

Tina, Emma and Annie wore matching conspiratorial grins.

But then, Leah couldn't stop smiling, either. "I can't believe you pulled this off—that I fell for your plan."

"It was easy," Annie admitted. "I think it was decorating the cake in front of you, and renting the movie you wanted. You figured I was planning a simple celebration for the two of us."

"It's that innocent look of yours," Leah teased.

Tina grinned at her. "I couldn't believe it when Emma got you to put on the Cinderella gown."

"And on my birthday." Leah groaned. "I must have seemed like the perfect dupe."

Tina held up her camera. "Let's just say we're glad we have pictures."

It seemed as if everyone Leah had met from the church and school was crowded into the B and B. She couldn't believe they'd all turned out for her birthday. Emma and her family. Ethan and the rest of the artistic committee. Principal Gunderland, Miss Randolph, several other teachers, Cindy Mallory, even the pastor, Katherine Carlson, and her family. Leah's eyes scanned the group. There they were, Danny and Matt. Leave it to Annie!

"Hey, Leah!" Danny hollered.

"Hey, Danny!" She grinned and waved.

He waved back, heading toward her.

Matt wasn't far behind. He looked so handsome. Dressed as Indiana Jones, Danny as the child who'd aided the action hero on his quest. Actually feeling like Cinderella, Leah caught her breath. "Don't you look…wonderful!"

"So do you!" Danny's eyes shone.

She bent to kiss his cheek.

"Yes," Matt said quietly.

Rising, she met his gaze. "Thank you."

"Happy birthday!" Danny chirped.

"Thank you again. I can't believe this party."

"You're really surprised?" Matt asked.

"Absolutely. I *saw* Annie making the cake from her special recipe. And she rented my favorite movie. This…this… Well, she really got me."

"We knew all along," Danny confided.

"Then you're really good at keeping secrets. I'm terrible at it." She glanced at Matt, wondering at the strange expression that flashed in his eyes.

"What we got you for your birthday is a secret, too," Danny told her.

Matt nudged him.

Leah smiled. "Oh, my."

"But I can't tell you what it is," Danny continued.

"Of course not." She smoothed the diaphanous folds of her gown, then glanced at Matt. "You didn't have to get me a present."

"Sure we did," Danny declared. "You always bring a present to a birthday party."

His simple truths were constantly amazing her.

"Just like you always get cake," he explained.

"Sounds like a fair exchange to me," she observed.

Danny glanced toward the other kids Annie had included in the party.

"If it's all right with your dad, you can go and play with your friends, Danny."

"Okay," Matt agreed, and the boy took off.

Despite the noise that filled the room, an awkward silence fell between them.

"Well," Matt said at last.

"Yes?"

"Are you missing your family?"

Surprisingly she wasn't. "No. As I was telling Annie, this is the birthday no one believes, my twenty-ninth. People always think you're holding out on the thirtieth."

"I'd forgotten you told me when you met John you were only—"

"Nineteen, just barely. With all the sense of a peanut." She laughed softly. "That seems like a hundred years ago."

"Do you wish you'd never met him?"

"If I hadn't, there'd be no Danny. I'd think you, of all people, would believe in greater plans."

"I do. But I got the best part of this plan."

She reached up to adjust her tiara. "Maybe I'm beginning to, as well."

Leaning forward, he closed his hand over hers, helping her right the crooked tiara. There was but a whisper between them, their gazes lingering.

Then he pulled back. "Your sunburn's all healed."

She lifted her hand to her face, remembering his tender touch, how he'd doctored her all through that night. She had counted only on herself since the day Danny had disappeared. She'd refused to trust, to lean on anyone. She'd never expected it to feel so good.

Several voices called her name.

"Your friends await, Cinderella," he said quietly.

"Right." Her ballgown rustled as she turned.

The house was filled with people, conversation and good food. The party seemed to go on and on.

Danny stood at her side as she blew out her candles and cut the cake.

Then it was time for presents. Leah was over-whelmed. She was a newcomer to Rosewood, yet these people had taken her into their hearts, given her a place in their community, welcomed her as a friend.

"You really shouldn't have done this," she kept repeating as she unwrapped each gift.

A lace shawl from Emma. A vibrant silk purse Tina had made herself. A bracelet from Annie with a single charm engraved with one word: sisters. Leah found herself hugging everyone after each gift.

Danny was bouncing up and down when it came time for his and Matt's gift. Leah's hands were trembling as she opened the box. Nestled carefully inside was a perfectly carved heart locket on a slender gold chain, her initials across the front. She'd never before seen a locket carved of wood, but this one... Like any piece of fine jewelry, it opened seamlessly, and inside was a picture of Danny.

She smoothed her hands over the fine grained cherry wood. "It's beautiful...just beautiful. Thank you."

"Me and Dad made it. Well, mostly Dad."

"You both did a wonderful job." Her gaze moved up to include Matt, her heart catching. "Just wonder-ful."

"Danny wanted you to have something special."

She swallowed. "It's more special than I can say." Ignoring Matt's exclusion in the sentiment, she hugged her son. "The best present I've ever gotten."

Chapter Sixteen

Matt didn't even open the envelope. It was the third letter from Barrington Industries in only three weeks. There had been calls, too, requesting a meeting. He hadn't returned any. And Nan had said a man in an expensive looking suit had been asking for him in the store. He'd left a card. One of Barrington's representatives.

Matt didn't have to ask why they were so determined. Nor did he delude himself that he was a modern day Michelangelo and Barrington wanted exclusive rights.

The Hunters wanted Leah in L.A. And Danny, of course. Getting him there, too, would assure them that he wouldn't try to take his son back to the wilds of Texas, he supposed.

They liked being in control. That was what John had told him. They wanted to run things. John was supposed to work for them, live where he was told, do what he was told. He hadn't wanted to live his life that way and neither did Matt. He was surprised Leah did. And disappointed.

Yet despite knowing this, he was still drawn to her. His defenses were crumbling.

He tapped the envelope. Was this why John had run? Had he felt trapped by the Hunters? He'd been young. Had he thought there was no other way out?

Nan breezed in to the back room. "That man's on the phone again. Same one who's been calling all week."

He shook his head. "Not interested."

"Shouldn't you tell him that?"

"Just take a message, Nan."

"Okay."

He remembered Leah's determination on the hike, her concern that Danny not be disappointed. It seemed at odds with this plotting and planning. She'd still said nothing about the proposed buyout. Had she thought distancing herself from it would remove the taint of deceit?

It was the deceit that made him question her relationship with Danny and the wisdom of revealing who she was. He knew how badly she wanted Danny to know. He'd been praying about it, but the answer kept eluding him.

He didn't want to disappoint Danny. Learning Leah was his mother, then having her let him down...that would devastate his son.

It wasn't her occasional irresponsible behavior that led him to think that would happen, but this...

this buyout offer. This deceit. Danny had so much trust, so much love to give.

Much like himself. He'd nearly let his resolve slip at Leah's birthday party. She'd made him want to forget old hurts, past differences as they'd laughed together at the Borbey House. She'd convinced him he'd held a genuine princess in his arms. But she was a princess with a secret agenda.

His sigh echoed in the empty room.

Leah's cell phone rang insistently as she walked to Borbey House. She took it from her purse, guessing who it was before she saw the readout. "Hello, Mother."

"Hello, dear. I've been calling and calling."

"I've been busy at the school. I had my phone turned off."

"There's not much point in carrying a cell phone if you're not going to answer it."

Leah counted to three. "Is something up?"

"Yes, darling. Westien Hotels just called."

"Oh."

"Is that all you can say? Leah, you worked for months to hook them. It's a huge entrée into the Scandinavian hotel business."

"I know. It just doesn't seem relevant right now."

"Not relevant? What's wrong with you?"

"I'm sorry, Mother, but I'm not thinking about clients these days."

"Is Danny all right?"

"He's fine."

"When will you two be coming home?"

Leah hedged. "Rosewood has been home to Danny all his life."

"But you can't just petrify out there, dear. Have you told Danny who you are yet?"

Leah fumbled with the phone, making a few buttons squawk.

"Leah?"

"No, Mother. I haven't told him yet."

"What are you waiting for?"

"The right moment."

"You need to bring him home."

It all seemed so black and white to her mother. Leah had tried talking to her father, who was more patient, but he was sticking with her mother on this one. He thought Leah should return to L.A. with Danny. As he put it: the boy had been gone long enough.

Leah did something she rarely liked to do. "You're breaking up, Mother. I'll talk to you later." She pushed the Off button, then snapped the phone shut. If someone needed her, they could call her at the B and B. She hardly used her cell phone in Rosewood, and it was an amazingly liberating experience.

Besides, she'd already planned to meet Danny and Matt at the drugstore for ice cream that evening. She grinned to herself, thinking of the high-maintenance places she'd gone to on dates in the city. Funny. None could compare to an evening on Main Street in Rosewood.

* * *

"Sprinkles?" Clyde, the clerk at the soda fountain, asked.

"Yes, please," Leah replied, as he built her banana split.

Danny dug into his double caramel and hot fudge sundae, which was loaded with cherries. "I got more cherries this time than ever!"

The clerk finished her sundae with a flourish of whipped cream and placed it on the marble counter in front of her.

"Ah. The touch of a master chef."

Hooking his feet over the stool, Danny leaned toward her. "The ice cream's already cooked."

She laughed, then hugged him. Not understanding the joke, he shrugged and turned back to his ice cream.

"You folks enjoy," the clerk said as he delivered Matt's sundae.

"Thanks, Clyde."

Leah glanced at his dish, then her own. "I feel kind of piggish. You didn't order nearly as much."

"I ate a steak for dinner. What did you have?"

She tried to remember. She'd been upset by her mother's phone call, then had to rush to meet them here. "Uh, seems I'm having it."

"Why don't you get a burger?"

"Then I wouldn't have room for all my ice cream. Besides, I have fruit, dairy, all the food groups I want right here."

"Want me to see if Clyde has some broccoli he can chop and sprinkle on top?"

"Gee, could you?"

Danny rolled his eyes. "You guys are silly."

Matt lifted the untouched cherry from his sundae and placed it on hers. "I seem to remember you like these better."

The simple gesture made her feel remarkably warm inside. "Yeah." She cleared the lump in her throat. "I do." She glanced over at Danny. "But I'm not the only one who likes them."

Danny shrugged. "It's okay. I got bunches." He took another bite of ice cream. "Are you goin' with us Saturday?"

"What's happening Saturday?"

"We're gonna go to the beach."

She glanced at Matt. "The beach? Aren't we quite a way from the ocean?"

"Galveston. It's about three and a half hours from here."

Was there hesitation in his voice? "Oh."

"I have to check out some special hardware a guy there produces by hand. Thought I might as well make a day of it with Danny. Would you like to come along? I have to warn you—we'll be leaving before dawn."

Which should she believe was genuine? The hesitation, the invitation or the warning?

"Yes, come!" Danny ignored his beloved cherries. "Please."

Her feelings pulled in opposite directions, she decided not to look at Matt again. "How can I say no?"

They reached the island city by daylight. Towering, fan-fringed palm trees and oleander bushes, ripe with fuchsia blooms, lined the center of Broadway. The wide boulevard ran through the center of the Victorian town, which was lined with mansions from its proudest era. Humid air carried the unmistakable tang of the ocean, of salt water, sand and tossing waves.

Inside the truck cab, the trio felt it. "Are we far from the beach, Dad?"

"Not too far. But we should have some breakfast, then swing by the hardware place. Get the business done first."

"Didn't you say the hardware place is on the Strand?" Leah shifted so she faced Matt.

"Yeah."

"Maybe there's a place close by where we can eat." She glanced down at Danny. "I did a little checking on the Internet. The Strand's supposed to be fun."

"Fine with me." He grinned at his son. "*And* it's in the same direction as the beach."

"Yay!"

The historic Strand district was once the heart of Galveston in the late 1800s and early 1900s. High curbs and overhanging canopies, meant to shade the streets, retained the charm of the era.

Leah was immediately captivated. "I love this!"

"They hold a Mardi Gras here every year, and at Christmas, Dickens on the Strand."

"I can see it now. With these Greek Revival and Victorian buildings…it must be fantastic."

"There was talk years ago of tearing this all down. But the historic society fought it, said it could be revived."

Leah shook her head. "Amazing. This area covers blocks, doesn't it? Now it's filled with stores and art galleries and restaurants. Good thing the historical society won. How do you know so much about it?"

"I've always liked Galveston. If it hadn't been for the hurricane of 1900, it would have been the biggest city in the state instead of Houston. It's chock full of history. Not too far from here you can see what's left of the pirate Jean Lafitte's house." He motioned around them. "There's living history, beaches and seafood fresh off the boats."

She laughed. "What's *not* to like?"

"There's a real submarine in the park by the ferry," Danny told her. "And a battleship."

She turned in a semicircle, gazing at the fascinating pairing of old and new. "I could spend all day right here exploring shops and galleries."

Danny's expression filled with genuine alarm.

"Don't worry," she was quick to reassure him, not hiding her wide grin. "I won't."

They chose a breakfast spot that was housed in what had originally been a coffee importing warehouse. Now they sold small burlap sacks of coffee beans. More importantly, they served tasty and quick breakfasts.

When they were finished, they headed over to the hardware store. Hand-tooled knobs and drawer pulls fascinated the designer in Leah as Matt spoke to the owner about creating some pieces for an armoire he was designing. Danny fidgeted even though it didn't take long, his mind on beaches and submarines.

Luckily they weren't far from the seawall. The sound of the surf and seagulls could be heard despite the traffic as they drove alongside the ocean. Matt kept his speed down so they could breathe in the tangy sea air and admire the piers that jutted into the ocean. Some were used for fishing, others had restaurants or were crammed with chintzy souvenir shops. The ones that thrust farther out held elegant hotels.

Matt continued driving until they reached the turn-off to Stewart Beach. Leah didn't argue when Matt insisted on renting a beach umbrella because of her fair skin. She'd stuffed enough sunscreen into her beach bag for several people, but why take chances?

Matt took Danny to the bath house to change into their swim trunks. When they emerged, he was surprised to see Leah wearing her T-shirt and shorts. She walked out from beneath the umbrella to meet them. "Aren't you swimming?"

"I'm not a swimmer," she confessed. "I dip my toes in along the shore, but that's it."

"But you live by the ocean," Danny pointed out. "You shouldn't be scared of it."

"I'm not scared of the ocean."

"Danny, why don't you grab the bottle of sunscreen out of our beach bag," Matt suggested.

"Okay," he said, racing over to the umbrella, where Matt had left the bag.

"Diplomatic." Leah brushed sand from her shorts.

"Afraid of the water?"

"Always have been. My parents gave me lessons, but I wouldn't put my head under the water. So one of the teachers decided the baptism by fire method was the way to go. I nearly drowned. And now I have a deathly fear of deep water. My parents insisted I keep going to the lessons, even though I just kept sinking like a stone. I went through all the motions, but I've never been able to go in deep water since then. It terrifies me."

"So we'll stay by the shore."

"No! You and Danny go and swim. I'm fine. I won't drown dipping my toes in the shallow part. And I like to dig my feet into the sand. I can amuse myself doing that. If I get bored, I'll lie down in one of those chairs you rented and listen to the ocean. It's been a while since I've heard the sounds of waves, you know."

"Yeah. Okay. Later, I'd thought about riding the ferry, but if that's going to bother you—"

"Not unless we have to swim for it."

He grinned. "I'm pretty sure that won't happen."

"Really, I love what I've seen of Galveston. It's just the deep water thing. Anything else is great."

Danny raced toward them with a bottle of sunscreen and handed it to her. "Will you do my back?"

"Sure."

When she'd finished, Danny turned and hugged her. "It's okay to be scared of the water," he whispered. "Everybody's scared of something."

Oh, how she loved this child. Then he was running toward the waves, Matt close behind.

She didn't want to transmit her fear to Danny, but she kept her eyes trained on him as they played in the surf. Matt was never more than a foot away, easily able to reach him if he needed to.

It seemed impossible to believe that they hadn't always been in her life, as important as both of them had become. She could see so much of Matt in Danny, but every now and then there was a glimpse of Kyle, as well. She supposed his memory would never completely disappear from their lives. And she wondered if it should. Children needed the truth. But she knew how the truth would hurt.

Retreating to the chairs beneath the umbrella, Leah continued to watch. She couldn't relax. Not while they remained in the water. Still, it was a beautiful day, the sun high in the cloudless sky.

There were plenty of people on the beach. Tourists had descended on Galveston like the sunshine and warm weather. Teenage girls walked by in pairs, giggling at teenage boys. And the surf was mild; swimmers carried inflatable toys, floats and beach balls.

Still, Leah felt huge relief when Danny and Matt headed for shore. She reached for the towels.

Laughing, Danny sprinkled her with water when he got close enough. She covered him with a towel. "Okay, smart guy." But she didn't mind.

"You want to build a sandcastle, Leah?" Danny asked, his voice muffled by the towel.

"Absolutely." She dried him off, then picked up the plastic bucket and shovel.

Matt dug in the cooler. "You two start. I'll get the drinks."

Danny grabbed her hand and they walked out to the damp sand and knelt down.

"This okay?" she asked, scooping up a bucketful of sand and upending it.

He patted the sand in place. "Yep. We'll need a big base."

They worked in silence for a few minutes. Matt brought sodas and joined the effort. While Leah formed turrets and a tower, she noticed that Danny was building a house that resembled his own.

Matt's large hands shaped the roof, occasionally grazing hers.

Leah tried not to make more of his touch than it warranted, but she found her gaze straying to his before she forced it back to the sandcastle.

"Hey, Leah, you just filled in the window."

"Sorry, sweetie." She dug the sand back out.

"When we finish this, you wanna look for shells?"

"I'm game."

"Dad?"

"Sure."

"I wish we could have brought Hunter along."

"He's fine at Roger's," Matt replied. "He's romping with the other dogs, having a good old time. You wouldn't have been able to do everything you wanted to if we'd brought him."

"Yeah, I guess."

Danny was content with building the sandcastle, a search for shells, then another swim in the ocean. After oyster po'boys, they headed over to SeaWolf Park to tour the submarine.

The ferry was close by, so when they'd finished at the park, they drove over to the dock and parked. They walked onto the double-decker boat that made the crossing to Bolivar Island. Once the commuter ferry was filled with cars and passengers, it pulled away from the pier, a flock of seagulls following in its wake.

Many of the passengers congregated at the rear of the boat, tossing pieces of bread to the birds. The three of them had crusts from their lunch and Danny threw the bits skyward, delighted when a seagull swooped to catch the piece midair.

After a while, they walked to the prow of the ferry. Matt pointed to one of the huge ships in the distance. "Ocean liners. That one's Greek."

"I can't see," Danny complained.

Leah lifted him in front of her.

"Oh, yeah."

Grinning impishly, she held Danny's arms up in the pose that the movie *Titanic* had made famous, then motioned for Matt to get behind her, and all three of them assumed the stance.

Wind whipped through their hair and clothes. It was unexpected. It was silly. It was a memory moment.

The ship lurched slightly and Matt leaned in farther to steady her. Everything in that instant was perfect.

Chapter Seventeen

Billy's family was overwhelmed by the cradle. His father, Cal Mickleson, kept running his hands over the smooth wood.

His mother, Belinda, had tears in her eyes. "It'll become a family heirloom. It's so lovely."

"So much work you put into this," Cal murmured. "I don't have the words…."

Matt put his arm on his son's shoulder. "It was Danny's idea and we worked on it together."

"You've always been a wonderful friend to Billy, and now you'll be like another older brother to the baby." Belinda hugged Danny. "You've raised a wonderful boy," she said to Matt, including Leah in her smile.

"Yeah!" Billy jumped up. "We can share him!"

"Him?" Leah asked.

Belinda patted her stomach. "We just found out. Billy's going to have a little brother."

"Wow!" Danny's eyes were wide.

"That's wonderful," Leah murmured.

"Yes, great news," Matt agreed.

Leah handed them a gift basket. "I went with yellow since I didn't know."

Belinda threw up her hands. "You shouldn't have. The cradle was more than enough."

Smiling, Leah shrugged slightly. "I love shopping for baby things."

Belinda pulled out a soft yellow blanket and pad that fit perfectly in the cradle. There was also a matching teddy bear. "How sweet!"

"I couldn't resist."

"You wanna see my new soccer ball?" Billy asked Danny.

"Sure."

They scuttled outside.

Cal was still admiring the cradle with Matt as Belinda tucked the teddy bear back in the basket. "You three make a lovely family."

Leah started to shake her head.

"Don't you see it?"

She glanced over at Matt. "I…I'm not sure."

"Danny's dying to have a mother," Belinda confided, "and a brother or sister."

Leah felt her heart still. "Oh?"

"Yes." She smiled kindly. "I hope you won't think I'm being intrusive. I love Danny. He and Billy have been best friends all their lives. I can see you've been good for him. I've been concerned that Danny would have a hard time with this little one coming along, but with you in his life now, he's accepted it well."

"I can't take responsibility for that. Matt keeps him on an even keel."

"He's been a wonderful father, of course. But he's not a mother."

Considering her words, Leah glanced again at Matt. The longing to tell Danny was strong.

"It bothers him when the other kids' mothers bring treats to class and he knows he doesn't have a mom to volunteer," Belinda continued. "Same thing when it was time to decide on a den mother for Scouts. They sound like small things, but no child wants to be different or left out. And every child needs a mom. Anyway, I hope things work out for all of you."

Leah tried to keep the huskiness from her voice. "Thanks."

The picture Belinda painted of her motherless child had Leah near tears. And far nearer to needing the truth to come out.

"What's the rush?" Exasperated, Matt forgot to keep his voice down.

Leah tilted her head, indicating the other diners in the café.

He lowered his voice. "Well?"

"I didn't say there was a rush, just that I'm ready to tell him. I can't see that waiting is a positive thing."

"This is awfully sudden."

"Sudden? I've been here for months now."

He remembered the increasing phone calls from

Barrington, pressing him to sell the business. "Any special reason why you want to tell him now?"

"He's a little boy who needs a mother. He has one and I want him to know it."

"Why now?"

She fiddled with her iced tea. "Why not? What are we waiting for?"

"The right time."

"And who gets to decide when that is?"

He hesitated. That was a tough call, one he knew would be hard to make for either of them. "I just don't want Danny to get hurt."

"What if waiting does exactly that?"

He was torn. She could be right. Maybe Danny would feel betrayed if they kept the truth from him any longer. There was an uneasiness in Matt, though. Probably because Leah could take Danny away once he knew. But that had been possible for some time now. If she wanted Matt to move to L.A., too, why didn't she just come out with it? Why the ploys with Barrington? Did she think he'd withdraw his consent? "And what if he doesn't take the news well? What then?"

Her hands trembled. "You don't think he'll want me for his mother?"

She'd gotten to him again and he placed his hand over hers. "Leah, this news will change him forever. He's a little boy and he's going to be confused. You've got to be ready for that."

She bit down on her bottom lip. "What do you think, Matt? Do you think I'll be a good mother for him?"

He searched his heart, reached past the doubts, and surfaced with the bare truth. "Yes."

She let out the breath she'd been holding.

"You're a good man, Matt Whitaker. The best I've ever known." Her eyes fixed on him as though wanting to say more, but she didn't.

"Then I guess we're going to tell him."

She nodded, looking close to tears. "I guess so."

"There's something I have to tell you then. Danny doesn't know about John."

"I kind of figured that."

"Not because I'm ashamed of him…just that Danny's always been like my own. I'd planned on telling him when he was old enough to understand. Guess this pushes up that timetable."

"About Kyle…John, I mean. I've been thinking…"

Tensing up, he waited.

"Whenever I think about him…what he did, or might have done with Danny, well, it's based on the little time I knew him. If he'd lived, I think he probably would have eventually brought Danny back. I mean…he was young, like me. He made a rash decision, and after he'd had time to think it over, he'd have realized it wasn't the right thing to do. But he didn't have time to fix it."

That was what Matt had concluded, too, but he hadn't expected Leah to see it that way. He stared at her. There was a lot of forgiveness in this unusual woman. John had stolen eight years of her relationship with Danny because of his mistake.

Leah sighed. "And there's one other thing. He didn't like the way my parents wanted to...well... kind of control things. Since I've been here, I've spent a lot of time thinking back. You know how, as the years go by, it's easy to lose perspective? I've had it in my head that he just wasn't grateful for all the opportunities they gave him. But...he resented the fact they got to choose what they wanted him to do, where we were supposed to live. He said they'd wind up doing that to Danny, too. I was pretty much used to doing what they wanted, so I didn't see it then. But it's been clearer to see since I've been here, away from them. And now, well...I guess I just want to say how sorry I am for all the things I said about him. I know losing him hurt you."

"I want to think he'd have come to the right decision, too, but he hurt you both by his mistake. John had to have been scared once he'd taken Danny. But he lied about you leaving." Matt knew that now, even though the truth shamed him. He cleared his throat. "And I'm sorry I doubted you."

"You didn't know me then. I just showed up out of the blue."

And now?

"More coffee?" the waitress asked. "And we've got coconut cream pie. It's real good."

Leah shook her head. "Not for me."

"Three-layer chocolate cake?" the waitress asked. "It'll melt in your mouth."

Maybe so, but her sales pitch had ruined the moment.

* * *

Leah wanted everything to be perfect. Well, relaxed. She'd baked oatmeal cookies, Danny's favorite. But her hands were shaking and her neck was as
tight as a stiff jar lid.

Accustomed to her coming over, Danny didn't
think it was unusual for her to stop by on Saturday
morning. Relax, she told herself. Keep it casual.

After they played with the dinosaur village, fed
his fish and turtle, Matt joined them and they headed
outside.

Matt put his arm on Danny's shoulders. "Leah
and I have something to talk with you about."

"Okay."

"Why don't you sit down over here?" she asked,
indicating the bench beneath the tree.

"Sure."

She ran a hand over his tousled hair. "Sweetheart,
you know how your friends have mothers…" She
licked her lips, so nervous her stomach was pitching. "I'm hoping you'll want a mother, too."

"Are you and Dad getting married?" he asked,
bouncing up from the bench in excitement.

"No, no. That's not it."

He frowned. "Then how can you get to be my
mother?"

Her voice quavered, her smile tremulous. "You'd
want me to be your mother?"

Matt took over. "Danny, do you remember what
I told you about your birth-mother?"

Danny slowly sat back down between them. "That

you didn't know where she was. But that wherever she was, she must be sad not to have a wonderful boy like me."

"Right. For a long time I didn't know where she was. And she didn't know where you were. And she was very sad to not be with you. She's been looking for you since you were born, and now she's found you."

Danny's eyebrows drew together, and he looked at them in turn.

Leah held her breath. "Yes, I've found you, Danny. I'm your mother."

"It's you?"

"Yes, sweetheart. It's me."

He looked at her in bewilderment. "How could you have lost me?"

She glanced up at Matt. "It's a very long story, Danny, but I never stopped loving you or looking for you. You have been in my heart since the day you were born." Her eyes moistened. "You're my little boy."

"But you shouldn't have *lost* me!"

Matt cleared his throat. "Danny, you know how much I love you."

Danny's voice was filled with caution. "Yeah."

"Well…you've been my boy since almost the day you were born and I've never wanted it any other way." He lowered his head, swallowing the lump in his throat. "But your natural father was my younger brother, John. He was confused when he was married to Leah, and he thought that bringing you back

here was the right thing to do. Only he didn't tell
Leah where he'd gone, and then he got into a real
bad car accident and died."

"So, you're not my real dad?" Hurt and shock
filled his quavering voice.

"In every way that matters. I've been taking care
of you since you were a tiny baby. You're in my
heart, Danny. I love you more than anyone else in
this world."

Danny looked so betrayed, Leah felt the crumbling fragility in her own heart. "How come you
didn't tell me before?"

Matt stared at him for such a long time that Leah
found herself holding her breath. "I was waiting for
the right time, until you were old enough to understand."

"But we never keep secrets," Danny accused.

Matt stared at him helplessly. This strong man
who loved his son with all his heart. Who wanted
only the best for him.

Danny jumped to his feet, storming away. When
Matt didn't speak, Leah did. "Where are you going?"

"Takin' Hunter on a walk."

"We still need to talk, Danny," Leah called out.

He didn't reply.

She sighed. Maybe he needed to work some of
this out by himself. "Don't go far. We'll be having
lunch in about an hour."

He disappeared behind the workshop.

She slumped back on the bench. "You were right.
As usual, *I* didn't think things out. Just blurted out

what I wanted him to hear, not realizing…I'm sorry, Matt. Why didn't you stop me?"

"I'd have had better luck stopping a train." His voice was dull, and he stood staring into the empty space where Danny had been standing. "Don't blame yourself. I agreed with you that we'd tell him. I probably should have told him before. Maybe there never would have been the right time."

"But you thought we should wait. And I just plowed ahead." Why couldn't she have listened? Done what Matt suggested? He was the one with the parenting experience. Now Danny distrusted both of them.

Chapter Eighteen

Half an hour after lunch was ready, Danny wasn't back.

Matt called Billy's house but Danny wasn't there. "I know he's got to think this out, but we've given him long enough on his own. He won't have gone far. We'd better bring him home."

"Why don't we split up and look for him?" Leah suggested. "I've got my car. We can go in opposite directions that way, cover more ground."

Matt considered this, the pain he was feeling evident in his face and voice. "You know the popsicle stand by the Little League field? He and Billy like to hang out there sometimes. You try there first and I'll go by the Mickleson house. Maybe he's headed that way. Stay on the main roads. I can go off-road in the truck."

As Leah drove, she looked into the fields, but saw no little boy. She chastised herself for letting him sit alone with his thoughts too long. All she wanted was to find him, to put her arms around him, pour out her love and explain how very sorry she was to have hurt him. She wished she could take all that hurt on herself. It was so much worse knowing it was his.

She was tempted to take the side road to the baseball field but remembered Matt's instructions. For once, she wouldn't take off like a mad hare. But he wasn't at the field.

Then she remembered the path to the riverbank. Danny wasn't supposed to go there alone. She'd gone there with him when Matt had been with them. Feeling betrayed, angry, maybe rebellious…would he disobey his father?

Acting on instinct, she turned in that direction. The elevated riverbank was surrounded by trees, wild grass and dense scrub brush. She could only drive the small rental car to the edge of the vegetation. Then she set out on foot.

And as she walked she prayed.

Matt took the shortcut to the Mickleson home. Belinda and Cal were concerned, but sure that Danny hadn't been there.

"Do you mind if I talk to Billy alone?"

"Of course not. Whatever we can do to help."

They withdrew and Billy perched nervously on the edge of the couch.

"You know, when I was your age, my best friend was Jason Deats. Wasn't anything I couldn't tell him. Like when my dad died. That was the worst thing that ever happened. And he understood, even though he had his dad. Do you know what I'm saying, Billy?"

"I think so."

"So, if I were Danny, I think I'd come to you if something pretty big happened and I needed to talk about it."

Billy ducked his head, staring at the rug.

"I don't want Danny to get hurt."

"He won't get hurt!" Billy blurted out.

"I'm glad to hear it. You'd better tell me where he is."

"But—"

"He needs me right now, Billy. Because I love him and want only the best for him. Can you understand that?"

"I guess so. He went to the river. But he's just gonna throw rocks and stuff."

Matt patted his shoulder.

Thanking the Micklesons, he headed south. The river was a quiet place to think. One that had drawn him when he was a teen. Danny was growing up. They'd pushed that maturing process forward today. His boy was hurt and he'd be hurting for a while to come. But most of what he was feeling was confusion. It would take time for him to understand. But now, he had to face them, get over this first difficult step.

Danny looked very small when Leah spotted him. He sat on the ground, his knees drawn up, his head resting against his dog.

Leah made her footfalls deliberately loud and rustled the grass so she wouldn't startle him.

Still he jumped up, swiping at the tears that had been running down his face. He tried to keep his lips from trembling, but failed.

"Hey."

He didn't reply, gripping Hunter's collar.

"I've made a mess of things again. And I'm the grown-up. I should know better. I just got so impatient to tell you who I am."

"Moms don't lose their kids."

"Not usually, no. But I didn't have a choice. Your biological father and I were very, very young. He made a mistake."

"Why didn't you stop him?"

"He ran away. When adults run away, it's not the same as when children do. I couldn't find him. I've been looking for you for eight years. When I found out he'd died, I was so scared that meant you had, too." Her voice quavered. "But the Lord has been good, Danny. He kept you safe and gave you a wonderful father to raise you."

"Then why didn't Dad tell me?" Still feeling betrayed, he wasn't willing to give an inch.

"He was going to, sweetie, when he thought you were old enough to understand."

"I'm old enough." The lip that trembled now turned stubborn.

"Maybe. But if that's true, can't you forgive him for this one mistake?"

Danny gripped Hunter even tighter. "Do I have to pick?"

"What do you mean?"

"Between you and Dad?"

"No, never."

"Maybe he'll get tired of me someday since he's not my real father."

Leah stepped closer. "Danny, your father chose you to be his son. He *chose* you. Can you see how much that means he loves you? That he wanted *you?*"

Danny's face crumpled. Leah stepped closer, thinking she'd persuaded him. Instead he turned around, scrambling down the riverbank.

She ran to the edge. At first Danny kept his balance, then he started skidding on the rocks. Out of control, he tumbled into the river.

Hunter barked furiously from the shore. Leah climbed down the side, then jumped into the water after her son. Waving her arms wildly, she tried to remember her swimming lessons, but all she could think of was saving Danny.

The river current swirled, splashing water over her face. The old panic was there, a hot, bubbling force, but the need to save Danny was greater.

She propelled her arms in the water and kicked her feet, but she didn't move forward. *What had they taught her in those lessons? Why had she blocked it all out in her fear?*

Danny was bobbing up and down several feet ahead of her. She reached out toward him, sinking beneath the water. Flailing her arms, she came up sputtering. Spitting out water, she shouted to Danny. "Don't worry! I'll get you."

She went under the water again. When she surfaced, she couldn't see Danny. Her heart nearly stopped.

The water covered her head again, carrying her farther downstream. She fought to get to the surface, not for herself, but for Danny. *Please, Lord, help him. Send us help.*

She broke through the water again, desperately reaching out to grab hold of something, anything to help her reach her son. But she still didn't see him. "Danny!" Her shout was more a gurgle, a plea.

Without warning she felt a rope come down over her shoulders and pull tight. Then she was being dragged to the shore. Dazed, she saw Danny sitting on the ground, Hunter licking him all over.

Matt, his face grim, pulled her with the rope until he could lift her to solid ground. She sagged against him, her breathing shallow.

"What do you think you were doing?" he yelled, shaking her.

"I—"

"You could have killed yourself. You don't know how to swim. You're scared to death of water. What if I hadn't had a rope with me in the truck? What then? What would Danny and I have done without you? Did you think about that? No. You just jumped in the river."

Her breathing was returning to normal, but she

wasn't sure her hearing was. Had he said what would he have done without her?

"Danny's only eight years old. I can see how he wound up in the river. But you're a grown-up, Leah. If you're going to be a member of this family, you're going to have to start acting like one. You can't jump into a river without knowing how to swim—"

She felt a surge of indignation. "I wasn't going to let my son drown without doing something."

"No, you weren't, were you?"

She met his gaze. His eyes were tender, full of worry. She shook her head.

"Even though chances were you'd die doing it." He stroked her cheek.

She swallowed. "What was that about being part of your family?"

Matt glanced down at Danny. "We okay now, pal?"

Danny nodded, hanging on to Matt's leg.

"This isn't the most romantic setting a guy could pick, but it might be the most honest. I love you, Leah. Every stubborn inch of you. I love that you stand up for what you believe, I love that you love our son. If you'll have me, I'll do everything in my power to make sure your life is as good as the one you'll be giving up."

Forgetting her soggy clothing and drenched hair, Leah beamed as her heart started to fly. "I won't be giving up anything. I'll be getting everything."

Chapter Nineteen

Annie carried her ever growing list into the parlor. "Apple and poppyseed strudel, maybe peach, too?" Leah and Matt's reception was going to be held at Borbey House and Annie couldn't resist fussing.

"Only if we skip the entrée," Ethan replied.

Annie looked up from her clipboard and blushed. "I thought I was talking to Leah."

"Will I do?"

"You'll more than *do*."

He took the clipboard from her and then took her hand. "We need to talk."

"Oh." Nothing good ever came of a conversation that started with those words. But Annie put on a brave face. After all, she didn't want Ethan to be a victim of her family curse. It was better this way.

"What are you keeping from me?"

The artificial smile slid from her face. "Keeping from you?"

"I can sense it, Annie, and I don't want anything between us."

"I guess I've been fooling myself thinking I could put it off." She turned away from him, wishing she didn't have to tell him, wishing tragedy hadn't dogged her family. But he deserved to know the truth. So she told him. "And when I found out that Leah almost drowned in the river, I thought I'd caused that, too, since she insisted on being my sister."

At first he didn't say anything. She expected the usual skepticism, denial or even mocking. Instead, Ethan took her hands. "Why don't we pray about it?"

His voice was quiet but strong as he asked the Lord for His guidance to get them through this issue that troubled her, to give her peace. Then he sat beside her without speaking for a while, the familiar noises of the house and the guests around them.

Unexpectedly, a sense of peace stole into her heart. Raising her eyes, she met his. "Thank you."

"I don't ever want anything to come between us again, Annie." He lifted a strand of her dark hair. "I love you."

"You do?" Hope infused her voice like scent in a budding rose.

He smiled. "I do."

Her smile grew. "Me, too. I mean, I love you, too."

He unfastened his music insignia pin from his jacket and carefully attached it to her collar.

Her lips trembled.

"It's not a diamond ring, but until we pick one out, I'm staking my claim."

"And you're not worried about the other thing?"

"No. All I'm worried about is picking the right strudel for *our* reception."

Leah had so much to do. There were arrangements to make with her assistant to get her L.A. apartment closed and the rest of her belongings shipped to Rosewood. Then, of course, the wedding. It would be simple. Beautiful, but simple.

And she knew that together they would ask the Lord to be in this union with them. In finding Danny, she'd also found the fullness of her faith. The Lord had protected her child, given them another chance, then protected him again. She'd learned what it was to live with faith.

She felt a new sense of completeness belonging to the Community Church as well, something she'd never had before. Something she treasured.

When she'd called her parents with the news, they'd mentioned that Barrington Industries would like to buy out Matt's business and market his designs around the country, but she couldn't see him giving up his individuality. After all, anyone could go corporate. But Matt, well, he was Matt. She told him about the offer, and he agreed with her that he preferred to keep his business his own.

Annie was fussing over the wedding reception and Emma had designed an original gown. Surprisingly, the details weren't that important to Leah. She trusted Emma to make a beautiful dress. She'd just told her to keep it simple and in keeping with the surroundings. Beyond that, her energies were focused on Matt and Danny. And the blessings that just continued to flow.

The evening was ripe with honeysuckle. It was a heady scent in the damp air. White picket fences gleamed in the moonlight and couples strolled down the well-swept sidewalks.

Matt and Leah sat on the swing of the wide front porch at Borbey House.

Matt looked into her shining eyes, amazed all over again that she'd said yes to his proposal, that they were going to live right here in Rosewood. "We have some unfinished business."

Questions filled her emerald eyes. But they were questions now grounded in trust. He reached into his pocket, pulling out a well-worn jeweler's box.

She sucked in her breath. Her fingers flew to cover her mouth.

He carefully opened the old box. Inside was an exquisite emerald cut diamond. She knew, before he told her, that it had been his mother's. It was a tangible sign of the depth of his commitment, the foreverness of it. Tears filled her eyes.

"She would have loved you as much as I do." He slipped the ring on her finger. It fit perfectly. "I don't think I actually said the words the first time. Will you marry me, Leah?"

Her voice was as soft as the moonlight. "Yes. Very much yes."

Moonlight shimmered over her unfettered blond hair. Her clear eyes shone close to his, their faces a breath apart. Her lips were soft beneath his, tender, giving, whispering the love they shared.

Cradling her in his arms, he breathed in the clean smell of her hair, warming his cheek against hers and feeling her entrenchment into his heart grow ever deeper.

Sunlight pierced the tall rafters of the Community Church, casting its bounty through the stained-glass windows that dated back to Victorian times.

Leah and Matt had chosen a nontraditional ceremony. Rather than Leah walking down the aisle on her father's arm, she and Matt entered from the sides of the nave, meeting at the center. Danny served as best man and ring bearer, Annie as maid of honor. They wanted to keep the ceremony simple, to express the making of a family.

Rhonda Hunter had a hard time with what she considered the no-frills service and reception. She requested an additional reception in L.A., but Leah didn't budge. When Rhonda saw that she couldn't win, she didn't give Leah a difficult time. While she would never be a soft and cuddly mother, she had stopped trying to run Leah's life.

And Leah was ready to embark on that life.

Do you, Leah Michelle Hunter, take Matthew Andrew Whitaker... In sickness and health...for

*better for worse...forsaking all others...until death
do you part?*

She repeated the vows, her heart singing the
words.

Matt stood straight and tall as he made his pledge,
committing his vows to her and to God.

Blessed. The word ricocheted through his thoughts.
It had been his mantra since the moment Leah had
poured out her love, accepted his proposal and cried
over the ring he'd given her. As it sparkled on the
hand he now held, it harbored a wealth of meaning.
And she'd known that instantly. This woman who had
come to know his heart.

As they gazed lovingly at each other, the congre-
gants, family and friends seemed far away.

"I do," Leah whispered again.

"Me, too," he whispered back.

"...now pronounce you man and wife. What God
has brought together, let no man put asunder."

Matt looked at her tenderly, his bride/wife.

"...may kiss the bride."

Gently he touched his lips to hers, feeling her
tremble. Then she smiled, that smile he loved. He
clasped her hand in his, letting his strength flow to
her. And together they turned to face the world as
one.

Borbey House hadn't gleamed this much since its
own debut. The dark walnut surfaces had been polished until shiny. Ivory lace net bunting, caught up
with nosegays of yellow rosebuds, draped the door-

ways. Annie's family silver shone beneath the crystal chandelier.

The one extravagance Rhonda had insisted on and Leah had given in to was a small string ensemble. They played softly as a background to the sound of happy voices.

"You look incredibly beautiful, Mrs. Whitaker," Matt said.

"So do you, Mr. Whitaker," Leah replied.

Matt lifted his eyebrows. "Can men be beautiful?"

Her eyes misted. "You are."

He smoothed her cheek with the back of his hand. "And you, my love, are a gift."

The pain of their pasts slipped away, forgotten. Only the future remained, so bright, so shiny, it reflected in the hope they saw in each other.

Danny tugged at Matt's coattail. "Dad. Is this it?"

"It?"

"Are you and Mom and me a real family now?"

Matt smiled at his bride as they each took one of Danny's hands. "Absolutely."

Danny looked up at them. "Is this just grown-up stuff now?"

The music swirled around them.

"No," Leah answered. "This first dance is for all of us." She gazed into the two faces so dear to her. "That okay with my men?"

Their chorus was music, it was wonder, it was all she ever needed to hear.

"You betcha."

* * * * *

Dear Reader,

I think there can be no greater fear than that of losing a child. For Leah Hunter, it's a loss she's lived with for eight long years. But when the search for her child brings her face-to-face with Matt Whitaker, it will take divine guidance to separate fear from fact—and one little boy from two people who love him with all their hearts.

Like most parents, stories with children touch my heart. And, also like most of you, I relish the special relationship that produces those children.

It's a tough world we live in today, but Rosewood is a gentler place where neighbors still care about one another, people matter and love flourishes. I hope you'll enjoy going there with me again.

God bless.

Bonnie K. Winn

Love Inspired®

Everything Montana Brown *thought* she knew about love and marriage goes awry when her parents split up. Shaken, she heads to Mule Hollow, Texas, to take a chance on an old dream— being a cowgirl…while trying to resist the charms of a too-handsome cowboy. A wife isn't on rancher Luke Holden's wish list. But the Mule Hollow matchmakers are fixin' to lasso Luke and Montana together—with a little faith and love.

Her Rodeo Cowboy
by Debra Clopton

Available September wherever books are sold.

www.LoveInspiredBooks.com

LI87691

REQUEST YOUR FREE BOOKS!

2 FREE INSPIRATIONAL NOVELS
PLUS 2
FREE
MYSTERY GIFTS

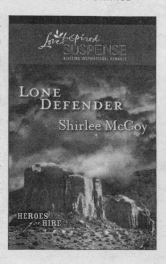

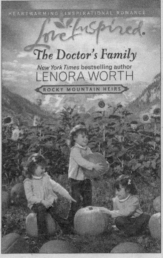

Raising four-year-old triplets and an abandoned teenager, single mom Arabella Clayton Michaels loves her big family. But when Denver surgeon Jonathan Turner arrives to announce that Arabella's beloved teenager is his long-lost niece, they find themselves becoming an unexpected family....

The Doctor's Family

By *New York Times* bestselling author

Lenora Worth

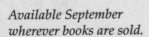

Available September wherever books are sold.

www.LoveInspiredBooks.com